Beginning a year ago, from time to time it seemed to him that when reading he met other readers *inside* the given text. And from time to time, only now and then but more and more vividly, he would later recall those other, mostly unknown people who had been reading the same book at the same time as he. He remembered some of the details as if he had really lived them. Lived them with all his senses. Naturally, he had never confided this to anyone. They would have thought him mad. Or at best a little unhinged. Truth be told, when he seriously considered all these extraordinary matters, he himself came to the conclusion that he was teetering dangerously on the very brink of an unsound mind. Or did it all appear to him thus from too much literature and too little life?!

AT THE LUCKY HAND

aka *the sixty-nine drawers*

GORAN PETROVIĆ

Translated from the Serbian by
Peter Agnone

DEEP VELLUM PUBLISHING

DALLAS, TEXAS

Deep Vellum Publishing
3000 Commerce St., Dallas, Texas 75226
deepvellum.org · @deepvellum

Deep Vellum is a 501c3 nonprofit literary arts organization
founded in 2013 with the mission to bring
the world into conversation through literature.

Support for this publication has been provided in part by grants from the
National Endowment for the Arts, the Texas Commission on the Arts,
the City of Dallas Office of Arts and Culture's ArtsActivate program, and
the Moody Fund for the Arts:

ISBNs: 978-1-64605-014-7 (paperback) | 978-1-64605-015-4 (ebook)

LIBRARY OF CONGRESS CONTROL NUMBER: 2020015911

Cover Design by Justin Childress | justinchildress.co
Interior Layout and Typesetting by Kirby Gann

Printed in the United States of America

CONTENTS

ENTRY TO THE MATERIAL

WHERE WE SPEAK
ABOUT AN UNCARED-FOR WORMWOOD PLANT,
A MYSTERIOUS TASK,
A MYSTERIOUS WRITER,
AND A BOOKBINDING OF SAFFIAN;
ABOUT THE HEIGHT OF OUR MOUNTAINS,
THE PLEASANT SMELL OF THE GIRL WITH
AND THE BELL-SHAPED HAT;
ABOUT A GLOOMY AQUARIUM,
POROUS WALLS,
AND WHETHER MOLD CAN START TO GROW IN A JAR
OF APRICOT JAM OPENED ON MONDAY

1

IT WAS A SENTENCE IN SERBIAN. As was the next one, after all. Typeset by hand. Printed in Cyrillic characters. Between the lines one could make out the impress on the back of the page. Originally a perfect white, the paper had yellowed in spots from time; time which insinuates itself everywhere . . .

As he waited for the youth to glance over the first page of the book, the mysterious man feigned interest in examining the office, a long-unpainted little room at the end of the left side of the corridor. Hardly more than a cramped space, this general-purpose room contained only a broken-down rolltop file cabinet, its lock forced open many times, a standing coatrack, two rickety chairs, a work desk, and the uncared-for stalk of a wormwood plant languishing in its pot. The rather small work desk, its edges chipped and the lacquer worn away, was scarcely large enough for the six prewar volumes of the *Dictionary of the Serbian Language*, the postwar edition of the *Orthography*, and a stack of the current week's freshly printed pages of news text.

The light in the room was weak, the view from the window being obstructed by the pockmarked shoulders of the adjacent government building, and so one had to wait till noon for the tiniest bit of rosy sunlight, which never lasted more than a quarter of an hour here, provided it wasn't overcast as it was that late November day. Probably for this reason the young man was hunched over, his face nearly pressed between the covers of the book. Having read the first page, he carefully turned it, but only hastily scanned the remaining lines; then he closed the book and began to examine its binding of cool-red saffian, a binding much too fine, of course, for present circumstances.

"Well?" said the man. Not a single line of his face moved to warrant any kind of description.

"Well?!" said the youth evasively, though he could surmise what was expected of him as he tried to afford himself another moment to think it over.

"Well, decide—will you take it on?" said the man, frowning slightly.

"I'm not sure . . ." said Adam Lozanić, a student in the School of Philology, a degree candidate in the Serbian language and literature program, and a part-time proofreader for the tourism and nature magazine *Our Scenic Beauty*. "I'm not sure what to say—this is a book, it's no longer a manuscript."

"Of course it's not. Now, it's important you abide by the conditions. And that means that you will not leave behind any kind of notes, or any other written trace despite the nature of the work. Discretion goes without saying. If you think the compensation inadequate, I am prepared to offer . . ." said the man, leaning forward confidingly.

Adam had choked at the first amount that was mentioned to him. From the now-doubled sum he would be able to live comfortably for five or six months, without having to worry about the rent, and finally finish, in peace, his thesis in order to complete his studies. Along with his part-time position at *Our Scenic Beauty*, he could just about make ends meet.

"That's awfully generous. But my job makes sense only if, how can I put it, it is practiced on manuscripts. A book is a printed, final thing, and proofreading or editing really can't correct much of anything here. Besides, I don't know what the author in question would say about all this," offered the young man shyly, once more opening the saffian binding. On the inner title page, in larger type, hovered the words *MY MEMORIAL.*, and somewhat below this, "Written by and published at the expense of Mr. Anastas C. Branica, man of letters."

"I believe he'll have no objections, since he died a good fifty years ago," said the man, somehow smiling stiffly. "I emphasize, there are no surviving relatives. But even if there were, this copy would still be my private property and I consider that I have the right to make certain revisions. I could, if I felt like it, underline sentences, fill in the margins with notes, even pull out pages I didn't like. Nevertheless, I want you to make some minor changes, in accordance with my specifications and the instructions of my wife. Your editor tells me that you're diligent. I myself am somewhat in the same profession, and so I suppose this is the nicest recommendation people in our line of work can receive . . ."

Adam Lozanić placed his palms on the covers of the book. When he was preparing for his examinations, when he was choosing what to read first from the long lists of recommended literature, it seemed to him that he could feel the pulse of each reading selection that way. Before entering it, he would always indulge in that innocent superstition. Despite the cool binding of the leather known as saffian, this book was warm, intensely alive, its hidden pulse beating below the pulp of the young man's fingers. As though written only a short while ago, it was indistinguishable from newly completed manuscripts, hotter still than the writer's feverish hopes and fears. Perhaps it was just this warmth that helped Adam make up his mind.

"All right, I'll give it a try," he said. "I can't promise you when I'll finish it. It's pretty long, and besides, the spelling rules have changed several times since then, the punctuation is unsuitable—you saw the full stop after the title—and then the vocabulary is the most sensitive part . . . And I'm really not sure where you would like me to make all the changes?"

"When can you begin?" asked the mysterious man, not hearing what was said.

"Tomorrow morning—in the evening I'm too tired. The newspaper text is so tiny and full of errors. I see letters even when I close my eyes. I can start tomorrow, in the morning . . ." The young man was talking at needless length, as if captivated by his own question: *What was he getting himself into?*

"At nine o'clock sharp, then. And don't be late. If I can't make it, my wife will wait for you." The client got up and exited the room.

Adam Lozanić remained to stare at the calendar, which was tacked askew to the inner side of the door that had just been closed. A square pencil mark framed the twentieth of November, a Monday. The man's wife would wait for him?! But where?! And what could all this mean, except that the mysterious man had found out his little secret?! He shuddered. Anyway, he was certain he had never revealed it to anyone. Beginning a year ago, from time to time it seemed to him that when reading he met other readers *inside* the given text. And from time to time, only now and then but more and more vividly, he would later recall those other, mostly unknown people who had been reading the same book at the same time as he. He remembered some of the details as if he had really lived them. Lived them with all his senses. Naturally, he had never confided this to anyone. They would have thought him mad. Or at best a little unhinged. Truth be told, when he seriously considered all these extraordinary matters, he himself came to the conclusion that he was teetering dangerously on the very brink of an unsound mind. Or did it all appear to him thus from too much literature and too little life?!

Now that he had remembered the reading, it was time to engage in that by means of which, at least for the present, he still earned his livelihood. New texts were waiting, and he sharpened a pencil and got down to work, rarely opening the *Orthography* or the volumes of the *Dictionary*. There were numerous articles, but his task was made easier by the editor in chief himself, who had instructed him to focus his attention exclusively on the proof-reading. Conversely, the changing of the order of the words, the words themselves, or the facts—he was not allowed even to consider these possibilities.

"Lozanić, mind you don't needlessly rack your brains, that's not one of your responsibilities!" the editor in chief had said just that harshly several times, not hesitating, in Adam's presence, to brush the dandruff from his shoulders and the collar of his dark blue, double-breasted suit jacket.

Once the young associate had stood his ground. "Sir, permit me, a factual error has crept in here. I can't allow this to state that Kopaonik is almost 2,500 meters high when the official altitude of Pančić's Peak—I consulted the map—is 2,017 meters?!"

"Almost! Does the word *almost* mean anything to you?! It's small, and exactly covers the difference. And where is the error here? Lozanić, you are a specialist in Serbian literature, albeit one that hasn't graduated yet, but a geographer you're certainly not. The wrinkling of the earth's crust is not a finished thing. Do you have a scrap of national pride at all? Why would you round it off to two thousand?! Economizer! Had I only asked myself, I would have written in a full three thousand! Let's go now, and don't come to me anymore with your petty quibbling and that miserable faintheartedness of yours." For a moment the editor left the dandruff on his collar, only to get rid of it with an intolerant sweep of the hand.

Our Scenic Beauty was issued bimonthly. Adam Lozanić was obliged to come in on Mondays, to look over the articles that had arrived from the regular correspondents from all the known and unknown corners of the world. The work ahead of him, from the mysterious man, had arrived at just the right time: he would have a whole week for the best-paying job of his career as a part-time proofreader. Perhaps for that very reason, the young man made sure he didn't miss the chance to correct the part of the holiday issue editorial in which the haunting riches of his native land had been wildly exaggerated. In the text he crossed out the reference to the controversial reindeer, and on the side of the page wrote in: "Untrue. As far as is known, no such Arctic animal exists here."

2

Finishing the last article around three o'clock, something about the boom in convention tourism, the young man put on his Vietnam field jacket and packed the books in a sports bag. The editorial department didn't have copies of the *Dictionary* or the *Orthography*, indispensable tools for a proofreader. Scrupulous when it came to even the slightest deviation from the rules, Adam was forced constantly to lug all that weight around with him, because in the afternoon the general-purpose room was used by the cleaning women, and at night the old watchman took a little nap there.

The November sky congealed into cuttlefish black, threatening to pour. Walking to his rented studio apartment on Milovan Milovanović Street, at the foot of steep Balkanska, and once more remembering the mysterious man, the youth changed his mind and, pushing his way into the crowded bus on Terazije, set out in the direction of the National Library. He intended to find out who this Anastas C. Branica was, the author of a book so estimable its owner had bound it in expensive saffian. There in the National worked Stevan Kusmuk, an industrious type who had graduated on time and, unaccustomed to being idle, taken a position as a volunteer in the main reading room. Fortunately, there were not many patrons at the library, and this friend helped Adam search through the catalogs, bibliographies, and lexicons of writers for nearly two hours. There was no Branica.

"Are you sure that's his surname? Strange—if he ever published anything, it would have to be recorded here . . ." This was afterward, in the library's snack bar, with Kusmuk knitting his brows. He could not endure the least bit of perplexity; at the university he'd been known for the enormous number of references in his seminar papers, often lengthier than the text itself.

"Yes, I mean, probably, I have to check . . ." answered Adam, not wishing to reveal the reason for his interest, and even getting ready to leave, when he saw a pretty girl with a bell-shaped hat descending from the reading room into that same snack bar, probably to refresh herself with coffee or tea, like the others.

"Tell me, which books did she take out?" he asked, following her with his gaze, not doubting Stevan would know something like that by heart, had the girl only handed him an order slip with the titles he was to bring from the stacks.

His friend truly had a prodigious memory, and he recited: "*The Encyclopedic English-Serbo-Croatian Dictionary* of Svetomir Ristić, Živojin Simić, and Vlade Popović, Volume One, from A through M, in the photo-printed edition of Prosveta, Belgrade, 1974."

For a few moments Adam Lozanić wondered whether he should wait; that is, whether he himself should go into the main reading room, order the same volume, and from there watch for her return. He rather hoped this might be one of those days when he would manage to enter the reading selection so far that he would become conscious of the other readers who were immersed in the same text at the same time. In just that way, at the end of the seventh semester, he had had a promising romance with a classmate, the prettiest girl in the World Literature Department, but when he had tried to approach her in real life, outside the text—that is, in the courtyard of the school—she had simply looked the other way.

"Would you like to walk beside the river?" he'd persisted, wishing to remind her not only of their simultaneous reading of a realistic novella—set along the meticulously described riverbank—but, even more, that yesterday they had spent the whole afternoon there. In front of the others, she'd quipped: "I'd like to, but only if you swim across to the other side."

That whole week following he hadn't set foot in the auditorium; it seemed to him that her ringing laughter was not at all attenuated by the building on the student square.

What, then—even supposing he would have managed to meet her inside a text—would have been the use now of approaching this beautiful girl with the bell-shaped hat, if she, too, really didn't know him? Reading together, Adam feared, was becoming an obsession that could take him too far.

"Kusmuk, when some book starts to thoroughly engross you, do you have the feeling you aren't alone, that besides you there are other people, similarly captivated, who by a concurrence of events, by the law of probability, have simultaneously begun to read on the opposite side of the city, in another city, possibly even in another part of the world?" As soon as he'd declared this, Adam regretted it.

His friend looked him up and down in astonishment. It took him some time to recover himself. But from that moment, Kusmuk simply rambled on matter-of-factly:

"There are three types of readers, says the old nitpicking Goethe. The first enjoys without judging. The third judges without enjoying. And the type in between judges while enjoying and enjoys while judging—the type who actually creates the work of art anew. Roland Barthes, however, says . . ." and now Kusmuk had really taken off, ranging from author to author and theory to theory: Yuri Tynyanov . . . Hans Robert Jauss . . . Wolfgang Iser . . . Nauman . . . The theory of reception of the literary work . . . The open-ended work . . . The horizon of expectation . . . The reification of the text . . .

The triangle of author-work-reader . . . Semiotics . . . The signifying chain . . . Even though it concerned the field of painting, Kusmuk recommended to Adam the recently translated study *Abstraction and Empathy* by Wilhelm Wörringer . . . But Adam Lozanić was not listening. He was looking at the girl with the bell-shaped hat. He watched her drinking tea, and found extraordinary graciousness in those quite ordinary movements. He watched her stand up and pass beside him, leaving behind a pleasant smell. Only the next day's heavy task kept him from getting up and following that smell and, in the reading room, asking for the same dictionary, so that they might simultaneously follow the same lines. Which is why, having exited the National Library building, he bore in his breast a feeling of regret. The autumn colors of Karadjordje Park had turned to darker hues. Little dogs on leashes pulled their owners along the paths and around the monument to the great leader. The gilded crosses of the decades-unfinished St. Sava Church kept vigil in the twilight, which hung low on the rooftops of Vračar. At about that time, the season's first rain began to fall.

3

To get to his studio apartment he needed a good, perhaps a very good, hour or more. You couldn't squeeze into a bus, streetcar, or trolley. Especially not with an overstuffed bag. Giving up on the idea of taking public transport, Adam Lozanić walked down to the rotary Slavija district, for some reason stubbornly circumventing the entire marketplace in a direction opposite the circular flow of the traffic. He walked past the neon McDonald's sign, the crowd at the bus stop for numbers 2, 19, 22, and 59, on past the close-packed tobacco shops and the rain-wet cardboard boxes on which street vendors were selling trifles, then stopped beside the famous Mitić's hole, the site of the largest department store ever conceived in the Balkans, at one time never erected and then never torn down. Then he continued past the vendors selling chestnuts, sunflower seeds, and chewing gum, past the somber outline of the old Hotel Slavija reflected in the darkened glass of its newly built annex, once more past the McDonald's sign in order to enter the river basin at Nemanjina, and on toward the main railroad station. The six volumes of the Dictionary of the Serbian Language, the Orthography, and the enigmatic book bound in saffian became heavier and heavier; the bag's shoulder strap cut into him painfully, no matter how often he shifted it from one shoulder to the other. The young man progressed with difficulty, barely making his way between the diagonally parked cars along the sidewalks of the capital, his hair wet and his clothes soaked to the skin. Having come within sight of the façade of the train station—the roman numerals MDCCCLXXXIV and the broken clock—he turned uphill. There, at the foot of steep Balkanska, was little Milovan Milovanović Street, named for a now-forgotten statesman, lawyer, and diplomat from the turn of the century. Adam lived only two houses beyond the Hotel Astoria.

No matter how tired he was, no matter how much in a hurry, he always stopped to observe the porter dressed in his pompous uniform, like a general decorated in imaginary ranks, gold braids, and trouser stripes, not entirely in keeping with the dingy lobby of the hotel. No matter how tired he was, he never missed the opportunity also to look in the direction of the tavern Our Sea, directly opposite his building. Judging by its name, the depressingly lonely, dusty stuffed green crab in the window display, and the pitifully limp and tangled fishing nets with which the rust-colored walls and ceiling had been decorated in not very inspired fashion, the dilapidated bar must have once long ago been a seafood restaurant. Of all that, the only thing remaining now was that Our Sea resembled

a large aquarium full of tobacco smoke, ruled over by a bevy of regular customers who were sitting over very sweet coffee and glasses
of vermouth, leaning on their elbows and saying nothing or forever
babbling on about the same old stories. The tavern could generally
be seen from the window of Adam's rented studio apartment, but
from up close the people crowded together in that gloomy aquarium
gave the impression they were cursed beings, having been entan-
gled in those barren nets from who knows when, beings in whom
no one took joy and whom no one needed; and so they spent a good
part of the day and night here, usually staying until the early morning hours, until closing time was announced. From outside, from
the street, the opening of their sadly downturned mouths evoked
something between difficult breathing and the inarticulate, sound-
less speech of fish.

On the door to his apartment Adam Lozanić found his own
message, which he had pinned there that morning. In it he had
informed his landlord that he would be paying him the rent any
day now, once he had received his fee from *Our Scenic Beauty*. The
loquacious, middle-aged Mojsilović, a man of private means, had
made agreements all over Belgrade with the most elderly owners of
various properties—who were always without relatives—to provide
them with lifelong care, in order thus, upon their deaths, to inherit
their apartments and then remodel and rent them out. He was forever complaining that his work was unprofitable, that he was on the
verge of bankruptcy, that medicines and foods were so expensive,
that the old people stubbornly clung to life, that they were always
grumbling about something . . . However, he claimed, his rental fees
were so reasonable. Just consider how to him, to Lozanić, he was
renting a studio apartment in a very good location at far below mar-
ket value . . . But even though the rent was sky-high, Adam thought,
the apartment, albeit located in the very heart of the city, was not
distinguished by any particular advantages. Rather small even for

a single person, it had come to be when Mojsilović "compartmentalized" a two-room flat, having subdivided it into three separate units—procuring as many occupancy permits as possible outside the law—then fashioning a circular patchwork of the electrical and telephone lines, of radiator pipes and tubes, and of water-supply and drainage pipes for the miniature bathrooms . . . Adam occupied the middle studio apartment; the one on the left was being rented by a family with two preschool children, and the one on the right by a scowling street vendor of souvenirs. At one time interior partitions, the walls were no more than three fingers thick and much too porous to hold back the constant quarreling of the little boy and girl, which was punctuated by the shouting of their parents. Opposite them, the vendor made his own pathetic souvenirs himself, mostly dried flowers in a frame, and so from there one heard the incessant hammering-on of slats, usually at the most improbable hours of the day. Silence in the middle apartment could be had only in the faucets, because for some incomprehensible reason there was oftentimes no water.

This time, perhaps because of the rain, the faucets were gurgling. The young man got undressed, with his forefinger straightened his eyebrows and the sparse hairs on his chest, took a shower, got into his cotton-flannel pajamas, threw a blanket over his shoulders, and snacked on whatever he could find, which is to say on a piece of yesterday's rye bread with last year's apricot jam.

"In a jar of jam opened on Monday, mold can never start to grow!" had said his mother, who weekly brought him homemade food by bus as well as her advice by telephone. "Never, not for anything, open a book on Tuesday. From time immemorial Monday has been a good day for beginnings. Tuesday is bad luck, on Tuesdays nothing ever goes right. Or ever gets done," she would add.

Smiling at this expression, as if it were the secret ingredient in apricot jam, Adam Lozanić remembered that today was in fact

Monday. Perhaps that was the only reason why, although he was tired, chilled to the bone, and on top of that discontented because he had missed the opportunity to try his hand at a simultaneous reading with the pleasant-smelling girl in the National Library—perhaps, that is, only because of his mother's adage, did he once more reach for the mysterious book bound in saffian.

"'MY MEMORIAL. Written and published at the expense of Anastas C. Branica, man of letters,'" he read out loud from the inner title page, and the blows of the hammer announced that the souvenir vendor had begun to frame his dry flowers next door.

"'Belgrade, nineteen hundred and thirty-six!'" he exclaimed, purposely shouting out those tinier letters and figures. He knew his neighbor couldn't bear it when he tested himself for exams aloud; more than once that frowner had told him he was not obliged to listen to his reciting.

"Neighbor"—the vendor had said when he met him at the bus stop, long ago, as Adam was preparing for his examination in Renaissance and Baroque literature—"I'd like to know where you dig up those little lyrics of yours?! Why don't you read things that other people do; up until the holidays I won't have time to follow the papers and it would be nice, while I work, to hear the news from you. We could share the costs. You buy the daily papers and I'll buy the weeklies . . ."

Turning now to the back of the saffian-bound book, Adam Lozanić, from the usual information on the last page, found only:

"'Globus Printers, Kosmajska Twenty-Eight; Telephone: twenty-two, dash, seven-hundred-ninety-four!'"

The hammering had quieted. And then an angry voice was heard:

"Can you please keep it down a little?"

Then the hammer started to metronomically bang again, and the young man began to examine the bookbinding. The Morocco, tanned characteristically thin, was a dyed goat-leather covered with finely cut pores. Of the finest quality and appearance, it was for centuries produced in the Moroccan city of Safi, whence the name saffian. The mysterious man's book—and, as it would turn out, the book of a mysterious author as well—had been bound in just this kind of leather, not in one of the cheap imitations bookbinders usually substituted today. Along the edges and on the spine was the imprint of an intricately detailed, masterfully wrought overlapping tendril of a vine.

Once more opening the book, but now skipping the title page, Adam read the italicized note framed in a black line:

This novel has arisen from a great and futile affection for Mademoiselle Nathalie Houville, a gifted painter and a cruel lover, and so I dedicate it, in its final version, to my people and to the blessed memory of my mother Magdalina, who succumbed to malignant fevr on the 3rd day of October in the year 1922. On St. John the Baptist Day 7/20 January 1936—Anastas C. Branica.

Indeed, the part-time proofreader for *Our Scenic Beauty* at once noticed that the full stops after the years were missing. And then a letter *e* in the word *fever*. But he was not sure if his client wanted exactly these kinds of corrections. He wasn't sure what exactly his client wanted at all. He only remembered the client's words, "My wife will wait for you!" Whatever that had meant . . .

Adam Lozanić concluded reassuringly that he had, after a fashion, begun the reading on a Monday, a good day for beginnings. Tomorrow he would be more rested and find out somehow what he needed to do to the book. Nevertheless, he couldn't resist inserting with a lead pencil the missing e between fev and r. Perhaps that word, that shivering word, reminded him that he himself was shivering slightly. Why had he caught a cold?! Right before such important work?! Right before such a well-paying job?!

"I'll make some tea," he said out loud; what with his neighbor's banging, he sometimes couldn't hear his own thoughts.

But you couldn't count on the rain. Although it was pouring and pelting outside, from the faucet in the improvised kitchen came only a wheezing, a gushing of perfectly dry silence.

"To bed!" now screamed the parents at the little boy and girl in the adjoining flat. "Go to bed this moment!"

The young man had never had words with them. He felt sorry, sometimes for the unruly children, sometimes for the nervous grownups. If they worked in shifts, when both the father and the mother found themselves on the night shift, Adam, in the evening— paying no mind to the protests of the souvenir vendor— would read through the thin walls selected stories from children's literature to the lonely little ones. Whether it was because of this or because of something else, on that examination he had displayed considerable knowledge, scoring a perfect ten.

"To bed!" the parents repeated. "Go to bed this moment!"

And as if this command had been meant for him, Adam Lozanić—degree candidate in the School of Philology, part-time colleague with the magazine *Our Scenic Beauty*, and subtenant in the building opposite the tavern Our Sea—went to bed.

But then he once more, for curiosity's sake, opened the book. This time at the beginning. It was a sentence in Serbian. As was the next one, after all. The same one he had hastily looked over today in his little room of an office. Typeset by hand. Printed in Cyrillic characters, on paper that had yellowed in spots from time; time which insinuates itself everywhere: "All around, as far as the eye could see, stretched a garden of ravishing beauty . . ."

And then, despite the hammering-on of slats to frames, he felt like sleeping. The book slipped slowly from the young man's hands, closing by itself.

FIRST READING

ON WHERE THE MOON WOULD BE
AS WELL AS THE NORTH STAR
WERE IT NOT OVERCAST WITH CLOUDS;
ON WHETHER A LIBRARY AND A BOTANICAL GARDEN
HAVE ANYTHING IN COMMON;
ON HOW THE SHINE RETURNS TO MEMORIES;
ON WHAT ONE SEES
IN THE EYES OF AN ATTENTIVE READER;
ON HOW ONE FORMS
THE SIMPLE FUTURE TENSE
OF THE VERB *TO BE*
WITHOUT THE LEAST BIT OF REGRET;
ON WHERE THERE STILL IS
SESAME SEED OIL AND REAL *BARBANATZ*;
ON WHERE THE LARGEST DEPARTMENT STORE IN
THE BALKANS IS LOCATED;
ON WHAT BECAME OF KING PETER II'S ORDERLY;
ON ALL THERE IS IN A YOUNG GIRL'S PILLOW;
AND ON WHAT IS TRUSTWORTHY LUGGAGE
FOR A TRANSOCEANIC CRUISE

4

Superficially glancing over the beginning of the just-opened book, Jelena suddenly didn't feel like reading. Would it help if she begged off because of weakness, or some other kind of discomfort? Was not the pecking below her breastbone the source of that nausea? There it was again: the dizziness she knew so well, and the sweaty palms . . .

However, casting a sidelong glance at Natalija Dimitrijević, the girl at once dismissed all the possible excuses. Behind the unnaturally strong lenses of her eyeglasses the old woman scarcely blinked at all, hardly waiting to drink up her tea—and to set out. First to do one part together, as they had so many times before; and then for each to follow her own destiny.

"Come now, the cold will do you good," said the lady of the house over her teacup. She had had to think long on how to articulate even that little bit of whispering.

It was chilly to be sure. Midnight was almost here. In the center casement of the latticed window, on the upper right-hand windowpane, on one of forty-five glass fields of the cuttlefish-black Belgrade sky, a chalk circle marked the spot where the full moon would be—and, on another windowpane, a little cross marked where the North Star would be, were it not overcast with November clouds. The rainy capital night was filled with the splashing footfalls of late passersby or the rumbling of vehicles rushing to deliver, before the event, tomorrow's edition of the newspaper; but amid the patter of raindrops one could yet hear the inexorable clanking of the cobalt tea service, adorned with painted gold constellations.

Jelena looked about the room. Everything was ready. Since

returning from the National Library, where she studied English on Mondays, since the lady of the house had announced her decision regarding her final departure, not so much as waiting for the girl to remove her wet little bell-shaped hat, since starting with the preparations, the companion had not taken a rest. There had been so much work to do. Except for a floor lamp nearby, the lights in the apartment had been turned off. Quite conducive to reading, the parchment lampshade softened each sharper edge of the adjacent light. A ghostly white linen had been draped across the chairs. As luck would have it, in the dressers and chests of drawers there were exactly as many bed sheets as needed to cover all the pieces of furniture. The remaining glasses of all types, in the credenza in the dining room, had been turned upside down so as not to collect dust. The lid on the phonograph had been lowered, the records wiped clean and finally put back into their corresponding jackets. The water in the vase of flaming-red fall flowers had been changed a short while ago; neither the girl nor the lady had had the heart to throw away a bouquet of flowers that had not yet wilted . . .

The required luggage was placed all around. And more than that: a chest, three large trunks, six suitcases, and a dozen round hatboxes, each with its own name tag or the embossed monogram of its owner. On this matter the old woman had never shown moderation, either, but this time she had really outdone herself. In a travel fever, from one moment to the next she thought of bringing also this or that. It was barely an hour ago that she had finally calmed down, because a place had been found for the insect net. The girl's luggage consisted only of a rather small varicolored rucksack with the most essential items. They still had only to finish drinking their jasmine tea and to leave. Because from here on there was no way out.

"Should I check whether I locked the front door well?" it occurred to Jelena to say, as an excuse by which she might delay, if only a while, the beginning of the end.

The old woman had never before been absent without first making sure the door chain had been securely latched and the key turned twice, that the faucets had been tightly closed and the blinds in the other rooms neatly lowered . . . But on this occasion it was as if she were no longer interested in all these usual precautionary measures. Although she had waited for more than half a century, she now wished for them to leave as soon as possible.

"Well all right—but hurry, I'm afraid I'll be late—if I'm still wanted anywhere . . ." she said in an agitated voice, expressing herself with difficulty because of her illness, so that out of every five or six words one would stick in her throat.

As she waited, Natalija Dimitrijević greedily swallowed some tea.

5

Yesterday marked one year since Jelena's arrival. A whole year since she took up residence in this building, in all respects a building just like all the others on quiet Palmotić Street. Diagonally parked cars. A row of plane trees, the bases of their trunks swollen right near the ground from some disease. Five. Seven. Nine. A row of drowsy pigeons on the safe height of the overhanging ledge of the roof. Curious little sparrows on the triangular lintels above the windows and on the tin cornices. A pair of strayed, trembling thrushes in the open mouth of one of the eight faithfully rendered lion heads on the façade, fashioned by the famous stonecutter Franjo Waldman. Balconies like giant nests, forgotten in the air, deserted until spring. It was as if the Belgrade architects from the turn of the century—Nestorović, Andra Stevanović, Dimitrije Leka, Aleksandar Bugarski, Savčić, Becker, Antonović, Konstantin Jovanović, Dragiša Brašovan—had competed over who (along with the many drainpipes on the faces of their buildings) would more abundantly satisfy the needs of birds.

The lobby laid in marble—and ringing with the echoes of stilettos—crisscrossed here and there with finely veined cracks and the scuffmarks of silence from newer footwear with rubber soles. The stylishly plaited lacework of the stucco, disfigured by the carelessly concealed scars of renovation and the subsequent installation of new wiring. Letterboxes with patinated brass nameplates, the surnames worn shallow, probably from the daily glimpses of owners hoping for a letter. The elevator car enclosed in a wrought iron cage. And a mirror, in a compartment so confined that Jelena, whether she wanted to or not, came face-to-face again with her melancholy, which was immeasurably large—so immeasurably large that it seemed the screeching steel cable would snap from the combined load. Later, Madame Dimitrijević would instruct her tenant in the secret ways of ameliorating sadness, thanks to which the girl at least ceased to pine because of her own overwhelming feelings.

"I know well from my own experience," the old woman would repeat at that time. "It will take time. You'll see, you'll learn that a person can get used to anything. A Russian émigré—a teacher of operatic singing—Paladia Rostovtseva taught me that. She said: 'Come, my dear, what's troubling you?! One: think of your demeanor! Two: cheer up! Three: a smile, a laugh—there is no more beautiful music!'"

However, that would all take place much later on.

The day of her arrival, when she stopped in front of Madame Natalija's door—a front door in no way different from the other apartments' on the fifth floor of that building on Palmotić Street—Jelena had only a little money left, a modest rucksack, that oppressive shadow of melancholy, and a doubly folded edition of *Politika*. From the time she had completed her studies, taking her degree only for the sake of her parents; from the time she had extracted from her father and mother permission to submit the documents to leave for some other country, so long as it was as far away as possible from her sadness; from the time she had filled in the questionnaires, drawn up the request, and awaited a favorable response from the embassy; from time to time she had supported herself by accepting all kinds of jobs, hurriedly studying the English language, the only knowledge she intended to bring from here. On the day of her arrival, her hopes had come down to a single want ad published in *Politika*, printed under the heading "Miscellaneous" and circled with a pencil stroke. "Older woman seeks diligent female companion. Room and board provided. Apply in person . . ." The girl had managed to read these words over tweed-clad shoulders, in between several open umbrellas, and in between sleeves of waterproof canvas. This had taken place at the bus station in front of the Balkan movie theater; to no avail she had moved from one end of Belgrade to another in search of something more certain, for anything by means of which, at least for a while, she could heal the rift between the past and present tense. She had managed to read just that much of the ad, and so, on account of the address, had had to buy a newspaper, strictly on her guard not to let her glance fall upon any adjacent heading, any other word . . . Namely, she had noticed long ago that the words of her native language increased the sadness in her, even caused her a painful feeling of discomfort—and so she avoided them as far as something like that is possible.

"Who is it? Come now, I won't harm you!" came a merry voice, before a peephole opened slightly and the key turned and the unlatched door chain rattled.

The door was opened by a frail little woman of a stature out of proportion to her high-sounding first and last names. Clad in a dress of raw silk, likewise too large for her, of a bygone cut. Wearing a straw hat, the brim glued at the front, a double necklace of mother-of-pearl beads, and beige cotton gloves. In contrast to the holiday details, holding in her hand her apron and some sort of knife, the kind used for cutting pages. Craning her neck and squinting, the way shortsighted people do.

"Forgive me," she smiled in embarrassment, flushed in the face. "A few uncut specimens have just arrived from the bookshop. Please come in, please do, we'll sit in the library room." She showed the young guest in. "Yes, I'm Natalija Dimitrijević. Miss Dimitrijević, actually. I never married. Nonetheless, don't ever address me as such. Now, at my age, that would be improper . . ."

Stepping out of the vestibule cloaked in semidarkness, walking straight ahead and then to the right, through the open double-hung doors, and into a room of books, Jelena had the impression that she was in a garden, although all around there wasn't a single plant, not counting the vase with a bouquet of flaming-red fall flowers. Where did such a feeling come from? she wondered. Yet afterward, for months and months, again and again, the girl would find a whole series of explanations.

Perhaps the feeling arose, she now thought, from so much teeming light and from the thickly woven drapes that had not been drawn. In the east wall was an enormous lattice window, where each of the five sashes was subdivided into nine equal fields, and these numerous panes, which made the room swarm with flashes, gave off the feeling of a glass botanical garden in which instead of plants thrived books.

Who knows, perhaps the impression of a garden was also imposed on one by the dense growth of titles along every free foot of the other walls, from the uncovered floor—a dried-out parquet, masterly fitted together in a mirthful mosaic woodwork with every nuance of fall colors—to the old-fashioned vaulted ceiling, which had shady nooks. At first the mottle of blooming titles could not be discerned, most of them being in two or three identical copies, just as in nature here and there the plantain continually replicates itself, and elsewhere shrubs of dogwood stubbornly spring up. Among the tendrils of this growth the girl immediately observed luxuriant titles in

English and other foreign languages in a separate glassed-in section of shelves, titles resembling some exotic transoceanic species that required special care and climatic conditions. To reach the highest rows there was a movable ladder, like those for trimming or grafting fruit trees, and so the separating of the uncut leaves from the samples seemed to Jelena to be a task one undertook in order to achieve a similar result.

Still, perhaps the unexpectedly modest furnishings also contributed to the overall impression. There were four cane garden chairs with high backs and armrests—as well as an easy chair with carved legs, as if taken from some other furniture set—indifferently gathered around a floor lamp with a parchment lampshade. There was also a little oval table large enough for a vase of always fresh mimosas, lilacs, roses—or those flaming-red fall flowers—according to the season of the year, and the table was large enough for serving tea and setting down one's eyeglasses or a book that has just been read. In addition, on the only swath of wall not occupied by shelves, above the low tiled stove lined in fire-baked bricks the color of evergreens, was a clock with weights in the shape of pine cones, its hands so slow that one needed time to determine whether the mechanism was ticking, whether it worked at all.

But at first (and then also for all those months during which she resided in the woman's home), the main reason the girl looked upon the library room as upon a garden was Natalija Dimitrijević herself. The well-preserved old woman would enter here, wiping her shoes on the doormat in the hall, dressed elegantly as if for some festive occasion, with an obligatory hat and cotton gloves, only to daydream idly, as in the mysterious shade of some thousand-leaved bower; or to tend patiently to her flowerbeds and treetops; to anguish over any spot gone bare, as over any branch removed; to distinguish each and every shoot; to expose to sunlight and to search through editions long sheltered away; to carefully protect loose pages from the disease of falling out; to listen closely, inclining her head, whether and where she heard the dry rustle of bookworms, the notorious book moth, chinch bugs, book lice, and other harmful insects; to finger the gilded spines and borders, the deep impressions of the ornamental vine leaves, the minute pores of the gravure, the cobweb-like vignettes, and the book covers of all types: from simple, coarse pasteboard containing tiny chips of wood to bindings of ordinary American cloth, from a pale rosy satin to a wine-red velvet, even from romantic jackets of starched needlepoint to the regal bindings of the red leather saffian.

And so their conversation, too, that day began in keeping with Jelena's conception of the room:

"From here the tree of my life branches outward . . ." said the old woman, making an uncertain movement of the hand. "Sadly," she added, heaving a sigh, "here it also converges. I've lived a solitary life for years now . . ."

6

Everything proceeded without further interruption. The woman gave a start, then briefly outlined her expectations. Jelena's employment would not be for the entire day. More accurately, they were to: chat over cups of jasmine tea; listen in silence to the clattering enamel of the cobalt tea service while counting the constellations painted on the saucers; very rarely venture out together, and only as far as nearby St. Mark's Church, for services on St. John the Baptist Day, high church holidays, and when St. Petka appeared to her in a dream. Truth be told, her legs weren't in the best shape, and she had never been one for walks; and at any rate, she had seen it all before. The length and the breadth of it.

"But only that far!" she said, and squeezed shut her eyes as if intending never to open them again.

There are people whose entire appearance is subject to one particular part of their body—connecting eyebrows, high cheekbones, inquisitive lips, sloping shoulders, unsymmetrical flanks, or flat feet. Natalija Dimitrijević no doubt could be counted among them. She was altogether defined by her large, tranquil-green eyes. Only when she closed them could one judge how feeble she had really become. From the shriveled eyelids, from the individual furrows—her face had been transformed into a meshwork of past tenses. Indeed, Jelena found that the woman had shrunk still more, that she had gathered into a wrinkle of life. The dress she wore, which was of a bygone cut, seemed like a withered pod. And that moving testimony of inextricable old age at once deeply touched and upset the girl, so much so that from the rest of that conversation, about further duties of the position, all she remembered was herself finally agreeing and Natalija Dimitrijević's childlike squeal: "Wonderful, we'll start at once!"

On the other hand, she mused afterward, regardless of what was going on here, such an opportunity was not to be missed. A quiet street in the center of Belgrade. A spacious apartment with a parlor. Admittedly, though, of a curious arrangement . . . Most likely partitioned several times, so that a way onto the balcony simply did not exist; that is, one could go onto it only from the adjoining apartment. Which was nothing in comparison to the pantry that had been mistakenly walled up during the reallocation of 1947, along with all the silver-plated candlesticks, the saltcellar, the molds, the strainers, the graters, and the other kitchen utensils. From where, in the dead of night, one could hear the muffled, persistent pounding of a wooden mortar, as if someone were preparing crushed grain for someone else.

In general, except for the library room, all the rooms had

been arranged in accordance with Natalija Dimitrijević's eccentric notions; it would serve no purpose to begin a more detailed description of the layout, for it was rearranged from one moment to the next, so that one would continually need to make changes to it. Notes on this were apparently being kept by the neighbor from the apartment that connected to the balcony, who took advantage of every moment the blinds were not lowered to constantly spy out something and write it down.

"Some things can never be found if they're always in the same place," the old woman would say, tirelessly transferring the phonograph records from jacket to jacket, the contents of the drawers in the dressing table to the drawers in the bureau, and vice versa, until she herself would no longer know where anything was, so that she would be pleasantly surprised the next time she listened to music or searched through her things.

"Let's see if there are any changes . . ." she would say, again sorting and arranging the photographs from the family album, comparing them with her memories of times long past.

"The moon should be here, and the North Star here," she would say, erasing the previous evening's circles and little crosses from the windowpanes, in order to mark with chalk the new positions of the heavenly bodies, even if the following night were cloudy.

"Even the finest crystal seeks moisture, and when it's not used or at least exposed to dew—I know from experience—it begins to crack," she would say to justify her habit of always drinking water from a different glass, ranging from ordinary table glasses to brandy glasses—somewhat larger than a thimble—and from round cognac glasses to various wineglasses or those from the Brothers Moser, especially the ones with the thin stems.

"It's nearly been a whole week since I moved the chiffonier, a lot of darkness must have fallen behind it." She would push and pull, to and fro, the most unwieldy objects, and the old furniture, with a stiff bearing, would initially resist her with a squeaking and squealing, but in the end would always, panting, occupy the position its owner had chosen for it.

And since she was in the habit of changing beds, in order to throw off track the sleeplessness that pursued her, Madame Natalija herself could not stay put and never reposed for three successive nights in the same bed.

"Even that double bed is narrower than the sofa, if I toss and turn all night," went the expression that accompanied the transferring of the bed linens and pillows.

All the rooms had been arranged in accordance with her eccentric notions, although the library room with the tile stove was unlike the rest of the apartment in that no central heating had been installed there: the old woman thought that only natural warmth was suitable for the books:

"Otherwise the paper blossoms uncontrollably, and on the bindings sprout kidney-shaped swellings or tiny bubbles, similar to suffusions and blisters."

A rather small, sunny room, once the maid's, had been set aside for Jelena. The squat nightstand and walnut dresser exuded hospitality, and the feather quilts and downturned sheets spoke of peaceful dreams. And there were other things one needed; here everything was at one's disposal. The agreement stipulated room and board and a modest allowance. As for household chores, the companion might see to the daily groceries or the seasonal flowers, take it upon herself to light a fire in the tile stove during spells of bitter cold, but without being obliged to, only whenever she was so inclined . . .

The woman's rambling advice for various aspects of housekeeping ran thus:

"To get rid of yellowish spots you have to use a felt rag . . ."

"Boiling it in a sodium bicarbonate solution, one teaspoon per cup of water, should bring back the shine . . ."

"Just to be safe, take in or hem the parts that are torn or have come unstitched . . ."

"Fill them with lavender or stuff them with ripe chestnuts . . ."

"It's intolerable this dust has been stubbornly building up for so long . . ."

However, although Jelena was not obliged to help with the above, she was obliged, and without fail, to assist the lady of the house in her numerous reminiscences. And since time settles atop the time that went before, the old woman found it increasingly difficult to recall in succession even her most indispensable memories.

Within a matter of days, once Jelena had moved in and become somewhat familiar with the arrangement of the rooms and the customs of the house, Natalija Dimitrijević added:

"My Lord, I almost forgot the most important thing! In the evening or during the day—I don't doubt we'll come to some agreement—I would like for us to read together. Everything else can be done this way or that, but during the reading, I would ask you to be meticulous. Your predecessor could hardly be called a companion, precisely because she was unthorough. In her precipitate haste, she skipped lines and whole pages. I put up with it somehow, I'd catch up to her. But when she started to doze off or quite superficially follow along, I was forced kindly to bid her farewell . . ."

Indeed, how lightly this last remark had been made, how innocuously. Remembering the books in English in the glassed-in section of the woman's library room, Jelena even began to hope that together with the old woman she would be able to study the very language indispensable for her departure. Definite and indefinite articles, comparative adjectives, the agreement of tenses, the inflections of irregular verbs—reading out loud, word by word, phrase by phrase, the better to learn. It was probably for this reason that she so rashly obliged herself:

"Of course. I'll do my best."

7

It was a December afternoon last year, also a Monday, from time immemorial a good day for beginnings. The woman left it to Jelena to select a cane garden chair in the library room, a chair that in the future would be considered hers. She herself sat facing the girl. She took the glasses with the unnaturally strong lenses that she had just wiped clean, put them on, and noticeably ceased to blink. Reading together implied a whole host of minor preliminaries.

"It's essential that a person be tastefully dressed; you never know whom you're liable to meet . . ." she said, fastening the buttons on her gown for traditional outings and needlessly straightening the fresh wave in her hair.

"Time there is compressed time. It happens that five minutes here last a full hour there, but also vice versa; our reckoning is of no consequence, so you can feel free to forget about your watch or to take it off at once . . ." she admonished the companion.

"Find the third chapter, the river—I often go to stretches there. I consider it very suitable for some preliminary observations," concluded the old woman, handing the girl one of two books with the same title.

Jelena at first resisted her feeling of astonishment. At the remark about dressing tastefully she had blushed; her canvas sneakers were certainly not in keeping with the fashion tastes of Madame Natalija. At the observation about time, she had confusedly undone the band of her wristwatch, putting it in a pocket of her cotton jogging suit. But when she realized that reading together meant reading exactly the same book at the same time, even the same pages, she could not overcome the impression that Madame Dimitrijević's actions teetered dangerously on the very brink of an unsound mind. Once more looking at the old woman's face, with the tranquil-green eyes and the beatific smile, she had no other choice but to respond to everything with a nod of the head.

"So?" she heard not long afterward, trying without success to concentrate on the reading selection in front of her.

"'So?'?" she repeated, trying to buy time, not knowing just what was expected of her.

"So: I'm interested in what you have to say. What do you think of it?" asked the woman.

"Well, it's nice . . ." she uttered vaguely.

"Nice?! Is that all you have to add?!" Natalija Dimitrijević stared at the companion, disappointed. "You probably see the smoothness of the water there?"

"No, I mean, yes . . ." the girl quickly corrected herself, finding rescue precisely in the old woman's eyes, where, magnified by the lenses of her glasses, the surface of the mighty river sparkled, agitated slightly in the middle by the sinews of the main current.

"Now you can see why I love to go there. And besides, a little August in December can't be all that bad for my joints. It's all about two worlds, you see. Rather similar and rather different. Concerning the river basins of the second one—more exactly, of the first—there are no reliable data, so that one doesn't know why some river there dries up or swells . . ." said the woman, satisfied that she had at last found a true interlocutor.

That December Monday there was something of the August heat in her eyes. Of the fluttering of willow and sallow leaves, of the trembling of birds in a nest built atop the bow of a boat that had been hauled out and then forgotten; of those suns above the rippling river, the steamy haze of the reed patch on the opposite shore, and the pale blueness of the huddled mountain range; of the distant clearings under a blanket of eternal snow . . . When the woman turned around there was the flickering outline of a single solitary house, two stories and a light and dark yellow, uncannily desolate on a gentle rise in the middle of a forested valley. In the library room, it was now even warmer than when they had begun; it smelled of the great waters, which for centuries, perhaps since the beginning of the world, had been flowing who knows whence, who knows whither . . .

On other occasions Jelena, too, began to avail herself of this small artifice, in order to demonstrate that she was carefully following along with the remarkable old woman. Namely, she sometimes read certain passages from her gaze, ever more rarely wondering how it was possible to meet there that which hadn't been mentioned in the books. Eventually she quieted her conscience; after all, her duties also consisted of fulfilling the simple-hearted expectations of Natalija Dimitrijević. That harmless indulgence would of course require no effort. There was vindication also in the old woman's eyes, in which the companion caught a glimpse of happiness despite the magnifying lenses of her glasses. And above all, for the better part of each day she was able to prepare for her departure. She studied the English language in her little room, as quietly as she could, forever delaying informing the old woman of her ultimate intentions.

"I shall, you will, he will, she will, it will . . ."

She recited from an ordinary standard dictionary, the kind with a brief overview of grammar, strengthening particularly her knowledge of how to form the simple future tense of the verb to be, without the least bit of regret.

"We shall, you will, they will . . ."

8

At the end of the year, almost overnight, snow completely covered the last traces of fall. People walked the streets hunched over, their hands buried in their pockets; the wind sneaked in through even the narrowest sleeve, and then blew out the other. To make matters worse, this was no ordinary wind, one that merely chilled the small of the back. This wind brought with it also the cold of surrounding, ever closer wars, filling the heart and soul with trepidation; one could hardly block out the ubiquitous fear.

"Savor the little joys. I fear there's really not much else left to us," said the woman, becoming concerned when she saw the shivering Jelena return from the city. She took down from the chiffonier one of her hatboxes. "Here, I set aside a little gift for you, the kind of bell-shaped hat that's now being worn again, and it will also suit you for our walks."

Natalija herself decided a fire would be lit in the tile stove in the library room, in the morning, at noon, and in the evening, and so one busied oneself with the flame, then went down to the basement for firewood hauled there long ago, and carried out the ashes from the extinguished fire.

The old woman personally, during frosts, checked de visu whether each and every book was in its proper dust jacket or protective box, whether any ribbon bookmarks were protruding . . . "Last year a collection of stories slipped by me; when I opened it in the spring, there was hardly anything left of it to see. It had completely rotted," she moaned.

And on Christmas Eve, Madame Natalija ventured out with the companion for the first time, bringing a bundle of oak branches and straw. And then on St. John the Baptist Day she took a cake decorated with the cross and the letters of Christ's name, and with birds, little barrels, and grapes, and with braids of dough glazed with diluted honey. But between these two visits to St. Mark's Church together, the old woman had also gone to the city alone, and even on three occasions.

Jelena had insistently discouraged the woman: "Just because of candles?! But don't, I'll buy them—it's very icy, you might fall and injure yourself."

There had been frequent restrictions on the use of electricity, and the question arose of how they were to read if they didn't have adequate lighting.

Natalija Dimitrijević, getting ready, paid the girl no mind. "The best candles are the ones with the Apollo brand—they have Viennese wicks; only with them do the letters remain clear. Nowadays they carry them only at the trinket shop At the Lucky Hand."

"Well, fine—I'll go, only tell me where . . ." pleaded the companion.

"Dear child, I must still do that myself. You wouldn't find it. Kalmić's trinket shop At the Lucky Hand officially no longer exists. It's closed and has been for decades and decades now . . ." She waved back from the door.

From the window Jelena watched the old woman, at a snail's pace, carefully make her way along glistening January Palmotić Street, squeezing precariously between the diagonally parked cars and sometimes leaning on tree trunks or the walls of buildings.

Whether it was because she had walked cautiously or because At the Lucky Hand was somewhere far away, she was gone just long enough for the companion to begin to seriously worry. But she indeed returned with a box on which was written "Apollo." This incident, too, might have perhaps remained unexplained had it not been repeated the following week, although for a different reason. Selecting recipes for the Slava feast, Natalija Dimitrijević discovered that she lacked certain provisions, which could not be procured in just the same way:

"Good Rangoon or Carolina rice, sesame seed oil, and real bar-banatz can be found only in Svetozar Botorić's grocery shop, and fine paté de foie gras, Dresdener, bratwurst, and Rokap ham only in the sausage shop of that thickset Czech, Kosta Đ. Rosulek. Both stores are on Terazije, but I'm afraid you won't notice them among all the present-day store windows . . ."

"Because they no longer exist," said Jelena.

"That is only so to speak! Indeed, I continue to be their loyal customer! And where do you think this jasmine tea came from?! It's true that Mr. Botorić hasn't replenished his stocks in a long time. He says that he's going to liquidate the business, so few people stop in to see him; he drives a hard bargain, that crafty grocer, but he always greets me with the words 'Miss Natalija, it can be gotten, for you it can always be found!'" the old woman declared curtly, and then returned, indeed, with an overstuffed shopping bag of delicatessen goods.

However, as it turned out the very next day, that hadn't been the end of it; what really topped it all was her trip to Mitić's department store, where Natalija Dimitrijević was going to supplement her collection of phonograph records for the Slava feast.

"Are you thinking of the one on Knez Mihailova they still call Mitić's?" asked the companion.

"No, I'm thinking of the fourteen-story building in Slavija, which was taller than the Palace Albanija by a full two meters." The woman pointed through the window, as if somewhere in that direction such a building stood.

"You're probably thinking of the foundation pit that the developer Mitić excavated just before the Second World War, intending to build the tallest department store in the Balkans?" said Jelena, deciding to clear up this matter about shops and stores that had disappeared long ago.

"Pit, pit, foundation pit—I've been listening to that nonsense for fifty years now! Do you know that Vlada Mitić decided everything, from the exactly twenty million dinars deposited in the National Bank for the construction of the building to the future appearance of even the smallest store shelf? Only he didn't succeed in building it! Maybe it was better that way: they would have destroyed it in the bombings, or the new government would have seized it. So it's still standing there the way it was conceived. When some newer buildings disappear, not much of them remains. Right up until his death, Mitić used to make the rounds of all the store's departments, to wait personally on customers and to take care of every little detail, helping his diligent workers with credit, pay raises, and money for medical treatment. Yes, that's right, the workers—don't shake your head at me. Mr. Virijević, whose specialty was the sale of fabric goods, arrived in Slavija every blessed morning at exactly eight and remained on his feet till eight at night. It was believed that he went out of his mind, but with one look he could determine, to within a centimeter, how much of a particular material or lining you needed for a suit. What's more—I'll take you with me sometime—on the ninth floor of Mitić's department store is a restaurant. The last time I went I sat there; the view is simply charming, and they serve wonderful raspberry juice."

Jelena said nothing. She had neither the right nor the heart to wreck Madame Natalija's world. That, of course, was only a fanciful story, but everyone has a right to their own one. Although, it was strange the old woman had returned with her arms full from this shopping trip as well. One of the phonograph albums was a rare recording by the young pianist Arthur Rubinstein, and on the quite new dust jacket from the year 1926 was the selected program: Beethoven, Scriabin, Liszt, and de Falla compositions.

9

Along with the foods and tiny cakes, family reminiscences were prepared, embellished until they started to shine, as if they had taken place yesterday and not in times long past. With a surprising sprightliness, the old woman kept going from kitchen to library room, one moment leafing through the famous *Great National Cookbook* of Spasenija-Pata Marković, and the next recounting how the holiday had once been spent . . .

"Then, after the coffee, my father would ask my mother or me to sing. Mother had a special voice, and that gift I inherited from her; the guests would leave repeating that the song had been hospitality enough . . ." Natalija Dimitrijević recalled all sorts of details in the companion's presence, sometimes forcing her breath outward, as if with a deep sigh she wished to remove from past events the fallen blots of oblivion.

All in all, during the preparations for the Slava feast, more memories were revealed to Jelena than had been during the nearly three months since her arrival. Thus did the girl, helping the woman to arrange in sequence and to recollect the most prominent of them, little by little obtain a picture of the old woman's life.

Her late father, Gavrilo Dimitrijević, had owned the Pelican Bookshop on Kraljevski Square, subsequently Students Square, the largest in the capital after the one owned by Goetz Kohn and the one owned by Svetislav B. Cvijanović. Because she had secretly fallen in love with a young writer, and because she was unable to share the secret of her love with anyone else, she withdrew from the Stanković Music School in which she had just enrolled—removing herself from the operatic singing class of Madame Rostovtseva—and devoted herself entirely to the more predominant feeling, helping her father in the bookshop only because that young man often dropped in there.

"Regardless of the fact that he noticed nothing, regardless of the fact that the young writer perished under unexplained circumstances just several weeks after the publication of his first book, one evening, alone in my bed, I swore to love him my whole life long, and so those words, spoken then, still remain in my pillow . . ." she flushed.

The German bombs had not yet fallen on the April ruins of Belgrade, and Gavrilo Dimitrijević voluntarily put himself at the service of those who were gathering the singed pages of centuries-old Serbian church books in the destroyed National Library. He looked like a man who himself had burned on Kosančić Venac.

"He would come home half-crazed"—broke through from out of the haze of the old woman's memory—"his pockets stuffed with the charred remains of burnt books shaken down from the trees around the site of the fire, at night trying to salvage from the ashes at least some discernible word. As it turned out, he deciphered some of them, transcribed them in his legible handwriting, and sent them in waxed envelopes to Professor Veselin Čajkanović, and later, covertly, to the monastery Ljubostinja, where the German authorities were holding the interned Bishop Nikolaj Velimirović . . ."

After the war this correspondence served as a legal pretext for seizing his property. In the name of the people, supposedly, and without further ado, the bookshop and a portion of the apartment on Palmotić Street were expropriated, together with the link to the balcony, while the pantry was by mistake completely walled up; and on another, less official visit which one might sooner call a search, most of her father's notes were confiscated. Afterward, silent people would come and cart away some of the books, leaving scanty written receipts for them.

"The books and notes I'll make sure to tell you about later, because I don't have the time right now. St. John the Baptist Day is almost here, and we still haven't decided which tiny cakes to prepare!" the old woman pointed out. Jelena remembered the empty spaces on the bookshelves, the empty spaces which recalled severed branches in treetops.

Following the seizure of the family property, Natalija Dimitrijević's mother was never again able to recover her lost peace of mind. She trembled at the slightest sound of the doorbell or the lift. She had a feeling of foreboding even when on the staircase silence was heard—imagining that someone was stealing up to the door. No one could any longer get her to sing, and from a clot of melancholy in the breast she died in the spring of 1956. Natalija Dimitrijević related the story in hushed tones.

"Doctor Arsenov—you'll meet him at the Slava—held out hope until her dying breath, trying to persuade her: 'Come now, I know you don't feel like it, but force yourself. Here, try Zajc's "Where Are You, My Love?"—give vent to your feelings!' She wouldn't listen to him; she would turn away her head and stubbornly compress her pale lips, fearing that the song would only prolong the agony of her final hours . . ."

Her widower completely withdrew into this very library room, going out nowhere for almost an entire decade: taking his meals here like a listless bird, sleeping lightly like a frightened-to-death wild animal, obdurately keeping silent like a fish at the very bottom of the sea. He suddenly disappeared from the library room one overcast day in 1965; no one ever found out where to.

"On the table was left only a single open book; sometime during the search for Father, it too was lost," Natalija added softly.

And since then Natalija Dimitrijević had lived her lonely, unattached life, working in that same Pelican Bookshop until retirement—that is, since the business was nationalized as the Pelican Stationery Store, sellers of office supplies and equipment, and blank business forms—finding her only satisfaction in tending to the family library and the memories of her futile love. Meanwhile, she occasionally managed to withdraw a portion of her father's prewar deposits from banks and credit unions which had disappeared long before Jelena's arrival, in addition to supporting herself by giving reading lessons, for example, to Professor Tiosavljević of the School of Philosophy, who sometimes came to her, taking like a freshman three two-hour classes weekly.

"A total reading, my dear," the woman now said, seizing the moment to reproach the companion, "and none of your hushing up! I see you try hard to satisfy me, and yet that is far from the genuine thing. You're no doubt gifted, but after St. John the Baptist Day I'll expect you to approach matters a little more enthusiastically, more intimately!"

The Slava feast was attended only by Jelena and Dr. Isidor Arsenov, who by every reckoning was as old as the century. One of the dinner plates remained unused. It turned out that an expected female guest, a certain Petrašinovićka, "was no longer among us," having passed away last summer. Perhaps this was the reason little cheer was to be found at the dining table. Natalija Dimitrijević unobtrusively served the food, while Dr. Arsenov smacked his lips and relished on his tongue the praises he spoke. No matter what he took in his hands, from the dish of boiled wheat to whatever else, he found a reason to emphasize the medicinal properties of natural foods:

"Boiled wheat relieves stomach cramps . . ."

"Parsley is an excellent antiseptic . . ."

"Leeks quiet a cough . . ."

"Marjoram has a calming effect: it is useful against uncontrollable hiccups, bronchitis, and other health-related conditions . . ."

Since after many attempts he had recently given up tobacco, and since one of the chief characteristics of a Slava feast is that everything is lei-sure-ly, between every course rather than smoke a cigarette he would doze off a while, during which the cinnabar polka-dotted bowtie would wiggle in the gray hairs of his drooping beard. Finally, after—as he progressed from one type of tiny cake to another—emphasizing with delight that the fruit of the walnut cures anemia ("And, hmm—pardon the expression—also enhances virility"), that blanched almonds alleviate stomachache while figs act as a mild diuretic, and so on, he fell into so deep a sleep that even after drinking a cup of black coffee he roused not a bit. He must have woken only when he began ingesting the grounds left on the bottom of the cup. He was confused and embarrassed, like a child who has been caught doing something impermissible:

"Forgive me, I dreamt that I was smoking. Although I don't have to go on about the harmfulness of nicotine, I confess that coffee without a cigarette is not much of a pleasure."

Afterward, Madame Natalija put the new record of maestro Arthur Rubinstein on the turntable of the phonograph. In the crackling pause between Scriabin's *Nocturne for Left Hand* and de Falla's *Fire Dance*, Dr. Arsenov asked:

"Early Rubinstein? Masterful! Where did you get it? As usual, at Mitić's in Slavija?"

"No," the woman answered sadly. "Can you imagine, Mitić's department store was closed in the middle of the day—I had to stop in the one they call 'Ta-Ta,' across the street from the Russian Czar."

It should be added that throughout the meal, the old woman was really not up to tasting anything.

"I have no appetite, I'm full from reading all of Pata's recipes," she said, excusing herself.

10

"It won't disturb you if we get away for a while, will it? I promise, we'll be back by dark . . ." The woman waited for the companion in the library room, at noontime, a week after St. John the Baptist Day, as usual handing her one of two books with the same title.

The earlier readings had usually lasted an hour or two. The girl was not really keen on giving in so to the old woman's caprices, or to being detained for so long, for the simple reason that, since receiving her first paycheck, she had enrolled in an introductory course in the English language, and made use of the afternoons to go over the previous day's lesson. But she had no way to refuse now, especially since the old woman went on, unfazed:

"We'll have lunch there! Some of Rosulek's Prague ham was still left—I made sandwiches."

Only then did Jelena distinguish, from the everyday interior of the room, a picnic basket right next to Natalija Dimitrijević's legs. From beneath its lid protruded the border of a red checkered tablecloth. She accepted the already opened book mechanically, not thinking to ascertain its title, feeling at the same time enormous astonishment and pity. Undoubtedly perplexed, she was later unable to recall how she had entered it so far. To be sure, she diligently followed along with the old woman—as she had before—from the indicated chapter, page after page, line by line, word by word, when she suddenly became conscious of the fact that instead of swarms of letters there stood before her a woman in a flowing dress of raw silk, with a shawl indifferently thrown across her shoulders, wearing a wide-brimmed straw hat and carrying a picnic basket in her right hand, a woman who went leisurely, but purposefully, along some kind of footpath . . . How this was possible, Jelena was unable to explain to herself. How she had reached a barren mountain height, overgrown only with grass, she didn't know either. Moreover, higher up in that clearing above the forested valley, the river, and the single visible house, blew a wind quite different from the one that wove its way through the streets and squares of the capital. This wind played intimately among the locks of her hair, while up above it dispersed the clouds and scattered the mild rays of the sun . . . They sat on a warm rock around the spread-out tablecloth eating sandwiches, and then, after drinking a quarter of a bottle of white wine, Madame Natalija put in the basket the corkscrew and the two glasses, the kind with fragile stems. All of this, then, was either real or mere semblance, but Jelena, doubtlessly for the first time in a long while, smiled. That could not be forgotten. They talked a little, observed the love gyres of the swallows, and laughed again and again . . .

"Just look at how mysteriously they fly, as if they're avoiding the—for us—invisible pillars and arches of the firmament . . ." said the companion.

"Pillars and arches, you say?! Yes, yes . . ." agreed the old woman, pleased. "It will turn out I didn't make a mistake when I hired you. You have a special gift for observation."

But how the journey home had looked, the girl didn't know how to describe. The lines of the book suddenly congealed, dimming in the early evening light, and then finally extinguished as the Belgrade night sealed up windowpane after windowpane of the library room. Madame Natalija set down her eyeglasses, removed her beige gloves, and, with trembling fingers, their joints and veins swollen, touched her freckled temples. Jelena turned on the lamp nearby and looked questioningly, now at her, now at the open picnic basket containing the crumbs of sandwiches, a carelessly gathered tablecloth, and an open bottle of wine.

"We're making progress, making progress . . ." said Natalija Dimitrijević, and then, as if wishing to prevent any further conversation on the matter, abruptly closed both books. "I'm a little out of strength. Let's go to bed."

11

"'The future perfect tense expresses action that will occur before some other action in the future. *As soon as I have written the letter, I shall return your pen.* This tense also expresses action that will occur and be completed by some definite time in the future . . .'"

Each day, in her room, the girl followed her lessons.

"'A, aback, abacus, abaft, abandon, abase, abash, abate, abatis, abbacy, abbreviate, ABC, abdicate, abdomen, abduct, abeam, abed, aberrance . . .'"

She systematically studied the words, being careful to pronounce them as familiarly as possible, taking rests by daydreaming about how she would speak English so well that when she left here, no one would guess where she had come from.

As was her custom, Madame Natalija spent her time in the library, erasing and drawing little circles or crosses on the windowpanes, tending to the books and the early lilacs, which had replaced the late mimosas, putting ever more effort into the preparations for a simultaneous reading. After choosing the reading material for a new promenade, she would then take a whole series of other necessary steps. For example, she would rapidly blink her eyes for several moments, in order to keep from blinking once she opened the covers of the book; however imperceptible, these blinks in fact caused cessations in the process of reading. And the opening of the bindings was itself preceded by the complicated calculation of the ideal width of the angle formed by the pages: for some books an acute angle of less than thirty degrees was sufficient, while others were of value only on the condition that their pages were at right angles, and for still others this relation ranged from 98 to 114 degrees—and then there were those for whom it was not worth the trouble unless you spread them open a full 360. In any case, now the woman more and more rarely set out without various necessities, sometimes taking only a travel icon of St. Nikola, sometimes an umbrella, sometimes transferring her women's trifles, a thousand and one things, from one handbag to another . . .

Jelena was discovering a completely new world. Approaching it made her stomach queasy, she felt a weakness, her palms were sweaty again, the terse opening words offended, but in order to proceed, regardless of what, where, and how minutely detailed it was written, she would find some unique quality that would make the world worthwhile to enter. With Madame Natalija she had learned that literary characters and events are not all that is offered to the genuine reader, that they are not, in fact, what is most interesting. If some street somewhere was cited or merely alluded to, Natalija Dimitrijević knew how to turn toward the public square about which there had been no mention, then to get from there to some other street from which she could enter any building she pleased—even climb if she wished to the attic, which might be filled with someone's wet, recently hung laundry—and then to aimlessly continue on to the first park—unerringly sensing it by the freshness of the air—where she would spend time on a bench feeding the turtle-doves, flown in from who knows where, or simply sit with her companion, away from the rows of seats that people typically used . . .

But not even that was what most surprised Jelena. With the old woman she became conscious also of the presence of others. Many different people were, at the same moment, in a completely different neighborhood of Belgrade—or in an entirely different city, even one on the other side of the world—reading the same book. And all of them had been gathered together by that book, that space. Some of them were able to recognize other readers, and some were incapable of identifying even themselves. When, despite the permanent and quite predictable subject matter of some long-forgotten sentimental novel, Jelena and the old woman almost bumped into Madame Angelina, the girl divined the all-encompassing nature of every literary space, even unimportant ones.

"My companion, and very talented besides . . . My friend from the Stanković Music School . . ." So Natalija Dimitrijević introduced them, noticeably in a good humor because of the unexpected encounter.

"Nata, Natočka, how long has it been since we've seen each other?! Since that travelogue it must be ten or twenty years?!"

"What's Najdan doing now? Still living in Argentina?"

"Until recently he was translating our poets into Spanish, but not long ago he underwent an unsuccessful operation for cataracts. The cataracts affected both his eyes. Now I read all alone, at night, so that I can recount it to him in the morning. That keeps at least him in an illusory state of existence . . ."

"Say hello to him for me!"

"Certainly!"

"You won't forget?!"

So chatted the two elderly women; occasionally you couldn't tell who was shouting louder than whom.

"Forgive me, I have to go back—it's daybreak there, maybe he woke up," Angelina offered as an excuse for her leave-taking.

"Of course. And don't tell him I've gotten old like this," Natalija Dimitrijević bade her farewell.

Jelena noticed that her landlady was returning somewhat unwillingly. Putting down that sentimental novel, she singled out her most important recollections, recalling them as if to fix them, as if to salvage for remembrance the outlines of history:

"Until that war, Najdan was an orderly for His Majesty King Peter II. Perhaps you once heard the phrase *ad usum delphini*. Namely, at the French court it was the custom to prepare for the dauphin's use a special selection of reading materials, from which everything considered detrimental to the exemplary upbringing of one who is to inherit the throne would ultimately be removed. With us there were no such stringent rules, but the young Peter II Karadjordjević, during his reading lessons, had a personal escort, Major Najdan. However, when the court and the government fled at the outbreak of the war, Najdan was left behind; someone had considered his employment of no great import to the country. He fell into German hands, and after '45, having an aversion to the new government and being offended by the action of the court, he roamed the world, finally settling down in South America. At that time, in the fifties, I read a great deal with Angelina, and so it also happened that we met him. At the same time, by some twist of fate or by pure chance, all three of us were beginning the same book. He in the morning, sitting in some modest emigrant's room in distant Buenos Aires, and we two in the evening in this apartment, all three of us dreaming of far-off places. Our soiree continued; some ten times more it was much the same but now by agreement; and then the two of them fell in love, and after many ups and downs Angelina managed to obtain travel permits, and from then on it was their story alone. At her parting she took along a travelogue that I had, too, and so we would meet there every first of the month, regardless of the difference in time zones and the distance of thousands of miles. After they had set up house, they would invite me to join them, but I couldn't leave my father, or afterward the library, the pillow in which I had sworn my love, and the sole language in which I'd lived . . ."

The girl imagined Madame Angelina there in Buenos Aires, in a cool house where despite the frequent whitewashing of the walls, the moist blossoms of nostalgia continually sprang forth; in a house with heavy carved furniture, with a boyhood picture of Peter II Karadjordjević, with drapes spread wide to no avail . . . She imagined Madame Angelina herself putting down that novel on the nightstand, then turning toward her husband Najdan, who was already awake: "You won't believe me, I saw our Natalija, the daughter of that bookseller who disappeared, Gavrilo Dimitrijević . . ." The companion imagined Najdan, onetime orderly to the king, raising himself up in bed and turning, the wrinkles of a smile appearing on his face as he remembered the bookseller's daughter, the distant pupils of his eyes sparkling: "Natalija, you say? Oh, Lord, after so many years! Tell me how she looks . . ."

Jelena now roused fom her reverie and asked:

"Madame Natalija, when we go there, I mean to that place, do we exist here?"

"Do we exist?!" repeated the old woman. "And where? That's a good question. I believe it's about some kind of mild presence or mild absence at the same time. Although, that relationship varies from person to person. And, I dare say, from nation to nation."

Thus were revealed to the companion the proportions of an unprecedented migration. There were no columns of people, they were led by no one in particular, they were not spurred on by the same reasons; after all, not even the realm to which they journeyed could be considered a foreign land, but the presence of so many could only be called what it was—a migration.

"Books are like sponges. Of unknown dimensions, full of small holes, the spongy tissue capable of absorbing countless many fates, even of taking into itself entire nations. What else are books about lost civilizations than sponges which have compressed within themselves entire epochs? To the last living drop, until they themselves begin to dry up, to turn to stone . . ." As she spoke, Natalija Dimitrijević would tap with her forefinger on the spine of some voluminous historical study, the sound resembling the means by which the stalactite makes itself known.

Truly, Jelena reminded herself, the spaces of some books looked as if they were petrified. Like cursed, abandoned cities in which everything stood fast in its accustomed spot, where one could dwell for days and hear nothing but one's own breathing. There were books that contained merely the past, a past so distant that shapes subsisted owing only to apparitions. Books through which human murmurings, music, and laughter resounded, in which the reader who entered them found an echo a hundred years long. Or books which only the enlightened visited, striving to restore from the remains the appearance of some building, or from out of oblivion, oblivion heavier than the heaviest, extract some worthwhile thought. And a reality existed which resembled those kinds of books, only unlike them one could not close it, lay it aside.

12

The omens started to appear at the beginning of the summer. That afternoon the lilacs relinquished their place to roses, and the woman nervously began to wander about the apartment as if looking for something in particular. She went from room to room, climbed the ladder in the library, stooped down to peep under the bed and the sofa, raised the rugs and tablecloths, opened the dressers, pulled out the drawers, turned pockets inside out, and overturned boxes of jewelry, letters, and sewing things; peered into corners, sighed, and wrung her hands. Alarmed, Jelena followed her about, never before having seen her like this and not knowing what to say until Natalija Dimitrijević threw herself into a cane chair, moaning helplessly:

"I don't have one keepsake!"

"I'm sorry . . ." the girl said awkwardly.

But for Madame Natalija that was little comfort. In a monotonous voice, she kept lamenting:

"I don't have one keepsake . . . I don't have one keepsake of my father . . . Oh Lord, how, how could I have misplaced it . . . How could I have been so careless; I can't remember the title of the book he was reading before he disappeared . . . I can't remember; if only I knew what was written on the binding . . . I was meaning to tell you about it, recently, at the Slava, but I neglected to . . . For this entire decade I've known what it was, but now . . ."

She apparently reconciled to her loss, but only after several days, and the whole incident remained what it in fact had been— the indication of an illness that, as it turned out, would progress unchecked. By the end of that month the old woman had forgotten, feature by feature, her mother's face, and photographs were of no help.

"These are only photographs, my mother was prettier, much prettier . . ." she said, and she turned her head away from the ten-odd photo albums the companion had opened along the length of the dining room table.

Not too long after this scene, her memory of nearly ten successive years faded; more precisely, her memory of the period from February 1981 to December 1989. From that fissure of many years, Madame Natalija Dimitrijević managed to evoke the memory of not a single nebulous day. All had disappeared as if it had never been. To no avail did Jelena recount in order, with the precision of a watchmaker, the events about which Natalija Dimitrijević had earlier talked at length:

"The seventeenth of April, nineteen hundred and eighty-four, at five in the afternoon, you told me, Professor Dobrivoj Tiosavljević visited you, at that time only a lecturer in the School of Philosophy, your former pupil in reading . . . You prepared tea and biscuits with lemon zest; Mr. Tiosavljević declined a glass of cherry brandy . . . According to what you said, you talked about the books that had been taken from you after the war; he asked you to name each individual title, showing especial interest in the thirty or so copies of the same book under the title *My Memorial*, by Anastas C. Branica . . . The professor, from time to time, would widen his eyes and repeat: 'Interesting! Are you certain?! I read all of them through very carefully, but that part was unknown to me?! May I keep the copy you lent me a little while longer? If I'm not mistaken, you still have two of them!' With your permission, he smoked a pipeful of tobacco the aroma of vanilla . . ."

"It could be, Jelena, it very well could be. I don't doubt it all happened that way. But don't substitute your memories for my own," said the old woman with a wave of the hand, like one insulted. And that was all she had to say.

Another time, Natalija gave the girl a linen traveling dress as a present, which fit Jelena perfectly. For the old woman it had been a worthless item of clothing ever since the moment she'd forgotten on which occasions it had been worn. And so it continued: the gaps multiplied, the past tense resembled a musical score from which, here and there, someone had cruelly torn out the pages so that just as the melody soared it also suddenly fell silent.

"Little can be done here," concluded the drowsy Dr. Arsenov—who'd been the family's physician—in Jelena's presence following a conversation with the patient and the companion. "Young lady, it's up to you to do what pleases her. Read books together, who knows, perhaps that prevents forgetfulness; every book is a nota bene, that is to say, a note that serves as a living reminder."

And so it was. More than ever, the girl and Madame Natalija Dimitrijević read. Now the companion importuned, suppressing the queasiness she felt toward her native language, pretending to be interested in this title or that, discovering a reason to remain a little longer among these pages or those. At first the woman, as she had earlier, gladly seized every opportunity to fill her ebbing existence; but eventually the illness of forgetfulness inexorably penetrated the fabric of language as well . . . It was some leisurely reading selection—they had decided to go for a walk—when the old woman halted and with her forefinger pointed to a dandelion.

"That?! I can't remember what that's called?!" she stammered.

"Who really cares, let's jump over it, let's go a little farther . . ." said the companion, taking the woman under the arm:

"But don't keep it from me, not by any means, every word is important! It's on the tip of my tongue it is, it's some ordinary word, isn't it?" Natalija Dimitrijević stubbornly stayed put.

"Yes—an ordinary word, *dandelion*. Would you like to rest?"

"Jelena, what does that word *dandelion* mean?" Natalija Dimitrijević stared blankly, even more blankly owing to the terrifically strong lenses of her glasses.

"At her age it is difficult to tell one symptom from another . . ." Dr. Arsenov later advised. "Senility, nominal aphasia, dyslexia . . . Perhaps she should go to a specialist . . ." He offered someone's calling card, on which was scrawled a host of titles, before he dozed off while probably "dreaming" that he was smoking.

Then he woke up coughing; he couldn't quite give up the tobacco. "Let her take as much food as possible with vitamin E; prepare fish for her . . ."

When Jelena later handed the old woman the card, Natalija Dimitrijević refused after reading the name. "It's out of the question; I'd never approve. Why, the man doesn't even know my name."

But she was not able to put into practice even the advice concerning diet. Natalija Dimitrijević forgot what the word *fish* meant and refused to taste even a morsel of "that grass." In general, her meals became more and more alike; the number of unknown, and for that very reason, unwanted, ingredients multiplied; she had already singled out every type of meat, onions, peas, and celery; and the companion wondered what would happen when the woman also forgot the word *water* or *air*.

However, something still more horrible occurred. Exactly on the day Jelena learned that her request to go to some other country had been approved, and that she had only to take care of a few formalities before her final departure—and, of course, to travel to the city of her birth to bid her parents farewell—indeed, exactly on that September day, Jelena, returning home intent upon announcing her decision to the old woman, found her on the floor of the library room, removing with a paper knife from a slit pillow feather after feather, examining each one and then throwing it away . . .

"I once said something important into this pillow, but now it's no longer here . . ." She momentarily lifted her tearful eyes, and then continued picking through it.

The freed white feathers alighted on her hair. They hovered all about the room. Here and there. Here and there . . .

13

A short-lived turn for the better merely foreshadowed the beginning of the end. During September and November tea was mostly drunk in silence, with little conversation, as they listened attentively to the clattering of the cobalt tea service adorned with gilded constellations. In the general silence, the old woman and the girl would incline their heads to the cups and saucers, to the creamer of unskimmed milk or the sugar bowl, following the pulse of the porcelain.

"Doesn't it seem to you that my cup is beating . . . a lot slower?" said Natalija Dimitrijević, apprehensively making the comparison. But she talked less and less now, at most a sentence or two, and, probably, only if she had thought them over carefully and decided nothing was missing, so that she could express with dignity what she had in mind to say.

"That's not possible; the enamel ages in exactly the same way. Here, listen for yourself . . ." Jelena would dissuade her, even though she herself noticed the difference no matter how hard she tried to arrange the pieces of the tea service differently.

"Really?" said the woman, cheering up. "Ah, real Meissen porcelain . . . Nineteen hundred and ten . . . This is nothing compared to how sharply it used to clatter . . . When the porcelain was young."

"I know you're only comforting me," she added when she had thought about it a little more. "I can just barely hear it . . . Pretty soon it will stop beating altogether . . . Promise me one thing. Don't let me die here, all alone . . ."

"I'll be with you," said the companion, even though the deadline for putting her papers in order at the embassy of some other country was inexorably running out, and now there was a real danger that the entire procedure surrounding her attempt to depart would have to be repeated.

On Monday evening, the twentieth of November, after returning from the National Library, she found the woman in a flurry of excitement, packing luggage sufficient for a transoceanic cruise. Dresses for the daytime and evening, warmer clothing, footwear, nightgowns, nightcaps, handkerchiefs, brushes for hair and eyebrows, a manicure kit, bottles of eau de cologne, photograph albums, and apples, in case they happened to get thirsty . . .

Jelena hadn't yet managed to remove her wet little bell-shaped hat when Natalija Dimitrijević said imploringly:

"It's time to go . . . Help me not to be late, if I'm still wanted anywhere . . . Only one more day, and I won't keep you any longer . . . Until I get settled in . . . And then, go . . . Go your own way . . ."

Having arranged everything as if they were abandoning the apartment forever, having checked whether the key had been turned twice, and whether the door chain had been latched, the faucets closed, and the blinds lowered, Jelena finished her cup of tea and, owing to some sudden warmth, undid the two upper buttons of her linen traveling dress. Only a few minutes separated them from midnight. Outside it was still raining. Two women, one young, the other on in years, held identical copies of the same open book. The first frightened stiff, with a queasiness below her breastbone, and sweaty palms. The second unflinching, her eyes ardent behind the magnifying lenses of her glasses. Before long one could hear in the library room only the turning of pages . . .

SECOND READING

WHERE WE SPEAK
ABOUT A SUMPTUOUS GARDEN
AND, A LITTLE FURTHER ON,
ABOUT A FRENCH PARK;
ABOUT A PERGOLA
WITH LATE-BLOOMING ROSES;
ABOUT A LIGHT- AND DARK-COLORED VILLA
AND AN INSCRIPTION IN A PEDIMENT;
ABOUT A BRIEF REPORT IN *POLITIKA*,
AN OUTSIZED SHADOW,
AND THE CONTENTS OF A GLASS PAVILION;
ABOUT A CONVERSATION WITH A MAN
WHO INCONSIDERATELY PRESSED THE DOORBELL;
AND THEN ABOUT THE QUESTION:
WHAT GOOD IS COOKING
IF YOU CAN'T ADD SOMETHING
ACCORDING TO YOUR OWN TASTE?

14

ALL AROUND, AS FAR AS THE EYE could see, stretched a garden of ravishing beauty. The road first wound between rows of larches, and then red oaks prevailed, and then, in perfect harmony, in a fireworks of form, the trees were interchanged, skillfully joined by bends of brushwood and low, shrubby vegetation. One could hardly take a step without the next angle of observation giving rise to some new delight. From the primeval lichens, tranquil mosses, stubborn mistletoes, and trembling ferns in the hollows, to the young ivy and the mighty trunks, to the alternately round, pyramidal, branchy, conical, sadly drooping, and bushy outlines of the treetops. Isolated here and there . . . Then grouped in small forest massifs of birch or conifer. Divided by forked trails of settled dust . . .

Solitary, disheveled English oaks on grassy plateaus swarming with mushroom caps. Then pastures, gentle slopes edged by wild blackberry bushes and low walls of stone stacked "on the dry," overgrown with creepers of ivy. Quite unexpectedly, steeper inclines and endemic flora nestled against bare, blanched rocks, as in the Alps. With seemingly carelessly spread-out contours, but always in such a way that the shady side never encroached on the sunny one, so that each blade of grass had sufficient light and cool . . .

Vegetation accentuated by a well-considered, seething palette of colors. Nuances of red, purple, yellow, blue, and green. Doubled in intensity by textures of shiny smoothness, mealy pubescence, or hoary shriveling . . . Receding in a perspective of lighter tones, which lent to the whole expanse a certain depth. Vegetation raised up always in such a way that the season of the year did not usher in monotony: a period of bloom began where some other variety was flagging, the needle-covered evergreen pines did not hinder the flaming beechen colors of fall, and the freshness of the firs and spruce found expression when the deciduous wood of maples and elms began to languish . . .

Adam Lozanić beheld all this, moving along the widest path, not knowing in the multitude of wandering descriptions where in fact he was going. The garden must have exuded an equally ravishing fragrance. But the young man had woken on Tuesday morning with all the signs of a bad cold; opening the window, he hadn't been able to very well discern the acrid smog of the capital. He was weak from an elevated temperature, and out of sorts on account of it all. Proofreading demanded complete concentration, but he scarcely managed to collect himself enough to even perform ordinary, everyday tasks. He cut himself while shaving; twice he failed to button his flannel shirt; for a quarter of an hour he was occupied with the lifeless knots on his sneakers, only to force them on; and the last slice of rye bread fell from his hands, of course onto the side spread with apricot jam. He decided he would have a bite in the neighboring milk bar when he got tired, when he took a break. It was still raining. The way things were going, something might well have run over him as he crossed the street.

"The simple truth is that Tuesday is bad luck. On Tuesdays nothing ever goes right or ever gets done!" he said out loud, trying to schedule the book bound in saffian into whatever free time he had at his disposal. But however he planned the work, he didn't manage to divide the number of pages into approximately equal parts, and so he finally gave up, resolving to cover as much of it as he could every day. Somehow he would manage to read it through by Monday; the souvenir vendor probably wouldn't disturb him too much.

Thus did the young man slowly make progress, no doubt oblivious to the numerous odors, sniffling, stopping here and there to blow his nose into a plaid handkerchief and to look over the details essential to the work he really knew next to nothing about. Nevertheless, his general impression of the setting gradually restored his mood: what he found there was well-done, irreproachable even: there were no lapses; nor was the vocabulary inappropriate; the sentences of Anastas C. Branica followed one another naturally; the punctuation stood in the proper places. It was only that, apart from the description of the garden, there was nothing else. Absolutely nothing else, except newer and newer vegetation. Nothing appeared; of events and happenings there was not a trace, nor an intimation, provided one does not count the slow rising of the solar orb, the flight of some distant birds seemingly lost in the blue firmament, the falling of pine cones, or the forming of dust clouds behind the young man's feet. Thus did the pages follow one after the other, perhaps even more quickly than that asthmatic afternoon on Milovan Milovanović Street. The time of reading is compressed time, an hour here is not the same as an hour there: sometimes it lasts ten times longer, sometimes it is briefer than the instant between two blinks of an eye.

15

For how long it had gone on this way, he didn't know. Although he read in a half-lying position, it seemed to him that his feet were already tired when there began to emerge from the garden the sides of a house—or, better to say, of a villa; in any event, of an unusually beautiful structure, in a style unknown to the young man. The presence of human hands became more apparent, the vegetation at once thinned out and gathered into the harmonious gardens of a French park, into ornate flowerbeds of rectangular and circular design and spherically cropped box shrubs, and the road spilled onto a symmetrical delta of footpaths covered with gravel crushed so fine that it rustled.

A woman approached on one of these meanders. Adam was certain that it was the wife of the mysterious client of yesterday. Whatever the case, to Adam it was one more bit of proof of his extraordinary ability to meet other readers: that woman was reading the same book he had in his hands—just where she was reading he didn't know—but in such a way that she was waiting for him exactly here. Dispensing with the formalities, she herself suggested something similar:

"Finally! You're late!"

"Forgive me, the garden is rather large, and it takes hours to see everything," he offered as an excuse.

"Young man, you're not here to poke your nose around, but to make the revisions I require of you," she said, looking him up and down. Each of her gestures evinced haughtiness. He didn't like her, but decided not to attach any great importance to it; after all, he had gotten involved not for satisfaction's sake, but rather to take on a well-paying job.

"That goes without saying . . ." he said apologetically, trying hard not to look at her.

"You're younger than I imagined . . ." the woman continued in an appraising tone. "And I hope not rash as well. My husband claims you have experience."

Adam opened his mouth to explain that he would soon receive his degree, that for two whole years now he had been a part-time associate at *Our Scenic Beauty*, that on three occasions he had done the proofreading for an anthology of stories, of poems rather, by some of his friends, beginning writers. He opened his mouth, but then changed his mind. For sure, that meager bio-bibliography would make no impression on the woman.

"There is nothing to be done about it," the woman shrugged

her shoulders. "Let's see how much you know. Take a good look at that pergola. I have never liked it. Be so kind as to get rid of it, but of course in such a way that no empty spot remains."

On the contrary, the pergola clustered with late-blooming roses was quite dazzlingly beautiful. Adam felt that he would be committing an unpardonable sin if he simply "got rid" of it. On the other hand, the instruction had been explicit. The woman had ordered the work to be done; if he wished to keep his job, he would have to accede to her demands . . .

Again he was unable to judge how much time had passed. His body temperature must have risen. His head cold rendered the smell of the roses useless. He approached several times the spot to be altered, picturing in his thoughts how the final version would look, and then what would happen to the surrounding sentences. Lastly, he decided where and how much to intervene. He stuck out the point of his pencil like a scalpel—more precisely, like a spade—and into the very roots of the description. He began to cross out, to reverse the order of words, to rearrange sentences, to write in conjunctions, to pluck out entire images, and, finally, to join passages together. He was all sweaty, unpleasantly sweaty, from a bad conscience; the pergola with the late-blooming roses vanished as if it had never been. The wound could already scarcely be discerned when the upturned clods of grass began to take root—the mournful scar would not show for even this long.

"Well, enough," declared the woman with reservation. "But that was merely a little test. We already have a gardener. Let's start for the house. Most of what I have chosen for you to do is there."

Confused, Adam did not budge.

"Well, why do you stand there? I don't have time to waste. Let's go to the house," the woman repeated coldly.

"And the pergola? Do you want me to put everything back the way it was?" said Adam, not moving.

"Oh, but you're a soft heart! A romantic. Forget about that now. Pokimica will be back. He has some free time on his hands, and gardening is more or less his passion . . ."

Adam's interlocutor turned in the direction of the villa and peremptorily strode off. The young man had no time to wonder who this Pokimica was and how the pergola would be built anew.

16

The sumptuous garden proved to be merely a worthy entrance to the beauty of the building. It was a two-story villa, its somewhat lower, ground-floor wings angled slightly backward, like a large bird just about to take flight. From where he stood Adam was unable to determine its style—he had never really understood architecture—but each individual element on its face was unquestionably a regular little masterpiece of structural engineering. The delta of paths converged in front of the marble pillars of an arched doorway, which gave onto a double door with a pair of bronze door knockers in the shape of a long-fingered woman's hand. By way of a wide, hugging staircase fringed along its balustrade with stone vases, one could then proceed onto a large terrace, a sort of esplanade onto which communicated the doors of all the upstairs rooms. Judging by the number of windows and doors, one might have concluded the house had ten or so rooms on the upper level. The numerous drainpipes and friezes enlivened the light and dark yellow surfaces of the façade. A person didn't know where to look first, didn't know upon which principle all the dimensions had been calculated such that the slightest deviation would disturb the harmony of the entire structure.

Unfortunately, the woman had walked so quickly that the

young man hadn't had nearly enough time to focus attention on every detail. Before he knew it, they were climbing up to the terrace via the outside staircase, not entering the house. There, exactly on the vertical of the middle section of the villa, not far from a little table and four chairs made of wrought iron, stood a ladder leaning to reach the triangular pediment. The cornice of the roof was adorned at regular intervals with the figures of eight broad-shouldered Atlases, their arms raised and spread wide, palms turned upward, as if holding up all eight corners of the world.

"We'll start with the pediment," said the woman, pointing her forefinger in the direction of the triangle. "You'll be doing an inscription."

Adam squinted. Where the name of the villa or the year of construction usually stood there was nothing, except for traces of the past removal of mortar. In the very apex of the triangle was a clock, its hands seemingly gone astray on a face without numbers.

"Do the inscription in bas-relief, and make sure that one can see it. The contents are these . . ." said the woman, handing the young man a folded slip of paper.

"'*Verba volant, scripta manent*,'" Adam read to himself. Searching through his rusty knowledge of Latin, he stammered: "'Words fly . . .'"

". . . 'written things remain'!" the woman finished. "And now I'll have to leave. I've some pressing matters to attend to. Be diligent. Tomorrow I'll return to see what you've done and whether we can agree upon future alterations. If you get hungry, go to the back . . . there you'll find the kitchen . . . The old housekeeper Zlatana never leaves it; I believe she'll have something to serve you . . ." The woman turned and quickly vanished down the stairs.

Now alone, Adam tried to compose himself. Once more turning toward the garden, he understood just how much everything here was made for pleasure. The Italian word belvedere was quite appropriate for the terrace. The view encompassed almost the entire estate. The edge of the property could only be divined by the coagulation of blueness. Beyond it, a many-days' walk distant, gray mountains rose up, their peaks white with eternal snow. Fog-shrouded lowlands and a great river stretched there, its source and mouth hidden in the indistinct haze of the horizon. Nearer still, he saw the road by which he had come, the now-shrunken picturesque forest massifs seemingly painted with the brush of a skilled watercolorist. He saw the geometric figures of the French park, the one near the approach to the villa, and saw what from below, from the ground, he had been unable to observe: to the south, a glass pavilion set alongside the cascades of a shimmering fishpond, and to the north, a genuine Renaissance maze-promenade of tall hedges and shady arcades in whose center swaggered the sparkling crest of a fountain, an empty statue pedestal, and—despite every expectation—two rather stunted palm trees.

Oblivious to all save this captivating splendor, the young man sat down on the wrought iron chair nearby, his back to the pediment.

17

The telephone rang. Probably for a long, long time.

"All right, Adam boy, why don't you answer?"

"Yes?"

"This is Kusmuk!"

"Kusmuk?!"

"Stevan Kusmuk, scatterbrain! Why do you sound like that, as if you're on the other side of the world?!"

"I have a cold, a cough, maybe a temperature too, and my ears are clogged . . ."

"What can you do? Just think of Thomas Mann; to him life seemed to be a fever of matter . . . Anyway, I found that Anastas Branica. By accident. There's no trace of his book in the reserves, you know that, otherwise it would be in the catalogs. I found a review of his novel. My friend, that's not a review, that's a site of execution. In *The Serbian Literary Journal* of 16 August 1936, new series XLVIII, number 48, page 646, under the heading 'Reviews and Notes.' The reviewer is one D. L. He's unknown to me. Nowhere else does he appear under the same initials. He worked over your Branica pretty well. Just listen to the title: 'A Scribbling Attempt.' And then the subtitle: 'Boredom in over six hundred pages.' Adam, my boy, are you listening to me?"

"I'm here . . ."

"Wait, I'll read it to you: 'For quite a while now we have not had the opportunity to have in our hands such a long and drawn-out text. However, in recent months Mr. Anastas C. Branica has seen to that. By his own admission a man of letters, he has published a novel under the title *My Memorial*. In any event, we thank this industrious practitioner of the written word, for now we possess a standard of what a literary work ought not to look like, and thus to what extent a person may become blind regarding his own, altogether unsupported intentions.' What do you say? Standard!"

"Scathing, no two ways about it . . ."

"Scathing. But that's nothing compared to what follows. I'll skip around a bit . . . Listen to this: 'We asked ourselves, and we ask ourselves, from where does one get such a far-fetched idea that he can write a novel in which, except for a description of some kind of forest, a park, and then a description of some house—a summer house, probably—there isn't, I emphasize, there isn't any kind of plot, any kind of action, nor even a single character? We asked ourselves, and we ask ourselves . . . Alas. No answer from anywhere. Except, of course, if everything cannot be properly explained by a lack of talent and a rudimentary knowledge of the structure of the literary work; by a lack of proportion and the mediocrity of the scribbler; by a lack of a basic good upbringing; and by an excess of the conceit that all of his subject will interest someone . . . ' Adam, are you there? Are you breathing?"

"I'm here, here . . ."

"I'll skip around again . . . And now the dagger: 'It would be easy for us to take up a page, or even an entire issue of the *Journal*, with an analysis of this novel, but we consider that this would make no sense, and sense is precisely what we have failed to find in the subject of our present concern. Accordingly, we finish with it here in order not to deny space to deserving contributions of the Serbian pen. In short, Mr. Branica, from the Lord we wish you good health, and we ourselves issue you the following request: Please refrain from bestowing on us any more memorials!'"

"You're right: he obliterated him . . ."

"No, dear friend, you have no idea how right I am! Kusmuk researches everything very thoroughly. D. L. really executed him. I found in *Politika* from September 5 of the same year—that is, at most a week or two after the review—a report: 'This morning fishermen pulled from the Danube, at Vinča, the body of Anastas C. Branica, a local homeless man with no known relatives. The drowning victim had on his person no identity papers. According to the condition of the remains, he must have been in the water about ten days, but the identity of the deceased was established beyond doubt with the help of a copy of a book that was found, a first novel recently published at his own expense. We have learned from reliable sources close to the coroner's office that in this disturbing case there is no confusion, and at issue is a self-drowning, most likely as a consequence of some nervous disorder.'"

"Suicide?"

"So it was. Suicide. The other papers didn't report this news, but in the obituaries in *Vreme* and *Pravda* from October 15, on the fortieth day after his death, it says that Branica lost his life in an accident. The usual soft-pedaling euphemism. But if it interests you, the remembrance in *Vreme* was signed by a certain Miss Natalija Dimitrijević, and the other one, in *Pravda*, I'm quoting now: 'Your housekeeper Zlatana.'"

"Natalija Dimitrijević? And Zlatana?! The housekeeper Zlatana?!"

"Uh-huh, Zlatana. Is that odd? Tell me, what kind of intrigue is this? Do you have that novel, maybe? I'd like to look through it."

"No, I don't . . . Kusmuk, I thank you. I have to end the conversation; the water is boiling for tea . . ."

"Fine, Adam boy—get well, get well. Just know that you're going to explain it all to me when we see each other . . ."

Feeling a small pang of conscience because he had lied to his friend, Adam decided to set the matter right a bit: he put on the pot for tea. As the water simmered, as his mother's steeping blend of sage, thyme, and chamomile released its soothing effect, as he sipped the warm potion in short quaffs, the young man stood beside the window, now looking in the direction of the tavern Our Sea, and now toward the bed where the open book bound in saffian was waiting. It was past noon and the tavern appeared to have no empty seats. From the apartment it was difficult to see, but it seemed that no one there was opening his mouth, as if Our Sea were full of silence. Alas, with how many veils of silence was the unhappy fate of that Branica hidden? To write a novel without a scrap of plot was, of course, a curious undertaking. Although, the young man reflected, regarding the descriptions of nature and the exterior of the villa, one would be hard-pressed to discover any serious reproach. From the style one simply felt a certainty, felt that it had actually been experienced. So much the better for him: there would be no difficulties with the editing and proofreading. But this whole assignment branched out in too many mysterious directions. Who was his client? Why wasn't that Natalija Dimitrijević somehow known to him? Was it a coincidence that the housekeeper Zlatana, of the death notice, was the same one the woman had mentioned? And with that name reminding him that he had eaten nothing today, Adam Lozanić began to waver between going out to the milk bar or continuing with the reading . . .

The silence decided. His neighbor wasn't there—no hammering-on of slats—and the young man resolved to work a little more, while there was any peace at all.

18

Sitting exactly where the telephone call had interrupted him, in the wrought iron chair with his back to the pediment and the doors to the rooms on the terrace-belvedere, Adam at once perceived a change. From somewhere behind him stretched somebody's elongated shadow. A triple shadow. According to the position of the sun this was in no way possible, but when the young man turned around he could not help but observe an unknown man, child, and woman huddled close together, nearly cowering; they gave off a reflection far greater than belonged to them by the existing laws of nature. The door to one of the rooms upstairs stood open; the three of them had just set foot onto the terrace, and the shadow still gathered behind them, like a puddle of dirty water, which always, unerringly, tends toward where it is most shallow.

It was not easy to measure whom this encounter had surprised more. They immediately flashed to Adam that at this very instant, the three of them were reading the same book, too. Together, gathered over it, what with being huddled up so close like that. After all, as he'd learned from Kusmuk, in Anastas Branica's novel, there weren't any characters. Opposite him, the man, child, and woman were visibly curious as to who might be this unknown youth in sneakers and a flannel shirt thrown on indifferently over his faded blue jeans.

"A very good day to you," the man decided to say first.

"And a very good day to you," Adam greeted him in return.

"How's it going? What's new?" added the man after a brief pause.

"Fine, it's pleasant here."

"It's always nice here."

"Do you come here often?" said the youth, not having to ask from where; the man's Jekavian dialect bespoke where this small family might be from.

"Almost every day. Of our entire library, only a few books remained." The man lowered his head. "We read together, with the little one; we think that this is time within time . . ."

"Time within time . . ." Adam recalled how two or three years before, he had heard of a man from a place where bridges and ferryboats were apparently built in peacetime only in order that, in time of war, there would be something across which to flee. This man allowed not a single book to be used to light even a meager fire— despite that everyone was freezing—before the family that owned the book had read it once more. Time within time . . .

"All that remained of our things was a big shadow . . . No matter how we move, it nestles up to us . . ." the woman joined in. She passed her foot back and forth through the dense shadow, which for a brief instant seemed to part and then revert to the way it was.

"And you, are you on vacation?" asked the man, wishing to avoid the depressing subject.

"No, on business. I'm supposed to make some changes—there, on the pediment, they would like a new inscription . . ." answered Adam.

"Uh-huh," the man nodded his head.

"This is what the owners want . . ." the young man apologized for some reason.

"The property is as much all the others' as it is theirs," the woman interjected, obviously upset. "It belongs to the owners neither more nor less . . ."

"Hold your tongue," her husband whispered in a frightened tone.

Adam blushed. He stood up. The little girl did not remove her gaze from him. She had large, sad eyes; they could be described in no other way. Sad eyes. She said everything with them, and absolutely everything had been said.

"The way it was explained to me . . ." began the youth.

"We don't know anything," the man interrupted him. "This is an old book, from back before the war, there are few who know anything about it in detail. Perhaps the housekeeper Zlatana, but that good old woman is hard of hearing and talks only of preparing various dishes. If there's anyone who can help you, then it's the professor."

"The professor?" repeated Adam.

"Yes. There he is, over there in the pavilion. They say he's writing some kind of study about all this here. He comes to do research, he collects things, sorts through them . . . A decent man; he always greets us . . ." the man explained sparingly.

"Thanks. And now I'll have to add the inscription," said Adam, remembering.

"Uh-huh," the man nodded his head.

"And we're leaving," said the woman coldly. "Behind the house there's a meadow to pick flowers. Pokimica lets the little one play there . . ."

Adam made for the ladder, searching meanwhile through his pockets for that slip of paper. The family with the big shadow started down the stairs. Huddled one against the other. As if afraid the reflection would creep in between them as well. Only the little girl turned and shouted:

"We're the Leleks!"

"Leleks?" the young man turned around.

"Yes. That's our last name. Lelek!" the child affirmed.

"Adam . . . Adam Lozanić . . ." the young man introduced himself, but the Leleks had already disappeared from sight.

Sluggishly gathering itself, as if it knew that no one could escape from it, the triple shadow lazily slithered after them, lower—downward—from the belvedere.

19

Assuming, at the top of the ladder, the safest and most comfortable position possible, and in the absence of a tape measure, Adam began to proportion with his hand the available space and the four words he was to put into that blankness. Traces of previous inscriptions were vaguely visible from below, but at close quarters they were distinctly legible. It turned out that the pediment had been some sort of architectural palimpsest, a place where atop an earlier text had come a newer one several times before. Judging by what remained of the mortar, the color, the protuberances, and the hollows, letter by letter the young man determined there might have been as many as four alterations. The original and oldest of them had been done in high relief; the strongly pronounced inscription in Latin letters, "Villa Nathalie," must have been spaced from the apex of the triangle by a good three fingers. Another, in bas-relief, considerably shallower, had been done in Cyrillic characters, and of all the words that were there, the only one that could be discerned was the one that read "memorial." Had he not remembered the dedication at the beginning of the book, the young man would have surely found it difficult to puzzle out its meaning, for the third alteration had in fact been done by knocking off, letter by letter, the previous one, somewhere down to the bricks, and then filling in the scars with new mortar and subsequently writing out in ordinary oil paint "1945." As for the fourth layer, it could not be reliably ascertained whether it was the simple result of yet another alteration of some fickle human temperament, or the accumulation of time, or the shifting rains that washed things away, or the beating down of the sun's rays, or the dampness, or the heat, or the pecking of icy winds—that is, it consisted of nothing at all.

Carefully removing what remained of the previous inscriptions, the young man decided on a type of square lapidary capital letter, then, invoking his knowledge of Roman epigraphy, and having proportioned the Latin words and the spacing between the letters, he wrote in the two lines:

VERBA VOLANT,
SCRIPTA MANENT.

It came out well. And it was not lacking in dignity. Scriptura monumentalis. The clock in the apex of the triangular pediment had no numbers, but it was still light out and one could determine that it was around three o'clock.

Having fulfilled the request of his mysterious clients, the young man was now free, and so he decided to take another walk around the property.

From the terrace, on the spot from which the pergola with late-blooming roses had been removed, he saw a man who was doing some kind of work. Adam headed straight for him. No sooner had their eyes met than Adam felt remorse. The stooping man in his seventies, inconspicuously dressed, with some sort of little insignia in his lapel, ascetically thin, with a leaden pallor, his hair cropped close in military style, had rebuilt the pergola the way it was. It was probably that Pokimica, surely the reader whose duty it was to take care of the garden—thought the young man, wishing to justify himself for this morning's act. However, the glance that the man briefly deigned to cast at him discouraged Adam from attempting to say anything at all. Namely, Pokimica slowly straightened up, wiping off his hands on his trousers, casually spat to the side, and then shot him a look full of scorn, whereupon he turned his head and kneeled again, resuming his work about the late-blooming roses, doing nothing to indicate that besides him anyone else was there. Crestfallen, Adam withdrew.

Where he was going, he wasn't aware. From the French park he once more entered the dense vegetation. In order to forget the unpleasantness with the gardener, he began to consider the tiny forms with which nature abounded everywhere, only people usually didn't notice them, occupied as they were with their own overly important affairs. He discovered, in the space between the branches of a tree, the weave of the cosmically perfect spiderweb and its bowlegged master, who nimbly danced around a small fly that had just been caught. He saw a young caterpillar clinging to the bark of a wild chestnut tree, leaving behind itself the slimy threads of the recent toils of creation. He stepped over a column of black forest ants that were busy dragging seeds and a dead cricket. He was startled by the cry of a peacock that suddenly crossed his path. Craning its neck and spreading its plumage of blinding embers, the bird seemed to have no intention of going away. And so he turned off the trail for a while, a maidenhair caught on his face. He nearly stumbled over a molehill, and the rustling disturbed a squirrel as well as a partridge on her roost. The bird flew off, and the small animal measured him with untrusting little eyes and then fled into a thicket of briars, which curiously enough were still full of swollen fruit.

Through the dense willow trees came a stray dragonfly, and then the flapping of the wings of a gray crane. The fishpond emerged in shimmers, and Adam realized where he was located in relation to the villa. It was a smooth surface of the shallow depth in which everything is transparent, and it sprang up from who knew where, and then, in miniature cascades, it silently overflowed onto the next level, which teemed with water lilies, lotuses, and other similar pond plants inhabited by bloated frogs idling atop them. On the bottom of the pond, the young man observed quite clearly a school of spotted fish wriggling around stones covered in dark green algae and around a wine bottle with a slender neck half protruding from the settled mud. Where this water went to, Adam didn't know, because his attention was then captured by the neighboring pavilion, a little house with latticed glass walls composed of myriad panes, on whose inner sides were the lowered waterfalls of white linen drapes. After hesitating a moment, the young man knocked on the door twice and pushed the door knob while calling out:

"Is the owner here?"

Inside, he found no one. The pavilion was actually a single room crowded with stuffiness and all manner of things. Upon entering, the young man caught sight of the following: scores of large and small boxes resting in isolation or stacked waist-high, or even taller than the height of a man; garden tools; a torn net for cleaning the fishpond and a mended one for catching butterflies; a forester's hammer for marking tree trunks; a row of flowerpots with seedlings just beginning to sprout; an unmade bed and a cold hot-water bottle; medium high-top shoes with metal braces; grafting shears; a frayed straw hat; freckled eggs in a jar with some kind of liquid; in a corner, pieces of a broken porphyry bust of a woman; a bowl painted with Hellenistic motifs, a little more than halfway glued together; a bundle of surveyor's rods; a ball of string; a small broom and another of sorghum; a metal brush; rusty stirrups; on some kind of flower stand, a pair of copper coins and a silver buckle; beneath the stand, a spatula; a rather thick herbarium from which protruded the stems of leaves; on the floor, assortments of stones, fragments of ceramics, and colored glass, as well as slips of paper with some kind of numbers; and on a large table of rough-hewn planks, vials of india ink, a map scale, a pair of compasses, a protractor, a magnifying glass, a pair of pincers, and a map of the entire property, with various hachured areas drawn in—as well as with the sites of buildings, with little crosses, and with elevations drawn in too—and a vignette in the right-hand title, where it was written in fine penmanship: "Imaginary reconstruction of the domain's inception, 1:10,000, by Prof. D. Tiosavljević."

20

Mojsilović inconsiderately pressed the doorbell. Adam recognized him by that inconsiderateness even before he peered through the peephole. The landlord actually didn't remove his finger from the button until the young man had opened the door.

"Lozanić, you sly bird, you're not perhaps trying to hide from me?" leered the apartment owner, as if threatening with the handle of his closed umbrella.

"But yesterday I left you a note that I'll pay next week, as soon as I receive my fee from *Our Scenic Beauty*," said Adam, wanting to be as brief as possible, since Mojsilović would never come around if he had to solve the matter of the disappearing water or whatever else. He only ever came to collect the rent.

"Eh, Lozanić, do you know how late you are? And what expenses I have! Do you have any idea how many elderly souls I'm carrying on my back? And how can I manage that if you are constantly telling me

'Tomorrow' and 'The day after tomorrow'? Don't think that I'm not capable of renting this apartment right in the center of town for a lot more money!" Mojsilović never used the words *studio apartment*, but stubbornly used the phrase *an apartment right in the center of town*, thinking this would more than justify the dizzyingly high price.

"Next week . . ." Adam replied.

"And what will there be next week? If not another 'Next week'? You see what uncertain times these are. I know it's not easy for you; I myself as a student had to make ends meet. But understand me, too . . ." Mojsilović's customary tirade could not be easily curtailed; the young man thought that the landlord, of all the things he could have studied, had for certain attended only lectures in anatomy, in how to fleece someone but not kill him off completely so that he would be able to continue paying . . .

"Next week, for sure . . ." said Adam, not offering much resistance so as not to continue the conversation.

"Next week?! That's pretty uncertain. On Monday, Tuesday, or Wednesday? Let it be on Monday. In the morning or afternoon? Noon, at the latest. Besides—so that you don't have the impression that I see absolutely everything in terms of money—I came to warn you. Your neighbor, who regularly pays his rent, complains to me that you make an unheard-of racket. He says that because of your testing yourself out loud, he cannot work. I, Lozanić, am not prepared to put up with that kind of behavior." Mojsilović again raised the handle of his umbrella; from such a type as him, one could expect a no less unpleasant situation.

"Listen, I'm not feeling well. Come in the middle of next week. Now, I have important work to do for which I'll be very well compensated. Maybe then I'll be able to pay you a few months in advance . . ." Adam said impatiently.

"In advance?! That would be a very nice gesture on your part. And how far in advance?!" the landlord softened.

"Yes, in advance, and all at once. Five months . . ." the young man tried to convince him, corroborating his statement with an upraised hand, fingers spread.

"But please be a little quieter . . ." replied Mojsilović almost paternally, now already quite in a good humor. "And so let's see, one of these days, what can be done about that water of yours . . ."

"Of course, of course; goodbye to you, goodbye . . ." said Adam, and he closed the door.

21

Not caring that he hadn't had a bite to eat since morning, the young man quickly went back to the open book. Burning with curiosity and fever, he searched for the place where he had left off, where he had seen the mysterious map.

Emptiness. Everything in the pavilion was in the spot it had been before, only he didn't find the spread-out map on the table of rough-hewn planks. Someone had come in the meantime. Perhaps Professor Tiosavljević himself, perhaps some other reader, but no one would have been able to tell.

Overwhelmed by his thoughts, Adam returned to the villa by the same route he had used to come to the pavilion. Pokimica was not there. The pergola stood in its utter beauty, as it had that morning. The first dusk lent the late-blooming roses a nuance of tragic red. The terrace-belvedere was deserted as well. In two of the rooms flickered the light of a candle; from the massive triple shadow in one of the window frames, the young man assumed that the unhappy Leleks had taken up residence there.

Circling the house around the east wing, Adam listened attentively in front of each of the three rear entrances, and hearing the clattering of dishes, guessed behind which of the doors the kitchen was. No one answered his knocking, and so the young man decided to go in.

Unlike in the deserted pavilion, here he found someone bent over a rather thick book. A woman, very old, wearing over her dress an apron with an embroidered hem, and holding a wooden spoon in her hand. In a twinkling she stopped leafing through the book and shouted out:

"Close the door—you'll cool my dough! It's just beginning to rise! Sit—wait—it isn't done yet!"

And Adam obeyed. He sat down at a table cluttered with heaps of vegetables, lumps of butter in small dishes, a bowl of fresh cream, an oval tray with thick pieces of cleaned fish . . . The old woman was very loudly reading some sort of recipe from the tattered pages, and he recognized the famous *Great National Cookbook* of Spasenija-Pata Marković, the very same one (but only somewhat newer) that his mother had at home. From a whole row of copper vessels on the glowing plates of the wood stove, there came at every moment a crackling, a popping, and a snapping, a gurgling, a spluttering, and a sloshing, a sizzling, a simmering, and a rattling . . . The housekeeper Zlatana—and it must have been she—took no notice of the new-comer, but instead outshouted her pots and pans, as if to that entire orchestra, having tuned it instrument by instrument, she were now giving final instructions before the big performance:

"Take one kilogram of sturgeon, a half kilogram of onions, and a quarter kilogram of fresh mushrooms, which should be boiled until tender before using. The sharp scales of the sturgeon are more difficult to remove than those of other fish; it is best that you scald it with boiling water and then peel off the skin, remove the gills, and discard. Chop the onions as finely as possible, add salt, and then put them into a quarter liter of good olive oil and place on low heat to fry. When the onions are half fried, chop the mushrooms into small pieces and then add them to sauté together with the onions. When the onions have turned to mush, add the fish—cut into pieces—and let sauté for two minutes. During that time, sprinkle on a little red pepper and ground white pepper and carefully stir with a wooden spoon. Then add warm water to the fish, but only enough to cover it, and cook for half an hour. While it is cooking do not stir the fish with the wooden spoon, only shake the pan. Before removing the pan from the fire, add finely chopped parsley to the fish and allow a few bubbles to come up. At that time remove the pan from the heat, serve on plates, and place them on ice to cool!"

Only then did the old woman look at the youth. "Mmm, how good this smells! So that it looks more picturesque, we'll add peas and slices of cooked carrots, and, on top, more finely chopped parsley leaves! What good is cooking if you can't add something according to your own taste! What do you say, son?"

"It sounds good . . ." said Adam.

"What's that? It's not done yet! It's not!" The old woman was stone deaf. "This is for tomorrow! Aspic of sturgeon! Lenten! Is tomorrow Wednesday!?"

"Yes," Adam shouted, too.

"But I tell you it's not done yet!" The elderly housekeeper had heard nothing. "Dinner's not ready! Wait a while!"

And the young man waited, watching how Zlatana went about her work with surprising vivacity: how she peeped under the covers of pots and carefully counted the rising bubbles, added water, skimmed off the froth, lighted a fire, opened and closed the draft of the stove, peeled, stuffed, grated, and strained, seasoned with pepper, salt, and sugar, cut into halves and quarters and chopped, greased baking pans, rolled out dough with a rolling pin, put into and removed things from the oven, occasionally shouting as if to hear herself:

"Cloves, two!"

"Poach it, poach it!"

"The recipe calls for a little something else here. We'll add another sprig of dill!"

Steam fogged up the walls, which were covered in faience tiles illustrated with idyllic motifs; it blurred the outlines of the hanging pots and pans, the small kitchen utensils, the bunches of dried herbs, the little boxes of spices arranged in order . . . From the pleasant warmth Adam's nose had quite thawed out, and he reached more and more often for his handkerchief. Suddenly the other door opened, the door by means of which the kitchen was connected to the interior of the house, and the young man recognized the girl with the bell-shaped hat, now in fact without it, but once again with an English dictionary, this time a small one, under her upper left arm. She—here! He set to musing while despite his cold he also recognized her smell, equally pleasant as it had been the day before, in the National Library.

"Soup coming right up, it's almost done!" shouted Zlatana, addressing the girl as well.

The girl sat opposite the young man and absently nodded to him. Looking askance, he was able to see her open the dictionary and, underlining them with her finger, read out the words *waggle, wagon, wagtail, waif, wail, wainscot, waist, wait*. She was so near that Adam Lozanić could discern each eyelash and brow, each strand of hair on her head, all of a light red that contrasted so starkly with the paleness of her regular features . . . She wore a linen traveling dress, the top two buttons undone, and the lines of her neck seemed so delicate that Adam began to fear she would sense his glance. He didn't dare to utter a thing, to add anything at all . . .

Meanwhile, the housekeeper ladled soup from a pot into a bowl for Adam, and then ladled more into a lidded tureen that she placed on a tray along with two spoons.

"Here we are," she said, handing Adam his bowl. "Say hello to

Miss Dimitrijević and be careful not to spill! I didn't skimp on anything, I put in everything I was supposed to!" She turned back to the girl. "By God, Natalija Dimitrijević is going to remember not only my cooking but even what she never tasted before, or my name isn't Zlatana!"

The girl had closed the dictionary, stowed it in a pocket of her dress, and now took the tray and walked toward the door through which she had entered. The young man jumped up to assist her. He held the door, she thanked him with a sort of melancholy smile, and then she disappeared down the narrow hallway into the interior of the mysterious house.

Returning to the table, Adam started to eat, not knowing which was hotter: the contents of his spoon or the feeling of bliss which, because of the girl's smile, coursed through his veins.

"Blow on it, child, don't burn yourself!" roared the old Zlatana. "Blow! And now for the other courses!"

22

It was all the same. Some peculiar feeling of fullness began to make him drowsy . . . In the studio apartment, it had grown quite dark . . . The neighbor was hammering the slats on . . . But nothing disturbed Adam. Resting the pencil and open book on his chest, not undressing, he simply drew the blanket over himself and started to drift off to sleep. He dreamed he fell asleep in that same garden and that he felt someone's breath on his cheek. He dreamed that he awoke, that he raised himself up and came eye to eye with a splendid white unicorn. He dreamed how that mythical creature nestled its head on his shoulder. And then he dreamed—a horrible nightmare— that he awoke and was unable to dream of anything more.

THIRD READING

ABOUT THE SEA,
SCRATCHED KNEES,
WET STRIPED BROCADE,
AND PAPER BAGS OF SAND;
ABOUT MILITARY SKILL
AND DRIVING THE JACKDAWS
FROM AROUND THE ROYAL PALACE;
ESPECIALLY ABOUT THE GYMNASTICS OF THE LUNGS
AND SUPERFLUOUS JOY;
ABOUT A FLOWER FROM A BALKAN MALLOW
AND THE WRITING OF NAMES IN MARGINS;
ABOUT PARADES
AND TORCHLIGHT RALLIES
AND LIPS BLUE FROM THE NIBS OF INK PENS;
ABOUT VITAL HEADINGS
AND PERFECTING A LANGUAGE FROM
OLD NEWSPAPERS

23

ON A DRIZZLE-THREATENED WEDNESDAY IN the fall of 1906, Anastas Branica, then only a twelve-year-old boy, sat at his stepfather's work desk reading a book and swinging his legs as he quietly whistled some children's march. This day was the official beginning of what one might later call his history.

The chair with its armrests, the walnut work desk, the thin-framed eyeglasses, the steel pens, the staid penholder, the crystal inkwell, the oval blotter, the ivory paper knife, the green-glass lamp, the doubly folded *Belgrade News*, *New Movement*, *Daily Record*, and *Business Journal*, the singly folded *Politika* and probably *The Press* (although it had been laid aside so that its headlines could not be seen), as well as the entire two-story house on Veliki Vračar, subsequently Zvezdara—all of that perfect order belonged to the boy's stepfather, the lawyer Slavoljub T. Veličković. As for the boy's mother, she lived in a room that everyone called hers, perhaps because there, on the dressers and chests of drawers, she kept a few mementos of her previous marriage. The nimble housekeeper Zlatana, who'd been taken on last year and whose face was now all flushed, was preparing aspic of sturgeon in order to demonstrate her culinary skill to the gentleman. And he, Slavoljub Veličković, had an important court appearance in town. He had recently begun to represent the interests of the Geneva bank Mirabaud, in the Kingdom of Serbia, and he was enjoying everything that the power of being an attorney entailed—a handsome salary, prestige, and the esteem of the community.

No doubt, had anyone been around, the young Branica would

never have dared to use his stepfather's chair, reupholstered in striped brocade. Nor would he have dared to even go near the writing desk, where the arrangement of everything was well-known. Still less would he have had the courage to sit exactly here, in his short trousers with suspenders and his drooping socks, and, captivated by the reading, whistle and (because his feet did not reach the floor) swing his legs.

And yet it all happened that way. Perhaps Anastas Branica, then only a boy, a first-grade pupil in the Second Boys Grammar School, might have discovered his particular gift on some subsequent, less painful occasion. On the other hand—perhaps like most of us, who never become conscious of our special abilities—he never would have discovered his own gift had that day not transpired the way it did. Perhaps, then, what took place years later would never have come about. But on a drizzle-threatened afternoon, a Wednesday, on Veliki Vračar—renamed Zvezdara only when the observatory was built—it all began that way.

The book in Anastas's hands bore, on its first page, the impressed seal of his father's ex libris—a miniature depiction of the universal world tree, and among its branches were the letters from the first and last name of Artillery Captain Sibin Branica, killed in 1903 immediately after the May coup. The book told of various adventures suitable for school-age children, and since it had been given to him on his birthday by his mother, the boy had several times, word by word, studied its contents. Anastas's favorite lines were the ones that described a view of the sea, and since the little boy had, until then, never been beside the great waters, he often stopped longingly at this very place, once an elevated cape, and in time had convinced himself that he really could hear the roar of the waves, smell the bracing sea salt, and even see what was not in the book, what the writer had not elucidated to the last detail. Because on this occasion he had also swung his legs in his stepfather's chair, Anastas Branica, in that year of 1906, was carried away beyond all measure—and is said to have raced toward the shore.

And once they had been set in motion, the boy's little legs rushed ever more unstoppably down the steep slope. No, there was no longer a chair, nor a desk; there was no longer a two-story house on Veliki Vračar. Anastas hurried along a narrow, winding path, nearer and nearer the vast waters. Along the way the sharp vegetation scratched his scrawny calves and bony knees. The rumbling of the mighty open sea and the constant chirping of small insects in the undergrowth deafened him more and more. Into his flaring nostrils came, ever more steadily, the smell of dark seaweed cast up from the ebb tide. Beads of perspiration gathered in the hollow of his feeble chest and ran down his back—the Mediterranean summer sun beat stubbornly down—but the boy did not give up, instead covering the distance in long, determined strides like those of people who well know where they are rushing off to and why.

Emerging finally onto the narrow beach, he suddenly slackened his pace by dragging his feet through the warm sand and letting it fill his shoes and socks, which had fallen down around his ankles, until it itched. With a primordial fear and curiosity, he approached the foam that divided shore from sea. And then for a moment he halted, in order to cautiously straddle the immeasurable white wreath, observing how the waves gently embraced him in a sort of submissive cringe, as if from time immemorial, since the beginning of the world itself, they had been waiting just for him.

Thus did Anastas Branica step into the sea for the first time. And then he went in farther, up to his knees. And then to his waist. Perhaps he would even have returned leisurely, by the same trail along the slope—along the low retaining walls of stones stacked "on the dry"—resting in the shade of hundred-year-old gnarled olive trees, picking the ripe fruit of the wild pomegranate, collecting round pebbles or anything else suitable for trading with his schoolmates—indeed, perhaps he would have done all of this had the door to the lawyer's office not been opened. In a twinkling, everything vanished; and now the boy was sitting in the chair of his stepfather, who shouted:

"What are you doing?! I'm asking you, young man, what are you doing at my desk?!"

Anastas made no answer. Embarrassed and confused, he did not move. As if he had been caught doing something indecent, he only sat there and, breathless, stared tremblingly at his stepfather.

The gentleman's raised voice alarmed the housekeeper, Zlatana. She came running and, not having the courage to say anything at all, convulsively squeezed the dishcloth in her hand while she silently observed the lawyer Veličković as, all blue in the face, he strode furiously about the room pointing his forefinger.

"Get up, you better get up at once!" he repeated senselessly, even when the boy had obeyed him, fearfully clutching the closed book to his chest.

"For God's sake, Slavoljub, why such a tone?" asked the mother, who had just come in, still absorbed in the mementos she had gathered in the room that everyone called hers.

"Do you need to ask?! Your son is playing at my desk!" the stepfather said, growing even more furious.

"Come now, all right," she tried to calm him. "It happened, he's a child, we'll discuss it . . ."

"Magdalina, there's nothing to discuss here!" said Slavoljub, precluding any further conversation. "Look at that chair! The brocade. Do you see?!"

Everyone—Zlatana, the mother, and Anastas—turned toward the lawyer's massive chair. The seat, reupholstered in a noble striped fabric, was wet; beneath the legs, on the parquet floor, spread a puddle of liquid, in places edged with dancing little bubbles of light. Zlatana placed her left hand over her mouth. The mother grew pale.

Anastas lowered his head and only then realized that his trousers, socks, and shoes were wet as well.

"And now you'll tell us what you've done!" the stepfather said, looking the boy angrily in the face.

The twelve-year-old bit his lower lip.

"What have you done?" the lawyer persisted with his question—he'd never gotten used to having even the slightest perplexity in his life go unexplained.

It seemed to the boy that he was shrinking, growing inward, gathering around the fateful answer. He hesitated between telling a lie and telling the way it was. And yet he was unable to do either one or the other; and the silence oppressed him even more. At length he decided and then somehow managed with relief: "I was swimming."

Slavoljub Veličković quite flew into a rage. "What?!"

"Well . . ." the boy faltered, "I was . . . reading about the sea . . . Then I went downhill . . . I went down to the water . . . I went in . . ." He bit his lower lip, for he felt that telling the truth was getting him into even more trouble.

On that Wednesday in 1906, there again reigned an unpleasant silence. Zlatana now covered her mouth with her right hand. The mother had grown even paler. The stepfather gradually got the gist of it.

"Went swimming, you say?"

The young Anastas Branica mutely nodded his head.

"And you thought to make a fool of me?"

The lawyer almost choked with rage, and, seeking to vent himself, he dealt the boy such a slap that from Anastas's nose there immediately unwound a short thread of blood.

"I went swimming," the boy squealed, not managing to wipe away the drops.

"And you're repeating it one more time?!" The stepfather again drew back his hand to strike him.

"Slavoljub, don't, enough now . . ." the mother managed to plead. "And you, Anastas, never—but never again—attempt to lie."

"Sir, don't—everything will dry, come out nice and clean—here now, supper's almost ready, I made Lenten aspic of sturgeon. I'll see to this now, at once . . ." Zlatana somehow found the courage to say, then immediately stooped down to wipe up, with a dish cloth, the puddle and bubbles beside the chair.

"You, keep silent." Veličković had somewhat calmed down, but his glance at the soaking wet brocade again enraged him and he turned and left the room, slamming the door so forcefully that along the wall there extended a whole vein of cracks.

Anastas Branica cried somewhere within himself.

"Promise you won't do that again, and then go change your clothes," his mother instructed.

Only then did the boy burst out into sobs. Not letting go of the book, squeezing it until his knuckles were white, hurt more by his mother's words than he had been by the slap, he ran out of his step-father's room.

In the evening Slavoljub T. Veličković returned to his desk, obliged to finish the work he had planned to do there earlier, and so as not to wet his trousers on the still-soaked brocade, but also not agreeing to change his habits one bit, he placed on the chair a small embroidered pillow from the sofa. There was something ridiculous in that sight. The lawyer put on and took off his glasses, gravely examining the tip of his steel pen—again meticulously wiping it on the rim of the crystal inkwell—then wrote out words, carefully pressing the blotter onto the regular lines—and all while sitting on a little pillow. Dissatisfied, as though he were conscious of all this, the stooping man continually frowned.

The mother, Magdalina, withdrew into her melancholy room, and the whole night rather aimlessly leafed through the books that bore the impressed depiction of the universal world tree, the humble legacy of her first husband. Either she didn't know what she was searching for, or it could in no way be found.

And the housekeeper? She set the table in the dining room, sat beside the kitchen stove, and waited for someone to try her handiwork, the voluptuously quivering aspic of sturgeon. No one was present to appraise her culinary skill: the thickened transparence with the uncannily hovering peas, carrots, and little pieces of mushroom and fish, all sprinkled with finely chopped parsley leaves. Realizing that dinnertime had long passed, the housekeeper put away the unused dishes, and then quietly started for the boy's room. Although she had thoroughly swept all the rooms that day, something stubbornly crunched beneath her slippers, as if someone had strewn sea sand all over the house.

The boy slept a troubled sleep: under the blanket his little legs made sudden twitches, each accompanied by a deep sigh.

"My son, I know I'm poorly lettered, but I believe you . . ." said Zlatana above the head of the bed, and then just as silently stole out of what might be called the very beginning of Anastas Branica's fate.

24

Many, many times Anastas Branica later went down that same steep slope, along the same sharp grass and winding stone walls in the shade of olive and wild pomegranate trees, onto that same narrow beach at the foot of the cape beside that same boundless water, all the while searching, stooped, for anything that would confirm he had been there as a child. The waves, with their high and low tides, had thousands of times already smoothed out the imprints. Nothing could be recognized. Nowhere was there a trace of his footprint.

It appeared that few dared go as far as the shore. New readers, boys in blue-and-white sailor's suits with anchor buttons, or precocious little vagabonds in borrowed, striped tricot bathing trunks on whose trouser seats was written in bold, oil paint letters STOLEN FROM VLAJKO'S BATHHOUSE, remained standing on the vertiginous height, contemplating the open sea, but they quickly went on to where the contents of their adventure book led them. Only the rare individual looked back at the human figure who, in the morning, legs and arms spread wide, lay face down on the shifting boundary between land and sea, and in the evening, doubled over, sat picking white pebbles on the wreath of foam. They probably weren't sure whether it was a drowning man who had just a moment before been barely rescued, or some desperate person who was drawing up his final account. They probably were not sure, for Anastas himself was undecided which one he was.

In the house on Veliki Vračar, however, much of that first trip on that drizzle-threatened Wednesday in 1906 would long remain in evidence. First of all, regardless of Zlatana's efforts, the sand continually trickled in from somewhere, continually spread from room to room. Amazed, the housekeeper had by Christmas collected a jar of it seven brandy glasses full. Afraid that lawyer Veličković would again accuse the boy, she told the gentleman nothing about the sand, instead hiding it on the highest shelf in the pantry, behind the large pots and tin cake molds. In the habit of adapting quickly, she eventually was no longer amazed and would patiently stack the jars, little sacks, and paper bags of sand there, as if it were a matter of the most ordinary duty, just one of the many responsibilities of her employment. During spring and fall cleanings, she surreptitiously carried the sand to the basement and continued to stow it there neatly.

With the creeper of cracks on the wall to the right of the lawyer's door, it was even more useless. From year to year, the interweaving lines grew longer, progressed in all directions. The original contractors, experienced construction engineers from Pančevo who had been responsible for the dignified façade in a restrained Art Nouveau style, came three times only to shrug their shoulders, roll their eyes, and, after the repair, offer as a pallative that from now on everything was going to be "just fine, more satisfactory." But not one of them managed to eradicate the cracks completely, nor would any of the future craftsmen. The whitewash would always flake off anew, the plaster would crumble, and in the root itself there would turn out to be a "you-can-put-in-three-fingers"-wide fissure in the brick, where there quickly grew and then multiplied the rustling of mice. Slowly, the vein of cracks spread through the other rooms, threatening once and for all to extend to the entire house.

"It's rotting! This is not covered with paint, sir. The house is on a fault . . . Once the water gets in, it can always come back . . . The vein of cracks reaches from below, from the foundation, from the ground," finally decided the last repairman, one Crnotravac, after he had tapped a long time here and there on the walls, listening attentively with his eyes closed to the spreading out of the echo.

Nor could the rift between the young Anastas Branica and his stepfather be narrowed in any way. After all, the lawyer looked upon the boy only as a necessary burden, as one of those things that Magdalina had dragged into her second marriage. He had agreed to it all only because of his immeasurable passion for the widow. Or perhaps even back then he had a set plan for how, in time, he would free himself from everything—save from her alone.

Indeed, Artillery Captain Sibin Branica had perished nearly three months after the May 1903 coup. The bloody traces of the assassination of King Aleksandar Obrenović and Queen Draga Mašin had long since been removed from the palace; a handful of high-ranking officers, the president of the government, the minister of the army, and the brothers Lunjevica were also killed, while others received a year or two in shackles. Still others were bought off with large pensions, and some at once swore allegiance to the new dynasty, made all the easier since the plot could be justified by well-deserved hatred for a despotic regime. Captain Branica, however, hid in Belgrade, stubbornly refusing to compromise his conscience. He had given his word before the anointed His Majesty and had agreed not to break it, and now he continually changed where he spent the night, sending word that "the regicides had already spelled the death of the Serbs," and attempted to begin a collaboration with Generals Jovan Belimarković and Antonije Bogićević, tried and true friends of the former ruling house. Secretly and at his own expense, he ordered at an unknown printer, probably Horowitz's, postcards with the likeness of a little boy of an aristocratic bearing, wearing a short jacket, hat, and gloves; postcards which he addressed to magazines all over Europe, and thus did the Parisian *Journal des Débats* receive a copy with the text: "You are mistaken; there is one more Obrenović successor to the throne." At the end of 1903, he departed for Vrnjci in the hope that the old General Belimarković, isolated from politics and the world in his summer house, would receive him there. But at the capital station, Branica found himself surrounded by men in uniform with their swords drawn. Dapples of summer sunlight stood motionless on the sharp blades.

"Sibin, give yourself up—you'll die in vain!"

They were commanded by Lieutenant of the Commissariat Vemić, the best friend Branica had had in his class and a blood brother, and whose chief responsibility, under the murdered king, had been to drive the jackdaws from the trees around the royal palace so that the annoying birds would not make a din beneath the monarch's windows. The lieutenant had never been overly brave, but now he was on the opposing, many-times-stronger side.

"Away!" Branica defiantly straightened up, reaching for the inner pocket of his civilian frock coat in which he kept not a revolver but the Order of the Cross of Takovo—only to fall immediately thereafter, pierced in so many places that it was never learned who had dealt the mortal blow, just as it would never reliably be established where he had been buried.

Slavoljub T. Veličković made Magdalina's acquaintance a half year later. At the time still representing less important commissioners, Tzintzar usurers, and credit unions, he had attended an appraisal of the widow's effects; she, meanwhile, had been supporting herself by continual borrowing. To deal with all this debt, to deal, namely, with the question of whether to turn to her dead husband's sole remaining relative in Kragujevac—by persuasion an enthusiastic republican, a sworn enemy of any kind of monarchy—or whether, on her own, to sell much more profitably the household furniture and settle her bills of exchange, she had not the strength. And of her own kin she had no one: her entire possessions consisted of that little house in Dorćol, along with all the outstanding debts associated with the purchase of the lot and the costs of construction. A letter of condolence and thirty gold ducats in aid from General Belimarković she refused to accept. She had already then resigned herself to melancholy, to the feeling that would accompany her her whole life long. She visited Belgrade's cemeteries, lighting candles and placing flowers at random graves, leaving brazilwood-colored red eggs on the second Monday after Easter, and tidying up the burial mounds no one had been around to see—and all while still not knowing where her husband's grave was.

At the appraisal, the sight of the exceedingly beautiful pale woman, proudly looking somewhere into her past, so swept away the lawyer's proverbial cool indifference that he nearly doubled the value of the confiscated goods, forgoing his usual, never paltry fee. While the lads carried out the bulky Gründerzeit beds, the provincial Alt-Deutsch dressing table with mirror, the cross-river porcelain wall clock, and the Slava silverware, Slavoljub Veličković gave himself up to the thought that she, that woman, could be the greatest benefit he might ever accrue in any similar mediation.

Being a man of order, the lawyer first measured his actions well, and then proceeded according to a set plan. Having found that the easiest way to approach Magdalina was by way of her memories, he purchased the cheapest items of all: the dead artillery captain's throttled pocket watch, the penknife with the mother-of-pearl handle, and several of the confiscated books with the impressed depiction of the universal world tree, the mark of the deceased's family library. Then he returned one spring afternoon in 1904, sitting down stiffly and placing his hands on his knees, and, kissing her hand, he said:

"I thought these things meant a great deal to you, and so I wanted to return them to you; be so kind as to accept them . . ."

"I . . . I don't know what to say . . ."

The pale woman, moved, began to cry.

"Madame, please do not hesitate. You'll repay me when you're able." The lawyer stood up, bowed and offered his neatly pressed handkerchief.

And so it continued. Slavoljub Veličković came at regular intervals, spending hours on end in conversation with the widow, thoughtfully commiserating with the stories of her previous marriage, standing up and offering her his immaculately pressed handkerchief, all the while speaking very little about himself. For months nothing changed in these meetings, except that Magdalina's home was becoming more and more empty; anything having the slightest value was now in hock, and the desolate corners of her unenviable life could already be discerned. They soon had to converse standing up, because there were no longer kitchen stools. For months nothing changed, except for the growing little boy who could scarcely remember his father, and probably for this reason grew up with a certain absence in his eyes.

Keeping abreast of the state of Magdalina's assets, the lawyer sped up his plan when he learned that the house itself was irretrievably burdened with debt, that the pitiless holders of the bills of exchange were preparing to go to court for payment, and so it was only a matter of time before the woman and her child would find themselves on the street. The offer of marriage was understood by the widow to mean the protection of her son and what remained of her keepsakes. And so on the Nativity of Blessed Virgin Mary Day in 1905, holding Anastas by the hand, she stepped into the carriage that was to take her to Veliki Vračar, subsequently Zvezdara. The coachman had already loaded the two modest suitcases stuffed full of all kinds of mementos; everything else had disappeared, had been swallowed up by the estate's mortgage.

"Let's go!" The lawyer somewhat triumphantly—unable to help himself—gave the sign to leave.

From the site of the house itself, at which people marveled because it had been built so far from town, to the restrained façade, on which were legibly interwoven the flourished initials S. T. V.; from the framed circular imprints of Latin maxims and popular proverbs, girded in laurel wreaths or four-leaf clovers purchased in Solomon J. Cohen's store At Napoleon's, or Kalmić's trinket shop At the Lucky Hand, to the bracing green eau de cologne made in Vienna, and the pomade, and the pair of wire pincers for shaping the twirled ends of his mustache—everything in the new home clearly pointed to or simply betrayed to whom it belonged. And it was over personal possessions that the first disagreement arose. Too overwhelmed by her gloomy reflections, Magdalina had no intention of making anything her own and by that very act surrendering completely. It was as if she had come to Veliki Vračar temporarily, and with a sense of unease used only what she needed to, otherwise quite satisfied with her own belongings, meaning her son and the contents of the two small cardboard suitcases. And when after only three months she openly refused to share a marital bed with her new husband, the lawyer realized that his preliminary calculations had been wrong, that he loved her to no avail, that what awaited him was a long and uncertain struggle with the woman's memories.

He agreed to separate rooms when she promised to come to him once a week. She consented—even though it was torment for her to lie in the dark beside a man who was forever panting and wet with passion—only when she observed that he badgered her with trivial questions whenever she surrendered to her memories. If she were to acquire her own room, she would be able to isolate herself, to give herself up to her reveries in peace. There, in the dressers and chests of drawers, she hid her things, because she noticed that whatever she casually laid aside or forgot in some other room disappeared, never to return. And on another occasion, when she was feeling weak and he kept entering her room, on the pretext of wanting to see how she was, but really to remind her of his presence, she instructed him to make her a key. Particularly because he had knocked from her nightstand, as if unintentionally, a glass rimmed with gilded grapevines, one of the objects having special meaning for Magdalina.

And it was here somewhere that the line was tacitly drawn. Slavoljub Veličković was in part satisfied, for he had managed to confine his wife's memories to that locked room. And Magdalina finally found a melancholy corner into which her thoughts could settle down undisturbed. Nonetheless, that all of this ostensible harmony was sheer illusion was demonstrated by the stepfather's relationship with his stepson. If he had succeeded one way or another in getting rid of a good portion of the contents of the two small suitcases, the presence of Anastas Branica was, for the lawyer, a constant reminder of what was probably the single most serious mistake of his life. Powerless to do anything, he kept himself as far away as possible from the boy, minding to share with him only as much as was required. As the years went by, the middle-aged man became steadily more oppressed by the question: for whom had he so long, so patiently created so much order and progress? For whom had he diligently acquired possessions; for whom had he prudently converted unsound paper money into always valuable gold coins; for whom had he, with tricolor paper bands, bundled each new dozen of the securities pertaining to the highest-yielding cooperatives, savings banks, firms, and credit unions; for whom had he assiduously kept a ledger of income and expenses, checking himself three or four times, to the penny, whenever he made an entry? As he grew into a young man Anastas withdrew to the side, feeling that this life was suffocating him more and more, compressing him into that which he wasn't by birth. The rift between the two of them had widened to a chasm. Divining how great this fissure was, Magdalina countlessly talked by turns with her husband and son. Her efforts to conciliate the two endlessly followed one after the other, but she never heard whether her words had been received, whether one of them had ever hit home. And the sad woman truly had less and less strength to watch over these matters.

25

As only fate would have it, the lawyer was especially troubled by those few books he had so generously taken off the creditors' hands; those few books with the impressed depiction of the universal world tree on the first page; in all, just seven books from various fields, for various age groups, and with the leaves carelessly cut and unevenly bound.

Slavoljub Veličković possessed—it wasn't as if he didn't—a quite decent personal library, and concerning the legal profession an exceptionally rich one. On the shelves in his study stood scrupulously chosen titles, legal codes with bronzed spines, meticulously bound, mostly in dark brown leather. But those seven little books spoiled everything. The lawyer had merely to pass his glance over them and the rage or envy would well up in him. His wife read the books with a special enthusiasm. He had never seen her surrender herself more unreservedly to any other kind of reading material. Everything else from his library, he was convinced, she read less intently—absently, indifferently, even with an expression of boredom on her upper lip and scorn on her lower one.

Not very long after the wedding, having returned early from the city one day, with Anastas in school and Zlatana buying groceries, Slavoljub Veličković found his wife on the sofa holding one of those books. It would be more appropriate to say that she was spasmodically squeezing its binding, as though after a long, long wait she were finally clutching at real life. She hadn't sensed him even when he crossed the threshold and stepped into the room. Her eyes, almost without blinking, flew ardently across the lines. She turned the pages with fervor, or self-indulgently went backward to reinforce what she had already read. Pressed up against the high back of the sofa as if by some force, she was breathing rapidly, her breast heaving, and was unaware that her legs were exposed and her dress was raised above the knee. She was barefoot, and her laced shoes lay several feet away, having been kicked off her feet. Always of a transparent complexion, she was now flushed in the cheeks, and it was only the lawyer who grew pale as he discovered in his wife a passion that she'd never revealed since arriving in the house on Veliki Vračar—that was, since their first night together.

"Magdalina . . ." he began dryly.

She gave a start, quickly standing up and letting go of the book. Growing embarrassed, she didn't know whether first to straighten her dress or to put on her shoes.

"What was that you were reading?" asked Slavoljub Veličković, scarcely restraining himself—it seemed that she had just deceived him.

"Well, in my free time . . ." she managed to collect herself and answer vaguely.

He walked up to her determinedly and picked up the closed book, of course one of those with the depiction of the universal world tree.

He emphatically read out the title as he examined it closely along its side: "*On the Art of War*, by German Chief of Staff Field Marshal Helmut von Moltke?!" Then he turned a few yellowed pages at random. "I didn't suppose that something like this interested you?! Allow me to keep it for a while. I would like to know what is hidden here . . ."

She didn't object. She only closed her eyes like one who was unable to deny her guilt, and then withdrew contritely into her room. The lawyer remained where he was, to run his fingers through his hair the whole night long as he squinted and read about military patrols, about methods of preparing, defending, and attacking, and about the organization of a supply unit and field hospitals . . . There was nothing here but endless speculation on military doctrine, but Slavoljub T. Veličković thereby felt the pangs of jealousy all the more painfully. He'd offered her everything, and she'd devoted herself more to a book than to him. Only his practice of not easily abandoning his principles kept the lawyer from throwing *On the Art of War* onto the rubbish heap. Just before dawn, dressed in a bathrobe, he went into the backyard, dug a hole with a small garden spade, laid the book in the bottom of the pit, covered it with dirt, leveled it out, and finally stamped on it with his feet. On his way back he turned around: in the light of daybreak, the spot could not be distinguished; there was no trace of it at all.

"It's probably here somewhere; it must have gotten misplaced . . ." he replied nonchalantly later on, when Magdalina inquired obliquely about the fate of one of her mementos.

26

However, this whole affair of the books from Captain Branica's legacy exceeded all patience when, on that drizzle-threatened Wednesday in the year 1906, the lawyer turned up just in time to see where his stepson was reading and swinging his legs, as well as what remained behind him on the striped brocade and parquet floor. No, we won't be doing it like this anymore, he thought that evening, as he sat on the little pillow so that the dampness would not soak his trousers.

"From now on in this house you will have to read what I choose," he said in the morning, without further ado, to his wife and the boy. "On Sunday at noon I want to see you two together," and that same day he began the preparations.

One should know that Slavoljub T. Veličković attached much importance to good health. Since its very founding he had been a prominent member of the Serbian Grand Lodge of Sobriety of the Neutral Templars Order, at one time an assistant to its officers, and credited with having developed a large number of elaborate rules and regulations which sometimes bordered on ritual. He spent his free afternoons at the meetings of this society, which were conducted according to strictly established procedure, of course never entering a barroom or taking a drop of alcohol. A sizeable portion of the lawyer's library was made up of books, journals, and brochures devoted to sobriety and to the general struggle to heighten bodily and mental health. Of the breadth of his interests, the following titles spoke most eloquently: *Nervousness and Its Principal Causes*; *Preventing Infection*; *Protect Yourself from Dysentery, Dandruff, and Baldness*; *Unstable Gases in the Air and Their Hygienic Significance*; *Marriage Between Partners of Widely Varying Ages*; *Petroleum Is Not Medicine*; *Quinine Against Dysentery . . .*

As a subscriber, from the very first issue, to the instructional magazine *Health*, and as an admirer of its editor, Professor Dr. M.

Jovanović Batut, Veličković had a quite specific aim in mind regarding his wife and stepson. In addition to the ones he already had, he procured two more copies of each edition of the aforementioned journal.

"On Sundays, at this time, in this spot, the three of us together must read this useful material," he announced, giving the young Anastas and Magdalina each a number from the same volume.

And from then on, with the boy and his pensive mother sitting next to each other on the sofa, and with the stepfather and husband at his work desk, his mustache freshly pomaded, and all of them dressed formally as if for an outing—from then on the three of them, at the same time and until dinner, read to themselves articles, advice, explanations, and aphorisms about life and human health. The lawyer occasionally raised his head and craned his neck to verify that the members of his household were carefully following along with what was written, and if need be, reminding them when to turn the page in order to begin a new heading or passage. Indeed, he would not abide by any absentmindedness, let alone cheating:

"Magdalina, concentrate! Anastas, stop fooling around, looking left and right—look in front of you! Let's go to page ninety-five!" he ordered, and the boy and the woman obeyed. "And now look for 'Fear and the Anxiety Attack' by Dr. Joksimović."

Afterward, at Sunday dinner, Veličković expressed satisfaction with their joint reading. He considered that he had finally established some kind of order. "You saw how dangerous fish is during summer heat spells? And you, Zlatana, you might have joined us one time; had you done so, it wouldn't have happened that you put so much salt in the soup. Spices are deadly for the stomach and kidneys. Anastas, have you remembered that maxim 'Things are better done in the morning than during the rest of the day'? Come, boy, repeat it." The lawyer spoke so much between each course that he didn't notice the silence of all the others at the table.

As only fate would have it, had there not been these compulsory gatherings around the old issues of *Health*, Anastas would never have developed his special talents for reading. No doubt the stepfather would never have obliged them to read together had he only known where it would all end. Or rather from where it would all begin.

At first fearing the gentleman's hot-tempered nature, the boy zealously followed every line and word in accordance with the program for that week. And then it slowly dawned on him that the lawyer was incapable of knowing how far he or his mother had actually entered the content of the reading. All external things—if someone were feeling drowsy or the like—Slavoljub Veličković immediately noticed, but inside the written material, Anastas could do whatever he wanted. In time, Anastas saw that his mother had learned to wear a look of rapt attention when she began a reading, as if it really did interest her, although immediately after the title she would stare indifferently while searching for her memories in her thoughts. The possibility that somewhere, if a text were being read at the same time, Anastas would meet another reader—during which both of them would be able to, but did not have to, sense his traveling companion—later determined the greater part of Anastas's life. However, then only a boy, he used what he had learned to defy his stepfather, to while away the hours out of spite for him, while in that same study in the house on Veliki Vračar he bent piously over *Health*.

A particularly vivid example was their joint reading in May 1908 of the article "The Gymnastics of the Lungs and Military Tuberculosis." Following the advice of the author, Veličković demanded that particular attention be paid to physical exercise as an effective way to prevent pernicious disease.

"We'll start from the sentence 'Crouch while at the same time raising your arms in all directions . . .' Did you find it? And then further on to the end of the page." He looked across his work desk at Anastas and Magdalina, and then he himself got down to work when he was convinced that the members of his household were diligently following his instructions.

But regardless of what kind of impression they gave on the sofa, within the world of the text—where it was explained how to do the exercises—it was altogether different. The pale woman stared somewhere into the distance, and even moved into the shady garden since the author had noted that gymnastics should be performed outdoors, in nature. Meanwhile, the boy simply clowned around by bringing his lips right next to the lawyer's ear and saying, "Two-two-three, faster!" The only one who compliantly crouched and raised their arms was he, Slavoljub T. Veličković, who was nonetheless quite winded. Some unknown voice was urging him to do everything several times faster than his God-given physical capacities allowed.

His brow sweaty, the ends of his mustache drooping, the middle-aged man stopped. He could do no more. He lifted his eyes from the open periodical. The boy and the woman were attentively reading. They were doing it liesurely, without the least bit of effort—so mused the lawyer while undoing the knot of his tie and unbuttoning his stiffly starched collar. When he'd caught his breath, in order to conceal his defeat he interrupted them: "Enough, enough for today!"

In a sort of torpor, Magdalina put aside *Health*, got up, and withdrew to her room. Anastas simply jumped from the sofa and hastily exited the study, afraid his stepfather would notice the smile in the corners of his little mouth.

The lawyer was at a loss for what to do with himself. There was still a whole hour until dinner, the reading had ended ahead of time, and Zlatana surely hadn't set the table yet . . .

Always helpless when his fixed schedule was disrupted, he propped up his head on his hand, and with the fingers of the other hand, he nervously tapped on the walnut top of his writing desk.

27

Perhaps this country is either too small or else is constantly being squeezed, and so fate must continually be repeated. At any rate, to get to the house on Veliki Vračar, today Zvezdara, where the unhappy story of Anastas C. Branica began long ago, one might go at a leisurely pace by way of the street that bears the name of Professor Milan Jovanović Batut, a physician worthy of much praise for, among other things, having been founder and editor of *Health*. Back issues of the periodical, printed in the tens of thousands of copies, were rarely read by anyone now, but there would still be a wealth of valuable observations in them. For example, in the editorial for the January issue of 1910, it is written thus: "Our people, too, value health, but somehow only halfway. Yes, to be sure, the word is often on our tongues; yes, we bid each other good 'health,' we drink toasts to each other's 'health,' and so forth; but all this is an empty wish . . . and genuine, rational concern for our health simply does not exist among us. On the contrary: in our lives, in our customs, habits, and opinions, there are a great many things inimical to natural development and good health, and we cling to them so tightly that it is truly odd that we do not become completely ill."

The possibility of moving about within a text as within any other space; the fact that all who were reading the same book at the same time were capable of meeting one another; that some of them were conscious of both the boundlessness of that space and each chance traveler individually, while for others such a feeling was completely alien—all of this no doubt spurred the young Anastas Branica from then on to try his hand at different kinds of literature. That was the period of his first raptures, but also of his first disappointments. The boy did not succeed in every instance in crossing that shifting boundary; often, he would strain for hours on end and not budge a jot from the ordinary. And if he did manage to move, he wouldn't later have the strength to concentrate for long; it seemed he would get tired just before the most interesting parts, before the ultimate discovery. Finally, as he read so much and so ardently, Anastas felt more and more alone; not a few times did it happen that during his classes in his native language, all of his classmates, as well as the teacher, were looking at him in amazement, sometimes also with a sneer; and so it was that not only did he go off to the distant Second Boys School unwillingly, but he then returned even more dejected. This was perhaps the reason why he began to withdraw into himself, and during his schooling avoided the prescribed program, the reading required of everyone. Although he was capable of recounting details that even Homer, Virgil, or Dante had not dwelt upon in their poetry, Anastas's grades were barely sufficient for him to scrape by from one year to the next.

"Magdalina, do you think everything is all right with this child? He spends so much time over books, and his success is not even average?!" said the lawyer, trying hard to strike up a conversation about his stepson.

"Boys at that age are so: their attention wanders, they can't settle down. It will pass . . ." Anastas's mother always gave the same answer.

"Oh really now. I knew what I wanted even then!" Slavoljub T. Veličković would explode. "If it continues this way, I am not willing to continue investing in his schooling!"

In those years, there was nothing to indicate that things would improve. Anastas shut himself in more and more, further and further from children his own age and from the members of his own household. He was not like his peers, and since he all the more often disagreed with the others, a great sadness came over him.

Only rarely were things otherwise. As when classes in nature study at the Second Boys School, once a week, coincided with classes in botany at the Girls Teacher-Training School. Namely, it often happened that both here and there they were reading the same material. It happened that members of both sexes, contrary to the recommendations of the Ministry of Education about not mingling the young people, gathered around some subject of study, for example the famous *Flora of the Kingdom of Serbia* by Josif Pančić, and in the shadows of the described spruces, on the vernal slopes of Kopaonik, with greater or lesser attention, learned about the characteristics of this rare genus, during which each of those present was oblivious of the one nearest them. With the exception, of course, of Anastas, who was flushed in the face, confused by the presence of so many young ladies, and especially by a willowy blonde girl, her hair braided into pigtails, a girl who didn't, like the rest, look through him.

And because such days were ordinarily accompanied by sleepless nights, it seemed to the young man that he lived for those special moments, for the nature-study classes, for that wonderful hour when in the crowd of chattering girls he would recognize her eyes, which were once more wide open, observing him. At one point, she stayed home for three months because she was ill with pneumonia, and her absence truly caused him much worry—and so, like a fool, he read for days on end everything that had any connection with flora and fauna, hoping in this way that he would again be able to meet her.

"Branica, you're not perhaps taking up the study of botany, are you? Get it into that head of yours: the rule is that you may take out only one book at a time!" Thus the suspicious supervisor of the little school library chastized Anastas when he asked to borrow a whole series of titles that dealt with the particulars of that science.

However, all of the acutely oppressing discomfort, all of the wringing upset in his stomach vanished at once when the girl suddenly reappeared inside one of his readings, noticeably feeble but with an inextinguishable warmth in her eyes; it would turn out that she, too, had been waiting impatiently for their next meeting. Love truly works wonders, as the saying goes. He didn't know how it was possible, but it happened while Anastas was reading *Medicinal Herbs in Serbia* by Sava Petrović. He bent down and picked a flower from a Balkan mallow—attached to the text's description of the flower, in parentheses, were the words *Kitaibelia vitifolia*—and she shyly accepted the little gift, lowering her eyelashes, and for a long time afterward the young man regretted that he hadn't said a thing then; he was somehow sure that she would have heard him even though she'd been sitting far away from him, on a different school bench, in a different school, in a quite different neighborhood of Belgrade.

"You stupid blockhead!" he would scold himself at night, tossing and turning in his rumpled bed, getting up and lying down in vain, sometimes until morning.

It is certain that precisely this oversight prompted him, on the occasion of their next meeting, to pull an ink pen from his pocket, lick its nib, and on the bark of a nearby birch tree write out his name. With a smile she acknowledged that she understood, that among all the things that were being learned in her class she had read that word as well. What's more, she reached out her hand and below the bold type ANASTAS wrote in the string of letters M-I-L-E-N-A . . . Yes, that was exactly how it stood on the whiteness of the birch bark . . .

"Branica, are you roaming around in that book?!"

The lanky nature-study teacher, who was called Forest Ranger by the pupils, stood up, walked around the rostrum, and pointed straight at the youth, who was still gazing into the girl's face. Anastas gave a start, became confused, and placed his hands on the open pages of the textbook, trying to hide the words that, in addition to on the tree inside the text, had appeared on the margin of the page. Alas, it was too late.

"'Anastas'?! 'Milena'?! Oh, so this is a romance! You should be ashamed, Branica. And be prepared to explain your vandalism to the director!" the teacher said, as cruel sniggering spread throughout the classroom.

It all ended in a severe reprimand. But for Anastas Branica the true punishment resided in the renewed absence of the girl. In fact, she never appeared again. The pneumonia had returned in the form of tuberculosis—he had heard the schoolboys whispering so among themselves.

As for Milena, her last day at the Girls Teacher-Training School was likewise darkened by the nudging and sneers of her schoolmates, and by the rebuke she received from her teacher because of the same names written in the margin of her book.

28

Our people have always gladly thronged within the pages of newspapers, but at the time of the war with Turkey, and later with Bulgaria, each of the numerous daily rags truly resembled a brimming beehive. These were the years of Serbia's powerful rise, years of regaining its old glory, years of general enthusiasm. The front pages of the *Piedmont*, the *Tribune*, the *Belgrade News*, *Pravda*, the *Press*, *New Times*, the *Bell*, the *Slavic South*, *Business Journal*, and *Politika*—all were full of blaring headlines, buoyant articles, and exciting reports. Announcements of successful military ventures arrived one after the other; promising diplomatic turnabouts followed in rapid succession. From everywhere, from all around, our stirred compatriots reached for these publications, from across the Danube and Drina rivers, from the seacoast, even from across the ocean—these, several months after the fact—in order to read with pride about the resurrection of the homeland. As never before, others arrived as well, inspired by the awakening of the Slavs, by the possibility of Balkan unification, by the pluck of a small nation that was throwing off the yoke of Ottoman oppression, by the discovery of an exotic corner of Europe that for centuries had been shrouded . . .

Through this entire tumult of astrakhan fur caps with white feathers, of polished cockades, of epaulets, of shoulder patches and braids, of blue tunics, of bright red trousers, of the scaly chinstraps of shining helmets, of saddle cloths, of parade-horse blankets, of ornamented girths, of high boots in stirrups, of infantry, of artillery, and of the newer uniforms of the members of the recently formed airplane and balloon corps—through all of this, a young man with unusually glistening eyes also moved. He made his way through the crowd, making sure that nothing escaped his view, rising on tiptoe so as not to miss a single part of the march past, rushing to where the people were gathering to await the victors with a torch-light rally, to warmly greet the heroic brethren from the Principality of Montenegro or the Greek allies, to with curiosity interpret both the consul's retelling of events as well as the unofficial positions of sources close to the ministries of foreign affairs in Western capitals. It was in this way, over the bundles of newspapers his stepfather had brought into the house on Veliki Vračar, in an agitated sea of big words, that Anastas Branica spent the year 1912. Thus did he have the opportunity to meet, even among the scarcely literate, an ever greater number of those who zealously entered the text as far as the most insignificant details, an ever greater number of those who were at least semiconscious of this community, who whether it was in worry or joy were brought together by even the briefest report from the battlefield.

When at Kumanovo the Vardar division of the Turkish army was defeated in a rout, and the Serbian army continued on in pursuit of Zeki Pasha, rebuffing enemy troops all the way to Bitolj, people read the news with a sense of relief, and it seemed to Anastas that everyone was shaking everyone else's hand, or, as they passed each other by, shouting for joy: "We won, we won!" Once more, as the advance guard liberated town after town in Kosovo, people stopped, embraced, toasted one another's health. Anastas would never forget the daughter of Peter I Karadjordjević; by coincidence the two of them, in the same morning hour, were reading line by line: he in his room, clipping out old articles as keepsakes and mementos of those glorious times; she, Princess Jelena—married in Russia to one of the Romanovs—poring over the newspapers which had just arrived some twenty days late, brought in by a servant along with a buttered roll and a small cup of café au lait.

"The unified Serbian and Montenegrin army has broken out to the sea!" she loudly repeated at the table on the porch of her summer home in Pavlovsk.

Anastas recognized the face from the enlarged daguerreotype displayed in the main auditorium of the Second Belgrade High School, during celebrations of the birth dates of the members of the royal family: the way her hair was twisted into a bun, and the silver brooch on the lace jabot of her white dress. He now looked around; there was no doubt that those words had been meant for him. He jumped from his chair and, thrusting out his chin, snapped to attention.

"Dear compatriot, why are you rooted to the spot—come, let us congratulate each other!" said Princess Jelena, and kissed the unknown high school student three times. For a long while, the whiff of French perfume would not fade from the young man's memory—despite the prevailing fumes of lead and printer's ink in *Politika* from the end of October 1912.

29

The mother, too, carefully followed the newspapers from the time of the Balkan wars. For hours on end the gaze of the pale woman flew over the spread-out pages and wandered off somewhere into distances known only to her. Anastas had long been troubled by the question of why she read exactly this way, equally passionately and absently, as if she possessed some special talent in excess but only used it again and again to try to flee from life. Several times he had decided to set out after her, but in the house there hadn't been another copy of the same edition. An unexpected opportunity arose on April 6, 1913, when his mother was sitting outdoors in a cane garden chair, with her back turned to the home of her husband, the lawyer Slavoljub Veličković.

At first Anastas did not intend to sneak up on her. Magdalina simply didn't hear him approaching, having just begun the news that His Majesty had yesterday deigned to sign a decree awarding the Karadjordje Star with Swords of the Fourth Degree to the heir to the throne, Aleksandar; to the commander in chief of the army, Radomir Putnik; to the generals Mihailo Živković, Stepa Stepanović, and Pavle Jurišić Šturm; to Prince Arsen Karadjordjević; to the colonels Božidar Terzić and Milovan Nedić; and so on and so forth . . . Over his mother's shoulder the young man began with the same column. Put more exactly, he hardly managed to see her, following his gut rather than his (so-called) literal sense of sight.

Usually wistfully unhurried, Magdalina now hastened on, not noticing the crowd swarming to congratulate the victors. The people moved apart to the left and right of the pale woman; an inexplicable shoving and jostling ensued, and curious innkeepers stepped back, as well as bakers and pastry makers, journeyman tailors, apprentice candlemakers and barbers, barely literate coachmen and water-cart drivers, idle city dandies, bank clerks, members of various choral groups, the Circle of Serbian Sisters association, and even a dishonored girl who was waiting here to throw caustic lye into the eyes of her unfaithful lover. Without a voice of complaint, the gentlemen too moved aside, most of them with a bow and a doff of the hat. Standing apart were three informants of imperial Vienna, who, reading the newspapers in Zemun all day long, followed with a scowl Belgrade public opinion on behalf of the Austro-Hungarian monarchy. Shadowing her as far as he could, Anastas hurried after Magdalina.

There wasn't much to go until the end, scarcely a few sentences; the list of those being decorated concluded with the name of Quartermaster Colonel Vemić, the former Obrenović lieutenant who had distinguished himself on the occasion of the death of his blood brother Sibin Branica. What she was intending to do as she frantically rushed that way cannot be confirmed with complete certainty, but to the astounded officer Magdalina said coldly:

"I hope I'm not disturbing you. I have come to say hello."

The colonel didn't know whether to back down in the face of the woman or to suffer the scorn that clearly took shape on her lovely face. For so many years he had avoided meeting her, and she had found him in this most solemn hour of his career, as he reveled in, perhaps for the umpteenth time that day, the decree proclaimed on the front pages of the newspapers, all editions of which were brought to him by an orderly, several copies of each.

"Magdalina, that's the way it had to be . . ." he attempted, trying to find an explanation.

"Of course—otherwise you'd still be shooing jackdaws from the trees around the royal palace." The expression on her face unchanged, Anastas's mother turned and slowly went back the same way she had come.

Retreating after Magdalina, the young man did all he could to avoid being seen by her. But such caution was unnecessary: the pale woman seemed absent from everything real. Once more the crowd parted and gathered. Behind them, quite near, the shot of a revolver was heard. Someone had likely given vent to his joy; in those days one celebrated even lesser things.

Only the three zealous Zemun informants, in black redingotes with Franz Josef sideburns, with neckties on elastic bands and bowler hats, with their eyes red from conjunctivitis, with their lower lips drooping, blue from ink pens used for frequent noting-down and underscoring—only they considered it necessary to confirm exactly what had taken place here. The reading service of the Austro-Hungarian Empire was the first such secret organization to draw a clear distinction between keeping a close eye on the newspapers, or any other kinds of text, and spying on those who frequented a certain reading selection. Judging by the voluminousness of the archival material, meticulously classified into reports and denunciations, the Viennese agency maintained a very extensive network in all geographical locations where one might learn something of benefit to the security of the Dual Monarchy. After all, one could write all sorts of things, and at one's own discretion, and so censorship was slowly becoming a less effective method of oversight; it was very important, however, to have a true picture of those who were reading various types of publications. Consequently the Belgrade press, especially dangerous because of the large number of Serbs in the Empire, was teeming with trustworthy clerks similar to these three informants, clerks who were prepared to note down who, and with how much fervor, was partial to the motherland—apparently down to the most insignificant details.

Magdalina had long since closed the pages of the newspaper and was pensively staring into the distance while massaging her temples with a cooling migraine stick: menthol in the shape of a pencil, a popular remedy for headache and toothache. In his room, Anastas tried hard to remember who that abashed colonel might have been who had known his mother so well. He couldn't free himself from the vague impression that his face and name were known to him.

And to Vienna, from Zemun, went out a dispatch that, sitting over *Pravda*—which had published the decree of the high honor that had just been bestowed upon him—in his office in the Military Affairs building, and under the pressure of some mental derangement, a Serbian officer had killed himself with a revolver. The three informants concluded, scowling, that there was no need to attach any greater political significance to the event described, but that the whole case was nonetheless a rather instructive example of how this unpredictable nation was given to "drastic" extremes.

30

In the middle of June 1913, after checking it several times, Slavoljub Veličković put everything down neatly on paper:

Anastas had passed his final examination with a higher grade than anyone had hoped.

If the young man were sent to study in France, it would serve as a quite suitable pretext to get rid of the most visible memory of the previous life of Veličković's melancholy wife.

And above all—although he wouldn't have admitted it even to himself on paper, he was losing hope that he would have progeny of his own—the lawyer considered the possibility of making his stepson a successful heir to his already established practice.

Of course, on the condition that he take the surname Veličković, he added in his thoughts, when the time came for him to worry about his own future.

And if he was to be heir to the practice, then it meant that in Paris he would of course enroll in the study of law.

"Here you have everything calculated in detail: how many dinars, francs that is, you will need for an apartment, for food, books, washing and ironing laundry, haircuts, postage stamps, resoling your shoes—in total, for each individual item of your stay there. I'm sure I haven't forgotten anything. Avoid women of doubtful character and avoid wasting time in cafés, and you'll have enough. An allowance will be deposited every first of the month in the Franco-Serbian Bank."

The stepfather handed the stepson a notepad ruled with headings for all the vital aspects of the latter's existence, under which followed columns of figures and, in somewhat bolder type, the phrase *sum total*; and at the end the concluding sentence: Ergo, this is to certify that the present book contains forty (40) leaves or eighty (80) pages that are to be written on. This gift was given to the young man at the central railway station, with the first bell sounding as a call to the travelers.

"Should any unplanned expenses arise, explain them to me in detail by letter, and I will send the money to you by cable when I have determined whether they are justified!"

"Young sir," said Zlatana, shedding tears as a second bell was heard, "I would kindly ask you, on an empty stomach take honey and don't skip any meals; I trust there are lots of good things to eat there . . . And if your feet begin to hurt when you're abroad, on the bottom of the suitcase you'll find a bag of sand, so pour it into your shoes."

"Write me what and when you read," his mother whispered to him, kissing him on the cheek and pushing into his pocket the throttled pocket watch and the penknife with the mother-of-pearl handle, just an instant before the whistle of the locomotive.

Whether it was because he had purposely forgotten the notebook in the compartment the first time he changed trains, or because Paris was not a place where everyday events could be classified under narrow headings, from his very arrival Anastas spent far more than Slavoljub Veličković had foreseen. Not wishing to explain himself to his stepfather, he had already by the second week quit the boardinghouse whose address he'd been given in Belgrade, and then rented a considerably more modest room, only as large as required by the diverse temptations of the City of Light. The advice of the housekeeper Zlatana he followed only in part. He very quickly dispensed with eating dinner, but regularly poured sand into his shoes; he somehow felt more secure that way among those foreign people, in a city which outdid his native Belgrade in all things. It could be that the sand was also to blame when he began to miss his lectures; he had never really gotten used to the legal field. Conscious that Slavoljub T. Veličković would call him back immediately, in his communications to his stepfather he took pains at least to use expressions from the attorney's profession.

"Obligation! Jurisdiction! Authorization! Monopolistic management! Prosecution!" Slavoljub Veličković singled out precisely these words, pleased with Anastas's letters. "You see, Magdalina, how one can do it if he wants!"

And she, Magdalina, received hand-painted postcards of bridges on the Seine, Notre Dame Cathedral, or the promenade on the Elysian Fields, on which her son, "in order to find his bearings," had marked the points of the compass, and on the back had listed what and when he was reading. In truth, for a long time the young man hadn't had much of anything to mention. His high school knowledge of French had a solid foundation, but was of course inadequate for him to feel more at ease in the land of great literature. Therefore, just as a newcomer abhors any sort of ridicule, he at first avoided literary works, wishing to appear there only when he was able to understand all the nuances that a particular language possessed. "I started with the newspapers . . ." he wrote his mother.

" 'I want to acquaint myself with those spaces where ordinary

people enter, and only then set out to conquer the poetic heights ...'"
she, in her melancholy room, in the house on Veliki Vračar, read her
son's words aloud.

By a turn of events, Anastas had access to an inordinate
amount of newspapers. Opposite his room lived a seamstress, born
in Provence, who was convinced that in Paris she would manage to
attain a successful career as a milliner. She bought almost the entire
press, doing her utmost to always be informed, to learn the most
recent gossip and the trends in all layers of society, or at least all the
layers that might fit the expression *chic*. She was certain that in this
way, when her hour finally struck, she would transform, from one
who cut and bordered little holes for buttons to a creator of haute
couture. That little woman regularly brought Anastas bundles of old
newspapers, last year's publications specializing in the opera, small-
game hunting, tennis, horse racing, interior design, gardening, end-
of-season fashion for Fall–Winter and Spring–Summer, the stock
exchange, agricultural fairs—and the so-called yellow weeklies from
the previous month, which wrote equally enthusiastically about the
lavish balls of the remnant aristocracy and the unsolved crimes in
the taverns on the outskirts of town ...

"Learn!" the seamstress always said in the same way, slamming
the stack of newspapers onto the floor, considering it compensation enough that she could act important in front of this shy Serbian
student.

Anastas read eagerly. Truth be told, it even suited him that
there, among those various articles, he was alone, that most of those
columns had been abandoned by the curious long ago, and so he
wandered the whole night, sounding out words undisturbed, even
where he otherwise would not have found the courage to peep in.
There is something strange in the contents of texts conceived for the
many, and deserted so soon as a new edition appears. Among once
important titles, footfalls now eerily resound. Where once the crowd

breathed ardently, there now is not a quiver; the air has grown stale, giving off a stench of mildew and the inevitability of decay. To the past greatness of events bear witness the outlines of fates, but they too are paler and paler, less and less convincing, and it is only a matter of time before someone will begin to doubt whether those fates existed at all.

Nevertheless, for the young man the spaces of the newspapers were an opportunity to comprehend the crucial difference between the full and empty words of a language. How statements, and even solemn oaths, can be skillfully circumvented, last year declaring one thing, yesterday another, and tomorrow something else—all of which he was able to learn only when the seamstress brought him a new bundle. This was an opportunity, albeit a late one, to adopt manners unknown to a person from the Orient, as that part of Europe was called there. An opportunity, without shame, to stop before the sumptuous bill of fare at some fine restaurant, and to eat his fill since he had deprived himself of this actual meal in order to save money; he would choose from the menu those dishes whose names themselves were testimony to the famous Gallic gastronomic art, not skimping in the least on poetical desserts or the most high-sounding, noble wines. Finally, this was a possibility also to meet those whom it would be difficult to recognize in the reality of the French capital.

"A person only loses his peace of mind that way; why would I throng with all the rest? I'll lay down a hundred-dinar note that I'll know more than you if tomorrow I glance over what you today have parsed between the lines." These were some of the headstrong remarks, repeated many years later in the Three Sideburns Barbershop or in the saloon at the Russian Czar, upon his return from Paris—and no doubt conceived during the time of his studies.

In a crowd, though we look each other in the face, rarely are we aware of ourselves, let alone of one another. Thus, when Anastas, having entered a newspaper, was observing people in a mass, he was able to read them even more keenly than if he'd been talking to them tête-à-tête. Anastas met prominent members of the government or parliament, who were attempting to go back, unnoticed, on the promises they had made to the voters during the previous year's elections; young historiographers, cataloging the merest mention of the research studies of their faculty mentors; a puzzle maker, in search of the word with which to complete his life's work, a crossword puzzle of ten thousand fields; a provincial, preparing to cram into his head and memorize by heart maxims and the most inconsequential details, in order to boast to his astounded compatriots, upon his return to his village, how for him there'd been no secret in the capital; the kind of people with unimportant names, who killed time by finding reasons to write vehement letters of protest, discovering grandiose affairs or pointing out the disturbingly frequent typographical errors of the given publication; middle-aged gentlemen, impeccably dressed, coiffed, and scented, with freshly trimmed mustaches, sitting nonchalantly over mineral water in a café in St-Germain, but without twenty centimes to buy the morning paper; a somewhat younger type of the same, striving to meet, as if by chance, some spinster, not necessarily attractive, but exclusively well-off; an unhappy woman from the suburbs, convinced that the useful advice on how to remove stains from damask serviettes, porcelain, silverware, and the like was enough to make the unbearably dark days of her marriage suddenly begin to shine; a winegrower from Champagne or Beaujolais, who at the conclusion of the picking at last had time to heave a sigh of relief, to wipe his hands on his apron, to raise his head and see what was new in the wide world; boys from good homes, who after stealing from their parents stared dumbfounded at the virtually unclothed coquettes provocatively pursing their lips in the advertisements for stockings, brassieres, whale-bone corsets, Lahmann's women's undergarments, or those undergarments based on the "Sanitary Woolen System" of Dr. Gustav Jaeger; a now-wrinkled leading lady of the National Theater, tearful behind a tortoise-shell lorgnette, sitting over the announcements and encomiums of forgotten premieres, in which she had masterfully—"When I say *masterfully*, I mean *masterfully!*"— interpreted the leading role . . .

And so on, from page to page, spinning and spinning as in a kaleidoscope . . .

Until everything, suddenly, was ended by war.

FOURTH READING

IN WHICH WE TELL ABOUT A DEFICIT
IN THE BALANCE SHEET OF LIFE;
ABOUT A CHEST LINED
WITH THE CREASED, AND THEN STITCHED,
ODOR OF ANOTHER WORLD;
ABOUT MADEMOISELLE HOUVILLE
AND GOVERNESS DIDIER;
ABOUT THE MIDDLE PART OF THE BREAD
ROLLED INTO LITTLE BALLS;
ABOUT PLUCKED DUMPLINGS;
ABOUT WHETHER OUT OF WORDS
ONE CAN BUILD A CHURCH;
ABOUT HOW SHORT A DISTANCE IT CAN BE BETWEEN
SENJAK AND VELIKI VRAČAR;
ABOUT PALMS THAT BLOOM
ONCE IN A HUNDRED YEARS;
AND ABOUT FINGERPRINTS
OF BOTH VIOLET INK
AND TRACES OF COLORED PENCILS

31

HE RETURNED ONE THURSDAY, IN THE FALL of 1922. He hired
a coach in front of the central railway station, the eastern wing of
which had been severely damaged in the ravages of war, as if broken in two, and was now wrapped in a patchwork of sackcloth ban-
dages, which still stood behind scaffolding that resembled crutches
and splints. Although it was a rainy day, he ordered the coachman
to lower the roof, to keep the large traveling trunk dry with the
varicolored rug that one ordinarily used to cover one's knees, and
to drive along the more out-of-the-way streets. They hadn't gone
very far along the Sava River, nor had they reached the outer walls
of Kalemegdan Park and the line of the baroque steeple of Saborna
Church, and he was already quite wet. Outside there were few people, but no one would have recognized him all the same. With a
clucking sound the little old man urged on the tired bay horse, its
headstall decorated with soaking tassels of red wool made heavier
by the rain, occasionally cracking his whip and turning to look the
odd fellow over: this young hatless gentleman, who, going nowhere
in particular, was jolting along the washed-out cobblestone road
and insisting on getting wet, asking even to take a roundabout way
through the Jewish quarter Dorćol, and beside the electric power
station, to the downtown district, and from there to head toward
the botanical garden, and then to emerge in a completely opposite
direction, onto Knez Miloš Street, all the way to Weifurt's Brewery,
and then diagonally across to the Kragujevac highway, and from
there to enter the city once more—a moment there, a moment
here, as if after a long absence in foreign parts he needed to get

accustomed to Belgrade slowly. Thus did it happen that into the house on Veliki Vračar, subsequently Zvezdara, he set foot late in the afternoon, his suit completely ruined—no one knowing where it was dripping from him more—spattered with a swash of mud from the wheels of the coach. The housekeeper Zlatana shuddered when she saw him like this.

"Anastas . . ." she said, collecting herself enough not to address him as "dear child," observing how much he had changed, having become irretrievably grave, having grown tall, and now wearing a thin scar, the length of a thumb, over his left eyebrow.

But the very next moment, regardless of all those traits of a grownup man, she understood just how much outward appearances can deceive. Straight from the door, as soon as he had paid the coachman and included a good tip, giving him the last franc he found in his pockets, and had seen to it that his traveling trunk was brought into the dry, into the anteroom, he entered his stepfather's study and sat in the massive chair reupholstered in striped brocade. Slavoljub T. Veličković was no longer alive to reproach him for it. Although the lawyer had awaited the establishment of peace safe and sound, in spite of everything still accruing capital through various shrewd speculations—taking advantage of the wartime shortages to cheaply buy up real estate, stock shares, and bills of exchange with safe rates of return—he felt all the more often that somewhere between his income and expenses something was continually creeping in, squeezing through, some sort of great error. One evening, immediately after Unification, while he was balancing his accounts as usual, an irrecoverable deficit in the balance sheet of his life turned up. Everything else agreed to the para, the grosz, the filler, the piastre, or the kreuzer, but in the main account there it appeared again and again: an absence of love. That fruitless one, toward Magdalina, was not nearly enough to cover a deficit so large. Realizing that he had gone bankrupt in spite of so much wealth, and in despair having drunk almost an entire bottle of grape brandy kept in the house for compresses, and because in his abstinent ways he was unaccustomed to drink, the lawyer first swooned and then stumbled onto the floor, and then sank down to death itself, silently, without resistance, like a stone that no one needs.

But Anastas Branica had been apprised of all this earlier, in his mother's letters. Now he had no wish to remember Slavoljub Veličković. He demanded that Zlatana at once remove from the work desk the crystal inkwell, the steel pens, the penholder, the oval blotter, the ivory paper knife, the green-glass lamp, the ledger book, the folded editions of old daily newspapers, all of the impeccable order that had remained of his stepfather. And when she had performed what she had been instructed to do, the young man leaned on his elbows, rested his head in his hands, and wept. His melancholy mother, Magdalina, had died of mouse fever just seven days before, and he had arrived too late to see her for the last time, even though on hearing the news of the pernicious disease he had set out immediately from Paris. Thus he sat, ghostly pale and weeping, until evening, perhaps the entire night, until his suit dried on him—refusing, while he had a tear left in him at all, to eat anything, to change his clothes, to indulge any of the entreaties of the good Zlatana.

He spoke only the next day, only after returning from New Cemetery, where for the peace of their souls he had lit candles for his relatives and for Milena, his high school sweetheart, and in the process soiled his shoes and trouser legs with droplets of wax, and caused a large blister to form in the middle of his right palm by using it to shield the flame from the rain.

"Mother should not have been buried next to him, she never belonged to him . . ." he said softly, while the housekeeper, according to a national recipe, rubbed salt into his wound, forcing him to repeat what he'd said because she hadn't heard it; one of her eardrums had been punctured back in the year 1914, owing to the constant roar of Austro-Hungarian artillery from the Zemun side of the river and from the monitors, warships on the Sava.

32

And then for days on end he opened, closed, and reopened the enormous traveling trunk, lined with the creased, stitched, soft odor of some other world, removing from its shadowy depths book after book, shaking them out, carefully wiping them down, stacking them according to size and field, in larger or smaller piles. The housekeeper was astonished: the luggage contained nothing but a good many copies of books—not a single item of clothing or personal effect, not a soiled shirt, or a handkerchief, or a comb, not even a button that had come unstitched from a cuff, not a photograph, or a toothbrush or tooth powder; in truth nothing else. When from the fabric of that ruined suit she tried to remove the moisture and the dried swarms of mud spots and droplets of wax, she found only the throttled pocket watch, a forgotten ten-centime coin, a round pebble from the sea, a rather dull penknife with a mother-of-pearl handle, and of his identity papers an invalid, canceled passport from the Kingdom of Serbia and the new, Yugoslav one from the Kingdom of Serbs, Croats, and Slovenes, issued in the Paris embassy following its proclamation, the details in both documents now washed away by the rain that had soaked into the columns.

For a week or two afterward he occupied himself with carrying from the study, to no one knew where, the legal codes of his former country, the lawyer's old statute books with bronzed spines, volumes and volumes of them bound in dark brown leather. He pushed the brochures, periodicals, and bound sets of Batut's instructional magazine *Health* to the back rows. He arranged his own reading material on the shelves and assigned a place of honor to those few books with the impressed depiction of the universal world tree. He interrupted this task only to light a cigarette. Zlatana frowned whenever she found him wrapped in a cloud of bluish-cold smoke, sitting over plates of food he had hardly touched, food she had prepared (while adding in her own babble ("Today we have dumplings, chicken, and quinces in sauce, and for dessert a chocolate cake!")) all in order to get him to like regular meals again.

"If I only knew where you got that awful habit from!" she complained whenever he smoked, waving her arms, a rag, or a duster, every Saturday removing the stale smell of tobacco interwoven in the drapes.

Having completed the chore with the books, Anastas turned to the balancing of his inheritance. In Slavoljub Veličković's work desk he found the power of attorney of foreign firms and concessionaires, plans for establishing an electric company called Light & Power, a substantial amount of money, the bulk of it in ducats of all types and denominations, and whole bundles of bills of exchange due for payment. There were also shares of stock from various stock companies, bankbooks showing considerable sums in savings banks and joint banking ventures, and deeds to several building lots throughout Belgrade, all neatly tied with tricolor bands. Anastas proceeded in a quite unexpected way. He returned the bills of exchange to the debtors, and the deeds to their previous owners, but without any kind of recompense. Some of the money he waived, donating it to charitable causes, without revealing the name of the contributor, most often to foundations that cared for orphans of war. A portion of the cash, he lent to Zlatana in order to buy a ramshackle little house near the Palilula Marketplace, and established that from her new, now tripled salary he would deduct a symbolic amount. And from the money remaining after all of these transactions, a still not inconsiderable sum, he took a portion every day, not caring when and how much, never again keeping account of the returns on his securities, hardly spending them on his modest desires—which consisted mainly of only a few habitual items—not for anything agreeing to repair or to change the time on his throttled pocket watch.

It was probably out of superstition that he was reluctant to allow others to do it for him, and so he took his own measurements, the girth of his neck, chest, and waist, the width of his shoulders, the two lengths of his arms, from the armpit and from the shoulder, and the two lengths of his legs, from the groin and from the waist. He stood barefoot on wrapping paper and traced the outlines of his feet, and in accordance with all this ordered that a wardrobe be made for him, with each item of clothing and footwear designated to a different fashion tailor or shoemaker. Nothing extravagant: a dozen soft shirts and ties, a mohair scarf, a heavy double-breasted overcoat of fuller gabardine, four pairs of shoes, four suits of various thicknesses, four vests, just as many hats and pairs of gloves, according to the seasons of the year, and then house slippers, summer and winter pajamas with wide and narrow stripes, a bathrobe of wine-red close-cropped velvet, all of it of a much too serious design for someone his age, and none of this was to mention the special linings for the suits, selected at Mitić's, of Lyon silk, at first dark ones, and when the year of mourning had passed more cheerful patterns. He distributed funds for the food for the house, for fuel to heat it, and for general upkeep, but first of all for sealing the cracks in the walls, so that the rustling of rodents would not multiply, convinced that the mice that had crawled out from there had driven his mother to her delirium of death.

He gave the amounts that were asked, never verifying whether the expenditure was justified, with complete trust in Zlatana's running of the household.

The only things he bought immoderately were tobacco and

books. Finely cut, loose Herzegovina, always in the tobacco shop of the Invalids' Association, and even more books than he could manage to read, regularly dropping by the well-known bookshops of Goetz Kohn, S. B. Cvijanović, Jovanović & Vujić, or the Pelican, run by Gavrilo Dimitrijević, and ordering foreign books from Paris out of catalogs, as well as out of the announcements of new publications pinned on the notice board in the newly opened Franco-Serbian reading room on Knez Mihailova Street.

He still followed only the newspapers, strictly from the previous week, going out on Saturdays to the Russian Czar for coffee with freshly whipped cream and a pinch of cinnamon, and on Mondays to the Three Sideburns Barbershop for a haircut and the often unneeded trimming of his fair, downy mustache and beard, which had been grown during the period of mourning for his mother.

Thus did Anastas Branica live a sort of retired life following his nine-year absence from the country. He did not go on visits. Nor did he receive them. After all, he scarcely knew anyone. And it was even more unlikely that anyone more intimately knew him. He spent his time in the endless reading of books in French or Serbian, books that he bought insatiably even after his return. Shut up in his former stepfather's study . . . Sometimes not emerging for days. Sometimes reading through the night, in place of elusive sleep. Sometimes dressed formally, as if for a celebration or reception, with a hat, a handkerchief in his breast pocket, gloves, and leggings. Sometimes barefoot, only in an open dressing gown, beneath which he wore absolutely nothing. Sometimes gone so long and so far away that he returned sweating and with sunken cheeks. Sometimes appearing fresh and alert, as if he had entered among the lines only a quarter of an hour ago, rather than since he had gotten up, since he had opened his eyes . . .

Whether he had completed the study of law, which he had taken up in Paris, and how he had gotten through the war years, he told no one; the grist of his history one could only surmise, in bits and pieces, whenever he said something sparingly. But even the little that he uttered sounded so improbable that only the housekeeper would indulge him, as when, as a twelve-year-old boy, he had gone down to the seashore for the first time. Perhaps because she felt a respect for everything connected with books. Perhaps because she had gotten used to being devoted to the young gentleman. But perhaps, above all, because with Anastas's return, the tender-yellow sand began to spread again throughout the house on Veliki Vračar. Not as it once had, not in such a quantity that a rather large bag would be quickly filled with it, but nonetheless in an amount sufficient that Zlatana never doubted another of the gentleman's words.

"Prepare a summer change of clothes for me, some light linen, white trousers, and a shirt. I'll be gone a few days," he said monthly, and she would act in accordance with his wishes, not entering the room with the books, instead patiently waiting for him, convinced that he really was absent, even though he hadn't set foot outside.

Only the first winter did she express fear that he would catch cold. A bitter frost covered the streets, everything metal stuck to the hands, and ice floes took hold along Great War Island and the islets and banks of the Danube; even the hungry weasels raced across the frozen Sava. And he went dressed so lightly, not even lighting a fire in the stove in the study.

"There, where I intend to go, it's sunny, very sunny . . ." he answered her concern, and then returned with a sunburned brow and nose, and with his chest ruddy down to the third, undone button of his shirt, his biceps darkened to his rolled-up sleeves; radiating some kind of warmth, as if he had truly spent the entire time in the heat—although there wasn't enough sun in Belgrade to set the eaves dripping, the drainpipes gurgling.

. . . How it happened that from these monthly retreats into

another world the story was concocted, no one will ever know. Namely, Anastas had been declared "a little daft" because he was said to be meeting in the books with some English woman, the wife of an owner of a large colonial estate, who thousands of miles from here was reading the same title during the long, tropical days that her husband was absent as he made the busy rounds of the rubber and tea plantations. Reading the same book, in order to "meet" with her young lover. How such a story had come about was unknown, but already then people were given to viewing Anastas as some sort of crank, as one of those types about whom everyone had the right to say whatever he liked, to sling mud at, to invent and embellish about, to whisper behind his back, or to wave at mockingly:

"But who is he?"

"The stepson of the late attorney Veličković. A born dreamer."

"All saints and good St. Petka forbid, what an incompetent heir to such a capable man."

"God knows what he did out there, in the wide world?! Surely he didn't complete the study of law, otherwise he would begin some kind of respectable job here."

"A failure! He does nothing. He loafs around, only reads!"

"As though it's better there than in real life. A Parisian! An eccentric!"

"To me it's quite romantic, sentimental . . ."

"Oh, come off it! Bite your tongue . . . He wanders around in books so much that he no longer knows where he's been or who he is."

"But he returns from the assignations with that woman with his back terribly scratched up and his shoulders all bitten. The English woman must be a passionate one."

"Although some Russian woman is also mentioned, an aristocrat; after the Bolshevik revolution, having settled the gambling debts of her dissolute husband, she was left, of all the wealth, with only a twenty-five-year lease to a deck chair on the beach in Biarritz and a moth-eaten family library."

"What English woman?! What Russian noblewoman?! No, she's some honky-tonk singer, one of those unhappy women who by night, for money, entertains crowds of men in questionable places and by day, in the pages of novels, searches for amorous feelings. At the Boulevard, Djordj Pašon's hotel, there was one such loose cabaret troupe . . ."

"English woman or Russian woman, noblewoman or night owl, they come to him just the same. Mrs. Kolaković swears to me that when she leafed through that book—at the moment I'm unable to tell you its title, since I don't want to corrupt the young people here—well now, that when she leafed through that book—not that she was listening in—she heard someone, forgive me now, moaning and sighing in a sexual manner!"

"So that's the story? And here he always wears that serious expression on his face . . ."

"Reprobate! It wouldn't surprise me if it turns out that, over there, he got himself a good case of the clap or some other gentleman's disease."

"But did you know that during the war he 'read' on a map, for the French general staff, the sections of the terrain where the decisive battles would have to be fought?"

"It's said not only that he was able to see every little hill, gully, or goat trail—and, with the greatest precision, how many hours of forced march would be needed for the patrols to get from elevation to elevation—but that he already knew the location of each tree that might serve as cover for a machine gun nest . . ."

"He also 'read,' it's claimed, nautical charts: maps with data on the directions of sea currents, the force of the winds, and the jaggedness of the coast, with the recorded positions of lighthouses and breakwaters. He was capable of observing each sandbar or reef, of discovering the locations of floating mines, the courses of Austrian naval cruisers and torpedo boats, the hiding places of German submarines. The scar above his left eyebrow, he earned when he had a run-in with an enemy scout and nearly lost his eye . . ."

"Come, come now! You don't believe that nonsense, do you?"

"Personally, no. I'm only telling you what is being said."

"He's a little cracked! Mentally ill!"

"Don't repeat every stupidity you hear; in the end it will turn out that he's smarter than all of us, us normal ones."

Anastas himself did nothing to prevent the rumors—even though he hadn't fueled them with a single word, save for his explanations of why he read only old newspapers. But the mysterious disappearances, the way he looked, his often bloodshot eyes, the dark circles beneath them from the long spells of reading, and his obvious attempt to avoid close contact with people—this all took its toll. And when the pocket watch was added to all this, its hands forever stopped, throttled exactly at the Roman numeral XII, and which was whispered to keep some magical time within time, it was unlikely that anything would tip the scales in his favor.

For about a year or two, all this was a favorite topic of town talk, and then the story ceased to grow; attention was turned to other, still less plausible visions. It was being said that across the sea, in the American states, they had discovered a way to transmit speech and music far and wide through the air, that they were inventing moving pictures that did not require the accompaniment of a piano, that a certain Lindbergh was preparing on a whim to fly across the ocean . . . Entertained by these and other follies of the 1920s, people simply forgot about Anastas Branica.

And he forgot about them.

And so he detached himself from people.

33

In the late spring of 1927, Zlatana brought out for the morning meal the last jar of locust tree honey with its comb, extracted by means of a separator in that especially efflorescent year of 1924, along with a glass of fresh tap water, all on an oval silver serving tray with a doily ordinarily used only for special occasions.

"Young sir, put down the cigarette now and take this. It's too bad there's no more, it was a good batch . . ." she said upon entering the study and finding Anastas already prepared for one of his readings, dressed up as if for a promenade, from leggings to hat. A book in French, its leaves just cut using the dull penknife with the mother-of-pearl handle, sat waiting in the center of the writing desk.

And so, as soon as Zlatana left the room, Anastas set out among pages bristling with accents, circumflexes, cedillas, trémas, and apostrophes, all essential for the many finesses of pronouncing the sonorous words of the French language, while also alternately turning over in his mouth a sweet globule of honeycomb. He went leisurely, his hands thrust behind his back and attentively observing the landscape that opened up before his piercing eyes . . .

It was a book about Hellenistic architecture (*Le Temple Grec* was written on its cover), replete with bleached-white temples and clear blue skies. It was not very popular, and so he didn't have to bump into a crowd of other curious readers. And besides, it was still early. The day was just beginning to flaunt its colors, and the students who'd opened the book were still sleeping; in the immediate vicinity, he saw only one man taking an interest in the proportions of some colonnade or frieze, he wasn't sure which. And frankly speaking, he had no desire to find out; in order to avoid catching the man's attention, he abruptly turned around, taking the footpath despite the gleaming flashes of the marble, and enjoying his solitude and each rustle of the gentle wind in the branches of the cypress trees. He walked on and on, long having abandoned the studious disquisition of the book's author, engrossed instead in these pastoral parts, when he caught sight of her sitting on a rock, a sketch-pad resting on her knees as she drew the outlines of the landscape. She had talent, he saw that for himself when he had gotten close enough: the mighty temples faded in the distance, the arches of the aqueducts smaller and smaller, the slender trunks of the cypresses, a herd of goats scattered about in the maquis, an eagle clutching a turtle in its claws, the dispersed blinking of the sun—all of that, as if copied from a photograph and softened by the deposits of pastel chalks, was captured on the paper that lay before her. Everything, even the figure of a pale young man, with a downy beard and mustache, coming toward her. Thus Anastas recognized himself when he had approached sufficiently near.

"Good morning . . ." he said in Serbian, flustered.

"And good morning to you!" She gave a start, confusing him even more. Still, here he had expected to hear the language in which he had also been reading.

"Forgive me for suddenly turning up like this. I've ruined your picture—had I known, I wouldn't have intruded . . ." he apologized.

Her accent suggested that she was a foreigner, undoubtedly a French girl, who knew Anastas's native language rather well.

"It doesn't matter . . ." she said, offering her hand and a smile. "Miss Nathalie Houville."

"Kindly allow me to introduce myself. Anastas Branica." He took the palm of her hand, the fingertips smirched with pastel colors, and made a bow.

And it all started exactly from there. To the young man it seemed that fate had granted him the faculty of total reading, had granted him all those lonely years, all of that superfluous joy, the smarting embarrassment and the travail of sadness, only in order to lead him to that young lady with the tender fingertips colored with pastel chalks. Yes, he had met many, had savored within books the passion of numerous enraptured women, but never before had he felt such closeness. Yes, it pervaded him, his entire existence had been merely an overly long and painful prelude. After much indirection, his life story had flowed into a meaningful stream, one bank of which was he, and the other this beautiful girl . . .

They eagerly became acquainted—as if to draw near to each other as soon as possible, as if to compress the distance between them into as impetuous and raging a main current as they could. Already that morning, up above the gleaming flashes of the Greek temples, in the swaying shadows of the cypress trees, he learned that she was the daughter of a mining engineer, César Houville, the director of prospecting and exploitation with the French Company of Bor Mines (Compagnie française des mines de Bor), a company known also as the Concession of St. George. He learned that she loved long descriptions of nature and romance novels with happy endings.

A widower and without kin, and having no one with whom to leave her in his native Reims, Monsieur Houville, immediately at the conclusion of the war, brought his daughter to the newly united south Slavic land of Serbs, Croats, and Slovenes, working twenty-six days a month beside the Bor excavations of copper ore—down to the penny responsibly looking after the interests of the concessionaires, the main office in Paris, and the Geneva bank Mirabaud—and spending his four free days in Belgrade, overseeing step-by-step the proper upbringing of his one and only. Little Bor was continually rocked by explosions of dynamite, the disagreeable odor of carbide wafted through the little town, sirens monotonously announced the changing of shifts and forewarned of the presence of treacherous poison gases as well as cave-ins of the shoring in the pits, and in the evenings one could go out only to the so-called Casino, the one decent place where every gathering in the small French settlement, on national holidays, ended in nostalgic drunkenness.

A further, more important reason for Nathalie's residing in the capital, in a rented house on Senjak, was the October visit of Marcel Champain, vice president of the company's board. During his regular inspection of the operations of the local Belgrade office, in the year 1921, at a reception organized in his honor, Marcel Champain fell in love with the young girl with the still-childlike eyes. For the next three Octobers, the vice president returned as if to follow how she was developing into a young woman, to savor how her youthful indications were becoming more and more feminine, ever rounder— in blunt terms, to ogle at how she was filling out—only giving as a pretext his yearly inspection of the work. One year he gifted her, through her father, a handful of candied confections in a metal box, each sweeter than sweet, each in a special wrapper of shiny, expensive tinfoil. To formally make her acquaintance, to briefly speak to her, he waited until she was sixteen, as decorum prescribed. That meeting happened in 1925, and now there was no doubt that with each arrival they were becoming increasingly close, and César Houville began to hope that he might marry off his daughter well. It was accordingly her lot to reside here, to prepare herself for those yearly meetings with Vice President Marcel Champain that accompanied his inspections. In order that the preparations be as successful as possible, and as the French boarding school for girls, St. Joseph on Ranke Street, had not yet opened its doors, the engineer brought from his homeland a certain Madame Didier, a former governess in a Catholically strict boarding school, experienced in the matter of an exemplary education—and after three marriages of her own, especially experienced in matters of accommodating the preferences necessary to bring about betrothals and weddings.

"*Calmez-vous.* Don't you worry now, I'll arrange everything just fine! As for my references, please feel free to check them out,

AT THE LUCKY HAND

but I think that the marriages of my young ladies to counts, ministers, bankers, and other prominent bridegrooms speak most eloquently . . ." began Madame Didier, taking the job.

"*Je suis désolée.* I am forced to ask for a raise. The conditions I am working in I consider primitive. In the event that you don't give me one, kindly accept my resignation . . ." tearfully began Madame Didier, whenever the girl's father would travel from Bor, emphasizing that any remuneration was small considering the difficult, Balkan circumstances here.

"*Retenez bien!* Young lady, you are here by some concurrence of events; you belong to another spirit, another culture, and I shall return you to it . . ." began Madame Didier, explaining her lesson plan to her charge, not at all sharing the interest of the good-natured Monsieur Houville and some of her fascinated countrymen in the customs and temperaments of the locals, instead going out willingly only when some French artist or professor gave a concert or a lecture in town.

"*C'est inouï!* With these people I'm not able to make myself understood. I finally had to point out the cotton thread I wanted with my finger . . ." began Madame Didier after she returned from shopping. Having not agreed to learn a single word of Serbian; having a difficult time buying the indispensable ladies' notions; having attempted to explain to the unlettered Zuzana, a young girl who had been hired to do the housework, how and what she should serve for breakfast, out of what to put together a good potage, and how many teaspoons of sugar went into lemonade and the like—having done all this, she was in the end always forced to ask Nathalie to translate somehow or other her directions.

"*Donc!* You must know how to embroider. You will give Monsieur Champain a handkerchief with his monogram as a present. It will remind him of your hands each time he reaches for it. You must know how to sing all of the vice president's favorite songs.

When he hears them in Paris, too, he will think of your throat and lips. You must know how to smile, to move gracefully, to dance at least the waltz; you must know how to keep silent, you must know how to converse with him about that which interests him. Have you remembered that last year, 7,132 tons of blister copper were produced? And that in each ton, there are an enviable 41.52 grams of gold and 116.38 grams of silver . . . ?" Thus persisted Madame Didier with her instructions.

"*Moins de bruit, s'il vous plaît* . . . I have a stabbing pain below my heart, I feel that next October he will ask for your hand in marriage, and with that my job here will be done. And I? I'll be able to pack; they have a prospective girl of marriageable age in Lille, and they're imploring me for the third time now and begging me to come and help out with the whole affair!" Thus did Madame Didier end each of her days in Serbia, adding once more her calming sayings and troubling impressions, putting on her head her starched nightcap, plugging her ears with rolled tufts of absorbent cotton, pulling down over her eyes a plush sleep mask to block out the light of the full moon, preparing to dream until dawn of her return to France.

Isolated by the many prohibitions of the stern governess, weary from the exhaustive preparations for the marriage and, in particular, from studying in detail tables of percentages of copper purity, which she was supposed to know by heart, Nathalie spent most of her free time in the courtyard of the rented house on Senjak, drawing with charcoal, pastel chalks, or graphite depending on her mood. This was a special way to express her thoughts about the world around her. In three portfolios of paper-covered pasteboard, tied with ribbons and stacked under the bed, the young lady sorted the sheets of paper according to the subject and technique of the drawing. The first was soon bulging with portraits of Madame Didier, done mostly on the sly and exclusively in charcoal, in sharp, compressed lines, especially the ones that were supposed to represent her face. The second portfolio was stuffed full with picturesque landscapes *en pastel*, done from memory, of her rare outings in Košutnjak or brief walks through Belgrade, in glowing colors or quiet shades. The third swarmed with the interiors and still lifes of the girl's everyday existence, deep shadows of rubbed-in graphite. Aside from this limited number of motifs, the only things remaining to Mademoiselle Houville were books, and she, under the watchful eye of Madame Didier, weekly visited the Franco-Serbian reading room on Knez Mihailova Street, little by little perfecting her knowledge of the local language.

Having the drawing kit with her more and more often, even when leafing through books in the reading room, Nathalie Houville ever more rarely made a distinction between the disciplines of drawing and reading, at first merely dashing off sketches, illustrations of favorite places from her reading; and then, as she allowed her imagination to wander—copying down the fullness of that which the governess, frowning, had called sheer daydreaming—the girl began her fourth portfolio. Thus in that year of 1927, by chance having become absorbed, at the identical morning hour, in the same book as Anastas Branica, on her drawing she found a pale young man, with a downy mustache and beard and a scar above his left eyebrow, who was dressed much too seriously; but, thanks to the wind, she discovered that his suit had an unusual lining, of a smooth sort. And not only on that sheet of paper. Closing the book on Hellenistic architecture around noon, having placed her thread between its pages to remember where she had left off—the embroidery lesson with Madame Didier was just about to begin—Nathalie found on each of her drawings that same— as he had introduced himself to her—Anastas Branica. Here— sitting and telling her something. There—attentively listening to her. Over there—picking her a sprig of myrtle. And over there— offering her his hand to step across a brook. Finally—arranging a meeting with her for tomorrow, on the same page, in the same passage. Each, each and every one of the drawings contained his pale visage or his lanky figure, and Nathalie Houville, from that closeness, grew flushed in the face.

"*Ah, non, pas comme ça!* And what about your hands?! You're not thinking of embroidering with palms like that, are you?!" said the governess, aghast, upon seeing how her charge was preparing to seize the white linen with fingertips smudged in pastel chalk.

"*Mon Dieu!* Child, what is the matter with you, you're skipping! Hem it in sequence," Madame Didier admonished, not missing a single stitch; the girl was absentminded as never before, stealing glances through the windows of the house on Senjak.

"*Ça suffit!* I'll close them; the spring here distracts the attention. All you need is to prick yourself and I'll be explaining to your father." The governess angrily got up and slammed the windows shut.

Indeed, that could be heard for a long time in the rented house on Senjak, because the maid, the unlettered Zuzka from the countryside around Belgrade, didn't understand French, and she dared not get rid of a single unknown word, sooner allowing them to disappear by themselves, to vanish.

And on Veliki Vračar, the housekeeper Zlatana prepared dinner and waited until she lost patience. Knocking on the door to the study, inclining her good ear and stopping up the other with her little finger, then entering upon Anastas's invitation, she found the young man looking blissfully into that same book, cravingly lighting one cigarette after another.

"You'll suffocate. Open them a little and go eat something!" she scolded him, and spread the window sashes onto that late spring of 1927.

34

The book on Hellenistic architecture for months remained a meeting place for the young lady and young man. On each occasion Nathalie Houville and Anastas Branica were on different pages, but always as far away as possible from the other readers, entering regions that the author of the study had only generally described as "Arcadian." The discovery of long-hidden details brought with it a feeling of excitement, but not nearly so strong of one as what was engendered when they were mutually discovering each other. With little inhibition, so common in the world of nature, here acquaintanceship quickly rounded into friendship, and then strengthened into a feeling of love. Did love truly have a definite form? wondered Nathalie, looking at the blurred pastels she had done on her outings with Anastas. Or was it a feeling describable only by those round chalks with their additives of gum arabic, wax, or paraffin, that varicolored, sticky powder rubbed into the paper, a feeling which, like the countless particles, entered each pore and fold of the coarse paper, each uneven spot of this coarse world, making it smooth, supple, more bearable? No, love possessed not a single known, sharply defined form; it was ungraspable like the mist of a rainbow, and everywhere present like the haziness in her drawings.

"*C'est trop.* This spring the air is too saturated," said Madame Didier, she, too, acknowledging the existence of love in the house on Senjak, not suspecting where that sticky fog, that damp, was coming from, but also not missing the opportunity, the next time the engineer César Houville arrived from Bor, to ask for a raise, on the basis of these climatic changes.

"*Cher Monsieur . . .* These are new developments. I am suffocating in this country, and our original agreement stipulated moderate weather conditions," she complained to her employer, until she got what she wanted.

"This spring someone is in love. Hanging wash doesn't dry in three days' time; even iron locks, hinges, and door handles perspire, not to speak of brass parts . . ." The housekeeper Zlatana was more discerning, looking the young man up and down suspiciously, wiping dry everything that might begin to rust.

Moreover, there were several other convincing signs of the presence of love in both houses. Meals were merely shifted by forks from left to right on their plates, and the middle part of the bread was rolled into little balls. From sleeplessness the bed linen was rumpled and the feathers in the pillows matted down. From everything woolen were unconsciously plucked tiny spheres of wool, so many of them that they gradually came to resemble whole dumplings and bunches of grapes. Pairs of gloves and socks were absentmindedly broken up, while hairpins, brooches, keys, a cigarette case, matches, and the ashes of cigarettes, without the ashtray, were misplaced . . . But the most reliable sign of the existence of love on Senjak and Veliki Vračar was the book on Hellenistic architecture itself. Although not excessively long, for weeks and months it stood constantly beside the head of Nathalie's bed and on Anastas's desk, its bookmark of thread protruding; both of them knew to the letter, at any time of day or night, where they had left off during their last meeting. As expected, Madame Didier interpreted this, too, quite mistakenly:

"*Vous m'avez déçue* . . . I can't believe you still haven't finished reading it! Don't try to lie to me, for days now you haven't turned a leaf of it. You're still on the same page. My dear, you're deceiving only yourself, and not me! I know all about it . . . Monsieur Marcel Champain is a great admirer of Hellenistic civilization, and you must know how to converse a word or two with him about that . . ."

It paid to be more cautious. Therefore, together they decided to meet every week in a different book, a book of which two copies could be borrowed from the Franco-Serbian Reading Room. Whenever they parted, they would agree on a new realm to explore together, the day and the hour of a new simultaneous reading. Having no obligations, Anastas was most of the time unable to remain patient, and he would rise early, as soon as it was daylight, and for several hours stare at the agreed-upon passage, waiting for her to appear as well. Try as she might—better said, wish as she might—Nathalie was often unable to make it on time. Occasionally her classes in embroidery, singing, or the waltz would be prolonged; occasionally Madame Didier, overcome by pathetic sentiments, would tell endlessly of the unsuccessful and successful marriages she had brokered; occasionally the girl was simply unable to withdraw into her room quite so easily, and it would happen that she would be very late. Just the same, he stubbornly waited, contriving where he would hide from the possible curious gaze of others.

35

And he was imaginative. Unpredictable. If in the book there was a city square, he would escape it through a narrow lane, then enter another one, laterally, farther and farther away from a plot that, as a rule, attracted a crowd of ordinary readers, and then show her into some deserted pub and order two glasses of sweet vintage wine . . . If in the book he sensed the least bit of freshness, he would find freshness, even if it hadn't been suggested by a single word—a park or a river where just the two of them could be alone, looking and looking at each other, skipping flat stones, counting how many times they would alight across the polished surface of the water . . . If in the book it was vaguely mentioned that a band was entertaining the strollers, he would approach the bandmaster and request something quite special:

"If you would, sir, I know this is quite unexpected, but I'm here with a young lady—please play me something melodic, something of your own choosing, I believe that you have experience with the lovestruck..."

The bandmaster, disconcerted, would remove his cap with the silver pin in the shape of a treble clef, run the palm of his hand across the sweaty bald spot on his head—he'd been here so many decades, and always the same old thing, mostly light music that no one listened to, no one had ever asked something like this of him before—and for a moment consider whether or not it was suitable, then clear his throat, cast a glance in the direction of the young lady, make a somewhat awkward bow, then smile, and why wouldn't he? Nowhere was it written that he shouldn't leaf through the volumes of sheet music, whisper the title of the next composition to the no less disconcerted band, tap the conductor's stand three times with his baton, and then begin to lead a tender melody for that strange, lovesick pair, finding that in all those years of diligent service he had never taken part in something so lovely.

Thus did Anastas Branica, in an altogether different novel, once rent an idle carriage, asking the coachman to drive them as far as possible, climbing in with Nathalie Houville even before the man had agreed.

"Faster! Drive faster!" Anastas shouted; the girl's hair fluttered, the wind spread the coattails of the young man's suit, until the coachman pulled back on the reins of the flushed little horse, with the excuse that from there they needed to go on foot.

"Sir, there is no more road," he added, frightened after the cobblestones had turned into macadam, and the macadam had become clouded with dust. "I'm sorry, there is no more road!"

"Just keep going, go on! There are still lots of other things there;

you probably see how the hollows and heights follow each other by turns, you can see those enormous English oaks in the clearings, you can see the birds above the river . . ." objected Anastas.

"It's possible, sir. Quite possible. But they are birds. By goodness, I'm not moving an inch from here. It's downright precarious. If you and the young lady wish to go on, by all means please do so. But I'm going back. You don't even have to pay . . ." The coachman shook his head and turned the carriage around.

And not long afterward—this time it had to do with the tale of a local writer—they traveled together to a monastery so isolated that its name was mentioned only in a copy of a copy of a now lost medieval Serbian church book from the first half of the fourteenth century. Everywhere else it was stated that its existence had not been confirmed, and the doubt was even expressed that the transcribers had committed an obvious error. The monastery, however, stood quite solidly there where its founder had built it, in a gorge in a ravine, between craggy, barely passable mountains. The two young people walked about the churchyard, entered the church dedicated to St. Nikola, crossed themselves—each in his or her own fashion, Eastern and Western—and lighted candles, wondering who tended to the floating wicks in the lamps in front of the icons, because they observed no one else around. It was unlikely that anyone had read about this, had read this far, in a good three or four centuries. And despite signs that there had been a fire long ago, and despite the damage to the mortar on the walls, Nathalie admired the paintings that hung on them, while Anastas discerned figure after figure of the sacred Serbian kings depicted in the composition of the Nemanjić procession above the portico—and then there suddenly appeared in the church an old man in a simple cassock girded only with a length of rope, and, as they would later learn, of the monastic name Serafim.

What both this superior and this subordinate, the only inhabitant of this place pleasing to God, related to them that day in the

shade of the pine trees in the courtyard, they would never forget. The founder of the Monastery of St. Nikola had been the despot Jovan Oliver, a feudal lord of Czar Stefan Dušan the Mighty.
Tradition holds that he spent the night reading the holy scriptures
right in that ravine, that he was beset by beastly visions and doubts
about the fullness of the words, and then from the other side of the
gorge appeared St. Nikola, who prayed fervently with the despot
until morning.

"At daybreak, when the apparitions had disappeared and St.
Nikola had gone to help another in trouble, our gentleman resolved
to found a monastery as a mark of his gratitude to the saint; to dedicate it to his savior, the protector of other wayfarers and seafarers, in
order that future chance travelers would have somewhere to refresh
their weary souls, in order that they would have somewhere to take
shelter for the night . . ." said the monk, offering them a cup with
freshly picked mushrooms, prepared in water.

"And gathering from the scriptoria of Constantinople, Salonika,
and Skoplje the finest religious poets and grammarians, lectors and
choristers, narrators and illuminators, built from the recorded word
of God is the monastery you see before you, bestowing upon it many
metohs . . ." said the monk, displaying the gold-sealed documents
with the inventories of church properties and goods from this and
that corner of the world.

"But, from then until now, many books have been burned,
many stories of our people forgotten, many inventories scraped
from our walls for the registers and protocols of foreigners, many,
many words profaned for haughty human needs . . ." said the monk,
accompanying them as they departed, his knees tottering.

"There has survived only a memory of this place, Usek, and
even it is scarcely believed in. I have been here for more than half
a century; rarely does anyone pass through, let alone stop. I live in
seclusion and serve as best I can, so long as the Lord wills it . . ." said

the monk as the monastery gates closed, as the gorge between the craggy mountains grew narrower in the suffusing twilight.

36

From page to page, Nathalie Houville, together with Anastas Branica, came to know the expanse of every domain. From page to page, the distance between her and the young man grew ever less. Although she sat on Senjak, and he in his house on Veliki Vračar, although they had never met outside the texts, they were closer and closer, so close beside each other that he alone heard her when, across the thousands of rooftops of Belgrade, across half the capital of that mysterious Balkan land, through the tumult of the June day, incautiously giving expression to, or perhaps only more insistently wishing for it, she thought:

"Anastas, kiss me . . ."

Did this really happen? Was this truly the first kiss? A real kiss? Or did she dream it, did it only appear to her that way?

These questions she pondered as she sat at the dressing table with the small cantilevered mirror, examining her face, looking for a change. She needed go no further than the eyes. It was there that everything was.

"*Attendez!* Somehow your eyes are very bright. From now on we won't be taking any romance novels out of the reading room. Avoid the superfluous; I don't wish for you to be disappointed when you learn the difference between life and literature. By the end of next week at the latest, I will make a list of the required reading that you are to study by Monsieur Champain's next arrival . . ." Madame Didier said, squinting at her charge that summer afternoon.

"Anastas, she, that woman, will forbid us—we won't see each

other . . ." said Nathalie the following day at the same place of the kiss; she was sobbing, frightened by the possibility of again finding herself alone, in a world of narrow motifs, in a world of cheerless interiors, still lifes, tables and columns of percentages and pro milles . . .

"We'll think of something," he said, reaching out his hand, placing his fingers on her lips. "Don't worry, we'll think of something . . ."

And, indeed, he thought of something. Not quite an hour before the weekly arrival of Nathalie and Madame Didier, he would show up in the reading room, his suit buttoned so that the lining could not be seen, and pretend he was studiously examining something on the shelves, leafing through it here and there, and when the room's supervisor turned his head, he would place a letter in the very book that had been set aside in accordance with the governess's list, the letter a copy of which had been left on his work desk. Not quite an hour after the young man with the downy mustache and beard would leave the reading room, Nathalie would arrive in the obligatory accompaniment of the governess; they would close their umbrella or parasol and politely request the title that had been selected for next week's reading—the title with the duplicate of Anastas's letter. Indeed, every evening in the house on Veliki Vračar, he placed a folded sheet of paper in front of him, tore it apart, and on both halves wrote out the same contents, taking care that they differed by not so much as a word, deviated by not so much as a period. For that letter, in two identical, matched copies, would in the future have to be their new, simultaneous reading selection.

Without opening it, merely by measuring the weight of the book that had been ordered, Nathalie was able to feel how many of his lines were waiting there. Without opening it, merely by touching its binding, she was able to feel the warmth of each line that he had stowed there.

Madame Didier was surprised at her charge's diligence;

immediately upon returning to Senjak the girl shut herself in her room to read. She was pleased:

"Oh, Monsieur Champain will not be able to resist . . . I can already hear him proposing to you . . ."

"What's the meaning of this?!" asked the housekeeper Zlatana, growing curious when she was instructed to return the oval blotter and the green-glass lamp to the work desk, finding there a small bunch of penholders of various colors, the crystal inkwell filled with a violet liquid, and instead of steel pens, gold ones.

"What's the meaning of this?!" she repeated, removing the everywhere-scattered spots of violet ink with so-called *eau de Javel*, lemon juice, or a powder of two parts alum and one part tartar, depending on the freshness of the flecks and the type of stained material.

And in the beginning, Anastas's letters, like all other such letters, occurred in some indefinite space, filled with soaring feelings of love and ethereal declarations. The young man endeavored to find in his memory the most condensed romantic structures of his language possible, sometimes making use of French, especially poetry in French, at least to express the outlines of his emotions. Often he spent the whole night searching for a single word around which he would construct an astral communication to his beloved, in order afterward, during the following week, to read it at the same time as the girl, carefully following whether he had left at least a slight impression, at least an indication of the cosmic movement taking place deep within him. Perhaps for this reason, Anastas's first letters contained a particular confusion, a fear of the certainty that the books of others were of no help to him, that now everything depended on his own personal abilities and choices. But as Nathalie, even despite his trembling insecurity, followed those letters even more ardently—most of all captivated by the knowledge that those pages were meant for her and for no one else in the whole wide world, no one else; and as he felt that she was surrendering to those lines even more completely than before, Anastas slowly grew bolder, stringing together words with ever more abandon, dreaming up sentences that would flatter her even more, sentences that would join them even more intimately, gradually curtailing the awkward ending of his letters from "Permit me on this occasion as well to express my esteem for you," to the less clumsy "Allow me to call myself your friend," to the simple "Love, Anastas."

And along with it all, in those letters, during their simultaneous reading, there would also be an invisible postscript—the young man's pocket watch was working. There was a regular ticking. The hands glided smoothly along, went from Roman numeral to Roman numeral, endlessly describing circles of time detached within time.

37

Whether by then the thought had been conceived in Anastas—the thought that would absorb and exult him, and later cruelly bring him back to his senses—is not certain. Whether all this was prompted by the forthcoming yearly inspection, the regular arrival of Monsieur Marcel Champain in Belgrade, and Anastas wanted to pit himself against his rival, is likewise unconfirmed. Whether already in that September of 1928 he had a clear notion of what he was getting himself into will perhaps never be answered, just like countless other questions. Namely, on one long night set aside for the writing of letters, he began further from everything he had ever read, furthest from all books; he began from a domain that, at least he so naively thought, no one had ever passed through before.

Surprised by the change of tone in his communications to her, Nathalie wondered aloud, underlining with her forefinger as she followed along with his first such letter:

"Anastas, what is this?"

"A novel. It will be a novel with us as the only characters. A long novel, with a happy ending . . ." he smiled and proudly threw out his chest.

"Really?" she asked, afraid she would blink, that she would interrupt him with this slightest of movements.

"Yes, you'll see. I'll arrange everything for the two of us. You only have to ask for what you desire . . ." He pointed to that domain, the furthest he had been able to move away from all known books; he pointed to at a forested valley between gray mountain chains, their peaks under eternal snow. He pointed to a river; whence it sprang and where it sank into the earth was unknown . . .

Knowing how much the girl loved descriptions of nature, Anastas first cleared a road, taking pains that the approach meandered as luxuriantly as possible, that it wended its way through a succession of the most beautiful landscapes. It then led onto a cleared pasture where he intended to build a house for the two of them. Simultaneous with the leveling of the land that had been set aside for building, and not wishing for his project to become known in the petit bourgeois parts of Belgrade, he began negotiations with the respected Budapest architects Laurent Balagacs and Paulus Winter, not caring how much they would ask for the building plans, insisting only that they conceive of a kind of villa that existed nowhere else. Soon after he had paid the agreed-upon, not inconsiderable sum, he began to receive sketches on transparent blue tracing paper, painstakingly translating line by line into words, sentences. On his descriptions of the foundation alone, he expanded five letters into eight pages each; and so that all these elements of structural engineering would not overly tire Nathalie, he somehow at the same time began to lay out the surrounding garden. The progress could be seen each week; she read those long letters with curiosity, following along with him as he explained to her everything he had imagined—what would be here, and what was described there—she herself already discerning something of the magnitude of that epistolary novel, that manuscript.

"And will we be able to build a glass pavilion, too, with a fishpond beside it?" she asked, bent over the letters in her room in the rented house on Senjak.

"Only command it, wish it, my dear . . ." he answered readily on Veliki Vračar, holding the duplicates of the letters tightly, in both hands.

38

"*Vous n'y êtes pas.* I don't know what it is they lack?! You young people are always asking for something!"

Marcel Champain, having arrived in Begrade for another regular inspection, was referring to the candies he'd brought to Nathalie again. The metal box was now of different colors, the tinfoil always shone in a different way, but it turned out that the difference was only in the wrapper. The taste of the confections remained just the same as in previous years; the marriageable girl politely tried one or two of the *petits fours glacés* from that handful. And yet, regardless of her handiwork, the monogrammed handkerchief she had given him as a gift, regardless of the three consecutive, irreproachably danced waltzes, regardless of the fact that the girl possessed a masterful command of the percentages and pro milles of copper production, the vice president still did not propose to the daughter of his engineer for prospecting and exploitation. Madame Didier was disappointed; she asked for and received a raise, for a certain time giving up on the idea of returning to France, promising to see through to the end the matter of her charge's wedding, more and more often helping herself to the candied favors, even though they hadn't been meant for her.

"*C'est bien savoureux.* If you don't want any, you don't have to eat them. I really like them. Oh, why aren't I your age . . ." The governess took from the candies immoderately, gradually polishing off to the very bottom the eloquent remains of Monsieur Champain's visit.

Meanwhile, and following the departure of the manager of the French Company of Bor Mines, Anastas Branica wrote his long letters, concealing them in the books in the reading room in order to immediately afterward pore over them with his beloved. He wrote them in increasingly tiny letters, so that there would be as much as possible on a single page, and so that the thickness of the sheets, inserted between the books, would pass without notice. He wrote them on extra thin and expensive paper, sensitive to the slightest touch of the pen, paper with a watermark of the contours of the universal world tree, paper which had been manufactured especially for him in Milan Vapa's domestic cardboard and paper factory, in accordance with the samples he had gotten from the best-known Italian stationers. He wrote the letters, engaging not only in a simple enumeration of the blades of grass, but also describing the blades down to the type of softness they possessed. He captured the crackling sound of each individual cone on the pine trees, he predicted the movement of the clouds during the various seasons of the year, he trimmed with his own hands the stones for the foundation of the house, which was slowly sprouting up.

When he saw her coming barefoot, unshod, he knew he had managed to achieve more than many men of letters before him. She arrived with a sketchpad under her arm, leisurely walking about the field, certain that he had examined every inch of ground, had cleared it of bottles and thorns. Only once did she hurt herself on some kind of word, relating to nature but protruding from remote antiquity, forgotten here who knows when. Madame Didier understood not a thing:

"*C'est à vous que je parle?* You're limping? That's what you get for going barefoot! What kind of primitive habit is that now?!"

Of how much effort on Anastas's part this all speaks, one can only surmise. How much time he needed for it all, one can only surmise as well. Zlatana wrung her hands and heaved a deep sigh, for the young man hardly left his room, instead remaining bent over the desk and leaving the house only on errands related to the manuscript: to Vapa's paper factory for sheets of the finest quality, and to town not only for vials of permanent violet ink and gold pens, for penholders of various colors—these from the long-closed trinket shop At the Lucky Hand—but also for both the books and the loose Herzegovina tobacco essential for his labors.

"Young sir, soon it will be winter, we should get the firewood ready . . . Would you like me to bake some crescent rolls with apricot jam? . . . The vein of cracks on the façade should be sealed up again . . . Do you know that they laid the foundation for the observatory; now everyone calls Veliki Vračar 'Zvezdara' . . . Sir, this morning they reported that the Croat representative Radić was killed in the parliament . . . His Highness King Aleksandar has suspended the constitution . . . A law was enacted regarding the new name of the country, and its division into administrative units . . . The Kingdom of Yugoslavia, that's what it will be called from now on, has nine *banovina* . . ." Thus the housekeeper would try to draw Anastas's attention to life's more ordinary aspects.

"Not now, later . . . Decide yourself . . . No more about that, I have far more important work to do . . . Interesting . . . And how does that concern me . . . Leave me alone with the politics . . . History doesn't interest me . . . Let them do what they like . . ." He would refuse, even for a moment, to take an interest in reality.

Probably wishing to dazzle Nathalie, probably wishing to

render to perfection even the merest insignificance, Anastas more than ever purchased books, prepared to read hundreds of pages in order to give at least an elliptical description of some single detail. Of course, he became the best customer of all in the bookshops of Goetz Kohn and Svetislav B. Cvijanović, and in the Pelican, and he regularly visited the National Library, which had been reopened to the public in a building on Kosančić Venac after many years of healing the wounds of the war's destruction and ruin. He began a correspondence with a well-known expert on parks, Pierre Bossard, a professor at the Paris National School of Horticulture, ordering from him plans for a garden that would combine: the elegance of the park of Versailles, Renaissance park labyrinths, the ostentation of Moorish fountains, the stark beauty of alpines, and indigenous and exotic flora—and of course paying an exorbitant sum for Bossard's drawings and advice. Moreover, he consulted with authorities in all professions, from stonecutters to logicians, from puzzle writers to biologists, from typesetters to geometers, from well-diggers to geologists, from dowsers to astronomers, from glassblowers to statisticians, saying a little something to each of them but revealing to no one the entirety of his literary firstborn. He sought advice at the Kalenić Marketplace or in Zeleni Venac, not afraid to bargain for a little of the experience of the peasants, who were astonished by this odd fellow who gave a new ten-para silver coin for each word he hadn't heard before. He soon became known for this, and they began to accost him on the street or to show up in front of his house on Veliki Vračar, that is on Zvezdara, offering him archaisms, localisms, diminutives, neologisms, synonyms, all sorts of less common dialectical forms, and even slang expressions. He bought them up without regard to whether or not he momentarily needed them. The housekeeper Zlatana often had to drive away the flock that had gathered intent on taking easy advantage of Anastas's passion.

"Young sir, some sailor has arrived. He says he's prepared, for a reasonable price, to tell you how palm trees that bloom only once in a hundred years look. He saw two such palms in 1897 or 1898 on some shore. If I tell him to go, by my reckoning, if he's even telling the truth, it turns out we'll have to wait more than sixty years . . ." said the housekeeper, trying to establish some kind of order.

"It's all right, it's all right, show him in. A palm tree is a symbol of divine blessing, of resurrection and victory over death . . . It would be worthwhile just to see, with Bossard, in which section of the garden it would be most suitable to plant them."

39

"Where is this from?"

"And that?"

"And that one?"

Not only did the epistolary novel begin to take on an indefinable form, but Anastas, when writing letters, more and more often found words that he was certain he had never read before. Where they were from, he didn't know. It appeared as if they came to him from nowhere, as if they had created themselves precisely in the spot where they were needed, where they were essential. He partly comprehended the secret only after a certain amount of time, observing that they arrived together with the easterly winds, sometimes entirely, sometimes like seeds which took root between the lines of his manuscript, sprouted, and bloomed. Yes, such words arrived from the east, he discovered, while the other ones, often meaningless, came from all the other directions; often he needed to enter his own neologistic words before taking them to where Nathalie would pick them up, often he needed to enter and cross out, to remove that useless chaff or to recopy certain pages.

And it happened that entire pictures were also carried into the manuscript. On one occasion the east wind blew more forcefully than usual, and when it ceased, Anastas found a flock of unknown birds, not at all similar to the more widespread species. They gathered, perched, on the branches of the trees; for some time they rested there, chirping, and then flew off again, filling his letter to his beloved with a hundred-winged flapping and the thousandfold colors of feathers. On another occasion, a unicorn found itself in the letter. Anastas recalled descriptions of that mythical creature, descriptions he had read in old books, but at the same time it was different—as if it were real, the one that writers and mystics of the Middle Ages had perhaps been the last to see and somehow portray. The white unicorn then disappeared in the underbrush, but later he and Nathalie would sometimes meet it, never quite certain whether it was appearing to them in a hallucination or if it really existed. It could stand stock-still for hours facing the villa that the young man was building, for hours prick up its ears, shake that head adorned with the twisted, spear-like protuberance; it could rear or sound its sad, inarticulate language, and then immediately vanish if the two readers, from Senjak and Zvezdara, so much as thought of approaching it.

The year 1928 ran out, then 1929 expired as well, then 1930 began. The manuscript progressed, many plants in the garden had already struck root and put forth leaves, the completed glass pavilion gathered sunlight and moonlight, and the roof of the villa was just about to be put on. Anastas, section by section, patiently decorated the residence. Nathalie seemed to live only for her sojourns in the letters of a person whom she had never seen in reality. Of Marcel Champain, her suitor from France, she was reminded only by the strong flavor of ever the same glazed confections. Eating them up in place of her charge, Madame Didier grew terribly fat from those sweets, voraciously wolfing them down with a roll of the eyes, amusing herself afterward by making a ball from the wrappers. Shining piece by shining piece of tinfoil, the brilliant ball grew quite large, reaching a diameter of nearly forty centimeters.

"*Plus précisément trente-neuf centimètres.* I've decided. One day, perhaps even during this fall's inspection, when the vice president proposes to you, this will be my wedding gift, a quite appropriate memento of your girlhood . . ." she used to say, measuring the weight and circumference of the ball after each wrapper had been added to it.

In truth, it sometimes seemed to Anastas and Nathalie, to the two of them together, that their romance was merely an illusion. To each of them, individually, that he, and more exactly she, did not exist; that they had dreamed each other up. Sometimes it seemed to them that the traces of their love would refute them, convince them. And that came to pass when Anastas returned with the palm of his hand smudged in pastel chalks, the palm in which he had held the hand of his beloved. And when she, after a reading, found on her fingers what were doubtlessly spots of violet ink. These different vestiges bore witness to the two's gradual discovery of yet another domain.

What occurred on that summer day in 1930, when the roof was finally put onto the structure, when they walked about the empty ground floor and raced upstairs, then once more descended the inner staircase, arranging here and there, like their first household furniture, the echo of laughter; what occurred when afterward, tired, they sat on the bare floor of their future, rather large music room (or rather small dance hall); what occurred then could perhaps not be described were it not for those fingerprints. Namely, putting down the letter in the rented house on Senjak, Nathalie noticed traces of violet ink on each and every button, covered with the same georgette of which her no doubt recently unbuttoned dress was made. Fearing that Madame Didier would see through everything, the girl hastened to change her clothes, discovering the reflections of

Anastas's inky fingertips on her stockings, from the knees upward, discovering them on her undergarments, and when she took everything off, to the point of nakedness, she found the same fingerprints on her skin, on the whiteness of her breasts, belly, and flanks . . . Namely, putting down the letter in the house on Zvezdara, Anastas Branica noticed traces of pastel chalks around the buttons of his shirt. Suspecting what this might mean, he nearly fled from himself, completely undressing, finding partial or whole print marks from pastel fingertips, everywhere those colors appropriate to a specific part of the body, most of all nuances of red, from blushing pink to seething purple . . .

FIFTH READING

WHERE WE CONTINUE TO SPEAK
ABOUT ZEALOUS DEVOTION
AND OTHER CONSIDERABLE EXPENDITURES;
ABOUT A JEWELER'S LOUPE,
A BUST OF PORPHYRY,
THUMBS STUCK INTO A VEST,
ARTISTS' NECKTIES
AND CLOAKS;
ABOUT THE TWISTING
OF BOTH A READER'S INTEREST
AND LIFE BETWEEN TWO LOVES;
ABOUT AN OATH
FOREVER AND EVER;
ABOUT UNBUTTONING WITH ONE'S LIPS
AND UNTYING WITH ONE'S TEETH;
AND ABOUT HOW INSIDIOUSLY REALITY,
SOOT, AND SPARKS
GET INTO EVERYTHING

40

DEVOTING HIMSELF ZEALOUSLY TO THE LETTERS with his entire being, down to the most refined quiver of feeling, Anastas Branica unsparingly spent large sums of money on the various needs of his manuscript. During the years of assiduously creating his novel, during the years of exultation, together with his detachment from everyday affairs, the cash he had inherited began to wither away, finally to dry up completely. Gradually, Anastas began to empty and then to exhaust one bank account after another, selling even the securities he had found after his stepfather's death. The bundles of stocks grew ever thinner; of some of them there remained only the sagging, tricolor ribbons with which the shares had been bound in crosswise fashion. Had the young man paid the least bit of attention to the state of his financial affairs, an accounting would have shown that he could not have endured such considerable expenses for much longer. But in the same way that he didn't spare his feelings on the letters sent to his beloved, Anastas also did not keep track of his expenses, continuing to take according to his needs, not caring how much was left. The basic rule to which he adhered was that Nathalie Houville deserved only the best and not for a single moment to haggle with himself over that, nor with others, beginning with Laurent Balagacs and Paulus Winter, the architects of the villa, and with the Parisian professor of horticulture, Pierre Bossard, according to whose blossoming conceptions the sumptuous garden was being laid out, and with those to whom he had entrusted the remaining, less extensive tasks, and with, finally, the unknown persons who brought rare words and multiple meanings. Sometimes he didn't haggle because he himself wasn't the one who had the time to enumerate all the many necessary details; sometimes he didn't haggle because he considered that he did not have sufficient talent to carry out some of those details to the desired perfection, should the deal be broken off.

It is not easy to ascertain how many times he was forced to hire helpers. When he contracted for work to be done, he usually concluded the agreement with a warm handshake, naively leaving a down payment and often not even presenting—still more rarely justifying—the reasons for his puzzling orders. For instance, immediately after putting the roof on the house, he turned up at a well-known dealer in rarities, Isaac Konforti, and made a wide selection of furniture. Not at all surprised—he was used to the customer always being right if he had the means to pay, and, being in the Balkans, he was used to one's eagerly snatching at extravagant fancies in order to compensate for what was lacking, even whole epochs or centuries—Isaac Konforti, during two years of collaboration, supplied pages and pages of descriptions in accordance with which every free corner of Anastas Branica's villa was furnished. To the house on Veliki Vračar—actually, to a large extent already, the house on a slope on Zvezdara—an assistant or the antique dealer himself would come personally every week, rubbing their hands together and then spreading out dozens of rolls of paper on which, from the first morning light until the evening shades extended into dusk, each individual sample was examined.

"Master Anastas, you are a lucky fellow. Today I have a rug from Bukhara; each knot has been woven by hand, with Oriental patience, without skipping a stitch."

"Let me say at once, I am offering this tapestry only to you, Flemish work. Read, and see for yourself . . ."

"Take your choice: Wedgwood-blue or Pompeian-red patterns of wallpaper?"

"For summer I recommend taffeta drapes, and for the winter frost heavier ones of velvet or brocade."

"Chairs with backs in the shape of fanlike shells, in six copies, without the slightest difference; the engrosser was respectful of each oblique and vertical and round and curling line."

"Please feel free to look it over! A bergère bordered in oak and laurel wreaths. A more exhaustive description you'll find not even in Balzac."

"Dining room tables of solid engraved walnut, and other types of smaller tables of mosaic woodwork, for afternoon tea, chess, solitaire; for vases of seasonal flowers, for forgotten trifles or placing odds and ends?"

"A secretary of rose and lemon wood. Indeed, perhaps it won't be clear to you at first, because it has to do with a genuine labyrinth of secret compartments. However, if each of its sixty-nine little drawers is opened in the proper sequence, the double bottom of the seventieth will immediately open onto a space without end."

"A potbellied chest of drawers of ebony wood. Each sentence has been lacquered twelve times."

"Dressers lined with the growth rings of the Brazilian rosewood, cedar, teak, cherry, or pear trees; if you'll lean closer, if you please, just a little, a little bit closer, you will smell each of the aforementioned types of wood . . ."

"A mirror of cut glass that remembers every reflection for exactly one century . . ."

"Chinese screens of rice paper. It is said that for thousands of years they experimented with the transparency of the silhouette until they achieved the right amount of shadow."

"A large selection of fine porcelain from Sèvres. Smooth or with bulges. However you read, not one of the decorative patterns is repeated twice."

"Unique glassware from the islands of Murano. Please, more

carefully! Move your head and don't breathe directly on it. It is very fragile."

"Miniature after miniature, enchased bronze consoles, door knockers for the entry door, hand bells for the servants, all kinds of appliqués, door locks, handles and hinges, burnished candelabra and candle sconces . . ."

Many of these items, of diverse epochs and variations, bore the original seals of the most famous old masters, decorators, woodworkers, goldsmiths, and engravers: Boulle, the brothers Gobelin, Thomas Chippendale, Hepplewhite, Ebben, Jacob-Desmalter, Le Marchand, Bélanger—who could remember all the names? In short, Isaac Konforti charged dearly for his services, but he cheated not a single one of his strange clientele. As Jews, fate had scattered the Konforti family throughout the world, and he received those copies of interiors from distant relations, who on his behalf diligently made a tour of the most high-sounding European palaces, or humbly waited in corridors in order to peep into the main auditoriums of town halls, or pounded the soles of their feet in museum salons until there were corns on them—and then dispatched to Isaac exhaustive reports, such that in Anastas's epistolary novel were to be found several faithful descriptions of pieces of furniture of exceptional beauty.

"But they were nothing in comparison with the memories of the impoverished nobility and the Russian émigrés," said Konforti, who occasionally made detailed comments on some of his favorite notes, never once setting down his jeweler's loupe, as if it were fused to his right, somewhat more sunken eye socket. "When they are all that survives, memories can be unbelievably detailed, to the point of self-deception. It happened that a lady-in-waiting of the Romanovs, through tears, told me how most of the Czar's collection of the jeweler Fabergé's Easter eggs appeared, carried off during the revolution. And I myself was amazed listening to her describe, carat by carat, the workmanship, color, and weight of each mounted precious stone . . ."

Several years later, putting together the final version of the manuscript, Anastas himself made numerous abridgments to it, giving in to a calmer style, without excessive adornment. Subsequently, after 1945, some of that sumptuousness went to outfitting the homes of the reestablished government, but not entirely, not all of it. Just as reflections stubbornly remained in the mirrors of the novel, so did those objects, no matter how their new owners moved them about in the rooms, remain unseen in theirs. And at that time the new government, in search of a secret repository, simply reduced the secretary of rose and lemon wood to its component parts, thereby irretrievably destroying as well the contents of the seventieth drawer, whose double bottom opened onto a space without end, worthy of a primeval, Arcadian world of innocence. Perhaps one should add that the dealer Isaac Konforti perished in the concentration camp in Sajmište, after first being stripped of all his property. The only thing he had managed to briefly salvage, actually to take with him, was a description of an ancient, seven-branched candelabrum, a description of the so-called menorah, on nearly a hundred closely written pages, which he had learned by heart, often reading it aloud to his imprisoned compatriots. During those several months of waiting, as group after group of Belgrade Jews were taken away never to return, Konforti's descriptions of those seven candles truly were, as Hebrew belief also relates, the only light in a darkness of life's chaos and uncertainty. And they themselves would be extinguished when the guards finally called the antique dealer's name. In the meantime, by personal order of Hermann Göring, the official collector of art for the Third Reich, Isaac Konforti's catalogs of rarities and antiques had already been sent to Germany in twenty-odd sealed crates, where they escaped any further mention.

However, Konforti was not the only one whose participation

in the letters sent to Nathalie Houville might be considered important. By the middle of 1930, Anastas had commissioned a bust of
her by the sculptor Platon Pilipović. A bust of enduring porphyry,
whose description was to be inserted into the section of the park
that was done in Renaissance style. For the sculptor himself—a
champion of classicist principles, who at the end of the thirties was
quite vociferous in a bitter newspaper polemic with Toma Rosandić
over whether the proper place for the bronze composition of "spir-
ited horses" was in front of the parliament building—this was at the
time, of course, an unusual task. The possibility that the model come
to his atelier did not exist, and so at the appointed time Pilipović
had to repair to the Franco-Serbian Reading Room and there,
unnoticed, make sketches of the lovely foreign girl, on the sly from
the rather plump and pretentious woman in her accompaniment,
whom they addressed as Madame Didier. Nevertheless, when it was
all completed, the one who had commissioned it arrived, looked
and looked, for more than three hours only silently holding the
palms of his hands on the stone face, and for an hour more touching each curve and hollow. He kneeled and leaned his forehead on
its forehead, and then made some kind of notes and left, settling his
account but not taking possession of the sculpture. He appeared
again the following summer, yet only to commission a figure of an
Atlas the natural height of a man, with its arms raised and its palms
turned upward to the sky, but when it, too, had been carved out,
he took nothing with him except for a description of the finished
work. The Atlas and the bust of the young woman remained in
the atelier to languish until 1944, when they were destroyed in the
Allied bombing of Belgrade. Pilipović was found in a heap of broken stone limbs, torsos, now formless plaster negatives and casts,
scattered sculptor's tools, overturned boxes of clay and wire skele-
tons; decapitated by a single shell fragment.

As for that highest art, capable of uniting into one even that which cannot be joined, and because in the rather large music room (or the rather small dance hall) there had been placed only a harp, Anastas missed none of the rare concerts for this poetical instrument, attempting afterward to conjure up in words the suppleness of the compositions he had heard there. But despite all his effort, even with the carefully chosen lyrical expressions, alterations, and euphonies, even with the appropriate stylistic figures, even with a suitable rhythm of sentences and timely pauses—and despite the conversations, lasting the entire evening, with the blind Stanislav Maržika, the authorized piano tuner of the orchestra of the Belgrade Opera and Ballet—Anastas in no way managed to conjure up such compositions, and so the woof of the strings would have surely remained sadly mute had it not, by a stroke of fate, turned out that the harp was able to begin playing by itself if, during the easterly winds, the tall windows in the music room were opened. Depending on how wide open or only slightly ajar the casements were, one received the melodic weave of distant spheres or even the endless glissando of distant spaces.

Naturally, when composing his letters Anastas relied most of all on beautiful literature itself. He read and ceaselessly compared his lines with those of other men of letters, making the acquaintance of several writers from whom he managed in various ways to extract a page or two for the communications to his beloved, sometimes paying for, sometimes pleading for assistance with that which he considered insufficiently inspired. There is a story that in the Three Sideburns Barbershop he once met Stanislav Vinaver, and the well-known Serbian essayist, translator, and parodist, an erudite nonpareil, while waiting for a haircut, stuck his thumbs into his vest and recited to Anastas verbatim a sentence from his "Manifesto of the Expressionistic School":

"Vision is always more powerful than reality itself, if, that is, reality at all exists for the artist!"

However, it is not certain whether the encounter even occurred, if only because Vinaver especially liked to parody himself, and was thus prone to fabrications. All one could be sure of was that the housekeeper Zlatana would remain the lone eyewitness to the visits of those strange people of the pen, people prepared haughtily to expect exaggerated praise, to fawn, covet, pout, and beat their breasts over a prize, while on other occasions they were unnoticeable; one wondered whether they even existed, or were really so magnanimous, willing to relinquish an entire life's work in exchange for the mere smile of an enraptured reader. Zlatana would remain an eyewitness who, of course, had no understanding of poetics and the artistic currents that were no doubt being quietly or heatedly discussed in the young gentleman's study. Bringing in refreshments for the guests, she would turn her head so that with her good ear she might more clearly distinguish the taciturn and withdrawn, and with the ear having the ruptured eardrum more feebly hear the noise and the bragging. Returning to the kitchen and putting on the water, lining up the cups and saucers, she continually grumbled because of the strong coffee that some of the guests were asking for so late in the evening:

"Black coffee in the black of night, where on earth is that done?!"

She grew angry because of all the bottles of Riesling and soda water, drunk strictly together by the early-rising visitors, those with the gaudy artists' neckties, cloaks, and wide-brimmed hats, who were always ready for a free drink that she had to take from the room the first thing in the morning:

"White wine in the light of day, that's not done anywhere!"

But above all, she was displeased because Anastas smoked too much and ate too little:

"It will all come to no good—spit three times over your shoulders! Over there, in those writings of yours, you're present more and more, while over here you've just about disappeared!"

41

Nevertheless, there was someone to whom fate did in fact vouch-safe the role of more reliable witness to Anastas's undertaking. The role of witness, and afterward accomplice as well. Namely, the large-eyed Miss Natalija Dimitrijević, the only daughter of the proprietor of the Pelican bookshop, gifted pupil of singing at the Stanković Music School, in the second operatic class of the teacher Paladia Rostovtseva. Sometimes she happened to be in her father's shop, and very quickly she noticed the young man with the downy beard and mustache, who was dressed too seriously except for the silk Lyon lining of his jacket and his right forefinger and thumb, which were ever stained with violet ink. He was without equal in being the best and most demanding customer Gavrilo Dimitrijević had. Not rarely did it happen that he would leave with an armful of books, first having spent hours in a finicky picking-through of the titles, and inquiring how he could most expeditiously order old editions of books, or last year's numbers of magazines, or new translations and poetic renditions, or announcements he had copied down from the previous week's advertisements. Balding from all the world's problems about which he passionately cared, the potbellied bookseller, who was the personification of a good nature, often found the young man all hunched over, wet or chilled and lighting cigarette after cigarette, having been waiting since dawn in front of the store with the low-ered shutter of green, corrugated sheet metal, the store that stood directly across the street from Pančić Park, only forty-odd paces from "the memorial to my homeland" of Miša Anastasijević.

"Had I only known—been able to suppose—I could have got-ten up earlier this morning to open . . . I overslept; last night I hardly got any rest thinking about the new cholera epidemic in Abyssinia . . . Have you read about it in the morning papers? You haven't?!

My Lord, how many lives are lost in vain each day, how many lives extinguished . . . Here we are, let's see now, just a little patience; these roll-up shutters should be replaced, they keep on getting stuck . . ." Master Gavrilo turned the crank with difficulty, the recalcitrant axle clattered, the metal sluice rose little by little, and through the store window peeped the covers of books, closed and opened pages.

Or the considerate Dimitrijević would wait only for him, when at nightfall he had to close the shop and Anastas was the last one present, refraining until the very last moment from disturbing him, making entries in the ledger, comparing lists of subscribers, putting his business papers in order, arranging the rows of books into perfectly straight lines, and finally being forced to clear his throat, take out his pocket watch, and sigh:

"Pardon me for interrupting you, but it's time for us to close . . . My wife has the stubborn habit of not eating dinner without me . . . She says that then every mouthful is rather dry . . . Pardon me once more and good night . . . I wish you a pleasant evening, Mr. Branica!"

It was not difficult, therefore, to observe that steady customer and his wide, one might say capricious, interest in all sorts of things. With attention and bemusement Natalija followed the unpredictable twisting of the young man's movement from shelf to shelf, from children's literature in the celebrated Lastavica editions to tables of logarithms and university textbooks on polytechnics; from small collections of verse by beginning poets to Zenithist tracts, manifestos, and the open letters of Ljubomir Micić and Branko Ve Poljanski, all the way to serious works by acknowledged national bards; from popular belletristic literature suitable for reading in summer resorts, on spa benches, and in physicians' waiting rooms, to capital Blue Circle editions of the Serbian Literary Society, and to voluminous scientific reports or mere offprints from all the departments of the Serbian Royal Academy; from numbered prints of coats of arms in the *Heraldry* of Hristofor Žefarović, to false genealogies that no matter the cost placed the people who had ordered them into direct kinship with the heroes of the First Uprising against the Turks, with lords of the Middle Ages, and even with personages of the Old and New Testaments; from primary school spellers to distinguished examples of Orfelin's calligraphy; from new contributions of collectors of proverbs and riddles, to the ethnographic studies of Veselin Čajkanović; from volumes of sheet music for ephemeral hit songs to grammars of all possible languages . . . Indeed, throughout all this roaming the young lady surreptitiously observed this Anastas Branica, and although everything that was seen agreed with the town's deep-rooted opinion of that odd fellow, she felt disagreement. Not only because she was willful like her mother and had been raised never to accept, at face value, the judgment of others, but also because somewhere deep within the girl a misgiving was being conceived: that all of this had to be some kind of crude error; that it had to be a misunderstanding that no one, up until then, had tried honestly to understand the eccentric.

She approached him by seizing on an opportune moment when her father was busy and then waiting on the young man herself. This continued when she found herself in the Pelican more and more often, pretending to help out and to fill in for others, being, moreover, the only one who wrapped the books he bought in plain straw paper, sometimes even working up the courage to say something, to include with the package an appropriate kindness, curled up and tied in a ribbon. But, to be more specific, it all began on that day when in the illustrated *Grafters Almanac* she found an article about a type of scion for late-blooming, tragic-red roses, an article for which Anastas had long been searching.

"In order to build a pergola . . ." he said, though he didn't say where.

From then on Anastas turned for help only to her, and Natalija endeavored always to be at his service. At first, ignorant of the ambitiousness of his plans, she honored his requests, agreeing to collect for him apparently senseless facts or to answer the pedantic questions that he would suddenly put to her. She waited for him more and more willingly, resolved to comprehend just what it was that motivated the actions of that young man, striving to penetrate his thoughts, sometimes convinced that she was on the right track, sometimes still more confused by new, unexpected requests.

"'Because of the slow movement of the earth's axis, every several tens of centuries the role of the North Star is assumed by a different star . . . This one, toward which we are pointed today, has played that role approximately only since the beginning of our era, and will so for only some thousand years more' . . ." She found this series of lesser-known facts during the period he was diligently engaged in the methods of reckoning the position of a given terrain in relation to the points of the compass.

"It is claimed that moles ensure there are stores of food for the entire winter in a very cruel way, by gathering a large quantity of rain worms, first partially maiming them, but not quite enough that they would immediately die . . ." She researched for him everything that Alfred Brehm, in his just-translated *The Life of Animals*, had recorded about moles, voracious creatures that Anastas despised—though he himself had stated that he didn't find them around his house on Zvezdara, until recently Veliki Vračar.

"Wedgwood-blue or Pompeian-red patterns? It depends on the taste, dimensions, and purpose of the room, but I would sooner advise you to order these other ones, they strike me as being warmer . . ." Thus did she resolve his indecisiveness about the kind of wallpaper he should get, an indecisiveness he represented to her as a dilemma of vital importance.

And so on from incident to incident. Until May 1931, when Natalija at last dared to seek but a single answer, to ask him openly the purpose of so prolix a reader's interest:

"It's on account of the writing . . ." he said, embarrassed; there was no escape, for she was looking at him squarely, straight in the eyes.

"You're a writer?" she asked, not desisting.

"Well, after a fashion . . . More exactly, only somewhat . . . For now I write only letters . . ." Anastas had said much more than he was accustomed to.

"Letters?! What kind of letters? You must maintain a correspondence with important and intelligent people, since you prepare them so thoroughly. As when our Andja Petrović exchanged letters with Count Lev Nikolaevich Tolstoy . . ." The girl wanted to get to the bottom of it all.

"No, they're—how should I say—letters of a personal, intimate nature . . ." Anastas flushed.

"Oh!" Natalija flushed, too, only then relenting. "Then forgive me, by no means did I wish to be rude, to be overly curious . . ."

"It's nothing . . . To tell you the truth, somehow I feel relieved . . ." said the young man, smiling, finding it pleasant to be able to share a secret with someone else. And the large-eyed girl behind the bookshop counter seemed to him to be just such a person in whom one could confide, without shame.

42

Thus did Natalija Dimitrijević, almost unwittingly, penetrate to the remotest, most hidden aspect of Anastas Branica's life. To be sure, because she had suspected—and later discovered—that the young man's letters were being sent to another woman, in her innermost self there arose the first pangs of jealousy. On the other hand, in becoming a witness ever more privy to Anastas's passionate love, she was unable to resist the inclination she felt for a man who was capable of concerning himself, at such great length and in such great detail—and nearly myopically—exclusively with that love. Finally, when it happened that he had quite revealed to her the domain he was creating with his pen at night; when, making use of Gavrilo Dimitrijević's departure for Vrnjci to drink its healing, sulfurous waters, because the world's troubles had caused him gastric ailments; yes, when Anastas brought one of his letters to the bookshop seeking Natalija's frank opinion; when, for the first time, she found herself so near him that she noticed the mingled odor of loose tobacco and compacted honeycomb; indeed, in that moment, she read only those few touching pages and then gently put them down, scarcely able to restrain herself from telling him how she . . .

"And?" he asked in a frightened tone, misreading the fact that she had tightly closed her eyes.

"And?!" She deferred opening them, knowing how much it would hurt to see a man who could only ever be an acquaintance to her, at most a friend.

"And, what do you think of it? If you were that girl, would it please you?" Anastas pestered.

"I think . . . I think . . ." Natalija searched feverishly for something to say, rather than show how engrossed she was, conscious of the impossibility of returning to less dangerous feelings. "I think the letter is quite good."

"Really?" He was delighted as a child. "By all appearances, she, too, reads them with pleasure . . . And yet, I'm doubtful, I worry that . . . She's grown used to great French literature . . . You know, Rabelais, Molière, Hugo, Stendhal, Flaubert, Maupassant; and even the poetic Parnassians de Nerval, Gautier, Mallarmé, Verlaine, Rimbaud, Baudelaire, Artaud . . ."

"But they're books for all of us. For the public, in general. You write, create, only for her . . ."

"Yes, one day I will have an epistolary novel in which, despite time, despite history, despite superfluous events, despite everything which is not absolutely necessary to man, she and I will be the only readers, characters . . ."

"I understand that, a novel just for the two of you . . . The villa is beautiful; by the inscription in the pediment, I see that you have dedicated it to her . . . The garden is even more beautiful . . . But truth be told, the molehills spoil it . . ." said Natalija, wanting to avoid the gist of the matter.

"Damned burrowers, I can't get rid of them anyhow! Now you see why I was interested in certain things earlier on . . ." said Anastas ardently, and then explained to her everything he intended to do, what else he would describe, what was the best way to word the drama of the rising and setting of the sun, the reflections of both the sky and the lunar orb in the fishpond, to elaborate each blade of grass on the circular flowerbeds, each twig of the spherically pruned box shrubs, each angle of the building . . .

"I'll help you exterminate the moles . . ." said Natalija, trying to confine her words to anything that would not offend *her*.

And thus was Miss Natalija Dimitrijević left to live between two loves: her own, never spoken, and his, declared at great length in each letter he brought her to examine, in order to advise him on which aspect he might clarify; in order to extricate him from any kind of confusion. Thus did she live perseveringly, taking pains that nothing should give away her love, knowing she would lose him the same instant for so little as that confession. Thus did she live perseveringly, forced to read about his love, even to support him if he should grow weary of that love.

"Isn't it too unrealistic—I mean to say, exaggerated? Yet, she and I have never seen each other that way, face-to-face, in the flesh. Do you think she understands my motives? Perhaps I ought to be more open, more to the point? It's true, she speaks Serbian well, but being born a French girl, I wonder if she understands the finer details of our native language . . ." Anastas would be seized with disquiet, in cases when Nathalie Houville had not sufficiently dwelt upon some detail which for her sake had been embellished during sleepless nights.

"Don't worry yourself; the feelings you write about are everywhere always understood in the same way, regardless of the differences in speech . . ." Natalija would reassure him, all the while suffering her own unrest.

"We spent the whole day in the music room, and even though the windows weren't open, the harp began all by itself to play the most passionate composition, of a kind I have never heard before; it seemed that the pegs would pop out, and the strings snap . . ." he said on another occasion, having run the whole way, hardly catching his breath, just to tell her how it had gone with the simultaneous reading.

"That's because of your inner trembling. Melodies also take rise from the graceful quivering of the senses . . ." She rejoiced aloud about his harmony, while trying to muffle within herself her own tormenting cacophony.

43

About the traces of pastel colors, which Natalija noticed more and more often on Anastas's shirt, he had no need to relate; she could already guess how their numbers multiplied. She found confirmation for this in the spring of 1932, when she was no longer able to resist seeing her rival from up close. (Or perhaps secretly hoping that she wouldn't meet her, that this other girl didn't exist, that she was imagined, an only somewhat more subsistent fancy of Anastas's.)

Knowing the day and the hour that Nathalie Houville had agreed to pick up a new letter, the daughter of the bookseller Gavrilo Dimitrijević nearly collided with her at the entrance of the Franco-Serbian Reading Room on Knez Mihailova Street. The mademoiselle had just exited, in the company of a more corpulent lady; she was in a good humor, firmly squeezing the binding of some novel, in which there were surely hidden communications from her mysterious lover. Natalija required only an instant to catch sight of a tiny dot of violet ink on the top button of her dress.

"Madame, *s'il vous plaît,* would you like to come in?" asked the supervisor of the reading room, a likeable fellow with a pince-nez on the tip of his nose, who had just ushered out the two French women and was now holding the door for Natalija as well, kindly inviting her in.

"No, thank you—perhaps another time . . ." said the girl, turning and continuing along Knez Mihailova Street, behind the foreign women.

She was ashamed of her behavior, but she walked only a few paces behind them. The older, considerably fleshier one chattered ceaselessly about something, spoiling her sonorous language with disdainful grimaces, pausing before fashionable store windows on the main street of the capital only to pass a curt judgment, insofar as one could understand her words:

"Do you see those so-called yard goods?"

"Those patterns?"

"They're so . . . so passé!"

Her charge was not listening; she walked beside Madame Didier, although she was really walking after her thoughts, hardly waiting for when, in the rented house on Senjak, alone, she could peer into the letter in which Anastas Branica was already waiting.

Yes, I suspected as much, concluded Natalija sadly.

While going at a snail's pace, the three women came to Terazije . . .

The central Belgrade square was full of leisurely strollers, the shrill honking of the occasional automobile, the clanging of street-cars, the clamor of children around the still-audible murmur of the relocated Knez Miloš Fountain, the shouts of street hawkers selling baked rolls, hard biscuits, and lottery tickets of the National Lottery Commission . . .

"Take a chance, people! Lottery tickets, lottery tickets! Each one surely brings a lot of hope, until the drawing!"

They were of similar ages. And even similar names. In quite female fashion she compared the girl's beauty with her own. But outward appearance does not exist for itself alone; it first depends on who beholds it—and how.

The square was abuzz with malicious remarks about a hat with enormous ostrich feathers—a hat belonging to the paramour of the elderly president of the court of cassation, a woman who had just boastfully passed by in a carriage—and with the jingling of small change doled out to beggars, and with the hard bargaining of the wholesalers and provincial merchants . . .

"Agreed then, four ducats per bale of cotton, including freight charges. Should we drink something in front of the Moskva to celebrate our agreement?"

Had they been twins, it would not have mattered at all; Anastas looked only at Nathalie Houville, even though he had never seen her in real life. Her, Natalija Dimitrijević, he didn't notice, though daily he could see his own reflection in her eyes . . .

The square was filled with the impatient snapping of fingers from the terrace of the Hotel Moskva, by means of which one summoned the waiters, their hair slicked down, in black waistcoats and long white aprons; the square was filled with the toasting, with raised glasses, of the mishmash of closing a deal; it was filled with the fizzle of tiny bubbles of fresh soda and cold raspberry juice borne on trays; it was filled with the tapping of blank on blank of dominoes on marble tables . . .

"Did you see that fashion plate in ostrich feathers a little while ago? How isn't she ashamed? Libertine! Is that any way to exhibit oneself, publicly, in sight of respectable people?!"

Natalija allowed them to go on toward the Old Palace. What can I do, she thought, somehow sliding downward from Terazije to the unfinished parliament building . . .

And not much could be done. Should she continue thus, to assist him with source material and literature, encourage him in his undertaking, read the first versions of his letters, and endure her futile love? Or should she give it all up, take refuge in her girlhood room in her parents' flat on Palmotić Street, go to her lessons in operatic singing, and not go out to the Pelican; should she ask him to go instead to Goetz Kohn's bookshop or to Cvijanović's—anywhere—just so as not to see him? There was no third option.

"I'll keep loving him . . ." was what remained when everything had settled.

"I'll keep loving him . . ." broke free from her one Friday in 1932.

"I'll keep loving him, come what may!" she repeated that evening, aloud, into her pillow, speaking solemnly, as if vowing to herself forever and ever.

The following day, she told her father and mother that she no longer wished to attend lessons in Madame Rostovtseva's class. They were disappointed, but didn't try to dissuade her, also accepting her desire to help out from then on in the bookshop. It is said that the old teacher Paladia, on hearing the news that she had lost a gifted pupil, sighed:

"That's how it is . . . You can never have two loves at the same time."

44

The minute hands of private and public clocks moved in circles, and the hour hands dragged stubbornly along behind them. Pendulums swung in houses or in the window displays of watchmaking and jewelry shops: left-right, right-left, left-right . . . With the striking of every quarter, half, and full hour, frightened sparrows and sleepy pigeons flew from towers. Timing how long it took to reach the top of Avala, cyclists were preparing for the mountain stage of the big race across the Kingdom of Yugoslavia. That eccentric national athlete Vejsilović, called Baš-Čelik, kept his promise, breaking his own Balkan record, standing on his head fifty-two minutes longer than last year. On the first track of the central railway station, the early arrival of the Orient Express from Paris was adjusted by the tardiness of that same train on its return from Constantinople. Over rare Telefunken radios the striking of gongs signaled noontime. The chronometer in the Central Bureau of Weights and Measures glided along flawlessly, a chronometer that, according to the Ministry of Trade and Industry, was modeled on the system of the English mechanical engineer Shortt, and had a maximum error of plus or minus one second in a whole year. And secured from any changes in pressure, temperature, and humidity, under glass bells in clock housing, placed ten meters below ground level of the new observatory building, the six astronomical clocks of Clemens Riefler, recently imported from Germany, were compared for accuracy. And so the seasons revolved across Belgrade. The cogged ending of the year of Our Lord meshed with the onset of the next one, set it in motion without the slightest pause . . . Only Anastas Branica's pocket watch, following his passionate love, had no time to follow the time of the exterior. Inasmuch as on one side of life it stopped, moving not a whit, on the other side it pounded, compressing whole weeks into mere minutes.

Truly, Anastas's existence was measured according to the time he spent in the letters, according to the time of their simultaneous reading, which he shared equally, down to the instant, with Nathalie Houville. Briefly explained, according to the psychology of perception, the process of reading can be broken down into the jumping, skipping motions of the eye, lasting the fiftieth part of a second, from fixed point to fixed point, in actuality from one string to another of lettered signs, words, or groups of words; motions interrupted by pauses or by going backward, in the event there has been a lack of understanding of the text that has been read. To put this into lay terms, then, the brief moments of reading were the longest moments in the world. Each was worth a small eternity . . .

. . . regardless of whether they moved about the most distant reaches of the garden, in search of wild-growing species, being careful not to offend them by their disbelief . . .

. . . regardless of whether they roamed after the unicorn, luring him with their purity of thought . . .

. . . regardless of whether Nathalie drew, while sitting on the terrace of the villa, indirectly from the pupils of his eyes, that which he daydreamed of from the belvedere. "But be still, don't turn aside your gaze—I haven't finished the outline of the mountain. Be still when I ask you!" She pretended to be angry if she saw Anastas mischievously pass his eyes over her neck and shoulders or let them linger for any length of time on her breasts and thighs . . .

. . . regardless of whether together they observed unknown birds, flown in from a distance with the east wind, that blinking creature, with splendid feathers, naively prepared to peck crumbs right from human hands . . .

. . . regardless of whether they allayed their hunger with only a heel of bread or with tasty walnut fingers, whose ingredients and manner of preparation Anastas had copied down from Pata's cookbook, the only book that the housekeeper Zlatana owned—"Mix 4 egg yolks with 3 tablespoons of powdered sugar, and stir a good ¼ hour. Then add 250 grams of crushed walnuts and 2 teaspoons of flour. Beat 3 egg whites, and then add . . ."—verbatim, all in the same order in which it stood in the recipe . . .

. . . regardless of whether, by smell, they tried to determine which of the seventy drawers of the secretary of rose and lemon wood opened onto a space without end . . .

. . . regardless of whether they sweetly nestled in each other's arms, listening closely to the rubbing of the silk of her stockings and the lining of his jacket . . .

. . . regardless of whether they undid bone buttons, hooked clasps, snap fasteners, and wiggling garters with their lips; whether with their teeth they untied or removed white lace ribbons, black elastic bands which kept shirt sleeves from falling down, bow-like belts, and tight straps; with their teeth, so that traces of pastel chalks and violet ink would not give them away upon their return . . .

. . . regardless of the differences, each moment was worth a small eternity. Inside the letters, clock hands moved more quickly than the unaccustomed eye was able to see, so quickly that they gradually wore away all twelve Roman numerals of the clock built into the pediment of the villa.

And probably so as not to shorten by a jot such valuable time, Anastas prolonged the ending of whatever they read together. Because he asked himself more and more often *What now?* Where to, once he no longer had anything to write to her about? Would she then return to ordinary romance novels, would she then continue to read on according to the governess's plan, according to the alphabetical arrangement of the titles on the shelves of the Franco-Serbian Reading Room? What then? How would he know where she was? Where?

"No, I shouldn't end it at all . . . I should write her while there's still a drop of ink left anywhere in the world . . . Revise, embellish, conceive of an entire life . . ." he once uttered aloud, stopping mid-sentence.

"You can extend the property to the east, all the way to the river . . ." Natalija Dimitrijević approved when he voiced his fears. "Don't despair, around the house there is always much one can do. Here now, what have you said about the kitchen? Nothing! And even if you merely list everything it contains, only list the dishes and plates, the cutlery and the basic provisions, you'll gain time. And why do you speak so sparingly about the parquet floor? You hardly mention it. If you put in a mosaic woodwork, the two of you can talk and talk, and you can also include a description of how it gives way beneath your footsteps or hers. And let me repeat, the domain can be extended to the east, to the bank of the river. It will be easy for you; many broad views reach the eye from the other side as well . . ."

"I thank you, you have rescued me," he answered, and that same day he enthusiastically proceeded to measure off the new area, to thin out the wild vegetation and add cultivated seedlings, to populate it with that tiny life of dew, maidenhairs, and insects, to stamp down trails this way and that, to connect them with existing paths, to expand the domain. He even intentionally spoiled something here and there, so that he would have a reason to describe it again— as when he later decided that the roof of the villa would be flat, and to arrange on the cornice the eight figures of an Atlas, the height of a man, the palms of their hands turned upward.

And of course, so that the weekly letters to his beloved would follow one after another for who knows how long, for an eternity, Anastas Branica did not shrink from exerting himself till he was out of breath, nor from spending his entire worldly possessions to the last penny, just so that it would be so—so that reality would not slip insidiously into everything . . .

45

As he paid no mind to ordinary days, still less to important dates and holidays, he was at first surprised by the crowd gathered around the Monument of Gratitude to France, at the entrance and along the main footpath of Kalemegdan Park. He intended to stroll that Sunday morning, after his customary coffee with cinnamon in the Russian Czar, despite a threatening wind, and then to return home and get down to work on continuing his letter for the following week, having just begun a description of the complicated shapes of the water flowers in the fishpond. However, on account of all the people one could go no farther, and so he himself stopped, quickly realizing the import of what was taking place here. It was a ceremony marking the passing of yet another year since the end of the Great War.

Having finished the national anthems, the guard orchestra had just set down their instruments. The exultant monumental cadences of speeches for some time intertwined themselves in the fringes of the national flags, and in the tassels of the banners from the bloody battles to breach the Salonika Front; and hovered in the crowns of the plane trees and the folds of Meštrović's bronze sculpture. The minister of foreign affairs, dressed in tails, top hat, and glacé gloves, had just laid a laurel wreath at the pedestal, together with the French envoy to the Kingdom of Yugoslavia, a tall, thin man with a tricolor sash across his chest. Two generals, one Serbian and one French, accompanied by several high-ranking officers from allied countries in decorated uniforms and with parade swords, prepared to do the same. Scores of those who had participated in the retreat across Albania and in famous battles, clean-shaven as if on a holiday or with twirled mustaches, their breasts emblazoned with the shining of decorations and medals for bravery, stood at attention and saluted. Many distinguished people—headed by the towering stature of Patriarch Varnava and the beatifically calm Belgrade bishop, by ladies and gentlemen, by humble wards of the St. Joseph Girls' Boarding School, by bereaved families of those who had not returned, and by numerous French school pupils—magnified with their presence the solemnity of the ceremony . . . Alongside Anastas also passed the writer Stanislav Vinaver, one of the celebrated Thirteen Hundred Corporals, greeting him with a smile and an amiable bow of the head. Now Anastas, too, moved closer, as far as he could, straining to hear the minister, as with new gusts the wind swept away the timeworn words of the speech:

". . . brothers, we have gathered at the Monument of Gratitude to the French people . . ."

Anastas vigorously rubbed his left eyebrow. Perhaps the reminder of the war years had made the scar begin to itch again. Perhaps he remembered his detailed reading of maps and nautical charts on behalf of the intelligence division of the French command. Reading which was afterward kept in the strictest confidence, about which he later told no one, nor bragged. Reading of which traces now existed only in some confidential archives. And he, recorded with the Latin initials A.B. as part of the operation under the code name "The Living Language," never received the least bit of official recognition. Even though he had nearly perished when it was discovered that one of the maps—the areas of offensive operations on the Salonika Front along the Sokol-Dobro Polje-Veternik line— was being interpreted by him at exactly the same time as the enemy assigned the same task.

". . . noble citizens of the Republic, whose government so selflessly came to our aid, having accepted . . ." said the minister of foreign affairs. The young man tried to follow along between the gusts of wind, when suddenly, becoming conscious of a familiar odor, he trembled within.

He had almost no need to turn around. To the right, a mere

two paces from him, stood Miss Nathalie Houville and the corpulent Madame Didier; they stood and listened. Yes, it was her slender neck; he had touched it just the other day. Yes, it was that charming ear; so many times before he'd gently caressed its well-known spirals with a whisper, until Nathalie would shiver. "Stop it, you're tickling me!" she would laugh, but she never moved her head. Yes, there was no doubt, it was she . . . The heat penetrated Anastas. They had been even closer within his densely written lines, but outside of the letters they had never met, especially not this way, within arm's reach. What was he to do? How was he to behave? Were two distant worlds, one imagined and the other real, being intertwined? Were parallel times, at last, converging in the true measure of existence?

". . . in the hour of our most pressing need . . ." the minister of foreign affairs went on. The wind again buffeted impetuously, a flock of titmice flew off to take shelter in the silent niches of the Kalemegdan fortress, the patriarch's and bishop's vestments billowed, a military cap began to roll along the ground, two or three hats took off into the air, and with the mention of relations who had been killed in the war, tearstained handkerchiefs began to flutter.

Did Nathalie Houville recognize a familiar odor as well? And could it be that by some special female sense she divined Anastas's thoughts? Or did she simply feel that someone was steadily gazing at her? She turned around and found a young man, soberly dressed, with a downy beard and mustache, and a scar over his left eyebrow—all in all rather familiar, but she was unable to remember if and where she had seen him before. For a moment it seemed to her that it was one of those déjà vu encounters, one of those illusions; it seemed to her that this man was similar to the likeness which for years had been recurring in her drawings, those done in pastels, after motifs from literary works. But that's not possible, Nathalie thought, dismissing the comparison; and if it is, it's a matter of pure coincidence.

". . . in the years of the Serbian Golgotha . . ." declaimed the minister, glancing up at the sky more and more often. Bad weather was brewing; the wind scattered the fallen leaves, drove the clouds ever lower, and the azure of the firmament was lost in a cuttlefish ink. It seemed as if the flags would break free of their poles.

Anastas's disappointed eyes must have expressed horror at the knowledge that his beloved was looking at him in wonder. Persistent, hoping she would recall him, he didn't bat an eye, not having the strength to begin to speak . . . Indeed, he tried hard to think of something to say, anything, something that would remind her, some tender phrase, at least a word from his communications to her in fine penmanship . . . He tried to smile, in the same way that she had seen him smiling scores and hundreds of times before; he distended his lips, conscious of the fact that what formed on his face was nothing more than a spasm . . . And the pocket watch was not ticking as in the letters . . . Time within time had ceased here, while in Anastas Branica a single, confounding truth stood out:

She doesn't know me, she didn't recognize me!

Though he could not be heard well, judging by his gestures and an occasional vowel, the minister of foreign affairs had not yet concluded.

Carefully observing all but the ceremony, noticing that some impudent young gentleman from these parts was extremely impolitely—even rudely and importunately—staring at her charge, the rotund Madame Didier took the young lady under the arm and abruptly pulled her aside. Nathalie Houville began to walk. And then she turned around, confused by the feeling that she was committing the greatest blunder of her life. Anastas's benumbed heart began to beat again, it leapt as if to step out in her direction . . . No, no, he'd nonetheless been mistaken, she hadn't recognized him . . .

Exactly at the moment when the wind ominously died down, the girl proceeded after Madame Didier, and as she was doing so she said to him, without knowing why herself:

"Pardon . . ."

That was all?! That expression one uses to excuse oneself when passing by, that established civility, that mark of a good upbringing, now hardly more eloquent than a shrug of the shoulders? That was all?! Despite the crowd of people, Anastas remained alone. Unbearably alone, only with his rending pain. Clearing his throat, His Excellency, the Envoy of the French Republic to the Kingdom of Yugoslavia, began a flowery speech:

"Mesdames et messieurs Serbes, je voulais vous dire . . ."

And then it started to rain. At first a heavy, pouring rain, and then a steady drizzle. Black umbrellas were opened, and even an occasional parasol that had been brought by mistake. The wet flags and ribbons of the laid wreaths wilted and drooped. People began to make their way to the edges of the park. The envoy quickly concluded. The officials began to disperse. There remained only a guard in an olive-green, homespun uniform, his right leg shorter by two genuflections, to fold up the rented chairs and carry them off somewhere. No more than a quarter of an hour needed to pass, and on the deserted main footpath of Kalemegdan Park, facing the Monument of Gratitude to France, stood one man alone, his shoulders stooped, soaking wet, as if he weren't in his right mind at all.

46

And it seemed that except for the unbearable pain he had nothing left of himself. He destroyed the letter he had already begun. In a rage he tore to pieces page after page. The clumps of water flowers that he pulled up began to diffuse a pleasant smell. He poured a dozen vials of violet ink into the widest crack in the wall. Thick as blood, the fluid slowly disappeared into the thirsty depths. Only a dried droplet or two of it remained behind to bear witness. He pressed pen after pen into the blank, thin sheets of paper that had been made especially for him in Milan Vapa's paper factory, in accordance with the specifications of the finest Italian stationers; pressed the pens until the gold-plated nibs would split apart, and on the surface of the table, under the expensive torn paper, there would remain indelible scars. He broke in two nearly all the penholders of various colors: each snapped like a breaking bone.

He shut himself in the study and despaired, not allowing the housekeeper Zlatana even to knock. Not having had a bite to eat in three whole days, not feeling the need for water, food, or sleep, nor feeling those other bodily obligations, he grew numb from emptiness; he lay on the sofa, listening attentively for any echo of life in him, leaving only to go to that beach, that foamy wreath between sand and sea, in the children's adventure book with the impressed depiction of the universal world tree, which he used to read as a twelve-year-old boy.

At last, when he emerged from the study, he could no longer be called a young man. Before, rarely would one have thought him a full thirty years old; now, he looked as if he were at least ten years older than his true age. The first shoots of gray appeared along his sideburns, and there sprouted in his eyebrows, each to its own side, protruding wild hairs. From somewhere issued sharper whiskers, rendering slovenly the once downy softness of his beard and mustache. The lining of Lyon silk, the lining of the suit in which he had spent those three days, smelled of cooled sweat and the pungent odor of rain. And his despondent shoulders could not be made to straighten up from that hunching storm in Kalemegdan Park.

He firmly resolved not to write her again. But he changed his mind only an hour before his customary outing to the Franco-Serbian Reading Room, composing only several lines, using the sole remaining, unsplit pen, the only intact penholder, and the very last of the violet ink, stating in those few bitter sentences how hurt he was—in two copies, but more for his own sake, not expecting her to come at all.

But Nathalie Houville appeared as before. She arrived, sweetly sounding out sentences in Serbian. Underscoring each line with her finger. With her sketchpad and box of pastel chalks under her arm. In good spirits and curious. As if nothing had ever happened. Perhaps with only a slight cold from last week's rain at the Kalemegdan.

"Forgive me," she said to him, surprised at the bitterness she found. "Forgive me, I don't know how it is possible, it was a misunderstanding . . ."

She was not lying. He understood that she was speaking the truth, her view of things, just as he understood that she would be incapable of recognizing him on the other side of the world, even if he were to sit facing her in the rented house on Senjak.

"A misunderstanding?!" he repeated dejectedly. "Yes, a misunderstanding; it seems that I wanted too much. Let's continue from the water flowers in the fishpond, let's continue, starting with the next letter, from the spot where we left off, before reality . . . before reality . . ."

47

On the face of it nothing had changed. Anastas continued to write his unavailing letters and to place them weekly in an agreed-upon book in the Franco-Serbian Reading Room. He continued to write in great detail, as before, patiently extending the domain to the east, toward the bank of the river, having purchased new fine-point pens and slender penholders, new double sheets of Vapa's sensitive paper, with the minor (or perhaps major) difference that now he used only black ink: his right forefinger and thumb grew darker and darker. Now that he had crossed the boundary of youth, there was no going back; he grew old sitting over his lines, conscious of the fact that outside the letters he did not exist; he accepted that he had to be satisfied with having only that form of her companionship, that during the hours of the reading his beloved at least recognized him indistinctly.

"Our language is what always remains to us . . ." he would comfort himself in his moments of discouragement.

Nathalie Houville continued to follow the sentimental pages that someone, always unerringly, left for her in the books that the stern Madame Didier had chosen. She continued furtively to read the tender communications which mysteriously awaited her there, in the meantime preparing for the moment when Monsieur Marcel Champain would propose to her, perfecting those skills that a respectable girl of marriageable age needed to master, drawing still lifes in charcoal and motifs from literature in pastels.

"Now he's middle-aged," she said, comparing the suppleness of line of the male figure that now appeared in them to the figure in her earlier work.

Madame Didier continued to help herself to the sugared confections that had been meant for her charge, growing plumper and plumper, ever more rotund and sluggish—just like that tinfoil ball of shiny wrappers from the candied offerings, received as gifts during the yearly inspections of the vice president of the French Company of Bor Mines. The monthly arrivals of her employer, the engineer Houville, she used to extort new pay raises, complaining about the local conditions.

"*On va voir ça.* Exactly eighty-seven centimeters!" Every first of the month she announced the circumference of the tinfoil ball.

César Houville continued, down to the penny, to faithfully look after the interests of the shareholders of the Concession of St. George, directing the prospecting and exploitation of copper ore in

Bor, and not losing hope that his daughter might marry well. During his short stays in Belgrade, in the rented house on Senjak, he reeked ever more persistently of the carbide used for the mining lamps and the homemade, local wine to which they had accustomed him in the little mining town.

"It lacks harmony, but its robustness cannot be denied . . ." he would say, trying to get his more reluctant countrymen to try at least a glass of it.

Zlatana continued to do the work around the house, managing from one day to the next to maintain a household, to eradicate the cracks in the walls, to buy the groceries, to make cakes of ground carob beans as equally tasty as those of walnuts, for Anastas now cared less and less about everyday life, selling the last shares he had inherited from his stepfather, pawning the more valuable items and more and more empty promises. At one time prepared to reproach him for his absentmindedness, Zlatana now pretended to see none of this. Actually, she pretended to see him even when it seemed he did not exist.

"The gentleman cannot receive you, he's busy!" she would say to protect him from creditors who moved in ever tighter circles around the house on Zvezdara.

Natalija Dimitrijević continued to help out in her father's bookshop, to keep the ledgers, to arrange titles, to wait on customers, and indeed to wait for Branica to arrive and bring for a first reading a letter that was intended for another. She continued to search for the facts he needed, to find them, to advise him, even to point out formal errors to him, but she continued first and foremost to love him in vain.

"I myself would begin a new part here; there's nothing else you can do; you've already finished the previous one . . ." she would say, stopping at some spot and raising her large, tranquil-green eyes toward him.

48

At the beginning of October 1934, after the battleship *Dubrovnik* docked in the port of Marseilles, no sooner had the open automobile in which he sat with virtually no security set out along the Boulevard La Canebière, than King Aleksandar Karadjordjević was killed, thereby beginning one more chapter in the history of Yugoslavia. Who was behind the assassination and what the consequences were of this murder would slowly become apparent in the coming years, but it was unlikely the dejected Anastas Branica noticed anything of all that, preoccupied as he was with his love. That fall a quite different occurrence spelled ill fortune for him. Vice President Marcel Champain arrived on his regular inspection, bringing along with the usual favors two or three phrases with which he asked for Nathalie Houville's hand in marriage.

"*Dieu merci!*" said Madame Didier, and she immediately began to pack.

"You have my assent!" said the engineer César Houville, before refusing from his future son-in-law a promotion and a transfer from Bor to Paris. "You know, I've somehow gotten used to . . ."

At last, Nathalie forever abandoned Belgrade with her fiancé, leaving under the bed, in her room, in the rented house on Senjak, the portfolios bulging with drawings and hundreds of letters from an unknown sender. Frau Henzel, maid to the new tenants, the six-member family of a representative of the German ironworks concern A. G. Krupp, Essen, was at a loss for what to do with all those papers, ordering the local servants to take them to the attic, where they would be eaten away by mice and the nights of the twentieth century. Nathalie left Belgrade bringing only that ridiculous ball of tinfoil, the wedding gift of Madame Didier. The porters barely managed to place the ball, now 114 centimeters in circumference, in the webbed luggage carrier above the passengers' heads. As the train departed from the central railway station, she lowered the window of the sleeping car and waved to her father, leaning out, looking at the many faces gathered on the platform, troubled by the feeling that she was forgetting to say farewell to yet someone else . . . The locomotive picked up speed, the view of the city moved in reverse, and that entire mysterious land, perhaps even the whole Balkan Peninsula, slipped backward. Soot and sparks flew into the compartment; the fiancé got up, raised the window, and peremptorily drew the little curtains closed.

That occurred precisely on the day that a simultaneous reading had been scheduled. Anastas waited in the heading of a letter, the sole copy of which he had brought to the Franco-Serbian Reading Room, smelling all the more clearly the odor of soot. He waited unflinchingly the entire night, blacker and blacker in the face, enduring swarms of sparks which flew into his eyes no matter how he turned his head. He waited the whole next day as well, his eyes filling to the point of tears with small particles, and then he put aside the letter and went to the Pelican Bookshop. Luckily, Gavrilo Dimitrijević was not there, and so Natalija was able to invite Anastas behind the counter and, with the tip of her handkerchief, opening his eyelids, remove the stinging motes.

"I'm going to make a novel out of the letters . . ." he told her, his eyes bloodshot. "I'm going to make cuts to it, I'm going to change the inscription in the pediment and publish a novel in which there are no characters, where the only events are the rising and setting of the sun, the growth of plants, the flight of birds . . . Do you think someone would want to read it?"

"I would . . ." said Natalija Dimitrijević, not daring to finish her thought.

And looking over all the letters he had sent to his beloved, thousands upon thousands of pages, Anastas took to putting together the final version of his manuscript, blind to all else. Having long ago spent his ready money, he sold the house on Zvezdara, not very profitably, on account of those cracks, and moved into a dank, tiny back room in Dorćol, where the housekeeper Zlatana was the only one to visit him, bringing him a little something cooked. He no longer went out to the Russian Czar, or to the Three Sideburns Barbershop, neglecting everything except the new goal he had set himself. As soon as he finished writing something, he would bring it to Natalija Dimitrijević to have it inspected.

In the middle of 1936, having finished the novel by placing three periods after the concluding sentence, he went in search of a publisher. But no one was willing to publish something like that. Selling off the rest of his property, even the books that he had collected his whole life long, with stacks of pages under his arm he set out for the Globus printing firm, at Kosmajska 28, and instead of the planned thousand, he contracted at his own expense for the printing of a mere hundred copies of his novel under the title *My Memorial*. Out of respect for the days when Anastas had been his very best customer, Gavrilo Dimitrijević agreed to sell the entire printing, while the author kept only one book for himself, gave another to Zlatana as a gift, and a third to Natalija. He no longer had money even for rent for that wretched room, and so he wandered around Belgrade, eking out a living by rooting up the grass that grew between the cobblestones of the roads . . . receiving, for free, a three-fingers' pinch of tobacco in the somewhere-hidden trinket shop, At the Lucky Hand . . . occasionally spending the night at the home of his former housekeeper . . .

When a decidedly unfavorable review of *My Memorial* appeared in *The Serbian Literary Journal*, he went down to the bank of the Danube and stood there to read his own novel once more. Once more he walked around the garden, the French park, the pavilion, the fishpond, all the rooms of the villa; opened the windows in the music room; listened to the hum of the harp; then started for the eastern part of the domain. And then by the narrow path went on toward the bank of the river that flowed through it.

There was nothing there in particular, only a few willows and sallows, a description of the wide water that flowed who knew whence, who knew whither, an abandoned rowboat in the underbrush . . . He waded in, went in farther, until the river climbed from his ankles to his knees, from his knees to his waist, from his waist to the line of his chest . . . Fishermen found him some ten days after this reading, in the Danube. Likely owing to a dearth of more important goings-on, several newspapers in the capital published brief reports of this unfortunate incident.

The housekeeper Zlatana continued to work diligently in well-to-do Belgrade homes until 1941, when she became deaf in the other ear during the German bombing. Although in the preparation of delicacies she had no equal, no one any longer desired those things. She disappeared in 1942, when for the first and last time she was seen in the window of her small kitchen reading aloud a book that was not the cookbook of Spasenija-Pata Marković.

True to the vow she had spoken into her girlhood pillow, Natalija Dimitrijević continued to subsist on the memories of her unrequited love for Anastas Branica.

SIXTH READING

IN WHICH WE EXAMINE AN INTERIOR
AND THE QUESTION OF WHETHER ONE CAN
FLEE FROM A LANGUAGE;
THE SIMILARITY BETWEEN THE FEMALE FISSURE
AND BOOKS;
WHETHER EVERY BOOK,
NO MATTER WHERE IT IS LOCATED,
IS IN FACT BESIDE THE GREAT WAY;
HOW AT A DISTANCE
ONE DETERMINES WHETHER SOMEONE HAS
BRONCHITIS;
WHETHER ONE CAN BE,
AT THE SAME TIME,
IN AN APARTMENT AND OUT OF IT;
AND, FINALLY,
WHERE THE PRINCE WOULD RIDE OFF TO ON
HORSEBACK
FROM THE PEDESTAL OF HIS MONUMENT

49

FROM WEDNESDAY TO FRIDAY, ADAM LOZANIĆ met briefly with his clients, and several times with the housekeeper Zlatana. The mysterious man and woman were pleased with the inscription in the pediment. The lady led the young man into the first-floor rooms of the house, prescribed what needed to be done there in the future, and, excusing herself on account of obligations, again vanished together with her husband. The student spent three days in the villa, not going outside till the late evening hours, not meeting the shadowy Leleks, Professor Tiosavljević, or the girl, paying no mind to his noisy neighbor and the teary-eyed children next door, bent over the book bound in saffian, nibbling on the end of a lead pencil as if delirious, reaching for the volumes of the *Dictionary of the Serbian Language* or the *Orthography*, only once interrupting his reading: Kusmuk called, thoughtfully taking an interest in whether he was battling his cold. In truth, he was unable to rid himself of the constant unpleasant feeling that someone was watching him; for instance, if he suddenly went back a page or two, it seemed to him that he recognized Pokimica, his hair cropped close, military-style, sometimes wearing a scornful expression, sometimes twisting his face in positive hatred. He dropped by the kitchen, to no avail; there he always found only the elderly housekeeper, absorbed in reading recipes aloud, adding in her own ingredients and preparing fancy dishes. No matter how hard he tried, the old woman understood not a thing; she always replied with answers from which he could learn nothing, save that one about testing the freshness of yeast by taking a tiny pinch of the pound and putting it in water, and if it floated, "Then the yeast is all right to use!"

And the like. Cooking was all Zlatana knew; everything else she was deaf to or wisely pretended not to hear.

In the late-night hours, Adam left off reading only to have a bite of all those goodies, to try the soup with homemade noodles, to nibble on a vanilla cookie or to drink tea, and then go back to work, looking to finish it as soon as possible, and in order to search for the female reader with the pleasant smell. However, contrary to what he had hoped, the work stretched on. The lady instructed the young man to examine all the fabrics and to get rid of or to restore their defects, but Adam became confused with the very first draperies. A lovely summer drape of tulle, embroidered in orange-colored laurel leaves, was, owing to someone's carelessness, slightly torn and frayed at one of its corners. The young man spent hours on end finding such thin and delicate words with which to repair the ruined spot. No sooner did he begin to hope that he had matched its fineness than it turned out that he had failed to match its color. No sooner did he locate that particular shade of orange than it turned out that the drape, in that spot, had too many folds, that it didn't fall as freely as it did on the opposite side. Everything, simply everything in the interior of the house—just as was the case with the outward appearance of the villa—had been done with the greatest of care. The first floor consisted of an antechamber with a wide, hugging staircase, a large dining room and parlor in the right wing, a spacious room in the left, and a room that might have served as a rather small dance hall or music room, considering the harp that was placed in its center, its slender neck still intact, but owing to countless drafts over the years, its strings mournfully out of tune . . . There were various types of furniture harmoniously grouped into ensembles, very much according to style, some of the pieces seemingly wrenched by force from some other furniture suite . . . Oriental rugs, a parquet floor of mosaic woodwork, cascades of draperies, elegant candlesticks, flaming tapestries, Pompeian-red wallpapers, pictures, every single one in technique a pastel, large and small mirrors which contained even more than one could see reflected in them, marble consoles, burnished handles, locks and keyholes, ornaments of glass or porcelain, all of which had been obviously selected with the greatest care and wrought with a masterful hand. Although it appeared the villa was not used very often, and that nothing more needed to be added here, it turned out that this little bit of work required a good deal of patience, sometimes a skill bordering on art. Adam had the impression that he'd wandered into some sort of *roman d'époque*, where like an unworthy apprentice to the great writers he had the task of revising a little of what time had abandoned or obscured. Thus did a whole Wednesday go by in getting rid of all the dust and cobwebs, Thursday in pouring vinegar into hundreds of wormholes, then plugging up the weevil holes with wax, and Friday in braiding fringes, taking in the faded areas on the tapestries, restitching the woof of some chair's slipcover, or removing stains from carpets of such colors that the young man needed to weave in five or six words for each one in order to obtain, let us say, precisely turquoise-green-with-a-touch-ennobled-azure-blue, or some other appropriate nuance. Something of that tedious work remained for Saturday as well. Contrary to his custom, Adam wound his alarm clock and rose early at the first signs of dawn. Rain had begun to fall again, or it had never really let up. His cold oppressed him even more, he felt weak, and yet he was determined to finish his well-paying job as soon as possible. Nor had the tavern Our Sea opened yet when he took up the book in the rented studio on Milovan Milovanović Street, at the foot of steep Balkanska.

In contrast to the ubiquitous solitude of the previous day, in the middle of the parlor he found an unknown woman, in a housecoat that was too long for her and felt slippers, somewhat younger than the housekeeper Zlatana, but no doubt in her declining years. That way, with her hair slightly disheveled, with glasses that unnaturally magnified her otherwise ample, tranquil-green eyes—her overall appearance as if she'd been sitting up the whole night—the old woman nearly frightened Adam Lozanić; she looked like a patient who had just been released from a long hospital stay, who herself didn't know just where she was and where she ought to go now. Perhaps for this reason the young man discerned an apology in her voice:

"I hope I'm not disturbing you . . . I had insomnia . . . Ordinarily I trick it by sleeping on the other side of the bed . . . But last night I forgot . . . And so, I haven't gotten a bit of rest . . . Though, to be honest, I'm not sorry, I don't feel like sleeping . . ."

Not knowing what to say, Adam politely introduced himself and in a few words explained what he was doing there. She listened to him, giving the impression that she only partly understood what he was talking about.

"And I'm . . . Natalija Dimitrijević, probably . . ." the woman replied, somehow sadly; each of her sentences seemed unfinished, as if she still had something important to add but lacked the will or strength to. "At least Jelena, my companion, says so . . . Although, to tell you the truth, I'm not altogether sure . . ."

"Jelena? The girl who studies English?" asked the young man eagerly, somewhere in the back of his mind associating the old woman's name with the obituary Kusmuk had found in that *Vreme* or *Pravda* of 1936, and with Zlatana's soup which the girl with the pleasant smell had taken to someone on Tuesday evening.

"Yes . . ." she affirmed just as cheerlessly. "She is very talented and considerate . . . I don't know what I'd do without her . . . However, Jelena thinks that she can flee . . . No matter where she goes, that is impossible . . . At least it's not possible to flee from one's native language . . . We've only just met, but I would ask you, keeping in mind your profession, try to dissuade her . . ."

"Flee? Flee from what?!" asked the young man.

The windows of the villa captured the spreading dawn; the soft light more clearly distinguished one object from another in the interior of the parlor.

"I don't know . . . from some malaise . . . from everything . . ." Natalija Dimitrijević shrugged her shoulders. "Oh look, was it you who repaired this . . . ?"

She pointed to the slipcover on one of the armchairs, the one Adam had found quite worn out; he had spent a good part of the previous afternoon reweaving the detached golden motifs into its fabric, the color of ripe tobacco.

"Just as it once was . . . Anastas, you know, whenever he finished something, loved most of all to relax here . . . If I didn't remember the way it looked . . . I wouldn't think so much time has gone by . . ." She passed her trembling fingers over the back and armrests, gently, as if she were afraid her fingertips would damage the interwoven pattern.

"Ma'am, forgive my curiosity, but why did Anastas Branica write exactly this kind of novel? For whom did he build this house? This garden? Why did he drown himself in the end?" asked the young man.

"I've forgotten now . . ." said Natalija Dimitrijević, shrinking back as if she had been touched in her most sensitive spot. ". . . I've forgotten . . . I can't remember . . . Sometimes I can't recall to mind several years at a stretch . . . Sometimes it's as if the memory were still alive . . . But I can't think of the words to express it with . . . So they're on the tip of my tongue . . . And yet, to get them out, I'm not capable . . . They say that this is an illness in me, but I know that those damned pests have eaten my words . . ." the old woman absently rambled on.

" 'Pests'?" Adam was confused.

"Bookworms and book lice . . ." said Natalija Dimitrijević, shuddering in disgust. "You've read, come across words that are no longer worth anything . . . That's their doing . . . Beware . . . They can steal the eyes right out of your head . . ."

Someone was descending from the second floor. Footsteps were heard coming down the stairs, and then across the antechamber. At the parlor door appeared the girl. She was dressed only in a nightgown.

"Ma'am, you're doing it again, sitting up late," she said reproachfully.

"I've waited so long to return here . . . I probably won't sleep now . . . Come closer . . . Come here, I want to introduce you to a young man . . ." The old woman didn't turn around.

Jelena's hand was so delicate. Adam quite shuddered at the thought that their palms fit each other so well. Not daring to look at her fully, dressed as she was, he did not withdraw his eyes from hers. There he recognized Jelena's gratitude even before she softly uttered:

"Nice to meet you, and thank you for watching over Madame . . ."

"You're welcome. It was my pleasure . . ." Anxious, Adam made a somewhat self-important bow.

"Come along now, you need to rest . . ." said the girl, now turning to the old woman, taking her under the arm.

As they were leaving, Natalija Dimitrijević didn't cease to speak:

"Only an hour or two, no more than that . . . I don't want to waste time . . . A very, very nice young man . . . And how wonderfully, so very wonderfully we conversed . . . You didn't see how he repaired the slipcover on Anastas's armchair . . . Jelena, dear, how will I go up now . . . When I've forgotten what these things we're climbing are called . . ."

"Stairs, Madame. An ordinary word, *stairs* . . . Just go slowly, follow the sentence, the meaning . . ."

"Ah, of course . . . St-a-irs . . . What would I do without you? *Stairs*, you say . . . Do you know that in the parlor I remembered the word *drapery* . . . A very pretty word . . . Sounds lavish . . . I like staying here . . ." the old woman said.

GORAN PETROVIĆ

At the door, a few rays of sunlight passed through Jelena's nightgown, making translucent the fabric down the long outlines of her legs. Adam almost grew dizzy; and for a moment he closed his eyes, fearing that this sight would disappear, fade away.

50

For how long he had held his eyes closed, he was not concerned. On previous occasions as well, especially when reading in the late-night hours, he had met girls and women who had been scantily clad in their beds somewhere, sleepily turning the pages of the same book. There had been something exciting in those encounters, in the way they surrendered themselves to the reading material, in their seductive intimacy, while incautiously appearing before strangers who that night were opening the same bindings, or as if they had taken up the book in order to show themselves to other readers, not caring whether their bed linen fell off, whether their nightgowns crawled up above their knees, whether the pointed tips of their breasts showed clearly through the thin fabric, or whether the fabric was forced to now follow the flats of their stomachs, the curves of their thighs. And the books themselves were similar to that female fissure, which was at first given shyly, and then completely, in order to give birth anew . . . But this kind of intimate warmth, heat, Adam had not felt before. He closed his eyes, imagining how it would be, upon his return to the villa, to search for the same rays of sunlight that had followed the outlines of Jelena's body, so that he might rest his forehead, cheeks on them . . .

Having finished the remaining changes in the parlor, the young man stopped again for a moment, wondering what there was for him to do. The companion was probably minding the ill old woman;

it would be out of place to disturb them, to go upstairs uninvited, to their room on the second floor. There would likely be other opportunities, he comforted himself, looking over the book bound in saffian. And so Adam left the villa, intent on finding Professor Tiosavljević, who would be able to explain just where it was that he found himself, who in truth his clients were, where Madame Natalija had come from, but first of all—who that girl was.

This time taking no notice of all that one could see when passing through the garden, swiping the maidenhairs from his face, stumbling once more on the molehills, merely glancing out of the corner of his eye at the smooth surface of the late-morning fishpond, he knocked on the door to the pavilion and, hearing an invitation to enter, stepped among all those curious objects he had found there on Tuesday. The map was on the table, and over it bent a bony, middle-aged man, now wielding the map scale and the pair of compasses, reaching for the magnifying glass, drawing in with black india ink the triangular symbols and figures for the heights above sea level, beside cross-hatchings, winding contour lines, and dotted peaks.

"Ah, it's you, the newest member of our little family . . ." said the professor, straightening up. On a leather cord, around his neck, he wore a compass; from the pocket of his shirt protruded the bitten stem of a tobacco pipe. His cream-colored trousers had forgotten all about creases, and now he was wearing those shoes with the metal braces. He was distinguished by a stern demeanor, a penetrating gaze, and slow, but not sluggish—one might say thorough—movements. It appeared that he knew who Adam Lozanić was, and on what business he had come to the villa. "After all," the professor explained, "this is a very rare book, having been published in only a small printing. It has had a curious fate: It has never been reprinted. It is known that fewer than ten-odd copies still exist, and so the arrival of every new reader is immediately noticed . . . The inscription in the pediment is your doing? And I hear you ruined the pergola with roses as well. Everyone who comes here spoils a little something, according to his own taste. And where did you get the very idea that you can rearrange things to your own liking?! Fine, that's just fine!"

"The property is not theirs to own," he replied even more gravely when he had heard Adam's excuse. "Here they're as equal as the next, just like that hard-of-hearing housekeeper Zlatana, you, or myself . . . Young man, I don't wish to embarrass you, but it is an equally weighty question whether Anastas Branica, the creator of this no doubt pleasant property, could lay entire claim to the domain himself . . . Sit down and listen!" The professor pointed to an empty chair and began to pace about the pavilion, speaking more and more rapidly:

"Here, within a circle of only several hours' walk, we have prehistory, indubitably Hellenism, the Roman epoch, renowned Byzantine examples, our Middle Ages, finds from Turkish times, from the period of the Serb migration, not to mention more recent centuries, everything as plain as day, in successive layers; wherever you point your finger, you come across traces of prototext . . ."

And Tiosavljević began to carry box after box from the shelves, to open them and systematically explain their contents. Adam remained silent as there unfolded before him a history covered in layers of time.

"A petrified conch. Malacology does not know of this fossil remain. Put your ear to it: You can clearly hear the asthmatic wheeze of the eons . . .

"Do you see this word? *Sidescraper*? Imprisoned in stone, it came to be through a patient trimming away of the superfluous, not all at once, mind you, but over scores of centuries . . ." He took out something that might have resembled a primitive cutting tool.

". . . A much later period. Nowadays it is easy for us to say *club*, but formerly much time was needed to obtain such a smooth, perfect shape, and in addition such a deadly one . . .

". . . Shards of a primitive rattle: Together with other words, it might have been a sorcery against spells or evil powers," he said and lined up several unconnected syllables. "Unfortunately, no matter how I turn them, there aren't enough of them for me to make a meaningful reconstruction . . .

". . . A diminutive, not very minutely detailed, but even then one babbled it to the youngest . . .

". . . Early Hellenism, an imported culture, probably received in a trade. Today we imprecisely call similar artifacts bracelets . . ." Tiosavljević unrolled a sheet of paper with a rather small display of affection.

". . . You study literature; this is an entirely classical copy of a tragedy; someone very faithfully rendered for someone else the first episode of Aeschylus's *Oresteia*. The weeping is that of the listener, I didn't want to remove it . . .

". . . A fragment of an ode by some Roman patrician . . . Provincial workmanship, with a lot of commonplaces. However, there were special, highly esteemed, and expensive composers of epitaphs, encomiums, satirical poems, and even those devoted exclusively to the writing of curses . . .

". . . The battle cry of a legion about to charge; feel free to form ranks, I have an entire cohort here, voice by voice . . .

". . . And here we have, how should I say, the entwined suspiration of a man and woman in a moment of lust. It is difficult to conjecture whether we are speaking of the early Middle Ages; some things have not changed since the beginning of the world . . .

". . . Nevertheless, all of this is merely a leisurely introduction to the following . . . Last year I found a hoard of more than ten thousand words, *Megale hodos*, that is, *Via magna*, from the times of all the Byzantine dynasties, extending from the Holy Roman Emperor Constantine, the founder of the celebrated Eastern Roman Empire, to the unfortunate loser of the same, Constantine Dragas

XI Palaeologus. At first I was unable to determine the meaning of all those ambiguous words, but I later associated them with the writings of the mystics of the Eastern Church, apocryphal texts, and also Latin sources, from which it followed that in this direction passed the so-called Great Way, the one that was believed to have led to the end; that is, to the beginning, to the first word of God . . . Whether anyone managed to get there, and in which direction that road stretched, today we have no knowledge. But this hoard no doubt proves that pilgrims went somewhere this way, perhaps even whole processions of them. It is not impossible that here, nearby, there were inns; I have in my possession finds of entire psalms, biblical quotations, and short prayers that were recited before retiring for the night. And here someone is saying to another: 'Hasten not; the Holy Scriptures should be understood, not merely read.'

". . . This collection of brief lives of the holy fathers, I attribute to Archbishop Danilo II. Nowhere does there exist a similar commentary, but there is no doubt that it was read at the same moment by the archbishop himself and at least three deacons . . . By the shouts and cries that reach us from afar, which we generally call unchristian, I have dated it to the year 1307, at the time of the famous attack of the pirates on Sveta Gora. One can easily imagine how Danilo, then *iguman* of Hilandar, together with his monks, in order to take heart, read aloud in some monk's cell, or in the tower of those besieged grounds dedicated to the Virgin Mother.

". . . What it was that someone whispered to this girl we cannot know, but her smile is pure Renaissance, very rare for these parts; it might have been that some Dubrovnik captain, trading far and wide, discretely wore it on his breast like a medallion, to refresh him and remind him of some unbridled night . . .

". . . In the manuscript library of the Duke of Urbino, Federico da Montefeltro, known for having employed some fifty scribes at once, there is an illumination under the title 'The Rose of the Winds,' where the arrangement of the stars coincides with a twinkle in the open sky above us; you'll find not the slightest aberration . . .

". . . At the beginning of the fifteenth century, the principality of Saxony attempted to join the universal race to discover new continents and colonies. Precluded from this mission by its location far inland, cut off from the shipping lanes, Saxony, for the then fantastical sum of ten thousand guldens in gold, in the greatest of secrecy ordered from the Dutch printer Enschede seventy copies of the book *A Travelogue of Unknown Regions*, a translation of a work by a certain Prudenzia de Salvo, the first mate of Christopher Columbus. In the months that followed, seventy volunteers from all over Saxony of various professions gathered in Leipzig in a converted grain warehouse, in a room with a walled-in door and windows reduced to skylights, in order to read this same book at the same time, setting out one after another on a voyage of no return. The entire affair had been largely forgotten, the enormous costs of this foolish adventure covered up, and the disappearance of the colonists suppressed, only for one of the readers, the woodworker Erhard, suddenly to turn up in his homeland after thirty years, claiming that he had founded New Leipzig, somewhere over there, in uninhabited regions of exceptional beauty and wealth. His descriptions of the parts through which he traveled are identical to the place where you and I now stand. As you can guess, the woodworker's fate was not a happy one; he was executed as a heretic, even though he knew how to duplicate on any instrument the music of the spheres.

". . . There is no need for me to add anything here: Turkish times—one hears well how some pasha or bey long kept silent, and then with a chibouk spoke through clenched teeth: 'Christiankind, may you be cursed.'

". . . It is thought that in the middle of the sixteenth century the brave nobleman Melchior von Seidlitz, from a journey to visit the holy relics in Jerusalem, returned through Niš, Novi Pazar,

Prijepolje, and Foča, but nowhere in that direction does there flow the river he saw and described, of which he was told that none knew whence it sprang and where it emptied; nowhere was there a monastery called Usek, whose church dedicated to St. Nikola had been built by the despot Jovan Oliver, reading there two centuries before him . . .

". . . The question 'Your Holiness, whither thou?' may have been addressed to Patriarch Arsenije III Čarnojević personally, at the time of the Great Migration of the Serbs . . .

". . . More recent times are not a subject of my interest, and so I have not classified them in any special way," Professor Tiosavljević said finally, and showed him the contents of one of the largest boxes in the pavilion, sitting in its eastern corner—fragments of a porphyry bust of a woman, as well as various types of memoranda, among them also Anastas Branica's contract with the designers of the villa, the Budapest architects Laurent Balagacs and Paulus Winter, uncommon names that Adam had remembered.

". . . And all this . . . all this you found here?" asked the young man.

"For more than ten years, I have seriously concerned myself only with this region. The location was obviously favorable; it's no wonder that Branica settled down here. One thing is certain: He redid much of it himself. For example, in order to lay out the French park, he had the terrain leveled, and with that act made any further research impossible. Nonetheless, on the basis of all that remains, I am very close to establishing that the traveler's inn along the Great Way was precisely here somewhere. Your clients are trying to . . ."

"Pardon me—who, exactly, are they? Who are all the others who stay here? The family with the shadow, Pokimica, the housekeeper, the old Madame Natalija, her companion . . ."

"Readers," the professor answered. "And what else would they be? Probably the last owners of a copy of this rare book. Natalija

Dimitrijević, unmarried, Palmotić 9, the street behind the parliament building . . ."

The telephone rang.

". . . Jelena's surname I don't know; all I know is that she's preparing to leave here forever. She's staying temporarily with Mrs., that is, with Miss Dimitrijević, where she works as her, as you said, as her companion . . ."

The telephone rang!

". . . The housekeeper Zlatana has been here a long time now. She was declared missing more than fifty years ago . . ."

The telephone rang!!

"Sreten Pokimica, former employee of the National Security Service, pensioned off early, works here and lives at People's Front 11. The ones who engaged your services . . ."

The telephone rang!!!

51

"Adam, my son, I was just about to give up. How are you?"

"I'm all right, Mother."

"Then why is your voice so hoarse? Do you have a cold? Don't try to lie to me! It rains in Belgrade, too, you know. I can just imagine how you got all wet. How many times do I have to tell you? You see how the weather is, you're not a child. You go bareheaded—dress more warmly, and dry your jacket well . . ."

"Mother, I've only got myself only an ordinary cold . . ."

"I knew it! Do you have chamomile, thyme, and sage tea? To drink the best proportion, always take a three-fingers' pinch of it! Do you have enough handkerchiefs?"

"I have enough, Mother."

"Don't neglect a cold. Are you coughing? Come, breathe deeply so I can hear if something's gone down to your lungs. Do you know how long you've been ill? I have a jar of young walnuts in honey left . . ."

"But, Mother . . ."

"Not a word! I didn't call to quarrel with you. Do you hear what I'm saying? Unbutton your shirt or whatever else you're in. Lift your T-shirt—you probably wear that one all the time—and place the lower end of the receiver on your chest and breathe deeply . . . L-i-k-e t-h-a-t . . . Now stop . . . Breathe again . . ."

"Mother . . ."

"Don't talk, you're disturbing me . . . How bad this connection is . . . Is that your telephone clicking like that, or mine? . . . Move the receiver to the right . . . Breathe deeply . . . I don't hear a thing . . . Thank God—it's clear!"

"I told you, I'm fine."

"And your father asks, do you need any money?"

"No."

"Are you sure? After the holidays there'll probably be a paycheck, and we'll be able to spare a little . . ."

"No, I really don't need it."

"Fine. And why don't you come for a while on the Day of the Republic? Aunt Roska is always asking about you; this morning she told me that she dreamed you were going through some forest, toward a pretty yellow house; she wanted to follow you, but it started to rain. It began to pelt down on the gutters and she woke up. Come tomorrow . . ."

"No, I can't, I'm reading something for my final examination—next weekend, for certain. What are you two doing?"

"Well, each his own thing. Your father regularly follows that magazine of yours, *Our Scenic Beauty*. He congratulates you; he didn't find a single mistake. And I've been making quince preserves.

Grated more finely, the way you like it. Will you definitely come? Or should I bring a jar by bus . . ."

"I'll come for certain, that Saturday."

"All right, my son, we'll wait for you and we send regards. And don't shame me around Belgrade; always take a clean handkerchief with you. And remember, take a three-finger pinch of tea and pour the water. Don't sweeten it by mistake; sugar weakens its medicinal properties. Take care . . ."

"Don't worry . . . See you soon . . . And take care of yourselves as well . . ."

52

However improbable the professor's words had seemed, Adam immediately had to confirm them. He put on his Vietnam field jacket and went out, as always slowing down opposite the tavern Our Sea. He could see the waiter, in a smock whose sleeves were too short, carrying around cups of coffee and glasses of vermouth. One of these days I'm going to go in there, he decided. To hear what they are saying when they open their mouths like fish. And then he started uphill, intent on looking for house number 9 on Palmotić Street.

But at the intersection of Balkanska and People's Front Street, Adam changed his mind. Pokimica lived in the area and Adam decided to first find out whether he really lived where Tiosavljević had told him. Yes, on the mailbox in the entranceway was the familiar surname. He had no intention of climbing up to his door, not knowing what kind of excuse he could contrive for his visit. And the young man would have continued on his way, had there not emerged from an apartment on the ground floor the building superintendent, a woman with a penetrating gaze, her hair undone and thinning, who without asking him a question spewed out a whole torrent of facts—where each of the tenants lived, when they returned, how they greeted her, how much water they used, whether they were fond of drink, what kind of habits they had . . .

"Sreten Pokimica is during the week supposedly away at work. He has no family. He comes only on Sundays, relaxes. But, if you ask me, he's here every other day. I hear him rustling, pacing about the room, sometimes I see him peeping from behind the curtain . . . And maybe his conscience won't allow him to appear. You know that at one time he . . ." Adam singled out from everything she had said.

Having reached Terazije, he took a little rest. He was still dizzy from the weakness; it was as if the entire central square of the capital was tipping this way and that, depending on how many passersby and vehicles there were, while the buildings—the Albanija, the Hotel Moskva, or the Iguman's Palace—seemed like weights that someone had for decades, without success, been adding on to achieve a balance.

How is it possible to weigh so many fates, he wondered. Then the answer came to him: It can happen only if it's a matter of thousands of different forms of one and the same destiny. And disquieted by this insight, nearly running, he descended from Terazije and set out in the direction of the parliament; and then cutting through the park entered quiet Palmotić Street.

Five. Seven. Nine. A façade with numerous drainpipes. The lobby laid in marble and the ringing echoes of stilletos, crisscrossed here and there with finely veined cracks and the scuffmarks of silence from newer footwear with rubber soles. The stylishly plaited lacework of the stucco, disfigured by the carelessly concealed scars of renovation and the subsequent installation of new wiring. The elevator with a sign: Out of Order. One had to go on foot.

He knocked for a long time right below the brass plate with

the shallowly engraved name Natalija Dimitrijević. Finally, footsteps approached, someone raised the cover on the peephole, a key turned, the door was opened as far as the security chain allowed, and in the gap he saw Jelena's face.

"I was passing by, and so I dropped in . . . How is the old woman, how are you? . . ." Adam said.

"And how did you know where we live?" the girl asked mistrustfully.

"Professor Tiosavljević told me. Forgive me if I'm disturbing you, but I was free . . ." The reserve in her voice had flustered the young man; there was no doubt that she had recognized him, but she acted as if somehow frightened by his turning up.

"Professor?" repeated Jelena, looking him straight in the eyes. "The professor is no longer alive . . ."

"Not alive? You're joking; not more than two hours ago we were reading together in the pavilion. He was showing me his finds . . ." Adam smiled uncertainly, gooseflesh creeping up his back, a spreading shudder of fear.

"Professor Tiosavljević did not die a natural death; he was murdered. Natalija Dimitrijević is very upset. She is unable to receive you . . ." said the girl, wanting to withdraw.

"Murdered?! For God's sake, who could do something like that?" Out of astonishment Adam Lozanić was unable to find any more fitting words.

"Murdered. And now if you'll excuse me, we returned for a hat with a black veil. The professor was Madame's pupil and she . . ." The closed door squelched the rest.

Having exited the building, walking several paces uphill, the young man turned around, he himself not knowing why. Coming from the opposite direction, along Palmotić Street, his landlord, half hidden by a large umbrella, went into the entranceway of Madame Dimitrijević's building. There was nothing to confirm it, except perhaps for those ugly traces of the installation of new wiring, but the young man could have sworn that Mojsilović was expanding his business to include the old woman's home as well.

53

The rest of the day passed like a nightmare. Immediately upon his return Adam seized the book bound in saffian, heading straight for the pavilion. He found the glass-walled structure empty, filled only with a stuffy loneliness and the smell of pipe tobacco with the aroma of vanilla. Nowhere were all those curious objects, tokens of the professor's studious residence of many years; the bed was made, nowhere were the boxes and boxes of finds, the stacks of written notes, the surveyor's rods, the mended butterfly net, the small brooms and spatula, the porphyry fragments of the bust of a woman; nowhere were the map of the domain, the map scale, and the magnifying glass; the large table of rough-hewn planks was bare; the sole testimony that something had taken place here were three or four dried darkened drops of blood.

Frightened, he threw down the book. With a trembling hand, barely guessing the main telephone number of the National Library, he called Kusmuk and requested him, as soon as possible, however he could manage it, and once more, however he could manage it, to find Tiosavljević, that's right, Tio-sav-lje-vić; the first name he couldn't remember, although he was sure he had heard it somewhere, or, better said, read it somewhere.

"Hold on, whoa, why such panic?! A university professor? What does he teach?" asked Kusmuk.

"I don't know."

"And in which department?"

"I don't know."

"Where did he publish his works?"

"No, I don't know that either."

"All right, Adam my boy, what *do* you know? What's all this mystery about? Certainly you're involved in something big. Can I help you in some other way, without my having to sort through the catalogues or get myself all dusty in the storeroom?"

"Please just find him. It's a matter of life and death. Do you hear me? As soon as possible, I need his address, telephone number, or where he works, anything at all, but as soon as possible . . ." Thus he ended the conversation, went to the window, stood, and waited.

Time passed terribly slowly. His neighbor, the souvenir vendor, was banging the whole time with metronomic precision. People went into the tavern Our Sea. Now he remembered the thick glass displays, those fish tanks at the Bajlonijeva Marketplace, where the caught carp or trout, cruelly crowded together, thrashed about sadly for a swallow of air, unaware that their fateful hour was near. The little boy and girl from the other apartment were quarreling. The children's clamor was punctuated by the shouting of their parents. The telephone had hardly rung once.

Kusmuk submitted his report, conscientiously listing the bibliographic data, books, and published articles for three different professors. "Adam boy, I found three Professor Tiosavljevićs. Božidar, Vladimir, and Dobrivoj. The first is a corresponding member of the academy, a lecturer in the Agriculture Department who specializes in hybrid varieties of grain . . . The second is a doctor of electrical engineering who left three years ago for some American institute and is not coming back . . . The third is in the School of Philosophy, in the history program; his narrower field of specialization is archaeography, although he also writes stories; in the next to last issue of *Literature*, there's one printed under the title 'New Leipzig'; I can tell you, it's imaginative prose, an idea worthy of a novel . . ."

GORAN PETROVIĆ

"Forget about the first two—what about the archaeographer?" Adam interrupted him.

"Well, nothing, except for one minor detail. When I called the School of Philosophy to get his address or home number, the secretary told me that Dobrivoj Tiosavljević, today, in the morning, died in his office. Of a stroke, or something similar . . ."

Adam Lozanić, degree candidate in the Serbian language and literature program, part-time associate with the magazine *Our Scenic Beauty*, and reader of the mysterious book by Anastas C. Branica, hadn't yet properly hung up the receiver and was already reaching for his Vietnam field jacket. In an instant he descended the flight of stairs and was climbing Balkanska Street not a whit more slowly. Probably because of the rain, the usual swarms of people on the Square of the Republic were not present. The dirty-yellow city lighting was illuminated as if to no avail; the figure on horseback in front of the National Museum stood suspended in half-motion; to the young man it seemed the prince would gladly pull back on the reins with his left hand and ride off the pedestal, if he only had somewhere to go. When the sculptor Enrico Pazzi cast it at the end of the last century, the right hand of Mihailo Obrenović pointed fixedly to the southwest, symbolically indicating the still-unliberated cities of Serbia. But where now? Where to? Everywhere? Suddenly that monument to victory and rewon glory, fringed with graceful lettering, no doubt among the more beautiful in Belgrade, seemed to him like sadness recast in bronze. And that echoing thought occupied him all the way to the School of Philosophy building.

In the corridors he found only the occasional student. He climbed up to the floor the History Department was on, and among those catacombs of narrow passageways looked for the professor's office. It was unlocked. Inside was a cleaning woman, her hands faded from washing, in a blue smock. Picking up the compass on the leather cord, the map scale, and the magnifying glass, he immediately observed that she was removing dried drops of blood from the top of the work desk.

"Are you looking for someone?" she asked.

"Professor Tiosavljević. I am supposed to do my senior thesis with him," Adam lied, looking around to see if he recognized any other objects from the pavilion.

"Son, the professor died today. He was gushing blood at the nose. In brief, he just fell and slumped over this here desk . . . That upset me very much; he was a dear man. He knew how to joke: 'Sofija, do you know that you're worth exactly half as much of all philosophy!'" said the cleaning woman. "And about your thesis, come back tomorrow, in the morning, and see the secretary . . ."

The woman turned her back and continued to expunge the traces of death: the cloth left a damp trail on the worn-out lacquer. Then he noticed, on a rather low shelf, a folder with the heading "Anastas Branica's Adjectives." He opened it. It was empty.

"And what's that you're searching through?" the cleaning woman caught him unawares. "For God's sake, put that down. It's a sin—they just drove the poor man away in that black car; some of them crowded in here, they went through his papers, carried out books. Where is the respect in that, where is the decency . . ."

"They carried out papers and books?" repeated Adam.

"All I know is that some man came and took at least one of them. He examined every scrap of paper, opened every binding, which are all the same to me," the woman said, putting her hands on her hips. "And the professor himself told me: 'Dear Sofija, no matter how different they may appear, books meet far away on the horizon line. When you read one truly carefully, with complete understanding, it's as if you've read many neighboring ones.' I memorized that. It pleased me. Go now, and come back tomorrow about your thesis . . ."

Although he had gone by the same streets hundreds of times,

on his way back it seemed to Adam that he was lost. He walked for quite a while, getting wet, feeling the gathering darkness saturate the lining of his jacket as well. And who knows where he would have gone to, he was convinced, had he not by pure chance turned up on his own street, finding himself in front of the window display of the tavern Our Sea.

"We're closing!" the waiter said to him ungraciously when he opened the door to the barroom. At the tables sat only a few patrons; the man behind the bar, using some kind of tally board, a thin wooden strip with notched lines, was measuring the levels of the liquids in bottles lined up along the counter.

"Just a cup of tea," Adam implored; in the apartment there was surely no water. The stretched out nets on the walls stirred not the slightest, as if he had said nothing, as if he hadn't come in, as if he weren't even there, in the glass aquarium, still full of tobacco smoke.

"Are you deaf, buddy?! Closing time!" the waiter answered gruffly, and then went back to counting his notches, copying into a worn-out business ledger the balance of the daily receipts with a ballpoint pen: four across, one down, four across, one down . . .

Squeezing with difficulty between the diagonally parked cars, crossing to the other side of Milovan Milovanović Street, climbing up to his studio apartment, Adam heard his neighbor's hammering-on of slats to frames more and more clearly. On the first landing he passed by a man with an upturned collar, and only when this man had passed did he become aware who it might have been.

"Pokimica! Sreten! Stop!" he shouted after him.

The man turned, and then quickened his pace down the stairs.

SEVENTH READING

WHERE A LITTLE SOMETHING IS LEARNED
ABOUT THE MEANING OF A CONCEPTION
AND A FESTIVE DINNER AFTER TWO DECADES
AND NINE MONTHS; ABOUT A STATE OF STUPOR
AND ENTRAILS FALLING OUT OF A THOUSAND HOMES;
ABOUT A MISUNDERSTANDING WITH AN ADVANCE
GUARD OF THE THIRD REICH;
ABOUT "BREATHING" OVER THE SPEAKER OF A RADIO;
ABOUT A GENTLEMANLY TURNING OF PAGES;
ABOUT STUDYING THE RUSSIAN LANGUAGE;
ABOUT A BULLET THAT MARKED
THE BEGINNING OF A SUCCESSFUL CAREER
AND STILL ONE MORE FUTILE LOVE;
ABOUT THE IMPOSSIBILITY OF THE SECRETARY
OF ROSE AND LEMON WOOD
BEING CARRIED OUT OF THE NOVEL;
ABOUT ANOTHER BOOK,
WHICH WAS ACTUALLY A TRAP;
AND ABOUT WITHDRAWING FROM REALITY

54

IN ACCORDANCE WITH FATHER'S BOASTFUL account—despite the fact that Mother, blushing, warned that common decency dictated one not speak of it—I record that I was conceived exactly on the twenty-eighth of June 1919, in honor of the signing of the celebrated Treaty of Versailles and the final collapse of the Central Powers.

"Bull's-eye! That will be our little contribution to the creation of world peace . . ." Father happily recalled saying back then, after the act, as he contentedly loafed in the conjugal bed, enthusiastically forging plans for his heir.

"You again with that?! How many times do I have to repeat it? One shouldn't talk about things like that . . ." my abashed mother interrupted him.

I note down that in March 1940, some two decades and nine months later, when I had reached my twentieth year, my family gathered for the last time. Not one of the four headstrong brothers, neither my father nor my uncles, particularly understood politics, nor did they practice governmental or public professions, but that—and still less the festive occasion of their communal table—did not keep them from bitterly quarreling in the middle of dinner. Each of them, as happens with our people, had his own opinion; the present was mainly of use to them to bicker over their views of past—and especially future—times.

"Happy birthday, Sreten! And consider well whom you'll vote for next year, when you get the right to do so!" went one sort of toast at the table, which was at the same time an utterance about which they were all in accord. This, however, only for each, immediately thereafter, to stand and present "his own view" and then find fault with "the opposing side."

"You should know that our friends the French, at the end of the twenties, granted credit to King Aleksandar upon, among other things, the extravagant condition that a monument of gratitude be built to them in as prominent a place in Belgrade as possible," caustically began the youngest uncle, who had recently secured a position as an itinerant agent with the Serbia Insurance Company. He was making use of the family gathering to present his fiancée to us; the freckled girl to his right, marveling at her betrothed, kept on blinking while a mouthful of food caught in everyone else's throat.

"That's simply treachery! German propaganda . . . Did that pro-fascist Dragiša Cvetković teach you that? Only a bad egg like him could dream up such a loathsome thing! Don't corrupt my child—and you, go right ahead, feel free to conduct a campaign for his government again . . . He'll bring all of you, one by one, to Berlin as a gift to Hitler! To be for the Germans today, after everything, is truly an affront! I'll remind you once more of the state of world affairs that preceded Sreten's conception . . ." said Father, who dapperly upturned his mustache and was a confirmed Francophile, and the proprietor of a small firm that manufactured natural dyes for textiles in Makiš, where I, too, helped out by keeping the books.

"Why, pray tell, do you address us in the plural?! You're generalizing. Let the boy get his atlas, let him find the old and new English seas and shores. Whoever has a brain in his head knows that even the most distant stream sooner or later inclines toward the open sea. If only we had relied more on the British. To them and them alone would I be prepared to entrust our fate," calmly stated another uncle, continuing to take interest in the movement of the chopped parsley in his soup. He was a confirmed bachelor and a senior supervisor of travel routes for the National River Traffic

Bureau who had been pensioned off early because of asthma, but perhaps also because of his Anglomania.

"Eh, if the good czar, our dear brother Nikolai, were alive, if our dear Mother Russia were resurrected, everything would be different, isn't that so, my dear?" said Father's third brother in a singing voice, every so often turning to his wife. The childless emigrant Afrosya Stepanenko sadly nodded her head; by Uncle's tearful eyes one could see that the fiery Pan-Slavist, who had proclaimed as his life's calling "his love for the beautiful Auntie Frosya," had in a fit of inconsolable sorrow drunk too much.

"Drop all that now. Go ahead, help yourselves to a little more; for whom did I prepare so much, it will go bad . . ." Mother urged and calmed them, suspecting where it might all end up.

But it was too late. And perhaps it had been so long before that dinner. A quarrel ensued. Soon it became more and more difficult to follow what anyone was saying to anyone else. The soup got cold, the finer glassware quite trembled from the serious words, and it seemed that the room would burst from so many raised voices, except that the third uncle repeated ever more softly the same old thing about Czar Nikolai. And when all the guests had left, each angry at the next, each offended, all four of them vowing to the other never again to set foot in his house, there reigned an unreal silence. Father propped his head on his elbows and sighed painfully:

"Did you hear, I ask you . . . How treacherously, straight in my heart, they went on about the French . . . If that's what they want, then let them go . . . I really had to keep myself from throwing them all out, from spoiling the celebration for the child . . . As far as I'm concerned, they can just forget about any kind of reconciliation . . ."

"And as far as I'm concerned, all of you Pokimicas, each and every one of you, are numbskulls . . ." Mother replied bitterly, clearing the table. "If by some chance there were five of you, the fifth would let his own blood just in order to prove to us how we need the

Etruscans, or some other extinct people, and how they no less need us . . . Look at how much food I'm throwing away; this does not bode well at all . . ."

"It turns out that it's best to be an internationalist. Actually, in some special, limited way, our family is already just that . . ." I added wisely.

"Internationalists?! Bolsheviks?! Communists?! What do you know, you sniveling brat?! You had better get out of my sight, before I report you to the first policeman I see! You got that idea by loafing around in the factory bookkeeping office, but tomorrow you're going to the drying kiln to sift soot for the black dye . . ." Father got up threateningly, but then immediately sat down tiredly once more.

Thus ended the last gathering of my family. And thus did I—for the first time, I carefully note down, in March 1940, a full year before obtaining the right to vote—let pass my lips the word around which, day by day, gradually, I would stack the dried twigs of my entire life.

55

And truly, the headstrong brothers did not go back on their word: from that time forward, no one ever stepped across the threshold of another's home.

In order to avoid the destruction of Paris, on the fourteenth of June 1940 the capital of France was understandably surrendered without a fight, and my father, overwhelmed by disappointment, likewise surrendered to illness, identified by Dr. Isidor Arsenov as manic-depressive psychosis, only thereupon to fall into a state of dull-witted stupor, a state in which the person reacts neither to external nor internal stimuli even though his consciousness is to some mysterious degree preserved. In such a form did the illness manifest itself for twenty-odd years. Until the day of his death, Father not only did not speak, but also did not perform the slightest action on his own. Mother cared devotedly for him, constantly having to lend him her own will, rouse his desire to live, initiate each of his movements, pull first his right, then his left leg through the apartment; relocate him, depending on the position of the sun, from a shady room to a sunny one; wrap his fingers round the eating utensil and then gently push the spoon to his mouth; straighten him into a lying position on the bed, in the evening, from a sitting one; close his eyelids, and in the morning open them again . . . She could have left him an entire month with his arms senselessly raised, for he felt no need to lower them. She could have left him standing in mid-step, on one leg only, for he felt no purpose in continuing on anywhere. She had just brought him thus into the hallway of the apartment, when at 6:50 in the morning, on April 6, 1941, the first bombs of the German Fourth Air Force fell on Belgrade: half our building, along with the entire living room, was simply destroyed. Mother lost consciousness, and when she came to, she found Father in that same unchanged position, staring at the gaping hole, a mere step away from the open breach of his whole life story. From all around came screams; the stumps of roof beams, the remains of demolished façades protruded outward, and through the broken flanks of walls tumbled the entrails of a thousand homes. As if nothing had happened, nor did he bat an eye when on the edge of town, from the direction of Makiš, there came a distinctive gray smoke. Although the small firm that manufactured natural dyes for textiles produced every possible shade of color, it was burning only in dark tones now.

As a reserve infantry lieutenant unwillingly mobilized in March 1941, in the first draft of the army of the Kingdom of Yugoslavia— he had just married that freckled chosen one of his heart, without having invited a single one of his relations to the wedding—the youngest uncle was taken prisoner during the April collapse. It was of no avail that somewhere near Sombor he had surrendered to a lost advance guard of a German armored unit; it was of no avail that he had run out onto the crossroads of two rural districts to greet the members of the Third Reich: a motorcyclist with an escutcheon on his chest and a dust-covered artillery scout in the sidecar, a sergeant gone batty from the local signposts and roads; it was of no avail that, meaning well, he had shouted out: "*Zurück*! You've made a mistake: to get to Sombor you should have turned sooner!" They almost shot him as a provocateur on that very crossroads. And considering the three years of slow dying in camps from the contempt of the other prisoners, in the end only to die of typhus in Osnabrück, only four hundred kilometers from Berlin, he would perhaps have been better off had they summarily executed him. Scrimping and saving during the whole war, Mother secretly sent my uncle packets of food and words of comfort, managing "like a real family" to compose nonexistent greetings from the remaining three brothers. He could never find the strength, if only in a censored postcard, to admit to her how remorseful he was, and perhaps he even hoped that the day would come when in Berlin, at the headquarters of the Reichswehr itself, he would personally set right his fateful error. The freckled young woman did not even look back at her husband, instead fleeing with some black marketeer only to return at liberation, and shamelessly demanding and receiving a pension on the basis of her brief marriage to the victim fallen in defense of his homeland.

And during all those years of occupation that asthmatic uncle, that passionate Anglophile, was visited only by myself. The bachelor, having quarreled with his closest relatives, never left his studio apartment on Englishman Street, nor did anyone come to him, until my mother would remind me that, for the sake of appearances at least, I ought to visit him, regardless of the row with Father. He had grown accustomed to requiring very little, surviving on a pension and savings that he had accumulated the whole of his solitary life, ever restrained as a Victorian. Rare is the person who recalls having elicited even a smile from that lonely man. I confess that I did not like those outings, and by all appearances neither did he; he never asked me anything, nor did he utter a word; we usually sat in silence for an hour or two, eyeing each other mistrustfully. The only sound present was his labored breathing, as if he were miserly even with the very air. I remember that he had once calmed his asthma attacks by opening a book—to be sure, a book inevitably by some English writer—and thrusting his face into it, but seeming not to read it and instead only inhaling there. Or perhaps that's how he had in fact contracted his asthma.

All the same, from the beginning of the war onward, when having an attack of suffocation, he applied a quite different "therapy": he would plug in the radio, scarcely waiting for the tubes to glow, and then turn the knobs on the dial, culling from the ether the purest possible waves of Radio London, or broadcasts in Serbian, and then he would incline his head, putting his mouth to the mesh-like speaker, until his chest was soothed, and a healthy color would again well up on his cheeks. Only once, after having listened to the news about the progress of the Allies, about encouraging reports from the government-in-exile, and about the pronouncements of the young King Peter, could there be seen in the corners of Uncle's mouth the hint of a smile. Later, undoubtedly gladdened by the development of "our cause," he would occasionally do something entirely out of keeping with his frugal nature: he would offer me Shonda's Best Cherry Liqueur from his own private, prewar stocks. He would also pour some for himself, although he wouldn't take even a tiny sip of it, but would instead ask me to smuggle the opened bottle onto the pontoon bridge on the Danube, so generously bestowed upon Belgraders by the occupying General von Weiss, and then to lower it—"Remember, that's important"—right into the middle of the river's main current. As a former senior supervisor of travel routes for the former National River Traffic Bureau of the Kingdom of Yugoslavia, he was convinced that every droplet of water, sooner or later, made its way to English waters, and so someone along the British coast would sooner or later be treated to the liqueur that had floated there. It would never have occurred to me to behave so wastefully; I regularly brought the refreshing liquid to his brother, the spouse of Afrosya Stepanenko, who, although he didn't care for sweet drink, accepted my gift in order to soothe the suffering in his soul. In the general confusion, during the incomprehensible Anglo-American bombing of Belgrade in 1944, I neglected my regular visit to Uncle. When I finally went, prepared to say nothing of how the Allies, in the first sortie alone, had killed at least six times as many of our fellow citizens as had German soldiers, and scores more of the long-suffering internees at the camp in Sajmište, and that the casualties of the subsequent waves of attacks had not even been counted, I found him fallen prone beneath the radio. He had been dead for several days already. One of the little tubes in the gadget must have burned out; the speaker crackled with static, as if the whole world were irretrievably evaporating. Not a word of what was being said, from somewhere far away, could be understood.

Quite on the other hand, I went to visit the pathetic spouse of the sad Afrosya Stepanenko, Father's brother the fiery Pan-Slavist, even more often than Mother demanded. Indeed, since the time nearly a quarter of a century before that he had proclaimed his love for the Russian emigrant as his life's calling, my uncle did nothing else but love that woman, "pretty as a picture," and no less so when it became clear that they would have no progeny. On what in truth they lived, only the good Lord knew. Apart from loving each other, they had nothing else to do. He had held a clerk's position in a large flour mill, in a rice husking concern, and in the woven goods factory Moravija—but each only for one "unbearable" day.

And she not even that much. It was rumored that they survived by having her recount, to some Jew, the antique dealer Konforti, in very beautiful fashion, carat by carat, how the czar's collection of the jeweler Fabergé's Easter eggs appeared, a collection that she as a girl had seen in St. Petersburg. They spent years together without parting, and even read each book together, side by side, lying in their marital bed with a canopy woven in the colors of pale night, Afrosya holding the binding, and Uncle gentlemanly turning the pages if she got tired, and vice versa. Finally, so closely did they grow together, identify with one another, that they would always, to the exact word, say: "Eh, if the good czar, our dear brother Nikolai, were alive, if our dear Mother Russia were resurrected . . ." And even though everyone in the family considered it downright irresponsible to spend the days of one's life that way, Auntie Frosya and her husband couldn't care less. The periods of poverty, they spent over weak, sugarless tea, splitting in half and dipping stale lamentations from the year before. If, who knows how, they came into money, they would indulge each other unrestrainedly, go to the opera and concerts, go to "circle" parties, balls, and outings, to fashionable spots, for aspic of goose liver, crab mayonnaise, *filet de boeuf*, pâté with truffles, and *Sachertorte*, all of that in the dreadfully expensive Hotel Bristol. Nor were they unfamiliar with carousing in cafés where it smelled of stew, boiled eggs, weak brandy, and linseed oil, filled with journalists, fortune-tellers, poets, somnambulists, actors, and other dubious clientele. Moreover, he was adept at finding and even bringing home Gypsies who sang Russian songs one after another; and from Botorić's store he would lug cases of imported wine, fill the largest silver bowl in the house with sparkling roe of beluga or sturgeon, and then invite whomever he met on the street as well, all in order to soothe a bit the sadness of the expatriate woman. And she, Afrosya Stepanenko, knew how to look at him and look at him, until Uncle would quite swoon from pleasure, prepared to demonstrate his love by various pompous acts of folly—challenging, to a duel to the death, anyone who refused to quietly stand in honor of the vanished Empire; draining to the last drop a half dozen bottles of champagne to his wife's health; or sitting on the window ledge, at dawn, as in some kind of expansive Russian novel, baring his soul and proclaiming his boundless feelings to the drowsy Voždovac district . . .

Truth be told, I didn't visit them on account of all that. After all, the antique dealer Konforti had back in 1941 ended up in a camp, and no one was interested in a mere story, no one had any need for memories of the expensive Easter eggs of the jeweler Fabergé; in their impoverished home, still-weaker tea and ever more stale, worn-out lamentations prevailed, while the silver caviar bowl was exchanged by its owner for only three small skins of sour wine . . . No, I went to them because they both flawlessly knew the language that was indispensable to me. My aunt knew it as her native tongue, and my uncle had learned it "to speak to his love." Had they only suspected why I'd so suddenly become interested in Russian, both would have of course refused to give me instruction. But I kept my intentions strictly to myself, secret, unassumingly agreeing with their reactionary views on the Bolshevik plague, and meanwhile, within myself, perfecting the language of the coming world revolution, the language absolutely essential in order for me to read the pamphlets I was receiving from my contemporaries; I was already deeply enmeshed in illegal activity. And perhaps had I only known in what a terrible manner I would repay their efforts and their kindness, I would never have become involved in something similar to begin with.

In this way, during the entire war, on Mondays, Wednesdays, and Fridays, I went devotedly to Voždovac, going over my Russian lessons with Afrosya Stepanenko (if Uncle was suffering from a hangover, or heartburn, from drinking wine), or conversely, acquiring knowledge with Uncle (if Auntie Frosya was sad, or had a headache from the chronic nostalgia). In this way, during the entire war, on Tuesdays, Thursdays, and Saturdays, I still more devotedly went always to a different address, consolidating my revolutionary views in various circles and meetings, preparing myself for the final victory of internationalism over the rest of the world. Once a week, on Sundays, I would help Mother with repairs in the cleft house, and with Father, who was sunk deep in a state of stupor. She required at least a day of rest to gather her own will; her own will, which had been prescribed to the patient by Dr. Arsenov "in as large a dose as possible, until the recovery of his paralyzed spirit."

56

For a long time I was unable to free myself from this period of my family's political misapprehensions. Because of them there was always a certain aversion, a certain suspicion toward me: not rarely would my comrades remain after the meeting to review my "bourgeois" case and the sincerity of my convictions, and even the questionable meaning of my conception—it had leaked out—on the very day the Versailles peace treaty had been concluded. I knew that they were watching me, appraising and weighing my every word or action, hesitating to take me with them on acts of sabotage and assassination attempts, or even when they distributed leaflets or collected aid for the combatants. When all was said and done, I acquired an advantage only through my exemplary knowledge of Russian; what the others followed in translation, I read without an intermediary, in the original, often explaining to the presidents of the districts the substance of the illegal material that had, who knows through what channels, arrived from the Soviet Ministry of Propaganda. Perhaps this ever present distrust and my special talent for interpreting the sources of communism were the fundamental reasons why I later chose precisely the field of state security. Although I would not exclude as a motive the constant need to prove myself, and also to gradually exact revenge for the humiliating surveillance to which I had been subjected during the war.

As it turned out, everything changed when at the end of 1943 there came into my hands the three-volume book *History, Theory, and Practice of the Reception of the Literary Work, with More General Directives in Conformity with the Decrees of the XV Congress of the SCP (b)*, S. V. Nikitin, B. Rosenstein, and M. M. Mukhin, authors, printed in Moscow in 1937. Naturally, it appears that this rather long title came into my possession by a twist of fate, or merely owing to the ignorance of the courier responsible for distributing litera-ture to the party cells, but at the time I was convinced that at stake was nothing less than what we mean under the vague notion of jus-tice. For the aforementioned tomes had been printed in a controlled, numbered lot, for limited use, only for the purpose of training the cadre of the most secret of all sections of the NKVD, and so not even selected students of the course had the right to study them on their own. Rather, this was done in threes, with the compulsory presence of a political commissar or superior officer who was always apprised of the activities of his two younger subordinates. Why this was so could be easily deduced from a cursory glance at the table of con-tents: the three-volume book had assembled all knowledge in con-nection with the so-called method of "total reading." It dealt with the evolution of this process; it gathered previous epochs' experi-ences with it, from the rise of literacy up to present times; it expli-cated the methods of perfecting the ability to penetrate a text further, to details that had not been cited although they doubtlessly stood among the pages of the literary space in question; and it analyzed the ability of two or more readers to meet in a reading selection, and then the methods for recognizing them in ordinary life, from a vague presentiment of them to the quite definite establishment of their identities; it illuminated the modus operandi of all the more major secret services in this domain, with case studies of successful operations; and, finally, it elucidated the benefits which a new society might derive from class-conscious individuals. I hadn't yet quite devoted myself to all this, and I could already see the tip of the iceberg, the power I would have at my disposal. One of the most intimate, most private, most personal of human activities was for me, from that time forward, open, plain as day.

Thus did my life acquire an added dimension. I wouldn't say a parallel one, for very quickly this new dimension outgrew the original one severalfold. Simultaneous with the drill, as I called the careful study of *History, Theory, and Practice of the Reception*, I rid myself of all the other titles in the family library, so as not to fall into the temptation to read out of that idle and no doubt superfluous, decadent habit. To Mother's question where I was going with the books that we had collected for all those years, I replied that I would exchange them for ration cards, and when I brought home a small sack of cornmeal, a half dozen *Milikerze* candles, and a pair of *drvenjaci*, shoes with fir-wood soles, she looked at me painfully—before the onset of Father's illness, she had loved to relax with novels.

"So little for all that?!" she said.

But I paid no mind. I had decided to break with the past, decided to make a future for myself. And I progressed—more rapidly than I had expected. Conscious of the other readers, I very quickly got rid of all those who doubted my revolutionary views, at the same time skillfully avoiding Gestapo raids and quisling break-ins. The special police of the infamous Dragi Jovanović employed traditional, decidedly more primitive methods: beating the prisoner on the soles of the feet until he confessed to things which he had never even imagined. Trained in and having a gift for spying, I now knew perfectly well where my comrades were, from the president of the committee to an ordinary courier; knew when they were supposedly reading attentively, but were in fact dozing off; what they hadn't understood, what they had skipped, where they had expressed disbelief to themselves . . . At the very next meeting I would reveal their weaknesses and their deviations: they would look at me in astonishment, stammer, grow red in the face, and lower their heads. I got rid of them one by one; the uncompromising comrade Sreten Pokimica was already becoming the talk of the Party, and they regarded me with ever greater esteem. And fear. However, I passed the final, official test only in 1945, six or seven months after the liberation of the capital.

The battles against fascism had not yet been concluded, but before its fall the victory of communism had to be won as well. In addition to military help, the Soviets also sent us cadre support. Along with numerous political commissars of the Red Army, along with numerous experts in all the methods of acquiring and preserving the achievements of the revolution, in Belgrade there arrived specially trained activists; one of them was named Galya Gorokhov, a specialist in the field, better to say, in the domain in which I, too, self-taught, was already considerably active.

A veteran Chekist who bore on his chest three rows of medals earned in battles with SR forces, Mensheviks, and the White Guard bands of General Wrangel; ever on his guard, with a Nagan revolver stuck into his belt, its safety catch unlocked, Gorokhov was genuinely elated by my abilities. He never asked how I had managed to progress so far in spying on other readers; in accordance with anticonspiratorial principles, the members of the secret services ignored one another's activities as much as possible. Each, however, was in fact able to keep an eye on everyone else, and, if he was scrupulous, even on himself. He never asked how I knew so much; he accepted me as a fellow combatant equal to himself, praising me countless times:

"*Tovarišći*, Comrade Sreten is worth more to you than a whole shock brigade!"

That pleased me. Flattered me. But I wanted even more. Insatiably. I wanted to prove myself to Comrade Stalin's deputy; I occasionally experienced Galya in precisely that way. And then, purely as a prank, on a whim, out of a need to distinguish myself, I brought to Gorokhov's attention *Notes of a Hunter* by Ivan Sergeevich Turgenev. To be sure, even without a directive I knew that we had to be especially cautious with the monarchists, the reactionaries, and the factionalists, with the Chetniks, Ljotić's supporters, and the followers of Nedić; with the dregs of a past time. I knew that everything else was less essential, but that didn't keep me from getting on Galya's better side, surmising how much the Russian emigrant population there would interest him. Namely, *Notes of a Hunter* was one of the favorite reading selections of my Aunt Frosya and my Pan-Slavist uncle; they would often go there, meeting with other expatriates; I had already witnessed the presence of many of them, easily recognizable by their tearful eyes at the very first sentence of their mother tongue. I met them often throughout the world, in Boston, London, Baden-Baden, Paris, or in my Belgrade, opening some Russian novel, novella, or story, and then reading aloud as if chanting in church, all of them weeping, holding their hands to their hearts, soothing their nostalgia in the only remaining way possible to "tread on their native soil." And I met them earlier as well, I say, including those who had stayed in Moscow or Leningrad, ostensibly recognizing government by the people, quietly reading in the metro station, standing in line to draw their ration of bread, pint of vodka, and coupons for the half-empty Univermag; dissembling, until a sigh escaped from them—to me, a reliable sign that I knew how bitterly they longed for past and future times . . .

"But it can't be! In Turgenev?!" cried Gorokhov, delighted by my discovery while there glinted in his eyes a single-minded hatred for czarist adherents. "And I mostly lurked in emigrant literature, searched through that miserable dissident slander and the pamphlets against Bolshevism. Rabble! They managed to organize, to plot and scheme, perhaps even to corrupt our youth in Turgenev, whom—come now—we had acknowledged and included in literary history by reason of his somewhat healthier attitude toward social reality. You, Sreten, deserve a medal from the hand of Lavrentiy Pavlovich Beria himself!"

"A medal? No, no, not for me . . ." I feigned humility.

"A medal, comrade, but of course! Come on, let's have a little fun, let's get rid of them! I'll buy us each a copy of *Notes of a Hunter* in Russian, and then we'll search through them! There's no way to get rid of the lice until you've exterminated the nits!" and Galya drew his cocked Nagan.

I accepted; having come even this far was not enough for me.

May 1945 bloomed; somewhere in this world it was exactly 8 p.m., somewhere it was two hours before midnight, somewhere midnight had just struck, somewhere day was bashfully dawning, somewhere the slough of night had mostly been shed, depending of course on the differences in time, when with Gorokhov I circumvented the narratives of Ivan Turgenev, not setting up an ambush at the beginning but rather at the epilogue, "Forest and Steppe," one of the most beautiful descriptions of nature in all of literature.

"Very clever, Sreten, to be sure, to be sure . . ." said Galya, lauding my talent as we stole up just when the wild game arrived, from here, from over there; we tenderly kissed and embraced the found words; or tenderly kissed and embraced each other; or merely, already bearing full loads on our chests, seized at the air of the elegiac landscapes in the closing pages of *Notes of a Hunter*.

Yes, here were gathered the shreds of a lost epoch . . . some noblewoman, dressed in pitch-black, her lips finely chiseled from employing elegant French phrases . . . a former czarist colonel, stooped over by his heavy military overcoat, stiff from long sitting at European gaming tables . . . some would-be gentleman, engineer, or musician, his fingers irretrievably grown thin, chilled through from hopelessness in his refugee's hovel, a subterranean little room . . . a gaunt, pious man who only crossed himself and bowed in prayer . . . even a whining foundling, from a generation that had come of age in exile . . .

"Let's wait a bit, let's wait a bit, until the little birds have gathered . . ." Galya whispered, though I doubt these people would have heard him over their own sounding out of the words.

"'An oak tree greedily spread its paw-like branchlets above the water; large silver bubbles, mimicking one another, rose from the bottom, covered with fine, velvety moss . . .'" the people read unquenchably.

"'The moist earth subsides beneath one's feet; the tall, dry blades of grass are motionless, the long strands glisten on the sunbleached grass . . .'" they repeated tremblingly, perhaps even to learn it by heart.

"'Breathe in the cold, brisk air, and blink spontaneously from the dazzling tiny flashes of the soft snow . . .'" they shouted out for joy; someone disrobed down to his *rubashka* and then completely opened it as well, down to the bare breast.

Thus did we wait in the mist a while longer. And then one by one the old Chekist Galya Gorokhov, alone—I myself really couldn't manage it—one after the other, very quickly, Galya put his hand over each of their mouths, tightly, so that they couldn't breathe. Some would squirm, some would moan, some would smile enigmatically, probably because they were dying in the embrace of Mother Russia; some merely slid back to whence they had come, so that the following day they would be found in Boston, London, Baden-Baden, Paris, or Belgrade slumped over on a park bench, in bed, or in an armchair, disunited from their dear souls with the book by Ivan Turgenev fallen in their laps or at their feet.

I admit, it wasn't pleasant for me. Galya did the liquidating, but it was I who did the denouncing. "And what were they searching for behind the revolution's back, anyway!" I said to myself, inventing reasons to ease my conscience. When I nearly stumbled over someone, an already fading body, I immediately recognized my exceedingly beautiful aunt, Afrosya Stepanenko, in a lace nightgown, smothered as well; fate would have it that she, too, that blooming May in 1945, would be holding that same book. *What have I done?!* I was probably thinking, when I scented that well-known odor of sour wine. The sole survivor in that place of execution staggered toward me in pain:

"Sreten, how did you get here?" cried my uncle, who as always had been reading right beside his wife.

"Unhappy man, what have you done?!" he wrung his hands over his beloved.

"How could you?! Why?!" he beat his breast in despair.

"Help me, holy martyrs Boris and Gleb, don't let my Frosya die, my life . . ." he begged, showering kisses on my dear aunt's blue lips and cold brow.

Who knows how long I would have stood there dumbfounded, listening to his cries, wailing, and curses, who knows whether I would have kept myself from telling him how sorry I was, how I hadn't wished for that, how I hadn't intended it, had Galya Gorokhov not reacted, not brandished his Nagan revolver, not taken aim. A gunshot resounded through Ivan Turgenev's "Forest and Steppe," and the bullet went straight through Uncle's right eye; it gushed blood while the other eye still wept.

"I salute you, Sreten!" Galya warmly clenched my hand afterward, when we had closed the books. "I congratulate you—exemplary behavior, a well-executed action. I'll pass on my observations to my comrades at the top . . ."

It turned my stomach. I was disgusted at myself. When I

returned that evening, dejected, to my parents' flat, when my mother made me tea of Klamath weed to soothe the sharp pains in my intestines, when she asked me why I was so leaden-pale, why I was unable to fall asleep, I answered in a delirium:

"I don't know; I have the feeling that Auntie Frosya and Uncle are no longer alive . . ."

We found them the next day in their marital bed, beneath the fallen canopy woven in the colors of pale night—she just as beautiful, as if asleep, at peace, and he with his eye pierced through. Mother looked at me oddly, somehow frightened. Luckily on May 9, 1945, Germany's unconditional surrender was signed in Berlin, and the victory celebration glossed over all the confusion surrounding the death of Father's last brother. All of Belgrade came out onto the squares to toast each other's health and to make merry; only Father didn't budge from his state of stupor, hovering on the fringe of consciousness. Seen from below, from the street, he resembled a large plant that had been left in the window.

57

Despite the official end of the war, fighting in the Yugoslav theater of operations continued up until May 15, and a wide front for the recognition of our struggle's outcome was opened as well. A front at which I directed a whole string of operations. It would happen that for an entire week I wouldn't raise my head, instead bent over pages and pages, illuminated day and night by a strong lamp, always in a half-darkened room of some confiscated home on Zvezdara, where a department responsible to me was temporarily housed. And even when the Service was divided into branches, when it was reduced by an entire government building and scores of vacant apartments used for spying, there was still so much work to be done; the people's government was threatened with danger from all sides, and one had to be equally wary of those who had until yesterday been enemies, inveterate supporters of monarchism and the government-in-exile, and equally suspicious of the arrogation of both communal and remnant private property, and analytical toward those who showed an inclination for a socialist-realist poetics of creation or were advocates of bourgeois tendencies . . .

I needed to stay awake because of all that, because of my passion for spying, but also because of my aunt and uncle's faces, which appeared to me whenever I attempted to close my eyes. The impossibility of my sleeping more soundly even made me quite famous. I was considered tireless, everywhere present, capable of foreseeing political turnabouts at least a sentence before the others. I passed for an incorruptible and uncompromising man of the Party; not for a moment did I hesitate when the clash with the Cominform became public. I was even pleased, I realized, that here I would always have something to do, a profession to practice; owing to me, many saw the sea around Goli Otok.

In my presence one lowered one's glance, looked for nonexistent bits of thread on one's lapel, and fastened the top button of one's shirt; subordinates trembled, and those in seemingly higher positions had sweaty palms. I conducted purges throughout many books of collected and selected works, autobiographies and biographies, war journals and historical studies, textbooks and encyclopedia entries. I wrote thousands of memoranda and reports. While the others compassionately refrained, I, in accordance with directives, filled the archives and the prisons; occasionally they would bury someone, no one knew where, without a grave marker . . .

But I have no intention of continuing in a similar vein here. About that you can reliably inform yourself when they open the archival material, when you read on the wall of some prison, deeply inscribed: "Sreten, may your eyes burst!" or "Pokimica, fuck you and everyone you know!" When here and there, during the laying of some foundation, blanched human skulls, vertebrae, and clavicles come rising to the surface. I record here what is not there, what is not cited . . .

But about those first years of the country's renewal, I really haven't much to add, because I had no private life. Nor friends. The old Chekist Galya Gorokhov was in March 1947 recalled to Moscow, only soon thereafter to submit a report concerning the doubt with which he had read a speech of Comrade Stalin in *Izvestia*, back in February 1938. In essence, he had eaten his last warm pierogi; he kissed his wife, saluted his lined-up children, and then with his Nagan, medals, and the confession about his own case, turned himself in to his superiors in the building on Marx Prospect. The trophy revolver and the confession ended up on a wall of the museum's souvenir room in Cheremodno, Galya Gorokhov's village of birth, and he in forced labor somewhere on the shore of the East Siberian Sea. Despite the nature of my work, I'd once been able to exchange at least a few words with him, but now he was no longer a person with whom I could exchange even that much.

On top of everything, although I don't remember the exact date, I moved away from my family, accepting the smallest apartment they allotted me, only because the new address was located on People's Front Street. I required nothing more. From Monday to Saturday, on all three shifts, I was occupied with reading at a record pace all manner of things, and on Sundays I would feign an ordinary existence in the real world, but rarely did I go out to visit my parents; I was ashamed of my father who, having lost his mind, remained stuck in past times. I spent my days off mostly rinsing my tired eyes with chamomile, or resting my overstrained vision alongside the Danube; strolling in the parks, inhaling deeply because of the leaden pallor that had penetrated beneath my skin; and, on holidays, leisurely arranging my collection of insignias. Mother at first reproached me for having become estranged, then she fell bitterly silent, and then, despite her timid nature, calmly uttered for the last time:

"I found out what you do. People told me. You spy. Aren't you ashamed? Your father was mistaken on June 28, 1919, about your illustrious conception. That wasn't any kind of bull's-eye, but the biggest miss of my and his entire life."

Until their deaths, I never again entered my parents' home. Sometimes I would merely pass beside the building that had been cleft in two by the bombardment, and could be neither demolished nor restored. I would stop behind some tree and from the street observe my motionless father, who was like a plant left in the window. In springtime, on open wings, birds would alight on his shoulders and head, shifting from leg to leg in his disheveled hair or whispering something confidentially beside the spirals of his ears. Mother would appear if the sun changed position, in order to bring him to the other, courtyard side, where the warmth still lingered.

I single out Kosana, who was the only one who behaved differently toward me. Having completed an accelerated course in shorthand typing, she was accepted into the Service as a secretary. We would often slave together late into the night; I would dictate my observations and she would record them, amazed at the pages of details I was able to extract from a mere few sentences. Yes, as I later found out, she was in love with me; she was not disturbed by my profession, by all those malicious stories behind my back, not even when I heaped abuse on her:

"All right, comrade, what's this you've written here?! No one can read that! Here, you omitted a letter! You're of no use at all! For God's sake, stop, you don't have to type what I'm saying now!"

"I remember, Comrade Sreten. I remember what you said last month. I'll correct it after my shift. Don't you worry, now—I remember every word you say; what others say I forget, even when they tell me I have nice knees," she said and smiled warmly.

"Knees? I hadn't noticed. I haven't time for that," I replied, embarrassed, returning to the reading and blind to Kosana's flirting.

And that is more or less the whole of it, until one Wednesday in November 1947, when I received authorization "in the name of the people" to attend the expropriation of the Pelican Bookshop, owned by one Gavrilo Dimitrijević. A routine affair for those times: an official decision, an inventory of the merchandise, a new padlock and a lead seal on the roller-door; nothing more would need to be said here, were it not for the bookseller's daughter, the large-eyed Miss Natalija. And her curt demand to keep several titles for their purely sentimental value.

"It's not in conformance with regulations, but go ahead; it's not the type of literature that would interest the class-conscious anyway," I answered. I myself couldn't believe that I was capable of being so compassionate, although I didn't fail to notice how she chose one after the other of that very same book, singling out from the shelves all thirty-odd copies of the novel *My Memorial*, by a certain Anastas Branica.

I became intrigued in two ways. Not only on account of a suspicious act, but also because for the first time I was aware of something that was not my specialty—the attractiveness of the female being. The first would have been reason enough for me to open the entire case. The second was sufficient for me to begin my own downfall. Putting aside all my other affairs, I devoted myself to an examination of the circumstances. I began to weave a web around the bookseller's daughter, not sensing how the fateful threads were in fact tightening around me.

The position I held enabled me to arrive unhindered at the desired information. I very quickly learned all there was to know about Gavrilo Dimitrijević, about his stand during the war, his voluntary rescuing of the words from the destroyed National Library, but also about the waxed envelopes of correspondence with Professor Čajkanović and Bishop Nikolaj Velimirović. I very quickly learned everything about his melancholy little wife, about her special voice, a gift that Natalija had inherited. But to the daughter herself I never got sufficiently close. Somewhat older than I, at the end of the twenties she had attended the operatic singing class of prima donna Paladia Rostovtseva, which she'd then suddenly discontinued when she accepted an ordinary job in her father's shop. She went nowhere in particular, nor did anyone visit her; she was merely in the habit of going on All Souls' Day to the grave of the author of the novel all of whose copies she had kept, the unknown writer. More exactly, the writer who was known, according to the facts I learned, for having drowned himself in the Danube following the poor reception of his first book. Unsatisfied, I decided to visit her at 9 Palmotić Street where she lived with her parents. I wrote "visit," but I meant to say to frighten her, to let her know just who Sreten Pokimica was.

"Go right ahead, turn everything upside down," she said ironically when I showed her my identification and the warrant to search the family library, located in a room with large, latticed windows, resembling a glass botanical garden.

"Don't be embarrassed, enlighten yourself," she added insolently when I handed her a receipt in exchange for the supposedly temporarily seized copies of *My Memorial*, but she didn't fluster me. A few of them were missing—she must have skillfully hidden them in that multitude of books.

"I would offer you *komisbrot* and tea, but your Commission for the Reallocation of Excess Housing Space mistakenly walled up the pantry, together with the reactionary cake molds and the opportunistic strainers." With these words, she coldly accompanied me to the door.

58

I read the novel very quickly.

"Comrade Sreten, what should I write down?" asked Kosana, pursing her lips, holding her pencil and notebook at the ready.

"Nothing, this time nothing . . . There's nothing here worthy of attention . . . There aren't any real events . . . There's no plot . . . Not even any characters . . . Idle fantasy . . . Imaginings . . ." I replied, absorbed in thought. The secretary looked at me with disappointment.

"And should I bring in something to eat? The Americans sent us a lot of fine fish in cans, and I have a ripe, juicy tomato; if you give me your little pocketknife to cut it right in half . . ." said Kosana, searching for a reason to remain in my company a little longer.

"What pocketknife? Comrade, what are you talking about?! I'm not hungry! You can go home!" I had been forced to raise my voice; she left a little offended, while I stayed behind to ponder what to do with my new, bewilderingly intoxicating feelings.

Regardless of their nature, I had never before concealed from the Party the results of my investigations. Nor had I ever attempted to withhold anything for myself. But Anastas Branica's story led me into temptation. A text without a story, pages and pages of descriptions done for the sake of a woman who had never met him outside of those pages. A garden and a villa built in such a way that you saw clearly also that which wasn't mentioned, heard sounds and smelled smells. Yes, smells. The novel was being read at the same time by someone else, the housekeeper Zlatana—that's how she introduced herself—who was stone deaf. As I subsequently verified, she was registered as missing in the lists of war casualties, although she in fact occupied herself all day long in the preparation of foods in the kitchen of the "memorial" of the tragic Branica, at once hospitably offering me all kinds of fancy dishes, probably on account of which I wasn't hungry when I closed the covers of the book before me.

Perhaps that night, in the office, I had no clear notion of what I wanted to do. Perhaps I didn't archive that unusual reading material because I suspected it would be better if it remained hidden from the Service itself. Perhaps I thought that this secluded spot might be a quite suitable residence, a home for the rest and relaxation of our highest administrators, a literature in which they, thanks to me, might forever assume the role of the absent tenants, the heroes. And assuredly I, with a little part of my consciousness, desired something similar also for myself and Natalija Dimitrijević. I was certain that she would often visit there . . .

In any event, I did the impermissible: nothing of what I found did I put into the files. More exactly, just in case, I followed procedure to a certain degree but in such a way as to better cover from future users the traces of what I had done, not issuing the directives prescribed by the regulations of the Service. Except for my personal copy I took all the others to the depot, established back during the old Yugoslavia, not filling out the forms for them, not entering in the register or card catalogs the name of the author, the title of the work, the year and place of publication. I knew that books without inventory numbers, in those catacombs of shelves and passageways, were better concealed than they would have been had I hidden them anywhere else. Afterward I even added to that subterranean abyss. I began to gather up what remained of that otherwise modest printing, finding them in private libraries and reading rooms, in secondhand bookshops and flea markets. I confiscated or cheaply bought up copy after copy, and then, by confidential memorandum—abusing my authority—I instructed my colleagues in other cities to undertake the same search. One book I even wrested from the hands of a little old lady in Kalemegdan Park; she screamed after me as if her skin were being flayed . . .

Taking into consideration the recent troubled times—the destruction and the way things are carried off in time of war—the ruined holdings of the National Library, and the traditionally short memory of our people, I could have been satisfied when I counted that I was missing only several copies. But I was more than satisfied, I was excited by—I shuddered at—the thought that of all the readers there might have been, the only copies of *Memorial* in the land, on the planet, were possessed solely by me and the large-eyed Miss Natalija Dimitrijević.

I read and read, waiting for her to appear as well. Whenever I was overcome with doubt, I went to Palmotić Street on the pretext that I needed to examine the notes of her father, still engaged in collecting the charred remnants of words from the site of the fire on Kosančić Venac. She would receive me and then show me out just as coldly, regardless of whether for hours I had interrogated her harshly about the activities of Gavrilo Dimitrijević, or whether I had offered—and later generously seen to it—that she would again be employed at the Pelican, now a seller of office supplies and business forms.

"Well now, you're not hiding anything from me, are you?" I laid bare tens of thousands of pages of her library.

"And the fact that you meet in travelogues with your schoolmate Angelina and the former king's orderly, the emigrant Major Najdan? Do you know that this is sufficient grounds for me to open a dossier on you?" I would say, trying to get her to talk.

"And where does that light and dark yellow house in your eyes come from, that pergola with late-blooming roses, those nonexistent birds—where are you when you see all that?" I stared straight into her pupils, to no avail; I only made her close her eyes when they met mine.

I quickly recruited the tenant in the adjoining studio apartment, which he had received upon the reallocation of their building and which gave onto the Dimitrijević's onetime balcony, requesting that he keep watch on her through the window. He reported to me on when she arose, on how the whole day long she tended to the flowerbeds of her library, how she searched through pages and separated the leaves of uncut editions, how with her father she listened attentively to the clattering of the cobalt tea service, how she urged her mother, ill from a clot of melancholy, to sing something all the same, how during cloudy evenings she drew on the windowpanes the locations of the lunar orb and the North Star, how before falling asleep she long spoke into the feathers of her girlhood pillow. Natalija's neighbor, in a patriotically devoted manner, submitted reports even long after I had retired early, when Natalija had been left without anyone, always emphasizing one and the same thing, understanding nothing:

"She tells the postman that she'll be gone for several days. She cancels her delivery of milk. Throws white linens over the furniture. Packs as if she's going on a trip across the ocean. She locks the door. And then she sits in a cane chair and reads. I don't know what you say, but to me that's extremely, extremely suspicious!"

"Sits and reads?! Did you perhaps see her sometimes holding this novel?" I showed the informant the work by Anastas Branica.

"That I couldn't say. But one thing's for sure: she reads as if she weren't here!"

59

I thought I was going mad. Or that I only madly, futilely loved her.

Once it seemed to me that someone had stayed in the villa while I'd been away on business, when we'd removed from copies of the Serbian church book every mention of St. Nikola Church, built of the solid word and bequeathed to pilgrims in the Middle Ages, by despot Jovan Oliver. Upon my return I found that the flowers in the stone vases along the balustrade of the outer staircase had been watered, the rooms aired out, the curled ends of the carpets straightened, the furniture and the frames on the pastel landscapes wiped free of dust, the cobwebs removed from the corners of the walls, the silverware freshly polished clean of old flecks, and that the armchair I'd moved to the middle of the parlor now stood once more beside the window.

"My name isn't Sreten Pokimica if she hasn't been here lately!" I blurted out, and Comrade Kosana squinted jealously.

Another time I saw someone with beige cotton gloves and a straw hat similar to hers, in a dress of raw silk, some fifty pages ahead of me alongside a great river that flowed through a valley; I quickened my pace and found no one, but the main current had not yet managed to carry away the countenance on the surface of the water along its bank. I stooped down, took the outline into my cupped hands, and immersed my face toward Natalija Dimitrijević's image, holding my cheek to hers until I choked.

"I'll bring a clean towel . . . Comrade, you might have called me . . . To pour it on you . . ." said Kosana, entering. She thought I had washed myself with water from the pitcher above the sink in a corner of the office; by the way she ogled me, it seemed that she would undress me completely and pour water all over me for a long time.

On a third occasion I followed along with some delegation of Slavists, tracking to each syllable what they were up to, when I heard the far-off sounds of a harp. Irresponsibly, I neglected the assignment that had been entrusted to me, and took up *Memorial*, which I always kept in the top drawer. The strings of the slender instrument were still quivering when I burst into the large music room (or rather small dance hall) . . . There was not a living soul. The ever present housekeeper Zlatana did not know how to answer me:

"And how would I, sir, being hard of hearing like this, be able to hear something like that? A harp?! That, too, I can read from your lips!"

I barely managed to cover up my oversight with the group of guest Slavists, having caught up to them after laboring at it day and night; who knows everything they had read without my supervision. Now rumors began to spread that I was no longer the same old Pokimica, that I was often absent, that I neglected things, that I lacked concentration. On the other hand, people began to gossip that many in the Service were going too far, that they had too much authority, that they were wiretapping even the highest government officials, that they were telling crude jokes at the expense of the president, who easily dozed off after the very first line of some book; I suspected that we were in store for a reorganization. What would happen if it were discovered that I had not acted in a principled manner with Anastas Branica's novel? With a heavy heart I was forced to do Internal Control one better; I resolved to make some changes, of a kind we had grown accustomed to in other works of bourgeois literature.

I started with the pediment. I simply knocked off the old inscription and wrote out in oil paint: "1945." Then I excerpted from the text some of the more successful descriptions of the household furnishings, copying them for the card catalogue of the central warehouse for period furniture, very popular with some of my comrades. Here were to be found several specimens of inestimable value: chairs, dressers, and chests of all eras; Flemish tapestries; oriental rugs; pieces of fine porcelain from Sèvres; gilded candlesticks; and especially mirrors: there was a very great demand for them even though they never reflected the so-called true images of their newfangled owners. But even despite the resulting gaps in the text, more than enough still remained. Only then did I completely understand how much effort and skill Anastas Branica had put into his manuscript. Particularly when I failed to discover the secret of the secretary with seventy drawers, of rose and lemon wood. I had to disassemble it, but I didn't know how to put it back together again; in no way did I succeed in lining up the words, in composing the sentences. Outside of the novel not one of the small compartments contained a space without end . . .

I knew she was aware that it was I who'd done all that when she nonetheless looked at me during my next visit to her house, only several days after her mother's melancholy had fatally congealed.

"I've opened my eyes because I've learned not to notice you," she said, and indeed I observed that I was nowhere to be seen in her tranquil-green pupils.

60

The reorganization of the Service ended the political careers of many agents, but me it spared; I retained all my former duties, and was even promoted. And yet I was far from happy. I loved, but my love was unrequited. I existed, but it was as if I didn't, at least not where I most desired. I senselessly passed the withered days, months, and years, but it constantly seemed to me that I possessed nothing of life.

Preparing dinner on Transfiguration Day of 1960, Mother felt weak. From somewhere she pulled out a small sack of wheat, sorted through the grains and picked out the cockles, dead bugs, and tiny stones, then let it stand in water to swell. The wheat cooked while she set the table for only one, while she brushed the black suit and again ironed the white shirt of her husband. Then she poured the boiled wheat into two small bowls, for the burial and for the weekly remembrance, including with each a glass of oil and red wine. Finally, she herself put on her best change of clothes, lay down in their marriage bed, and closed her eyes forever. Father remained in the open window for days, visited only by the birds, washed by drops of summer rain, wiped dry by the scorching edges of the August heat. There was no one to move him from the spot where he found himself, or perhaps he gathered the will to perform his first independent motion after so many years of being absent from reality. One evening, as if nothing had ever happened, he calmly took one step forward, closed the window sash, and mortally doubled over.

At that time I somehow came upon the thought that would spell my complete ruin. According to the reports of the studio apartment tenant I had recruited, Natalija spent a good part of each day caring for Gavrilo Dimitrijević, and I decided to get rid of him, hoping that she would then turn to me, that she would at least notice me. Of course I could have done this in various ways, but I wished to do things in a manner that would not arouse her suspicions. I began the writing of a book that would cost her father his life, but also a book that would, as it later turned out, end my career in the Service. The plan was quite simple. In the utmost secrecy from my superiors and subordinates, I composed, line by line, a manuscript about an alleged toppling of the government, knowing that on such reading material would gather like flies all possible manner of émigrés, opponents of the regime, and for certain the old bookseller himself. And when this indeed occurred, I reckoned, I would easily conduct a purge as I had in *Notes of a Hunter*—and suddenly close the bindings of that trap and imprison those vermin.

It went better for me than I ever supposed. Probably because no one knew so well the difference between what the regime proclaimed and reality, probably because no one knew so precisely, down to the inch, how to predict where that rift would extend in the future. The opposing side is usually blinded by petty personal reasons or a generalizing hatred, but I was the man on the inside, calm and collected, farsighted, informed in detail and by nature systematic; the manuscript I had undertaken outdid every other, usually merely maudlin dissident literature. Using the pseudonym "Inside Man" I signed the first fragments, which were published as an experiment in the émigré press abroad. After only two articles appeared in *The Voice of Canadian Serbs* and in the London *Our Word*, it was being rumored that there was some new, virulent enemy of the regime; within the ranks of the security division panic set in, and contrary to custom even the minister called me:

"Sreten, this is dangerous. He knows things . . . Do you have any clue, have our analysts determined the style . . . ? See to it that you unmask this good-for-nothing as soon as possible . . ."

"Don't worry a bit, Comrade Minister, we'll find out who it is . . ." I answered, and continued to retype my notes myself. I was just finishing the eighth chapter and Kosana was astonished that I was not dictating to her.

"I see that . . ."—she said, on the verge of tears when she found me at the typewriter—"I see that I am no longer of use to you . . ."

I confess, it might be that I even got a little carried away, that I forgot that my convictions were not in accord with what I was writing, and it also might be that I did everything only in the way I had grown accustomed to: responsibly, zealously. Namely, after two years of work, I had found a way to send a copy of the manuscript out of the country unnoticed, and before long there stealthily began to arrive from there printed copies of the book about which people were whispering, the book which was being passed from hand to hand . . .

"Have you read it?" went the most frequent question then if two men happened to meet, neither daring to utter its title.

"They're collapsing . . . From within . . . Only one of theirs could know that information and those events, all those names . . ."

one of them would say, leaning toward the other and briefly relating its contents.

"It has begun . . ." and they would take leave of each other, encouraged.

I gained an insight into the thought processes of many. I learned of new enemies of our government, I exposed the waverers and the misguided, the weaklings who were always prepared to agree, the purely disgruntled, the perpetual antagonists and the repulsive flatterers; but only Gavrilo Dimitrijević interested me. I waited for the moment when the book would ultimately fall into his hands as well. Once I got rid of him, I'd get rid of all the others, too; only then, it was my intention, would I reveal who the author of this brilliant ambush and decoy was—in a single stroke widening the prospects for my love, and forever consolidating my position as the finest operative in State Security.

But alas, everything ended only with partial success. On the day Dimitrijević finally entered the book from which he has never returned, on the day there remained on the little table in the family library on 9 Palmotić Street the title whose mysterious author I was, on the day there remained of Master Gavrilo's presence only the crackling of the cane garden chair, just as I was ridding him from the life of the woman I loved, just as I was contentedly musing on how Natalija would now turn her attentions to me, just as I was deciding to go to her, to offer her my condolences, and to personally offer myself as support, there came into my office three sullen men accompanied by Kosana.

"This is the manuscript . . . Here, this is the machine it was typed on, as you will easily confirm; the hook on the letter a gets stuck, B is a little slanted, b is always smudged, g protrudes above the line . . ." she enumerated, while the three men listed the contents of my desk.

"How dare you . . . You are making a mistake . . . Comrades, wait until I explain . . . I did it intentionally, to get close to them from within . . . So that we could trap them, like flies . . ." I recall saying, but the three men remained silent.

The only one who turned to me was Kosana. She began to cry as they led me away. And she said:

"You fool. I loved you so much, but you had eyes for everything but me."

61

Had all this happened at the end of the forties or during the fifties, I would have surely been shot, or, more optimistically speaking, imprisoned. As it was, though, I was merely disgraced and pensioned off early. The dissident book long remained a gruesomely simple trap in which troublemakers of all stripes were caught. I never did prove that I had written it with the best of intentions; my former merits went unrecognized, and there were many who could hardly wait for my headlong fall.

But what pained me still more was the futility of the sacrifice. While for many I passed as a revolutionary, worthy of loathing or admiration, Natalija Dimitrijević deigned not to pay me the slightest attention; on the street she continued to pass me by as if she hadn't seen me. In the Pelican she would wait on me as she would on any other customer; I soon had entire stacks of blank order forms that I really didn't know what to do with. And on top of everything, after her father's disappearance, she began to go to places which, because of our different memories, I had no access to. She bought delicatessen goods in Botorić's grocery on Terazije, odds and ends in the trinket shop At the Lucky Hand, which had ceased to exist still earlier; she patronized Mitić's largest department store in the

Balkans, designed from the foundation to the very last store shelf, but never built in Slavija; she even managed to withdraw deposits from prewar banks and credit unions, and thus spend ten days each September in Vrnjačka Banja, always staying in the villa Serbiada, immediately below the famous summer house of the Obrenović general Belimarković. In some of those years I set out after her, but in the Serbiada they were unable to give me a bed, and the old man at the resort's central reception desk assured me that such a villa did not exist here:

"You are asking the impossible; the Serbiada was destroyed back in 1946 or 1947, and the building material was hauled off to wherever one pleased. If it means anything to you, I can tell you how it looked."

"And Miss Natalija Dimitrijević, check your guest registers, she spends the night there . . ." I insisted.

"No, there is no such person," he said, once more looking at his books.

"I'm telling you, she stayed there . . ." I repeated.

"Perhaps if the lady in question remembers how the interior looked, I can tell you how the outside, the façade appeared . . ." The old receptionist looked me up and down sympathetically.

The sixties ran out; both of us were already middle-aged people. I gradually withdrew from the reality I had conceived; now I waited for her six days a week exclusively in Anastas Branica's novel, in the only book I possessed, in the only book I read. Having long ago lost the ability to sleep soundly, I didn't let her out of my sight from Monday morning to Saturday evening, at the beginning of the seventies virtually moving outright into the vacant light and dark yellow house, settling in one of the rooms upstairs, tending to the surrounding garden, or writing my autobiography, setting aside only Sunday for my habitual way of life on People's Front Street, to get a haircut or to leaf through the newspapers, to go out to the parks or to stroll beside the Danube. As before, it occasionally seemed to me that I had discovered signs of her stay here, that I had seen her in the clearing of a villa higher up, or in the distance, along the bank of a river, but we actually never met. I was certain that she had kept several copies of *My Memorial*, which was indeed confirmed when there began to appear a certain Tiosavljević, a student to whom she was giving lessons in total reading and subsequently a professor in the School of Philosophy. He moved into the glass pavilion beside the fishpond and, as he claimed, was engaged in archaeographic research of this domain. I was unable to shed my professional habits, and so I spied on him until I was convinced that he really did dabble a bit in ancient words, which he found here and there, or, during the east wind, simply gathered from below. All in all, including the housekeeper Zlatana and myself, this was one more person who'd been bewitched—it appears that literature brings together only suchlike. I avoided meeting and conversing with him as much as I could, usually exchanging with him, but only as much as I needed to, a perfunctory greeting:

"Good day."

"Good day, Pokimica, good day . . . I would just like to ask you—you surely know, you've been here a long time . . ." Tiosavljević would say. He was always rummaging around for something.

"But I don't know anything . . . I read for myself . . . You read for yourself . . . It's all written out for you; leave me alone . . ." I would reply, usually able to avoid saying anything.

And then in the eighties, still someone else, a married couple, began to arrive, the first time seemingly lost. Who knows where they had found the hidden novel; perhaps they had taken it out of the depot, perhaps they had even lost their way here by chance. Further, they more and more often held the same book at the same time, toured the grounds, measured off the property, the villa, the rooms, appraised the household furnishings, copied down some of the words, which I afterward found on the other side of reality, in speeches and in the newspapers, words that had become insubstantial as the shadow of a shadow; expended. That they had something serious in mind, I suspected, when on one occasion as I worked around the pergola with late-blooming roses, I heard them planning to bind their copy of the book in expensive saffian.

"There are no other characters . . . We still have to get rid of that professor and the gardener. With the hard-of-hearing old woman it will be easy; she doesn't exist there either, and she has absolutely no right to be here . . ." I heard them saying as I hid behind the rosebushes.

"Look! The word *thrive*! It's quite common, but I always need some fresh word," said the man, stooping down and writing something as he dug through a bed of marigolds, which had never been so thriving as they were that summer.

62

The arrival of the Leleks perhaps disrupted the slowed course of events. Which meant that an isolated copy of Anastas Branica's novel still remained. The three fugitives had also taken up residence in the meticulously described house; no matter how they moved, a very large shadow accompanied them. To be sure, the married couple was unable to look on all this, that is, to supervise it. Probably for that reason, hastily, they decided to bring in someone who would make alterations to their liking, who would rearrange what was there, make the two of them sole owners of the property.

"I found a gifted student, a part-time editor and proofreader, who has agreed to undertake everything discretely; we'll begin with the pediment . . ." I heard them conferring.

But only several hours before that young man arrived, she, Natalija Dimitrijević, appeared quite unexpectedly, surrounded by luggage sufficient for a transoceanic cruise, accompanied by a certain Jelena, her companion during the hours of reading together. Shrunken as if grown inward, with a wrinkled face and pronounced joints, she seemed to be caught in a cruel vise of a past that continually welled up and of some arrested future time, a future that no longer had anywhere to move, to retreat. All that remained substantial were her tranquil-green eyes, made even larger by the lenses of her glasses. And I myself was weighed down by time, hunched over, permeated to the pore with leaden pallor probably not unlike that young man of fifty years before, but my love had remained unchanged. I endeavored to read up to where she was, to the line, stopping where she would stop.

"Doorstep!" Thus said the companion, who helped her straddle objects here and there because she walked unsteadily and had forgotten certain words.

"Grass, ordinary, freshly mown grass . . ." On the very first afternoon, the girl brought Natalija out into the French garden, just as I was finishing the restoration of the pergola, destroyed by the vandalistic act of that pretentious student.

"My Lord, I still remember this tragic red of the roses," she said quite collectedly, so as to get a better look at my face. "And you . . . I can't remember . . . Have I met you before . . . ?"

"I don't know . . . Perhaps . . ." I stammered; for the first time I was in her eyes. "I am, you know, Sreten . . . Pokimica . . . I take care of the garden . . ."

"Very nice of you . . . I thank you . . . Thanks . . ." she whispered, while I was filled with shame. I didn't have the strength to tell her who was really standing in front of her.

EIGHTH READING

DURING WHICH WE SPEAK
ABOUT ONE MORE CLOUDY NIGHT,
AND, FORTUNATELY,
ABOUT A FULL MOON WITHIN A BOOK;
ABOUT HOW MEATLESS DOLMAS ARE PREPARED;
ABOUT THE PASSIVE VOICE;
ABOUT STRINGS SO SENSITIVE
THEY CAN BE RENDERED OUT OF
TUNE BY DRAFTS, CHANGES IN TEMPERATURE,
OR ONE'S MOOD; AND THEN
ABOUT THE DELUSION OF ONE'S OWN SHADOW;
ABOUT AN INTIMATION ENCLOSED WITHIN
A PIECE OF PORPHYRY;
ABOUT AN UNPLEASANT CONVERSATION
WITH AN EDITOR; AND
ABOUT A FINAL ADJUSTING OF PAGES

63

ON SUNDAY ADAM LOZANIĆ CHANGED his mind several times, breaking off work on the novel more than once, getting ready to leave the apartment, only to return again to the book bound in saffian. No, this time it was not a matter of an actual meeting with Jelena, Pokimica, or any other reader. He had spent a good part of yesterday morning with the girl, keeping her company on her walks with Madame Natalija Dimitrijević. Indeed, following the mysterious death of Professor Tiosavljević, the old woman had found herself here, dressed in black and wearing a hat with a nearly opaque veil; her bouts of forgetfulness grew worse, or perhaps on account of that dark veil Madame Natalija's words, less and less coherent, were even more unlikely to get through to the person with whom she was speaking. Together with the companion, Adam tried to make the woman's lack of memory more bearable, taking pains despite his assigned task to afford her a little contentment, as when from the harp, its strings rendered out of tune by many summers of drafts, he attempted to coax music anew. Although not particularly gifted, although he had never before held any kind of instrument in his hands, the young man tinkered for a long time with the pegs, tightening them and loosening them, testing the harmony of the tones by lightly pulling the pulp of his fingers across the strings, without any great success, until he discovered by chance the secret of creation. And everything was, at the same moment, so simple and so complex: Adam rose and opened the casements of the nearest window, and in the same way that he had sighed over the harp, the east wind stole into the room and softly began to pluck the strings. Madame

Natalija Dimitrijević unexpectedly raised her head and, having remained silent the whole day, whispered:

"Saint-Saëns, *Fantasy for Harp*."

"Did you say something?" the girl started.

"*Fantasy for Harp*, I'm saying . . . Camille Saint-Saëns . . . I once heard it . . . If I'm not mistaken, in the Manège Theater . . . I was still a child . . . Father took me, probably . . . They gave a bravura concert . . . Madame Nicole Anquier-Casteran, a professor at the Stanković Music School . . . In the second half of the program, with the accompaniment of the Orchestra of the Royal Guard, a selection of various works . . ." said the old woman, excited.

"But how? Are you certain? I mean, are you completely sure that this is that *Fantasy* . . . ?" the young man asked.

"Hush . . . !" was heard below the old woman's veil. "Quiet . . . Listen to it, surrender to it . . . And it will tell you everything on its own . . ."

Thus did the harp play. Jelena and Adam would open wide or only ajar one of the tall windows in the music room, open or draw the draperies; the wind would stream or glide through the curtains unhindered, and then weave itself with virtuosity among the scores of strings on the slender-necked loom, spinning tender compositions while Natalija Dimitrijević recognized the titles of the short pieces, interpreted transcriptions, expounded on performing techniques, and explained the makeup of the instrument.

"Fauré's *Impromptu* . . . It's as though I'm listening to it now . . . Debussy's *Arabesque* . . . Berlioz . . . Pierné . . . Milojević . . . Binički . . . This improvisation is unknown to me . . . It should be written down . . . Lest it disappear . . ." She recognized movements as well, flawlessly it seemed, although she'd forgotten how to applaud; after each rendition she would raise her hands, better to say her black cotton gloves, but her palms would sadly fail to meet. At a certain point she would give up, and on the dark veil would appear the damp tracks of tears; beneath it all she must have been bitterly weeping.

Perhaps the music helped Adam to decide.

On Sunday evening his client appeared to compare passage by passage what the young proofreader had done. The corrections that had been requested and then made were more numerous than in previous days: from the new arrangement of the furniture in the parlor, to the altogether unwarranted building of an interior wall, by means of which the dining room had been needlessly partitioned into two cramped spaces; from the addition of an entire catalog of clothing and other personal items of the new "owners," in chests, wardrobes, commodes, and nightstands, to the replacement of the adjective *light and dark yellow* of the façade, from the beginning to the end of the book, everywhere it was mentioned, with an ordinary, *ash-white* color. There had been many many alterations, but the young man was especially boastful of the harp, demonstrating it all by once more opening a window: below the touch of the enraptured wind, the curtain again began to dance unrestrainedly and the slender instrument played.

"And who ordered you to waste time on that?! In the future you will strictly adhere to our agreement. You will do only what you are told. Here, in any case, I had planned something quite different. We have no need of a music room. Tomorrow get rid of the harp—do with it what you will—and after that, since the pavilion is finally free, you will have to finish there . . ." the client said coldly.

"Yes . . . Of course . . . I understand . . ." Adam confirmed, while surrendering more and more to the thought that forced itself on him all day long, revolving in his head, striking painfully against the inner side of his parietal and occipital bones: *Tomorrow get rid of the harp! Tomorrow get rid of the harp!*

And so on Sunday evening he went out to buy paper, for many hours wandering the streets of Belgrade, climbing all the way to

Slavija in search of an open store, and at last finding a shop, exactly as narrow as its front door, seemingly wedged between the close-packed fronts of the buildings. And only as he was leaving the store did he recognize the name of that strange place—At the Lucky Hand. He'd traveled quite a ways down the street before he realized what he'd just read. He went back, but now he was unable to find the store, nor anything even similar to it. Had he not been holding the notebook purchased just a while before; had he not remembered the tinkling of the little bell, the room that widened out like a funnel, and the elderly clerk, who'd been surprised that anyone at all would enter; had he not seen him slowly straighten up, single out from a shelfful of all types of goods precisely this little notebook and from its cover shake off the dust; had he not found in his pocket a pair of coins long out of circulation, in fact the change he had received from the old man—it would have seemed that he had imagined it all. He had no one to ask; each passerby seemed himself to be in search of that long-vanished trinket shop.

Now he was even more firmly resolved. Despite the express condition that he not make any kind of notes, he decided that during his work he would write down something of what he had encountered in the ambiguous novel of Anastas C. Branica. Despite the danger that he would lose a well-paying job. Depite everything. At least to save the harp. Really not knowing musical notes, at least to record the names of the compositions he had listened to with Madame Natalija and the girl. At least to leave behind some trace of Professor Tiosavljević's mysteriously vanished finds, of the unhappy Leleks, or of the housekeeper Zlatana's recipes. To leave behind testimony of Anastas Branica's life, and that, just noted, of Natalija Dimitrijević. And of Jelena, of course. Of her in particular. Let us say, to describe the diaphanousness of her nightgown of the day before. At least to write just a sentence about it:

"It might read: 'At the door a few rays of sunlight passed

through Jelena's nightgown—making translucent the fabric down the long outlines of her legs,'" he formulated under his breath as he returned to the studio apartment.

There had been too many mysterious occurrences. It wouldn't hurt to set it down on paper in its basics. For the sake of comparison. In order to find his bearings. And he surely wouldn't remember all the details. After all, he had best prepared for examinations when during the reading of each book he had singled something out, written it down; one word might later grow into whole pages. Now he felt the need to record what had happened to him here. Or what had seemed to. And so he set out come what may—thrusting that notebook into the belt of his faded blue jeans and covering it with his loose, untucked shirt. More exactly he didn't set out right then; he turned off the light in the apartment, moved the chair close to the window, placed the book bound in saffian in his lap, and waited for everyone else to fall asleep, for night to take hold everywhere—both here and over there.

64

The rain stopped, and then it began to fall again. Ten o'clock had passed and the last patrons had unwillingly left the tavern Our Sea. The souvenir vendor ceased hammering on his slats about eleven, and a half hour later a couple in their declining years, each clinging to the other, sought shelter in the Hotel Astoria. Just before midnight Milovan Milovanović Street, at the foot of Balkanska, sank into silence; one could hear from afar anyone who was approaching. Adam hoped that there, too, in the novel, all had grown quiet.

Fortunately, he already knew the winding approach well and a full moon revolved above the villa, for the city lighting was weak, and next to the window of his studio apartment it was difficult to make anything out. This way, it was as if it shone from the open book itself. From somewhere there appeared those irksome little bugs that swarm toward the light; the garden breathed with dense, darker colors, but there was much that was still visible. He proceeded carefully—taking pains that nothing should give away his presence, that he not tread on any quarrelsome twig, nor stumble on a molehill, not encounter the strutting peacock of several days before, nor set to rustling the white gravel with which the delta of paths in the French park was strewn. Making use of the piercing hoot of an owl to take each new step, the young man simply stole up to the house, going all the way around to the rear entry, for the main one was locked.

Through the still-fogged window of the kitchen the coals in the stove were giving off their last red glow. The housekeeper Zlatana sat hunched over the table; she had lowered her cheek onto her spread-out hands and was sleeping the sleep of the just, surrounded by countless bowls and heaps of vegetables, occasionally talking in her sleep, very loudly, in the way she recited aloud when awake; from time to time noisily munching or smacking her lips, as if in sleep she were trying her own delicacies.

"To prepare meatless dolmas, scald the Swiss chard until tender! Like that, just like that!

"We put into the rice filling ground walnuts to taste and a tiny, teeny, teeny-weeny pinch of pepper! Then fold each dolma and arrange them in rows!

"With every tenth boil, shake the pan so that it doesn't stick to the bottom!"

Apparently not only was she unable to hear him, but he saw for himself that she had never even been outside her own kitchen. The young man opened the door and on tiptoes stole past the housekeeper, then went down the narrow hallway and emerged into the main antechamber of the villa. Behind him he still heard Zlatana scolding someone in her sleep:

"Keep your hands to yourself! Wait! It's not done yet! It's not!"

To be sure, inside it was still less visible; he needed some time to get accustomed, to reconcile the outlines of the furniture and other objects with his memory, from previous readings, of where things were. During those first several moments he did not stir in order to avoid stumbling over something, again listening intently; he had the feeling that his ears were growing, that they were receiving every murmur, every worm-wiggle of the rearranged furnishings of wood, which seemed little by little to be returning to where they'd been before; every gnashing of the desiccated parquet floor; every clatter of the enamel of the porcelain ornaments; every beat of his own heart; even the sand-like heaping up of the present atop past times . . . Yes, he could distinguish, above all, that upstairs someone was still awake. The unhappy family with the shadow, perhaps Pokimica, the old Madame Natalija, or was it Jelena reviewing her lessons in English?

Making his way step by step, Adam climbed to the second floor. There were several doors. Three of them, locked. From behind one of them came the heavy breathing of multiple people; there the Leleks were no doubt staying. From behind the second door nothing was heard. Pokimica was above all a quiet man: often there was nothing to indicate his presence, except for the uneasy feeling that he was carefully watching everyone else, following their every move. Conversation was coming from the third room; in the crack of the threshold wavered a thin strip of candlelight, and one could easily discern which voice belonged to Natalija Dimitrijević and which to Jelena.

"Madame, don't tire yourself. Lie down and rest; it's late."

"I can't sleep . . . I've just been counting sheep . . . No, for goodness' sake, not until I tell you what I've been meaning to, even if it's my last . . . You don't notice how he looks at you . . . He stares for a whole hour at one paragraph, waits for you to come to him . . . My dear, he likes you . . . There's no other explanation . . ."

"You're exaggerating."

"Don't you tell me . . . Even without my glasses it's obvious that you like him . . . That you find him sweet . . ."

"Well, all right. I agree, I'm not displeased."

"Then why are you behaving this way . . . ? Don't flee from him . . . He is a man whose glance you can rely on . . . Child, that's no small matter . . . That's everything . . . That's love . . . Perish the thought that tomorrow, as they say, you regret it . . . Jelena, if he's managed to see you here, then how will he look at you over there . . . ? Come now, promise me that tomorrow you won't pull away your hands when he . . . When he . . ."

"Looks at them? Madame, you're not well again, lie down and rest."

"No, not until you give me your word . . . No, not even if I have to hold my eyelids open with my fingers . . ."

"I promise; just lie down."

"Well all right, then . . . We've agreed . . . Tuck me in now . . . And don't forget to spread the insect net . . . If I say something in my sleep, tell me it tomorrow . . . Don't keep it from me if I've conversed with St. Petka . . . I know that I'm near the end, that it's time to confess my sins . . ."

"All right, don't worry now, don't worry . . ."

Slippers flopped on the floor. The rustling of bed linen was heard. And then someone blew out the candle; the wavering strip of light died down. And then, for a long time—silence. Then, Jelena began to go over her lessons in a whisper. Adam didn't dare move, thinking about everything the girl had acknowledged to the old woman: that she found him sweet, that his glances pleased her.

"'The passive voice,'" the girl whispered to herself. "'Only transitive verbs can take the passive voice. The passive voice indicates that the subject does not perform the action, but that the action, which we express by means of the verb, acts on the subject: *The boy was beaten to death.* We can transform an active sentence into a passive one if we put the verb into the passive voice; the object of an active sentence becomes the subject of the passive, and before the subject of an active sentence one places the preposition *by.* An active sentence: *I wrote this letter.* A passive sentence: *This letter was written by me.* Intransitive verbs can become . . .'"

Her voice grew more and more quiet. The young man descended the stairs only when he was sure the girl had fallen asleep.

65

Thanks to the many tall windows in the music room, a good deal of daylight still lingered there. From the chairs arranged along the wall he selected one, moved it closer to the slender instrument, reached for his notes, and began to write down everything by means of which the harp was distinguished, everything that he saw and that he had learned about it from Madame Natalija, in as detailed a fashion as he could. As he had nothing with which to measure it, he stood up and compared it with his own height. About 180 centimeters. In the shape of a three-sided frame. A rather small pedestal or pedalbox, as if through the centuries its builders had endeavored to make the harp depend as little as possible on the earthly, that it make as little contact as possible with the ground. From the pedestal, quite vertically, there grew a hollow post, the forepillar—richly decorated in floral motifs, particularly at the top, called the head—rendered like Corinthian capitals. Slanting upward from the pedestal there extended the resonant body, rounded underneath, one might say of Brazilian rosewood, with five slits, outlets. The upper surface of the resonant body, the sounding board, was of fir wood, and along its middle ran a narrow, bored lath, through which were pulled the strings, tightened by pegs. But the harp owed its poetic appearance most of all to its neck, the third, upper side, by means of which the forepillar and body were joined, bent into the shape of an italic letter S. Through the neck were inserted hooks. The union with the neck formed a bridge in which was located the upper part of the mechanism, connected through the interior of the forepillar to the pedals in the pedestal. By releasing and depressing the pedals, through a system of scores of little copper pulleys, one could elicit from the strings pitches differing by three tones. The basic key of the harp is a diatonic C-flat major. If all the pedals are in the middle position one obtains a C major, and in the lower one a C-sharp major. A combination of the various positions of individual pedals can produce any other scale, except for the chromatic. The tonal range of the harp is six and one-half octaves; the total number of strings is forty-eight. All of the C-strings are colored red, and all of the F-strings blue. The eleven lowest, and at the same time longest, bass strings have silken cores wrapped with silver threads. The remaining strings are made of gut and are very sensitive and easily snapped; they can be rendered out of tune by a draft, a rise or fall in temperature, a sudden change in the mood of the harpist . . .

Thus did Adam Lozanić write down an abundance of words. The harp took up page after page of text, the night slipped by; in the silence could be heard only the scratching of the point of his pencil across the paper, only an occasional quiver of the strings, and if the young man drew breath more forcefully or exhaled into the weave of the instrument . . .

Finally, it came time to grasp with words the most ungraspable thing of all—the music. The young man began to open the windows, guided by sheer feeling, at first cautiously, in order not to tighten or relax the strings too much, not to entangle them. And then, in accordance with Madame Natalija's explanations, he began to follow the movements of the wind. Described them as merging, faster, or slower *glissandi*. The performance of compact chords in short, rapid succession was called *arpeggiato*. Conversely, when the tones of a chord began to sound simultaneously, in a tweaking fashion, *strappato*. Then there was soft, lyrical *flageoletta*. The halting of the strings' vibrations immediately upon plucking them was how *staccato* tones were formed. And *lasciare vibrare*, if one wished for a single string or more of them to sound freely until their natural dying out. The act of playing *bisbigliando* was the alternating of plucks to a soft whisper. And then, directly along the resonant body, *alla cassa*, in sharpness similar to a harpsichord. Followed by *con sordino*, a short, rustling tone obtained by the wind's weaving between the strings a slip of paper that it has carried in from somewhere. *Timpanato*, the full, brusque striking of a group of strings, was the means by which one produced a hollow sound, similar to the sound of a tympanum . . .

All the elements were gradually assembled, one with the other. Component by component. The harp tipped backward and would have surely fallen had the wind not shored it up on its shoulder, had it not possessed skillful hands. The pulp of its fingers was soft; it had nails, to thrust in furiously, to pluck painfully, to tear out from the middle; it knew how to curl its fingers caressingly, to strum delicately and to pick; to stop for a significant moment, and then tirelessly to flurry again; it knew how to cover a single tone, the way one traps a butterfly with one's hand, and from beneath one's palm there magically fly out hundreds of them . . . The music grew ever more sonorous. The author of the novel, Anastas Branica, had expertly designed the proportions of this room for listening, the corners, ceiling, and walls all in accordance with the laws of acoustics; and yet the music was best and most clearly heard probably there where the young man's soul was . . .

Adam didn't know how to name the titles of all the compositions he heard that evening, in the book brimming with the full moon and the east wind. He didn't know how to write out the notes, and so the only thing he could do was, upon each new scheme for opening the window casements, to record in his notebook only his own feelings. This would have to be nearly the same thing, he consoled himself. How long had Anastas Branica needed to build all this here, when Adam, on a single word, on the word *harp*, had already spent several hours, noting down merely fragments . . .

As dawn approached, it seemed that the wind, together with its music-making on the harp, brought in other instruments as well: from various directions would sound the call of the clarinet, the dark bassoon, the thunder of horns, or the rise of the exotic oboe, and then strings joined in more and more—and even a human voice. From the river reached the murmur of a piano, and at the crack of dawn, as the birds in the garden started to wake, there began to well up a true concert for flute and harp, so similar to Mozart's lively compositions . . .

The reborn day brought new happiness and new trepidation. It was dangerous to stay too long in this place; someone might appear, discover him. He most likely had accomplished something, preserved it, for consolation's sake. Adam hid the notebook under his untucked shirt, and then with a heavy heart, exactly as he had been instructed, erased every mention of the harp from the novel bound in saffian. The music room grew deaf. The sun shifted from daybreak toward morning; the young man saw no purpose in returning to his studio apartment for such a short period before it was time to wake up, and so he and decided to rest there where he found himself, curling up on the bare floor.

66

He was quite late. Even though he hadn't slept well. His back hurt from the uncomfortable position: He'd been reading, captivated by the novel, for nearly thirty hours over there, with short breaks.

"Adam!" he heard a child's voice as he was taking a shortcut in the direction of the glass pavilion, where in accordance with the schedule for that day his clients were waiting for him.

He turned around. Not a living soul anywhere. However, no sooner did he hurriedly continue on his way than the call was repeated:

"Adam! We're over here, up here!"

He lifted his eyes and indeed had something to see. On the first thick bough of a nearby edible chestnut tree, half-hidden by leaves with prominent ribs, sat two of the three Leleks. The little girl and her father.

"A very good day to you," the man again addressed him first.

"And a very good day to you . . ." the young man said, bewildered by the unusual sight. "And what are you doing there?"

"Resting," answered the man.

"We're resting a bit from the shadow," added the little girl, swinging her frail little legs back and forth.

And truly, a shadow several times larger than the man and the child was lying curled up at the base of the trunk; one of its ends was attempting to shimmy up the tree, but kept sliding downward.

"We're deluding ourselves," the man smiled sadly. "What else can we do?! My wife didn't want to come with us; she claims it's senseless, says that everything will be the same when we come down. As if I didn't know that. But anyway, I feel better for at least this much . . ."

"Now it can't do anything to us," said the girl, pointing to the outline curled up on the ground.

"Nothing, absolutely nothing. You're in a safe place." Adam tried to sound as reassuring as he could, deciding to write all this down faithfully, this entire meeting and conversation, so that it would last as long as possible; he could do no more than that.

That was the reason why he was even more late. He found his clients in an ill humor, impatiently standing beside a regularly cut piece of stone of red porphyry, with sides approximately three feet by three feet, raised breast-high and fixed into the grips of some kind of wooden base, in the very center of the glass pavilion from which all traces of the professor's existence had been removed. He suspected as much when he saw the tools prepared and a single stool, so he was not too surprised by the new demand. He was to do a bust of the woman. Nor did anyone have to tell him—a bust that would be placed on the empty pedestal in the section of the park that resembled a Renaissance labyrinth. A new bust that would occupy the place of the broken one whose pieces he had noticed on the occasion of his visit to Professor Tiosavljević.

"Consider this section of the book the most important one of your stay here!" the man added, but perhaps he had no need to; Adam quite saw through the purpose of his labors, of all those revisions wrested from Anastas Branica's novel.

The ill humor, on account of the young man's being late, that already familiar, haughty expression of the face, could not be ignored, however much the woman tried to assume as relaxed a bearing as possible, readying herself to pose for the basic proportions of the bust. But that was not his concern; Adam stepped back, sketching on the stone the basic lines of the shoulders and neck and the contours of the head. It was his task to do the sculpture in her likeness, as he had been told, he reassured himself, taking careful blows. The porphyry at first resisted; the chisel would glance across its surface, a swarm of sparks would fly, the angry echo of the stone would cause the numerous panes of the glass pavilion to rattle. To find the true measure of lightness and vigor—the secret of all that exists resides in that, and the secret of this work as well—the young man circled round, striking out with his hammer, now more feebly, now more forcefully. Only calmly, patiently, the partings of the hair were somewhere here; he had only to find them, probing with the chisel this way and that. An excess could be removed only with a single, savage blow, but the danger that the essence would be forever broken off as well was then the greater. It was necessary to envision, to approach from several angles, to adapt oneself to the billions-of-years-long petrified way of reasoning with the porphyry, to enter the train of its thoughts, and only then to accommodate oneself to them. Interpret them.

When under his chisel the first fragment broke off and dully rolled down, Adam knew by some special sense that he had managed to come to an understanding with the stone, to establish an initial trust between them. He knew that the porphyry would no longer be so obstinate, just as he knew that he didn't dare deceive it, force it to do anything contrary to its nature. They continued to regard each other in an ever greater cloud of dust, and it happened that the young man saw neither his hands nor the tool; the woman grew lethargic and left the pavilion, but Adam went on working despite the absence of his model. Hours went by. If for a moment he rested, the young man felt how the trembling within him did not subside, how it echoed in his head, how for a long time his muscles would not calm down, and that hectic look in his eyes, that feverishness, had seemingly returned.

"This is all you've done—can't you go any faster?" the woman said with disappointment the next time she entered, finding the piece of stone merely something like a babushka doll, a preliminary, amorphous shape, hardly like the shape of a bosom, neck, and head.

He made no reply. He silently seized the chisel, now the pick, and then various other tools; he sought angles, reduced mass, attempted to shape the protuberances, the expressive points of the forehead, the pulp of the cheeks, the nose, the tip of the chin, the collar bones at the base of the neck . . . Well into the afternoon he reached for the sculptor's brush, a kind of serrated chisel, and there emerged from the stone the beginning of an intimation.

"We'll continue tomorrow," he said suddenly, laying down his tools, not really sure whether he was merely tired or whether he wanted to put off the final revealing in order to enjoy that intimation for as long as possible.

"Stop—come back . . ." he heard an angry voice behind him, but for the first time he didn't care how the woman would interpret his disobedience.

67

The water poured over his face, slid down his chest, down his upper and lower stomach, down his thighs, lower legs, and ankles, then spiraled down one of those nickel-plated, grated openings, and then onward into the subterranean outflow of the big city. Ah, if only besides the stone dust clinging to his sweat, it could free him of his pangs of guilt as well, if besides that film it could wash away his rash assent to make changes in the mysterious novel, if only it could unclothe him of his feeling of bad conscience. Or, if it still wasn't too late, if only he could do that by himself. By himself, as was the only possible way of doing it.

"Yes, as is the only possible way of doing it . . ." Adam acknowledged his thoughts aloud, drying his hair in the tiny bathroom of the rented studio apartment, changing into clean clothes, discerning more and more clearly what it was he might do.

And at once. It was unlikely that he had much time left. At most a day or two and his client would ask for the return of his book bound in saffian. He turned this thought over and over in his mind while he again stuck that notebook into the belt of his blue jeans, while he sharpened his pencils and considered where the best place was to begin, that is, to continue what he had already started, noting down everything about the harp, describing his meeting with the Leleks . . . There is no doubt that had the telephone not begun to ring, he would not have hesitated another moment.

"Hello, Lozanić?!" he recognized the voice of the chief editor of the tourism and nature magazine.

"Yes, speaking."

"Just you wait, Lozanić. Just you wait. When I get my hands on you, believe me, you will no longer be you. In front of me are the proofs, the texts for the new issue. The holiday issue! And on the first, inner page is my editorial! Do you remember, Lozanić, my editorial?"

"Of course. Some mistake hasn't crept in, has it?"

"No, nothing's crept in! You purposely corrected my text! Purpose-ly! You abridged it! And you wrote in your own observations!" shouted the man on the other end.

"But I had to. Arctic reindeer don't exist here . . ."

"And who are you to decide that? Who?"

"I'm telling you that . . ."

"Not a word! How do you even dare?! And I had so much trust. Do you understand, trust! It's a good thing I looked everything over again before it went to the printer!"

"Do as you please. It wasn't the truth. There aren't any—"

"Ingrate! Say goodbye to your fee! Any fee! And say goodbye to your job! I've had enough of your sophistry! Don't let me see you again in my office. Do you think I won't find someone like you?! And better?! *Our Scenic Beauty* no longer requires your services!"

"But wait!" Adam shouted now, afraid the editor would hang up. "Wait, so that I can tell you something!"

"I've already made up my mind. It's not worth your trying to explain!"

"No, not at all . . . I just wanted to tell you that I couldn't care less. Do you hear me—that I couldn't care less," said the young man, trying hard to communicate as clearly as possible just how he felt, and then he leisurely lowered the receiver onto the cradle of the telephone.

68

He didn't have to try very hard in order to forget the unpleasant conversation. The mysterious novel by Anastas Branica preoccupied the young man as never before. Perhaps because now he took a different view of it. Perhaps because now he took a different view of himself.

The fact remains that although he didn't know quite well why, he began to copy whole sections, to transcribe entire descriptions, sometimes in no particular order, at random, diligently noting down tens and hundreds of details, unaware of most of them until they fell into his hands, and then entering the expansive discussion on the appearance of the intimidatingly vast vault of the sky or the surrounding mountain chain. Without any particular plan, but with the hope that it could all be put together in a narrative, a story without end.

During daylight hours he wandered through the splendor of the garden, noting down the crossways and intersecting lines of the trails, entering also beside the meander of the paths, to evoke the lush growth of the vegetation and the seething life of the neglected microscopic world within it; and when the daylight began to wane he worked no less diligently around the once more light and dark yellow façade of the house, striving to conjure up all its architectural elements, all the proportions of Anastas Branica's futile memorial. Of the residents he met no one, not counting the fact that he was being closely observed by that Pokimica. Always at a respectful distance, the young man walked toward him several times so that he might explain why he was spying on him, but the stiff figure, the man with the hair cropped close, military-style, would then immediately disappear and the feeling of unease would remain, whispering to him that someone was watching him.

Just before sunset, by the outer staircase, he again climbed up to the terrace-belvedere, sat in the wrought iron chair, and attempted to compose one more description of the domain. Had he been an artist, he would have surely used pastel chalks, in this way endeavoring to employ the softest possible words, those words that fill in every pore, each uneven spot. Thus did he write everything down, even with the pulp of his right forefinger sometimes passing over the lines, softening further the letters done in graphite, when he first smelled that familiar, pleasant odor, and then heard her voice. It was Jelena.

"Are you working?!" she asked, halting in front of him. She was wearing that linen traveling dress and holding an English dictionary under her arm.

"I'm writing," he answered.

"But erasing a little something, too," she added sarcastically. "In the music room there is no longer a harp, and on the bureaus and chests of drawers are someone else's things. The old woman is beside herself. How could you have spoiled things for her that way?! Why? And for whose benefit? That is so very, very cruel; she didn't have very many memories left, and you . . ."

"Just hold on, allow me to explain . . ." he opened his mouth to say.

"There's no need. Now it's clear that you've been dissembling. And that you are one of them. One of those who whatever the cost snatch things right from under people's eyes," she scornfully interrupted him.

"But you're mistaken! For goodness' sake, allow me. Look, everything is written down here, as much as I understood of it, as much as I was able and knew how. Read it," he said, almost begging her, setting down the notebook on the wrought iron table.

"It doesn't interest me! It doesn't interest me in the least . . ." she said stubbornly, closing her eyes. "I no longer wish to have anything to do with this lying language! Anything at all. I'm sick of everything . . ."

"Read it! Just a little . . ." Adam Lozanić beseeched her in a cracked voice.

"*Life, lift, ligament, light, like, lilt, lily, limb* . . ." She still held her eyes closed, spitefully reeling off, by heart, her English lesson.

"Just a sentence . . ." the young man implored.

"*Pace, pachyderm, pacific, pack, pact, pad, paddle, paddock, paddy, padlock, page* . . ." She took no notice.

"A word, just a single word . . ." he concluded, brokenhearted.

"*Pageant, pail, pain, paint, pair* . . ." The girl went on speaking for a little while longer, now somewhat less convincingly, and then she fell silent and slightly opened her eyes.

Adam didn't speak. He no longer had anything to say. Everything depended on her, Jelena.

She leaned forward. Mistrustfully. From somewhere the wind picked up. The east wind. It riffled through the pages. And then suddenly stopped—when it had found the place where the previous evening the old woman, the good Natalija Dimitrijević, had said with difficulty to her companion: "Then why are you behaving this way . . . Don't flee from him . . . He is a man whose glance you can rely on . . . Child, that's no small matter . . . That's everything . . . That's love . . . Jelena, if he's managed to see you here, then how will he look at you over there . . ." The young girl read this. And then lifted her altered eyes.

"And as for the harp . . ." he said, turning the pages. "It's here somewhere."

Leaning forward together, so close, one right next to the other, closer even than every bodily closeness allows, Jelena and Adam read side by side all that he had written about the music room and the slender instrument, about the windows and the virtuoso wind . . .

"It's not exactly everything as in Anastas Branica . . . I singled out only the most important . . . But I forgot about the chairs . . ." he apologized with a smile; they had nowhere to sit.

"It doesn't matter . . ." she said, and lowered herself to the bare floor.

"Do you see this interweaving pattern . . . Perhaps I haven't captured precisely every tone . . ." he said, and joined her.

"Forgive me . . ." she said as softly as she could and rested her head on his shoulder.

Adam Lozanić didn't dare to add a thing, so as not to spoil the converging of souls that he had so dreamed about.

EPILOGUE

ABOUT HOW SOME THINGS ENDED,
AND HOW SOME OTHER THINGS BEGAN

NATALIJA DIMITRIJEVIĆ DIED ON TUESDAY morning, on the terrace-belvedere of Anastas Branica's house. She had no longer been able to remember a single, solitary word; she had kept silent for about a quarter of an hour, gazing fixedly at the horizon, the illusory junction of earth and sky. And then she gave up waiting. For some time yet the landscape remained in her open, tranquil-green eyes . . .

That was on the morning when Sreten Pokimica picked a bouquet of late-blooming, tragic-red rosebuds, preparing to confess to her who he really was, preparing to ask for forgiveness, to tell her how he had done everything with the best of intentions, out of love, on account of her. Instead of all this he only reached out his hand and closed Natalija's eyes, confining all which was still reflected in them: the French park, the contours of the forked trails, the crowns of the hundred-year-old oak trees, a distant flock of birds, that entire domain, and even his own mournful countenance, his very self. And then he again went down among the flowerbeds, sank to his knees, and remorsefully continued to tend to the seedlings in the garden . . .

The family with the shadow never again appeared among the pages of Anastas Branica's novel. Just as one did not know where they had come from, so one never learned where they had disappeared to. Perhaps the Leleks fled into some other crevice of the quotidian, taking refuge from their own unhappy life.

Contrary to their custom, the owners of the copy of the book bound in saffian that very same morning dropped into the kitchen, from which cries and shouts were heard; only two hours later the good housekeeper Zlatana found herself on a Belgrade street corner, without any identity papers. After fifty-odd years of being absent from reality, she didn't really know where she might go now; at nightfall, they brought her to the nearest police station, and as they had no idea what to do with her, she was placed that same evening in an appropriate institution for the uncared-for.

"How many of you are there?! Not a single story wants any of you either?" she asked the passersby just as loudly as she did the homeless people in the shelter.

Meanwhile, that couple went to the glass pavilion, where there doubtlessly awaited an unpleasant surprise. The bust of enduring porphyry not only did not resemble the wife of the man who had ordered the work, but had been sculpted in the likeness of that girl, Jelena. When the two went to discuss the matter with Adam Lozanić, they found the door to the studio apartment on Milovan Milovanović Street open, and in the tiny flat a certain Mojsilović.

"I evicted him. He moved out this morning. I kept all his books until he settles the rent he owes," he explained.

"This is ours," said the man, pointing his finger and picking up from a pile beside the bed a title bound in saffian.

"It's all right with me. Take it; I don't know what to do with all of them anyway . . ." said the landlord and shrugged his shoulders.

"Can you imagine? He did nothing; there's not a single correction anywhere. He even returned everything to the way it was—he didn't even leave our names . . ." said the woman, leafing through the pages, as all three of them descended the staircase.

"You'll have to forgive me, I'm in a hurry . . . I have important business to attend to on Palmotić Street; one of my female wards has passed away . . ." Mojsilović took his leave on the street and enthusiastically moved out of sight toward Balkanska.

The woman and man still stood there, facing the tavern Our Sea. She was the first to remark:

"If I'm not mistaken, only the end is somewhat different. It's written here: *Adam and Jelena untied a rowboat on the bank of a river, took it out to the middle of the main current, and set sail. The young man rowed, while the girl read to him from a small notebook on her knees . . .*"

The husband bent over the concluding pages and said:

"It's too late to do anything . . . They've already crossed over the horizon line . . ."

NOTES

9 *Dictionary of the Serbian Language*: The reference is to the famous *Matica srpska* (literally, Serbian queen bee) edition. Its emblem was a beehive, which was usually stamped onto the book's covers.

13 *Kopaonik*: mountain resort in southwest Serbia.

14 *Terazije*: literally, balance or weight scales. A main city square and business district in Belgrade.

16 *Roland Barthes* (French, 1915–1980), *Yuri Tynyanov* (Russian, 1894–1943), *Hans Robert Jauss* (German, 1921–1997), *Wolfgang Iser* (German, 1926–) and (Bruce) *Nauman* (American, 1941–): all are cultural critics of a postmodernist stripe.

17 *Wilhelm Wörringer* (1881–1965): German Expressionist painter and art theorist.

Vračar: also known as Vračar Hill, a district in central Belgrade in which Karadjordje Park and the modern National Library are located. Vračar is mentioned for the first time in the Turkish plan of Belgrade in the year 1526.

Slavija district: Slavija is a district in central Belgrade, in the shape of a rotary.

18 *Mitić's hole*: the foundation pit for a planned department store in the Slavija district. Somewhat before World War II a wealthy wholesale merchant named Vlada Mitić decided to build what was to be "the largest department store in the Balkans," most likely his fourth such store in Belgrade. Then came the war and the arrival of a new communist government, which promptly seized everything Mitić owned, including the foundation pit. The department store was never built. The foundation pit remained for thirty-five years until the early 1980s, when an ambitious city government decided to fill it in and build a park without any trees to hinder the sundial that was to be placed there. One member of the city council, Tirnanić by name, argued vociferously against the sundial, but it would have been better had he not; the property was again bought in 1992 and the hole re-excavated for a new building. This venture also fell through and the foundation pit remained until 2000, surrounded by a fence of green plywood, when it was converted into a city park.

the old Hotel Slavija: The reference is to the original Hotel Slavija, on the Square of Dimitrije Tucović, built in 1887. In 1962 a new Hotel Slavija was built alongside it. On city maps the "old" Slavija is referred to as "Slavija I" and the annex as "Slavija II."

22   *St. John the Baptist Day 7/20 January 1936:* re: the notation 7/20: Within the
      Eastern Orthodox Church, feast days and fast days are reckoned according
      to two distinct calendars, the Julian calendar and the Gregorian calendar.
      Until the end of World War I all Orthodox Churches had strictly abided by
      the old (Julian) calendar, which is at present thirteen days behind the new cal-
      endar adopted by the rest of Christendom. Several Orthodox Churches (the
      Churches of Constantinople, Alexandria, Antioch, Greece, Cyprus, Romania,
      Poland, and Bulgaria) eventually agreed to adopt the new calendar, while the
      Churches of Jerusalem, Russia, and Serbia all continued to adhere to the old
      calendar. The result of this situation is that the Orthodox Churches that have
      adopted the new calendar observe Christmas with the other Churches of
      Christendom on December 25, while the Orthodox Churches that have not
      adopted it celebrate Christmas thirteen days later, on January 7. And so it is
      with all the great feast days of the Christian calendar, except for Easter, which
      continues to be calculated by all Orthodox Churches to the dates of the old
      calendar. Hence the designation 7/20 January for St. John the Baptist Day.

      the full stops after the years were missing: In the writing of Serbo-Croatian
      dates, a period is normally placed after the year when this is expressed in
      numbers, even if it is not at the end of the sentence.

25   *BARBANATZ:* a special type of oil on which float the wicks of certain
      candles.

34   *St. Petka:* (Sveta Petka): a woman saint of Eastern Orthodox Christianity,
      also known as Paraskeva of Epivatos and St. Petka the Bulgarian. She was
      born in the eleventh century in the city of Epivatos, which is between
      Siliviria and Constantinople. Following the death of her parents, St. Petka
      strictly devoted herself to the monastic life. After five years of fasting and
      prayer, she went to the Holy Land (Palestine) to live in the desert in Jordan.
      In her old age she returned to Constantinople to the Church of Holy
      Theotokos in Blachernae to revere the miraculous icon of the Mother of
      God. In 1238 St. Petka's relics were moved from Epivatos to Tarnovo, then
      the capital of Bulgaria. After the Turkish occupation of Bulgaria, the rel-
      ics were moved again—this time to Vidim, on the Danube. In 1396, when
      the Turks conquered this area as well, the Serbian princess Milica acted to
      bring the holy relics to Belgrade. In 1417 the Church of St. Petka was built
      in Belgrade, and her holy relics were placed there. In 1521, after the mighty
      Suleiman II conquered Belgrade, St. Petka's remains, along with many
      Serbian families, were moved to Constantinople. In 1641, with the per-
      mission of Constantinople's patriarch, Parthenius I, the pious Moldavian
      ruler Vasilije Lupul brought St. Petka's remains to Moldavia's capital, Jash,
      where on 14/27 October they were placed in the church of the Three Holy
      Hierarchs, where St. Petka's holy relics still remain. St. Petka-Paraskeva
      is the second-most venerated woman after the Virgin Mary in the area
      stretching from Greece to Russia, including Romania, Serbia, Bulgaria,

and North Macedonia. She has become the protectress of the area between Paradise and Hell where the souls of unbaptized children are said to go.

36   *Brothers Moser*: formerly Ludwig Moser & Sons, a renowned Czech glassworks.

42   *this was no ordinary wind*: The reference is to the *košava*, a southern or southeasterly wind that blows across the Serbian plains.

     bringing a bundle of oak branches and straw: Serbian Orthodox Christmas custom. Traditionally, on the day before Christmas (January 6), in the morning the male head of each household goes in search of a *badnjak*, a young oak tree from which branches and leaves are cut and carried home along with a handful of straw. These Yule branches are then burned in the family hearth (in villages) or placed on or in front of the door of the home (in cities); the straw is scattered onto the floor. The Yule branches are symbolic of the branches used by the shepherds in Bethlehem to light a fire beside the newborn Jesus and his mother, while the straw represents the straw of Christ's manger.

     she took a cake decorated with . . . the letters of Christ's name . . . honey: The reference is to the so-called Slava cake. The Serbian Orthodox Slava is a yearly family feast in honor of its patron saint. Each Serbian family has its own patron saint (e.g., St. Nikola or St. John the Baptist, as is the case here with Natalija Dimitrijević), who is ordinarily passed down from generation to generation along male lines (from grandfather to father to son). On the day of the Slava, family and friends gather for the feast, a part of which is the Slava cake. This cake is actually a sacrificial bread which has its origins in pre-Christian times, always round in shape (symbolic of the sun), and specially decorated with small dough birds, grapes, and braids glazed with diluted honey, symbolizing fertility, prosperity, and a good harvest. In addition, four letters are impressed into the cake's upper surface: Is.Hs. Ni.Ka, which means *Isus Hristos je pobedilac* (Christ is victor). During the Slava feast, it is not eaten like ordinary bread; instead, each guest symbolically takes a small piece of it. In this instance, Madame Natalija is bringing a Slava cake to St. Mark's Church.

44   *Palace Albanija*: (Palata Albanija): a thirteen-story office building on Terazije (Knez Mihailova Street 4–6) which was completed in 1940 and, at sixty-five meters high, long remained the tallest building in the Balkans. It derived its name from the café that previously occupied the spot on which it was built. It was designed by the architect Milan Prljević and constructed by Đorđ Lazarević.

46   *Stanković Music School*: a famous music school in Belgrade that exists to the present day.

47   *centuries-old Serbian church books*: The reference is to the *srbulja*, a medieval Serbian church book of Eastern Orthodox rites.

Kosančić Venac (venac = wreath): the street on which the old building of the National Library was located from 1920 to 1941. On April 6, 1941, this building was destroyed in the German bombing of Belgrade along with most of its priceless collection of books and manuscripts. At the time of the bombing the library consisted of some 140,000 volumes (among them about 1,800 rare books dating from the fifteenth to eighteenth centuries), 1,400 manuscripts and other historical documents, and approximately 2,000 letters. In its long and stormy history, the National Library has changed buildings several times. It is now located in the central Belgrade district of Vračar, near St. Sava Cathedral, in a building that was completed in 1973.

Veselin Čajkanović (1881–1946): a corresponding member of the Serbian Academy of Arts and Sciences (SANU) and professor at Belgrade University, translator of classical languages. An ethnographer and ethnologist, he published important studies on the religion and folklore of the Serbs.

Bishop Nikolaj Velimirović (1880–1956): bishop of the Ohrid and Žiča monasteries. He was arrested by German authorities on July 12, 1941, and imprisoned in the monastery Ljubostinja until December 3, 1942. In 1944 he, along with Patriarch Gavrilo, were taken to the camp at Dachau and subsequently released through the efforts of Dimitrije Ljotić, a Serbian politician who has been accused by some of having been a Nazi collaborator (see note for "Ljotić's supporters," p. 253, below).

48 *Zajc's "Where Are You, My Love"*: The reference is to the song by Ivan Plemenit Zajc (1832–1914), a Croatian composer.

77 *on the fortieth day after his death*: The reference is to the so-called *četresnica*, the fortieth day after a person's death. The liturgy of the Serbian Orthodox Church prescribes that a requiem for the deceased be held seven days, forty days, six months, and one year after their death; announcements of these memorial services are usually published in the newspapers along with the remembrances of relations and friends. The četresnica is especially significant because Serbian Orthodoxy holds that only after forty days is the soul assigned the place where it will reside until the resurrection of the dead. Until then it is free to wander the heavenly habitations and the abysses of hell, not knowing where it will remain.

79 *Jekavian dialect*: Three distinct basic dialects exist in spoken Serbo-Croatian. They are referred to as *Čakavian, Kajkavian,* and *Štokavian* according to whether the word "ča," "kaj," or "što" is used, respectively, as the interrogative pronoun *what*? Štokavian is by far the most widely used in the former Yugoslavia. The Štokavian dialect itself has three subdialects, which emerged as a result of different developments in the pronunciation of the long vowel ě. The speakers of one subdialect came to

pronounce it as *i*, those of the second as *e*, and those of the third as *je* or *ije*. The word for *child*, for instance, is "dite," "dete," or "dijete" according to which sub-dialect is used. Jekavian (or, alternately, Ijekavian) is the third of these subdialects of Štokavian. It is spoken in most of Croatia, in western Serbia, Montenegro, Southern Dalmatia east of the Neretva, and in Bosnia-Herzegovina east of the rivers Bosna and Neretva. Serbs living in Croatia west of the rivers Bosna and Neretva speak Jekavian (*Serbo-Croat Practical Grammar and Reader*, Monica Partridge).

95   *Veliki Vračar*: a wooded, hilly area on the eastern edge of Belgrade; formerly part of the greater Vračar district.

96   *renamed Zvezdara only when the observatory was built*: The reference is to the Belgrade Astronomical Observatory on Veliki Vračar. The name *Zvezdara* derives from the word *zvezda* (star).

universal world tree: a rather complicated symbol associated with Orthodox Christianity, represented in various ways, usually as a connecting of three worlds, rooted deeply in the earth and in contact with the waters. The tree grows in a world of time, and its branches reach to the heavens and eternity. *Axis mundi*—axis of the world. *Imago mundi*—image of the world.

killed in 1903, immediately after the May coup: The reference is to the assassination on May 29, 1903, of King Aleksandar Obrenović and Queen Draga Mašin and the subsequent election to the throne of Peter I Karadjordjević. This spelled the official end of the Obrenović Dynasty and the beginning of the Karadjordjević Dynasty.

103 *brothers Lunjevica*: the two brothers of Queen Draga Mašin. In the summer of 1900, against the express wishes of his closest advisers, King Aleksandar rashly decided to marry his mistress, Draga Mašin (née Lunjevica), the widow of a Czech engineer and a woman much older than him. During the widespread unrest in Serbia in April 1903 following Aleksandar's suspension of the more liberal constitution that he himself had promulgated two years earlier, wild rumors circulated that Queen Draga intended to secure the succession to the throne for her two brothers. The brothers Lunjevica were assassinated along with King Aleksandar and Queen Draga in the Belgrade Royal Palace in the May 1903 coup.

104 *Order of the Cross of Takovo*: a military decoration given exclusively to artillery officers.

105 *Gründerzeit beds, the provincial Alt-Deutsch dressing table*: *Gründerzeit* and *Alt-Deutsch* refer to German/Viennese stylistic periods in furniture and architecture, circa 1870–95.

cross-river porcelain wall clock: a porcelain wall clock made across the Sava and Danube Rivers, in the now northern Serbian autonomous province of Vojvodina and beyond.

107 *Nativity of Blessed Virgin Mary Day: Mala gospojina*: September 21.

111 *Helmut von Moltke* (1800–1891): Prussian field marshal.

118 *Josif Pančić* (1814–1888): famous botanist and first president of the Serbian Academy of Arts and Sciences (SANU). In 1875 he discovered on the slope of Tara Mountain, in Kopaonik in southwestern Serbia, a unique kind of conifer, named Pančić's spruce.

119 *Sava Petrović*: nineteenth-century Serbian physician, one of the founders of the *Srpsko lekarsko društvo* (Serbian Medical Society) in 1872. His book *Medicinal Herbs in Serbia* was published in the same year.

121 *the year 1912*: The reference is to the First Balkan War (1912–13), in which Bulgaria, Serbia, Greece, and Montenegro, as allies, fought against Turkey. When war broke out, all of North Macedonia, Albania, and Epirus still formed part of the Ottoman Empire.

   Kumanovo: town in North Macedonia at which Serbia scored an important victory against the Turks on October 25, 1912.

   Vardar division of the Turkish army: The reference is to the Vardar River in central North Macedonia, to which the Turks retreated following their signal defeat at Kumanovo. In 1912 Turkish regular forces comprised twelve divisions of very weak establishment in Thrace and twelve similar divisions stationed at various points in the Ottoman territories farther to the west. The Vardar division was one of them.

   Zeki Pasha: Turkish general of the cavalry, adjutant general of the Turkish sultan, and military envoy plenipotentiary to the German emperor. He commanded the North Macedonian army during the Serbian onslaught of Kumanovo in the First Balkan War.

   Bitolj: town in North Macedonia.

122 *Peter I Karadjordjević* (1860–1921): son of Prince Aleksandar Karadjordjević (ruled 1839–1858) and grandson of Karadjordje Petrović (ruled 1804–1813), the founder of the Karadjordjević Dynasty. Peter I succeeded to the throne after the assassination of King Aleksandar Obrenović and Queen Draga Mašin in the May 1903 coup. He was king of Serbia from 1903 to 1918, and afterward king of the newly formed Kingdom of Serbs, Croats and Slovenes from 1918 to 1921. He led Serbia through the Balkan Wars and World War I.

   Pavlovsk: an imperial Romanov summer palace outside St. Petersburg, Russia.

124 *the Circle of Serbian Sisters*: a Serbian women's association involved in various religious, community, and charitable activities of interest to Serbs. Many chapters of this organization exist abroad in the Serbian diaspora. The organization takes its name from the word *kolo*, a Balkan circle dance

without the accompaniment of musical instruments that Serbs performed during the centuries of Turkish rule.

Zemun: town on the right bank of the Danube and separated from Belgrade by the River Sava. In medieval times it was the site of fighting between the town's inhabitants and soldiers of the First Crusade (1096). During battles between the Byzantines and Hungarians, the Byzantine czar Manojlo I Komnin destroyed the Hungarian fortress in Zemun (1154), but later restored it. In the fifteenth century the town belonged to Serbian despots and Hungarian magnates. In 1521 Zemun was attacked by the Turks, and in 1717 the Austrian army attacked the Turks. In more recent times, the World War II Nazi puppet Independent State of Croatia included all of Zemun, extending to the bank of the Danube River.

132 *the "Sanitary Woolen System" of Dr. Gustav Jaeger*: Gustav Jaeger was a nineteenth-century German professor of physiology at the University of Stuttgart who in 1884 developed "scientific" theories about the wearing of hygienic wool next to the skin. The health culture known as Dr. Jaeger's "Sanitary Woolen System" sought to encourage people to use wool fibers in all domestic textiles, from clothing to bedding. The wearing of such textiles, claimed Dr. Jaeger, was "healthy." Writer George Bernard Shaw was among the first to boldly don a "straight-from-the-sheep" Jaeger suit and tie in fashionable London.

135 *Kalemegdan Park*: park on the Kalemegdan, a hill overlooking the confluence of the Sava and Danube Rivers, in the oldest part of Belgrade. In Roman times it was known as Singidunum. Owing to its strategic location it has throughout history been the site of fortifications, which have been besieged, destroyed, and rebuilt successively by Celts, Romans, Byzantines, Slavs, Hungarians, Turks, and Austrians. In 1867 the Austrians were the last to restore these fortifications, so that the fortress that exists today is composed of Roman ramparts, Serbian medieval fortifications, and Turkish and Austrian buildings.

Saborna Church: a cathedral just outside Kalemegdan Park, built in the period 1837–40. *Saborna* means "gathering," hence the appellation "the Gathering Church."

137 *mouse fever*: known medically as hemorrhagic fever, an infectious disease of rodents caused by a virus. From the time of infection to the appearance of the first symptoms of the disease usually takes between three and seven weeks. The illness begins suddenly and is accompanied by fever, chills, headache, sore throat, dry mouth, and a feeling of thirst. In its first phase, redness may also appear on the mucous membranes of the eyes and the skin of the face and neck. The disease most often appears in mild form, but if left untreated it can develop into hemorrhagic syndrome—bleeding of the skin, mucous membranes, and internal organs, notably the kidneys—and ultimately lead to death.

139 *Palilula Marketplace*: a marketplace in Palilula, a district in eastern Belgrade.

152 *Košutnjak*: literally, "deer preserve;" a park in southwest Belgrade.

158 *medieval Serbian church book*: see note for "centuries old Serbian church books," p. 48, above.

Nemanjić procession: The reference is to the frescoes depicting the Serbian kings of the Nemanjić Dynasty, founded by Stefan Nemanja, Great Župan (head of tribal state) of Serbia from 1166 to 1196. Stefan Nemanja founded the Hilandar monastery and many others. He died as Monk Simeon in Hilandar in the year 1200.

159 *the despot Jovan Oliver, a feudal lord of Czar Stefan Dušan the Mighty*: The term *despot* should not be understood in a pejorative sense in this usage: a despot is a Byzantine emperor or prince, or a bishop or patriarch of the Eastern Orthodox Church. Stefan Dušan the Mighty was king of Serbia (1331–46) and czar of the Serbs (1346–55). His wife was the Bulgarian princess Helene. He was the founder of many monasteries, including Archangel of Prizren (Kosovo) and St. Savior in Skopje (North Macedonia).

mushrooms, prepared in water: the Lenten preparation of mushrooms, as opposed to cooking them in oil.

metohs: (hist.) a small church, monastery, or the land around it that is given as an appendage to a large monastery.

167 *banovina*: (hist.) a regional administrative unit ruled by a *ban* (civil governor or viceroy). For instance, *bans* were civil governors of Croatia and Slavonia.

177 *the islands of Murano*: Murano is a town in northeast Italy in Venetia on islands in the Lagoon of Venice, north of Venice.

179 *Sajmište*: literally, the Old Fairgrounds, a stretch of land on the bank of the Sava River across from Old Belgrade. It was first opened in 1937 and successfully served as the location of various fairs. During World War II it was the site of an infamous concentration camp operated by the Germans, in which Jews and Yugoslavs were killed in a bestial manner. It was run by the German Gestapo until May 1944, when it was handed to the Croatian Ustaše, Nazi allies during the war. See, for example, *Götz and Meyer*, by David Albahari, Random House, New York (2005), Ellen Elias-Bursac, translator.

180 *Toma Rosandić* (1878–1959): Serbian sculptor.

181 *Stanislav Vinaver* (1891–1955): Serbian Jewish poet, essayist, humorist, and satirist. In Rebecca West's famous 1937 account of her visit to Yugoslavia, *Black Lamb and Grey Falcon*, the character Constantine was in fact Stanislav Vinaver.

183 *the memorial "to my homeland" of Miša Anastasijević*: The reference is to a palace on Belgrade's Student Square, known as "Captain Miša's Building," which was built in 1863 by the rich merchant and former mayor of Belgrade Miša Anastasijević. Written in golden letters across its façade is *Miša Anastasijević presents this to his homeland*. The building is today the site of the Rectory of the University of Belgrade.

184 *Zenithist tracts, manifestos, and the open letters of Ljubomir Micić and Branko Ve Poljanski*: Zenithism was a Yugoslav movement of the 1920s begun by two avant-garde artists, the poet Ljubomir Micić (1895–1971) and his poet-painter brother, Branko Ve Poljanski (1897–1947). The official organ of this movement was the magazine *Zenith*, which was begun by Micić in Zagreb in February 1921. Zenithism heralded "the new man" and the dawning of "a new age of creation"; its motto was, *Not to live out of duty, but out of inspiration*. For a short while the most distinguished Serbian modernists (Rastko Petrović, Stanislav Vinaver, Dušan Matić, Miloš Crnjanski, Stanislav Krakov) wrote for the *Zenith*, but later broke with it over the publication in June 1921 of the *Zenithist Manifesto*, whose authors were Micić, Yvan Goll, and Boško Tokin.

Blue Circle editions of the Serbian Literary Society: One of the oldest publishers in Serbia, the Serbian Literary Society (founded 1892) has for more than a hundred years issued its Blue Circle edition of books, whose print style and classic blue-gray bindings have not changed over time. As part of this edition, the most important Serbian writers and foreign translations have been published. The term "circle" (*kolo*) refers to the cycle of books that has been published in a period of one year.

the Heraldry *of Hristofor Žefarović*: Hristofor Žefarović was the first Serbian lithographer. His important book of engravings *Stematografija* (Heraldry) was published in Vienna in 1741.

185 *Orfelin's calligraphy*: The reference is to Zaharija Stefanović Orfelin (1726–1785), a polymath who was a man of letters, historian, botanist, physicist, theologian, painter, and brilliant calligrapher. Around 1850 he wrote a book entitled *The Great Serbian Herbarium*, in which he described the sanative effects of some five hundred herb species.

the ethnographic studies of Veselin Čajkanović: see note for "Veselin Čajkanović," p. 47, above.

186 *Alfred Brehm*: Alfred Edmund Brehm (1829–1884), German zoologist. He published in 1864–69 his immensely popular illustrated *Tierleben* (*The Life of Animals*) in six volumes, in which he showed himself to be a superb prose writer.

192 *the relocated Knez Miloš fountain*: a fountain in front of the Hotel Moskva on Terazije (see note for "Terazije," p. 14, above). At the urging of Prince Miloš Obrenović in 1860, the fountain was placed on Terazije, but was

moved in 1911 to Topčider, a wooded region near Košutnjak in southwest Belgrade and the site of Prince Miloš's palace ("Konak Kneza Miloša"). The fountain was returned to its original location on Terazije in 1975.

Moskva: Hotel Moskva on Terazije. In its present form it was built in 1906 by the Serbian architect Jovan Ilkić, and is the most famous hotel in Belgrade.

193 *Old Palace*: *Stari dvor*: Built in 1882 by the architect Aleksandar Bugarski, it was the residence of the last rulers of the Obrenović Dynasty, King Aleksandar Obrenović and Queen Draga Mašin, who were assassinated there on May 29, 1903 (see note for "killed in 1903...," p. 96, above). From 1903 to 1941 it was the residence of rulers of the Karadjordjević Dynasty. The Old Palace is today the seat of the Belgrade City Council.

194 *Avala*: a mountain (511 meters high) eighteen kilometers from Belgrade. Heavily wooded with deciduous trees and conifers, it is a popular picnic grounds for Belgrade residents.

Baš-Čelik: literally, "true steel," "man of steel." Baš-Čelik is a villain from Serbian folklore whose tyrannical rule is challenged by a young hero, Nebojša. Baš-Čelik kidnaps the girl that Nebojša loves and imprisons her in his castle, intending to make her his bride. Since ordinary swords cannot kill Baš-Čelik, Nebojša goes on a quest to find the only sword that can, the legendary sword that can cut steel, only to find out, after many adventures in faraway lands, that such a sword can be made by simple peasants. Nebojša organizes an army and in the end destroys Baš-Čelik's castle, frees the girl, and kills Baš-Čelik, ending his tyranny forever. Baš-Čelik was also the title of a popular children's comic strip by the cartoonist Đorđe Lobačev, a Russian emigrant who died in 2002.

Clemens Riefler: a Munich-based German company that produced precision pendulum clocks at the turn of the twentieth century.

198 *Monument of Gratitude to France*: a bronze sculpture by Ivan Meštrović (1883–1962), erected in 1930 in Belgrade's Kalemegdan Park in gratitude to France for its military assistance to Serbia on the Salonika Front (see following note), for its educational assistance to Serbian students who studied in France during World War I, and for its support of Serbia during the course of that war. The sculpture is a monumental allegory, reminiscent of Nike, the winged Greek goddess of victory.

Salonika Front: World War I theater of operations. In October 1915 Bulgaria entered the war on the side of the Central Powers and attacked Serbia, with an eye to seizing Bulgarian Macedonia, which Serbia had claimed as its share of the spoils in the Second Balkan War in 1913. Facing this threat, Serbia appealed to Britain and France for military assistance. At the same time, Greece sought help from the Allies in honoring their treaty commitment to defend Serbia in the event of war. The British and French sent a small force that landed at the Greek port of Salonika (Thessaloniki) in early October. They advanced into Macedonia and engaged a Bulgarian reconnaissance force, but too late to help the Serbs, who had to retreat westward across the mountains of Albania to the Adriatic Sea. The Allies then withdrew to Salonika and set up an entrenchment camp, waiting for the Bulgarians to attack. The Bulgarians did not attack Salonika but instead consolidated their gains in Macedonia. The Allies continued to build up their forces and advanced to the Serbian frontier, liberating the town of Monastir. In the spring of 1917 the Allies again attacked but failed to break through. However, in September 1918, they attacked once more and within two weeks' time obtained Bulgaria's unconditional surrender.

199 *Patriarch Varnava*: Varnava (Petar Rosić) was Patriarch of the Serbian Orthodox Church from 1930–37. In July 1935 the government of Dr. Milan Stojadinović signed a concordat with the Vatican that, in the eyes of many in the Serbian Orthodox priesthood, granted the Roman Catholic Church special status in Serbia. Patriarch Varnava vehemently opposed this concordat. It is said that he died "a mysterious death" just two hours before the concordat was passed in the lower house of the parliament. Stojadinović, fearing the consequences—a procession of priests who had taken to the streets to pray for the patriarch's recovery had been attacked and beaten by gendarmes—decided not to submit the concordat to the upper house of the parliament, the Senate.

celebrated Thirteen Hundred Corporals: In the Balkan Wars of 1912 and 1913, and in battles with the Austro-Hungarian army at the beginning of World War I in 1914, many senior and noncommissioned officers of the Serbian army were killed. To make up for the severe shortage of military officers, the Serbian Supreme Command was forced to send college and even high school students to Skoplje (now known as Skopje, North Macedonia) to train as officers. On August 31, 1914, the battalion was formed that would become known as the Thirteen Hundred Corporals. On November 15, 1914, the Supreme Command promoted all the students to the rank of corporal and sent them to various fronts. By the fifteenth of December some four hundred of the Thirteen Hundred Corporals had been killed on the Kolubara Front in Serbia. Many more would later die defending Belgrade and on the Salonika Front, in the retreat across the mountains of Albania to the Adriatic Sea.

207 *King Aleksandar Karadjordjević*: son of Peter I Karadjordjević (see note for "Peter I Karadjordjević," p. 122, above). He ruled from 1921 to 1934, when he was assassinated in Marseilles.

222 *Megale hodos* (Greek): the Great Way; *Via Magna* (Latin): the Great Way.

Constantine: also known as Constantine the Great; full name: Flavius Valerius Constantinus (ca. AD 274–337). Roman emperor from 306 to 337, the first Roman emperor to be converted to Christianity, and the founder of Constantinople, which remained the capital of the Eastern Roman (Byzantine) Empire until 1453. Born in Niš in what is now Serbia (*Funk & Wagnalls New Encyclopedia*).

222f. *Constantine Dragas XI Palaeologus* (1404–53): Last of the Byzantine, or Eastern Roman, emperors (ruled 1449–1453). Constantine was despot of Morea before succeeding his brother John VIII to the throne. He inherited an "empire" that the Ottoman Turks had reduced to the city of Constantinople and the area immediately around it. In April 1453 a great Turkish army under Sultan Mehmed II laid siege to the city, which was defended only by a few hundred Greeks and Genoese. Constantine was killed in the fighting during the final Turkish assault (May 29–30, 1453) that ended the Byzantine Empire (*Funk & Wagnalls New Encyclopedia*).

223 *This collection of brief lives of the holy fathers I attribute to Archbishop Danilo II*: Archbishop Danilo II was a well-known Serbian writer and architect of the Middle Ages, successor of Archbishop Nikodim I at the monastery Hilandar. Around the year 1330 Danilo II built a church dedicated to the *Putovoditeljka* (guide to travelers), *Bogorodica Odigitrija*. He also built the church of St. Nikola between 1330 and 1337. He wrote a collection of hagiographies entitled *Života kraljeva I arhiepiskopa srpskih* (*Lives of the Serbian Kings and Archbishops*).

famous attack of the pirates on Sveta Gora: The reference is to the monastery Hilandar on Mount Atlas, also known as the Holy Mount (*Sveta Gora*), which is part of the Chalcidic Peninsula in northern Greece. It is surrounded by the Aegean Sea and populated exclusively by Eastern Orthodox monks. Hilandar was founded in the year 1198 by the monk Simeon, who had formerly been ruler of Serbia under the name Stefan Nemanja (see note for "Nemanjić procession," p. 158, above) until he abdicated in favor of his son Stefan Prvovenčani (Stefan the First-Crowned) in order to become a monk. Simeon, with his youngest son, the monk Sava, received permission from Byzantine Emperor Alexios to build on the site of an older Greek monastery, also known as Hilandar.

iguman: prior or head of a Serbian Orthodox monastery.

Dubrovnik: city on the Adriatic Sea in Croatia.

Duke of Urbino: Federico Paolo Novello da Montefeltro (1422–82), Duke of the Duchy of Urbino (Italy), who made his fortune as a mercenary and then turned to art. He was one of the most brilliant and cultured men of his day, the paradigm of a Renaissance man. He gathered around him the greatest painters, poets, and scholars of his time and sheltered them all in one of Italy's most beautiful Renaissance palaces, a palace that still stands today. He was the subject of a famous painting by Piero della Francesca in the Galleria degli Uffizi in Florence. It is said that he had thirty to forty writers busy working on his library, two organists, and five men to read the classics aloud at mealtimes.

224f. *Niš, Novi Pazar, Prijepolje, Foča*: Niš and Novi Pazar are cities in eastern and southwestern Serbia, respectively; Prijepolje and Foča are cities in eastern and central Bosnia-Herzegovina. Melchior von Seidlitz's journey, therefore, ran from east to west.

225 *Patriarch Arsenije III Čarnojević*: Patriarch of the Serbian Orthodox Church from 1674 to 1706. He enthusiastically supported a general uprising of the Christian population of the Balkans against Turkish rule, which had been encouraged by Leopold I following the Turkish defeat outside Vienna (1683). With some 20,000 men Patriarch Arsenije joined the Austrian army in its drive southward, during which Kosovo was liberated all the way to Prizren and Skopje. But when the Austrian drive was broken at Kaçanik (1690), he was forced to move his people (some 30,000 families) north to Hungary in order to escape Turkish reprisals. This has historically been known as the "Great Migration of Serbs." This tide of Serb emigration continued: in the eighteenth century the Serbs established flourishing centers in Karlovići and Novi Sad, now part of the autonomous Serbian province of Vojvodina.

229 *it was as if the entire central square of the capital was tipping this way and that*: The reference is to the city square Terazije, a word that literally means "balance" or "weight scales."

232 *a corresponding member of the academy*: The reference is to the Serbian Academy of Arts and Sciences (SANU), established in 1842.

233 *the figure on horseback*: The reference is to Prince Mihailo Obrenović, who in September 1860 succeeded his father Prince Miloš Obrenović as ruler of Serbia. Considered by some as Serbia's greatest modern leader, he introduced more Western methods of government, completely reformed the Serbian army, contributed to the final liberation of Serbia from the Turks, and founded the National Theater. On June 10, 1868, he was assassinated in the park of Topčider, outside Belgrade, by a rival dynasty.

240 *Dragiša Cvetković*: Yugoslav prime minister from 1939 to 1941. Like Dr. Milan Stojadinović, whom he replaced as prime minister in 1939, Dragiša Cvetković maintained a pro-Axis foreign policy. Following the German annexation of Austria in 1938, the Yugoslav government tried to maintain a position of independence but was increasingly pressured by Hitler's Germany, Yugoslavia's closest economic partner during the late 1930s, to ally itself more closely with the Axis powers. Thus Yugoslavia joined the Axis on March 24, 1941, when it signed the Tripartite Pact in Vienna—an act that sparked demonstrations in Belgrade. After signing the pact, Dragiša Cvetković assured Hitler that "Yugoslavia would be ready to maintain its position of independence and cooperate with the Third Reich." However, the Yugoslav army soon overthrew the government of Prince Pavle and Dragiša Cvetković, and vowed to resist the Axis. It was an event that triggered the German invasion of Yugoslavia in April 1941.

244 *a motorcyclist with an escutcheon on his chest*: During World War II some German soldiers wore a duty gorget known as a *Ringkragen*. This was a half-moon-shaped, thin sheet-metal stamping usually bearing a swastika, a spread eagle, and the identification number of the unit to which the soldier belonged. The gorget was hung from the neck by a neck chain and worn partly over the neck and across the chest.

247 *Sachertorte* (German): a chocolate cake with truffle and raspberry filling.

248 *Voždovac district*: area in southern Belgrade.

250 *NKVD*: In December 1917 the first Soviet political police agency, the VeCheka (Russian acronym for All-Russian Extraordinary Commission for Combating Counterrevolution and Sabotage), was created under the leadership of Felix Dzerzhinsky. In 1922 the VeCheka, also known as the Cheka, was replaced by the GPU (Russian initials for State Political Administration), which in 1923 became the OGPU (Joint State Political Administration). A succession of different police organizations then followed: the NKVD (People's Commissariat of Internal Affairs) in 1934; the NKGB (People's Commissariat of State Security) in 1943; the MGB (Ministry of State Security) in 1946; and the MVD (Ministry of Internal Affairs) in 1953. The death of Soviet leader Joseph Stalin in 1953 initiated another reorganization of the political police, and the KGB was formed in 1954 to take over state security functions from the MVD.

251 *Milikerze* candles: German candles of white wax.

Dragi Jovanović: Dragomir "Dragi" Jovanović, Belgrade chief of police and city administrator during the German occupation of Yugoslavia, 1941–44.

252 *Chekist*: member of the Cheka (see note for "NKVD," p. 250, above).

SR forces, Mensheviks, and the White Guard bands of General Wrangel: SR forces were forces loyal to the Socialist Revolutionaries (*Sotsialisty-Revolutsionery*, SR), a peasant party during the Russian Revolution and a faction in the subsequent Russian Civil War (1918–1921). Along with the Mensheviks and Bolsheviks, the SR made up the Petrograd Soviet, a governing body (together with the Provisional Government) that was formed when the imperial government was dispersed in 1917. Unlike the Bolsheviks, who demanded the immediate seizure of land for the peasantry, the Mensheviks placed emphasis on reform, envisioning a period of capitalist development and complete political democracy as the essential prerequisite for a socialist order. The Socialist Revolutionaries, on the other hand, maintained vague socialist aspirations.

Baron Pyotr Nikolaevich Wrangel (1878–1928) was a Russian military leader and counterrevolutionary commander during the Russian Civil War. He was born into a noble family in St. Petersburg. Late in 1917, after the Bolsheviks seized power, Wrangel joined the anti-Bolshevik forces, known as the Whites, in southern Russia, and became their commander

in chief in 1920. In the conflict with the Red Army, Wrangel was successful for a time, but the Soviet-Polish armistice of October 1920 enabled
the Red Army to concentrate its full force against Wrangel. He fled to
Constantinople with 150,000 followers in November. The Bolsheviks' ultimate victory in the Russian Civil War led to the founding of the Union
of Soviet Socialist Republics in December 1922 (*Encarta Encyclopedia*,
RUSSIAN REVOLUTION, WRANGEL, PYOTR).

253 *Tovarišći*: Russian for "comrades."

Notes of a Hunter by Ivan Sergeevich Turgenev: *Notes of a Hunter: A
Sportsman's Sketches* (1852), a collection of short stories. Turgenev's attacks
on feudalism in these stories, together with his enthusiastic obituary for
Gogol in the same year, led to his confinement at Spasskoe, his country
estate, but which reportedly contributed to Czar Alexander II's emancipa-
tion of the serfs in 1861.

Chetniks: World War II Yugoslav guerrilla and resistance movement led
by Serbian general Dragoljub "Draža" Mihailović. On April 6, 1941, Nazi
Germany and the Axis Powers invaded Yugoslavia. On April 17, 1941, the
Yugoslav High Command surrendered at Sarajevo, Bosnia-Herzegovina.
But in Doboj in northern Bosnia, Mihailović, then deputy chief of staff of
the Yugoslav Second Army, refused to surrender, gathering around him a
group of officers who would continue the struggle as a guerrilla war. This
guerrilla movement, known as Četnici (Chetniks), was composed over-
whelmingly of ethnic Serbs, and it relied on the Serbian tradition of resistance to the Ottoman Turks; the First Serbian Uprising against the Turks
in 1804, for example, had been led by the *hajdučke čete* of Karadjordje
Petrović, and Serbian guerrilla operations had been used during the
Balkan Wars of 1912–13 as well as in World War I. In their struggle against
the German occupiers, Mihailović's Chetniks were initially given Allied
support. The other major Yugoslav resistance movement of this time was
known as the Partisans. It was led by the Croat-Slovene Josip Broz Tito.
Unlike the Chetniks, who remained loyal to the exiled Yugoslav king Peter
II Karadjordjević, Tito's Partisans wished to establish postwar Yugoslavia
as a communist state. The Chetniks and Partisans soon came into open
conflict, and a civil war ensued. It was Tito's Partisans who ultimately won
this war when Allied support was switched from the Chetniks to them. In
March 1946 General Mihailović was captured and brought to Belgrade,
where he was tried as a traitor by the new communist government and
executed.

Ljotić's supporters: The reference is to Dimitrije Ljotić (1891–1945), a
Serbian lawyer, political leader, and member of the World War II quisling government in Belgrade. Like his grandfather, he was an ardent sup-
porter of the Karadjordjević Dynasty and of monarchy in general. When
King Aleksandar suspended the Yugoslav Constitution in 1929, Ljotić and

like-minded people were very pleased. As a well-known monarchist, Ljotić was appointed minister of justice in the Petar Živković government in February 1931, a post that he subsequently resigned over differences with the king regarding a new Yugoslav Constitution. Ljotić continued his political activities and founded the Yugoslav National Movement (ZBOR) as well as a number of newspapers in which he espoused his openly anti-free-masonry, anti-communist, anti-Semitic, and pro-monarchy views. When war broke out, he joined the so-called Government of National Salvation. He was one of the closest friends and associates of General Milan Nedić, the World War II quisling leader (see following note). When it became apparent that Germany was losing the war as the Red Army approached, Ljotić proposed that all Serbian nationalist forces evacuate to Slovenia where, together with Slovenian nationalists, a united front to combat communism would be formed. This plan was never realized because of disunity among the various nationalist groups. On April 23, 1945, while traveling to a meeting with nationalist and church leaders, Ljotić was killed in an automobile accident in Slovenia, where he was later buried.

followers of Nedić: The reference is to General Milan Nedić (1878–1946), the World War II Serbian quisling leader. On August 21, 1941, Nedić, a World War I veteran and former Yugoslav minister of war, was made president of the new German puppet Government of National Salvation, assigned with the task of ending the terrorist actions of the communist gangs of "partisans." Well aware of the atrocities being committed by the Croatian Ustaše and Bulgarians against the civilian Serb populations of Croatia, Bosnia, and Serbia, and faced with the German threat that Croats and Bulgarians would head the new Yugoslav government if he refused to accept the post of president, Nedić set about forming units of Serb volunteers to fight the partisan gangs and come to the aid of the Serbs. Thus Nedić assisted in the formation of the Serbian State Guard (SDS) and Serbian Volunteer Corp (SDK). In this regard, it is an open question whether Nedić was a quisling in the ordinary sense. On the other hand, he visited Adolf Hitler on September 19, 1943, informing him that thousands of Serb patriots were voluntarily fighting to protect their country from the Red terrorists. Nedić was apparently a virulent anti-Semite, and has even been accused by some of having facilitated the killing of Jews at the German-run Sajmište concentration camp (see note for "Sajmište," p. 179, above). On October 22, 1941, his government organized the famous "Grand Anti-Masonic Exhibition," whose central theme was the Jewish-Communist-Masonic plot for world domination. At the end of the war he was captured by the Allies and sent back to Serbia into the hands of Josip Broz Tito's new communist government. He was brutally murdered on February 4, 1945, by agents of communist police chief Aleksandar Ranković and buried in an unknown place.

254 *Lavrentiy Pavlovich Beria* (1899–1953): security chief of the NKVD (see note for "NKVD," p. 250, above), a precursor to the KGB. The chief method of the KGB's predecessors was terror, implemented by such security chiefs as Nikolai Yezhov, who directed the Great Purge in the 1930s, and Beria, who took over the organization in late 1938 and ran it during World War II.

255 *rubashka*: Russian for "shirt."

256 *holy martyrs Boris and Gleb*: alternately, Baris and Gleb. Brothers martyred in 1015, and who were among the first Russian saints. Their mother was a Volga Bulgar.

258 *Goli Otok*: literally, Bare Island; an infamous island prison camp off the coast of Croatia in the Adriatic Sea, to which the Yugoslav government in the 1950s and 1960s sent all those who disagreed with its policy toward the Soviet Union. Many of the approximately fifty thousand men and women who passed through this camp died there or perished soon after being released.

262 *All Souls' Day*: (*Zadušnica*): for Orthodox Serbs the day when the graves of relatives are visited, usually several times a year. Candles for the dead are lit and sometimes a requiem mass or memorial services are held.

komisbrot (German): similar to *milchbrot*, milk bread.

269 *Transfiguration Day*: *Preobraženje*: Serbian Orthodox religious holiday, alternately known as Transfiguration of Our Lord, on August 19.

Then she poured the boiled wheat into two small bowls, for the burial and for the weekly remembrance, including with each a glass of oil and red wine: Serbian Orthodox religious rite. Boiled wheat (*koljivo*) is ordinarily prepared along with the Slava cake (see note for p. 42, above) and for requiem masses in remembrance of the souls of the dead. In Christianity in general, wheat is a visible symbol of resurrection: Just as it is sown in the earth and does not die but brings forth life anew, so will the souls of the dead be resurrected by God on Judgment Day. Representative of Christ's blood, wine is one of the most basic symbols in Orthodox Christianity, not only during the Slava feast, but also in honoring and remembering the dead; it is a custom among Orthodox Serbs, during certain religious rites or feasts, to pour a little wine on the ground as a sacrifice to the subterranean gods and to deceased relatives. Wine mixed with oil is poured on the ground as a sacrifice to the deceased during their burial. Since ancient times wine (and oil) have been thought to have medicinal properties, and so at Slava feasts a little of it is drunk even by children. In this instance, Pokimica's mother is preparing the boiled wheat and wine/oil mixture for both her burial and for the weekly remembrance (see note for p. 77, above), which would ordinarily occur seven days after her death.

274 *Vrnjačka Banja*: spa about seventy-five miles south of Belgrade famous for its mineral baths.

the Obrenović general Belimarković: see page 104 of text, where General Jovan Belimarković and General Antonije Bogićević are described as "tried and true friends of the former (Obrenović) ruling house."

282 *Pierné*: Gabriel Pierné (1863–1937), French composer. He was a pupil of César Franck and Jules Massenet, and successor of the former as organist at Ste. Clotilde in Paris.

Milojević: Miloje Milojević (1884–1946), Serbian composer.

Binički: Stanislav Binički (1872–1942), Serbian composer.

286 *dolmas*: stuffed leaves of cabbage, sauerkraut, or grapevine. Dolmas can be stuffed with various meats or, for Lent, with meatless products (e.g., vegetables or rice).

PETER AGNONE (1948–2011) was a renowned translator who studied Serbian literature and culture at the University of Pittsburgh. His translation of David Albahari's novel *Bait* was nominated for the American Association of Teachers of Slavic and Eastern European Languages Book Prize. He also translated works by Goran Petrović, Vidosav Stevanović, and Mihajlo Pantić.

GORAN PETROVIĆ, born in Kraljevo in 1961, is an international bestselling author who studied Yugoslav and Serbian literature at the University of Belgrade. Petrović has been awarded numerous prizes in Serbia and abroad, including the NIN Award, Serbia's most prominent literary prize, for *At the Lucky Hand*. In 2019, he received the Ivo Andrić Prize for his lifetime contribution to literature. Petrović is a member of the Serbian Literary Association, the Serbian PEN Center, and the Serbian Academy of Sciences and Arts. Petrović's novels and books of selected stories have been published in two dozen languages around the world. He works and lives in Belgrade.

Thank you all
for your support.
We do this for you,
and could not do
it without you.

PARTNERS

ADDITIONAL DONORS, CONT'D

Cone Johnson
CS Maynard
Daniel J. Hale
Daniela Hurezanu
Danielle Dubrow
Denae Richards
Dori Boone-Costantino
Ed Nawotka
Elizabeth Gillette
Elizabeth Van Vleck
Erin Kubatzky
Ester & Matt Harrison
Grace Kenney
Hillary Richards
JJ Italiano
Jeremy Hughes
John Darnielle
Jonathan Legg
Julie Janicke Muhsmann
Kelly Falconer
Kevin Richardson
Laura Thomson
Lea Courington
Lee Haber
Leigh Ann Pike

Lowell Frye
Maaza Mengiste
Mark Haber
Mary Cline
Max Richie
Maynard Thomson
Michael Reklis
Mike Soto
Mokhtar Ramadan
Nikki & Dennis Gibson
Patrick Kukucka
Patrick Kutcher
Rev. Elizabeth & Neil Moseley
Richard Meyer
Sam Simon
Sherry Perry
Skander Halim
Sydneyann Binion
Stephen Harding
Stephen Williamson
Susan Carp
Theater Jones
Tim Perttula
Tony Thomson

SUBSCRIBERS

Audrey Golosky
Ben Fountain
Carol Trimmer
Caroline West
Charles Dee Mitchell
Chris Mullikin
Courtney Sheedy
Dan Pope
Daniel Kushner
Derek Maine
Elisabeth Cook
Hillary Richards
Jason Linden
Kenneth McClain
Kirsten Hanson

Lance Stack
Lisa Balabanlilar
Margaret Terwey
Martha Gifford
Megan Coker
Michael Binkley
Michael Elliott
Michael Lighty
Molly Bassett
Nathan Dize
Radhika Sharma
Ryan Todd
Shelby Vincent
Stephanie Barr

AVAILABLE NOW FROM DEEP VELLUM

MICHÈLE AUDIN · *One Hundred Twenty-One Days*
translated by Christiana Hills · FRANCE

BAE SUAH · *Recitation*
translated by Deborah Smith · SOUTH KOREA

EDUARDO BERTI · *The Imagined Land*
translated by Charlotte Coombe · ARGENTINA

CARMEN BOULLOSA · *Texas: The Great Theft · Before · Heavens on Earth*
translated by Samantha Schnee · Peter Bush · Shelby Vincent · MEXICO

LEILA S. CHUDORI · *Home*
translated by John H. McGlynn · INDONESIA

SARAH CLEAVE, ed. · *Banthology: Stories from Banned Nations ·*
IRAN, IRAQ, LIBYA, SOMALIA, SUDAN, SYRIA & YEMEN

ANANDA DEVI · *Eve Out of Her Ruins*
translated by Jeffrey Zuckerman · MAURITIUS

ALISA GANIEVA · *Bride and Groom · The Mountain and the Wall*
translated by Carol Apollonio · RUSSIA

ANNE GARRÉTA · *Sphinx · Not One Day*
translated by Emma Ramadan · FRANCE

JÓN GNARR · *The Indian · The Pirate · The Outlaw*
translated by Lytton Smith · ICELAND

GOETHE · *The Golden Goblet: Selected Poems*
translated by Zsuzsanna Ozsváth and Frederick Turner · GERMANY

NOEMI JAFFE · *What Are the Blind Men Dreaming?*
translated by Julia Sanches & Ellen Elias-Bursac · BRAZIL

PERGENTINO JOSÉ · *Red Ants: Stories*
translated by Tom Bunstead and the author · MEXICO

CLAUDIA SALAZAR JIMÉNEZ · *Blood of the Dawn*
translated by Elizabeth Bryer · PERU

JUNG YOUNG MOON · *Seven Samurai Swept Away in a River · Vaseline Buddha*
translated by Yewon Jung · SOUTH KOREA

FOWZIA KARIMI · *Above Us the Milky Way: An Illuminated Alphabet* · USA

KIM YIDEUM · *Blood Sisters*
translated by Ji yoon Lee · SOUTH KOREA

TAISIA KITAISKAIA · *The Nightgown & Other Poems* · USA

JOSEFINE KLOUGART · *Of Darkness*
translated by Martin Aitken · DENMARK

YANICK LAHENS · *Moonbath*
translated by Emily Gogolak · HAITI

FOUAD LAROUI · *The Curious Case of Dassoukine's Trousers*
translated by Emma Ramadan · MOROCCO

MARIA GABRIELA LLANSOL · *The Geography of Rebels Trilogy: The Book of Communities;*
The Remaining Life; In the House of July & August
translated by Audrey Young · PORTUGAL

PABLO MARTÍN SÁNCHEZ · *The Anarchist Who Shared My Name*
translated by Jeff Diteman · SPAIN

DOROTA MASŁOWSKA · *Honey, I Killed the Cats*
translated by Benjamin Paloff · POLAND

BRICE MATTHIEUSSENT· *Revenge of the Translator*
translated by Emma Ramadan · FRANCE

LINA MERUANE · *Seeing Red*
translated by Megan McDowell · CHILE

VALÉRIE MRÉJEN · *Black Forest*
translated by Katie Shireen Assef · FRANCE

FISTON MWANZA MUJILA · *Tram 83*
translated by Roland Glasser · DEMOCRATIC REPUBLIC OF CONGO

ILJA LEONARD PFEIJFFER · *La Superba*
translated by Michele Hutchison · NETHERLANDS

RICARDO PIGLIA · *Target in the Night*
translated by Sergio Waisman · ARGENTINA

SERGIO PITOL · *The Art of Flight* · *The Journey* ·
The Magician of Vienna · *Mephisto's Waltz: Selected Short Stories*
translated by George Henson · MEXICO

EDUARDO RABASA · *A Zero-Sum Game*
translated by Christina MacSweeney · MEXICO

ZAHIA RAHMANI · *"Muslim": A Novel*
translated by Matthew Reeck · FRANCE/ALGERIA

C.F. RAMUZ · *Jean-Luc Persecuted*
translated by Olivia Baes · SWITZERLAND

JUAN RULFO · *The Golden Cockerel & Other Writings*
translated by Douglas J. Weatherford · MEXICO

TATIANA RYCKMAN · *The Ancestry of Objects* · USA

JESSICA SCHIEFAUER · *Girls Lost*
translated by Saskia Vogel · SWEDEN

OLEG SENTSOV · *Life Went On Anyway*
translated by Uilleam Blacker · UKRAINE

MIKHAIL SHISHKIN · *Calligraphy Lesson: The Collected Stories*
translated by Marian Schwartz, Leo Shtutin,
Mariya Bashkatova, Sylvia Maizell · RUSSIA

ÓFEIGUR SIGURÐSSON · *Öræfi: The Wasteland*
translated by Lytton Smith · ICELAND

MIKE SOTO · *A Grave Is Given Supper: Poems* · USA

MÄRTA TIKKANEN ·*The Love Story of the Century*
translated by Stina Katchadourian · SWEDEN

FORTHCOMING FROM DEEP VELLUM

AMANG · *Raised by Wolves*
translated by Steve Bradbury · TAIWAN

MARIO BELLATIN · *Mrs. Murakami's Garden*
translated by Heather Cleary · MEXICO

MAGDA CARNECI · *FEM*
translated by Sean Cotter · ROMANIA

MIRCEA CĂRTĂRESCU · *Solenoid*
translated by Sean Cotter · ROMANIA

MATHILDE CLARK · *Lone Star*
translated by Martin Aitken · DENMARK

LOGEN CURE · *Welcome to Midland: Poems* · USA

PETER DIMOCK · *Daybook from Sheep Meadow* · USA

CLAUDIA ULLOA DONOSO · *Little Bird*, translated by Lily Meyer · PERU/NORWAY

LEYLÂ ERBIL · *A Strange Woman*
translated by Nermin Menemencioğlu · TURKEY

ROSS FARRAR · *Ross Sings Cheree & the Animated Dark: Poems* · USA

FERNANDA GARCIA LAU · *Out of the Cage*
translated by Will Vanderhyden · ARGENTINA

ANNE GARRÉTA · *In/concrete*
translated by Emma Ramadan · FRANCE

GOETHE · *Faust, Part One*
translated by Zsuzsanna Ozsváth and Frederick Turner · GERMANY

JUNG YOUNG MOON · *Arriving in a Thick Fog*
translated by Mah Eunji and Jeffrey Karvonen · SOUTH KOREA

DMITRY LIPSKEROV · *The Tool and the Butterflies*
translated by Reilly Costigan-Humes & Isaac Stackhouse Wheeler · RUSSIA

FISTON MWANZA MUJILA · *The Villain's Dance*, translated by Roland Glasser · *The
River in the Belly: Selected Poems*, translated by Bret Maney · DEMOCRATIC REPUBLIC OF
CONGO

GORAN PETROVIĆ · *At the Lucky Hand, aka The Sixty-Nine Drawers*
translated by Peter Agnone · SERBIA

LUDMILLA PETRUSHEVSKAYA · *Kidnapped: A Crime Story*, translated by Marian Schwartz
· *The New Adventures of Helen: Magical Tales*, translated by Jane Bugaeva · RUSSIA

JULIE POOLE · *Bright Specimen: Poems from the Texas Herbarium* · USA

MANON STEFAN ROS · *The Blue Book of Nebo* · WALES

ETHAN RUTHERFORD · *Farthest South & Other Stories* · USA

MUSTAFA STITOU · *Two Half Faces*
translated by David Colmer · NETHERLANDS

BOB TRAMMELL · *The Origins of the Avant-Garde in Dallas & Other Stories* · USA